Sham

by T S James

Copyright © 2024 T S James

ISBN: 978-1-917293-51-8

All rights reserved, including the right to reproduce this book, or portions thereof in any form. No part of this text may be reproduced, transmitted, downloaded, decompiled, reverse engineered, or stored, in any form or introduced into any information storage and retrieval system, in any form or by any means, whether electronic or mechanical without the express written permission of the author.

Acknowledgements

Firstly, I would like to thank my wife Linda for all her encouragement and help in writing this book. Her support has been unwavering and indispensable, providing me with the strength and motivation to persevere through the numerous challenges and obstacles I faced during this journey. Linda's insightful feedback, endless patience, and belief in my vision have been the cornerstone of my progress, and without her, this endeavour would have remained a distant dream.

I would also like to express my sincere gratitude to Charlotte Oldridge for her help in designing the front cover.

I would like to add my thanks to all my friends and family who have helped in spreading the word about this book and hopefully making it a success.

A BIG thank you goes out to Publish Nation for making the path to becoming a published author an easy and painless route.

And finally, may I ask the indulgence of the people who have bought and read this book. If you have enjoyed reading this book as much as I have enjoyed writing it, please spread the word, and please leave a review on Amazon.

A MASSIVE thank you for your support.

Please keep an eye on my website for news and updates. www.tsjames.uk

Pronunciation

Aysgarth = Ays-garth
Eldermar = El-der-mar
Elvenii = El-venn-e
Ethaenian = E-theen-ian
Hellvelyn = Hell-vel-in
Khuldehern = Kool-der-hern
Kuu-Luna = Ka-you Luna
Shu-Fray = Shoo-Fray
Sloendor Valley = Slo-en-dor valley
Stefremmus = Stef-rem-mus
Thashona = Tha-shona
Treonia = Tree-onia
Tres Shellon = Tray-Shellon

Prologue

In the Second Realm, there is a young Ethaenian boy of barely 17 years. His name is Shamera, he has always dreamed of becoming the sorcerer's new apprentice. Shamera lives in a land where strange and wonderful creatures live, and in a time of magic. Verazslo, the sorcerer, is attending the Ethaenian's summer festival and, as every year, he is looking for someone to become his next apprentice. Will today be the day he gets his wish?

Shamera lives in a village called Elms Hollow, which is in the south of the Sloendor Valley. It is a beautiful picturesque village with its stone houses and cobbled streets. Hanging baskets, and window boxes full of colourful flowers and plants adorn a lot of the buildings and they fill the air with the sweet scent of summer. Elms Hollow is best known for its summer festival they call Stefremmus, and of course the friendly Ethaenian inhabitants.

The Ethaenian's are an unusual people. They have the body of a human, the pointed ears of an Elf, all have black hair and, of course, they are friendly, sociable, and welcoming to all. It is said that they are a distant relation to the Elvenii, a fact highly disputed by the Elvenii as they believe their histories evolved along different paths, but the genetic similarities are there nonetheless. Close to the village stands some ancient ruins of a stone circle. Rumour has it they hid somewhere a great treasure in those stone ruins. It has been searched for, but in all these years, it has never been found and is now believed to be just a story handed down from generation to generation.

Overlooking the village and the stone ruins stands Khul Mountain; it wasn't a mountain but was an extinct volcano which had long since gone cold. The Khul' Dwarvian's used to mine gold and precious stones from deep inside it in the long distant past. A relation of the Dwarves, they are also known to work hard, play hard and drink hard. The Khul'Dwarvian now hail from Khulderhern; a mining region to the northeast. To the west of Khulderhern is Selvenora, the mountain home of the Elvenii people. The Elvenii are a very distant cousin to the

Elves. The Elvenii now spend a lot of their time contemplating life and being at one with their environment. They believe that all power emanates from the force of nature, and that being at one with nature; you can harness its power. These three provinces have lived in peace now for roughly 500 years, following many years of warring during the period in their history known as the 'Dark Times'.

These were now peaceful times and once a year Elms Hollow holds Stefremmus, its famous summer festival in which everyone from near and far attends. The festival would go on for two days and has been known in the past to have gone on for longer. It is at this festival that an event takes place called 'The Choosing'. This is when Verazslo, the Sorcerer, attends looking for a suitable apprentice. Should there be anyone worthy of that post, that is. Many had tried over these past years, but all had failed. Verazslo's apprentice would have to be someone worthy of that position, someone touched by magic. He would be a very special person indeed.

Chapter 1

Shamera walked slowly through Thornbeck Meadow. His deep red and royal blue summer cloak trailed ankle length, soaking up the early morning dew as it brushed past the grasses and small plants which flourished here. He stood looking towards the eastern sky as the first rays of the summer sun broke the gleaming horizon.

With both hands, he slowly dragged back his hood; his long black hair flowed down past his shoulders. He flicked it backwards from his face as he ran his hands through it. He watched as the sun rose steadily upwards. His kingfisher blue eyes sparkled in the early morning light. His skin had a sun-kissed glow, similar in colour to toasted almonds.

This was Shamera's favourite time of day. He loved watching the rising sun enliven the morning with its golden glow. He took a long deep breath of the fresh morning air, sweetly scented by the fragrance of the newly opening flowers. As he watched the sun rising upwards with majestic splendour, he clasped his hands together, paused for a moment and whispered to himself, "Is today the day?"

Shamera had wanted to become a sorcerer ever since he could remember, and he spent the last five years learning all about the medicinal plants and herbs which grew locally. He also learned how to make the lotions and potions created by Mirabilis the apothecary, by helping her in the shop during his free time.

Shamera was one of only six hopeful candidates from the region of Sloendor who were eligible to be tested to become the sorcerer's next apprentice. It would not be a straightforward task, yet, as he watched the sunrise; he felt a quiet confidence growing inside him. The sun was a large orange disc balancing on the horizon; its golden light illuminating the valley. Shamera looked around him as the new day dawned, drew another long breath of the sweet morning air before making his way home for breakfast. The village was quiet, but it was Saturday, it was also a festival day, and soon the entire village would be alive with the hustle and bustle of people arriving from all over the region.

By the time Shamera arrived home, he could see smoke spiralling upwards out of the chimney and, as he reached the front gate, he could smell the unmistakable aroma of bacon cooking on the open fire. As he entered the house, he closed his eyes and filled his lungs with the tasty aromas; this made his mouth water as he was ready for something to eat.

"Is that you Shamera?" shouted his mother. "I have made you an extra-large breakfast this morning. You will need all the strength you can muster for the Choosing." She said, with a proud smile. She rounded up the rest of the family so they could all sit together around the table.

His father, a portly gentleman, peered at him over the rounded rims of his glasses and, with a deep yet reassuring voice, said. "It's a fine day Shamera, all you can do is your best, as, I am sure you will." He blew across his teacup and took a sip of his favourite hot nettle tea. "I am sure you will make us all proud." He continued, and with a smile and a slight nod of his head, he took another sip.

Gwen, his little sister of eight years, waved a small wooden spoon, pretending it was a magic wand.

"You can magic up a unicorn for me to ride upon." she said excitedly. Shamera glanced at her and smiled.

"I am not a sorcerer yet, and I am sure there will be a lot of training and learning to do first... and besides, I might not get chosen, they have chosen only one person in the past sixty years, and he didn't last long. He apparently blew himself up, making a concoction called black powder?" He said, as a look of doubt appeared on his face.

"Be positive dear, no one deserves it more than you." His mother said reassuringly.

"You're justifiably biased mother."

"Even if I am biased, you would still make a great apprentice." she proudly remarked.

"Ah well, suppose I will have to make do with my rabbit, oh great sorcerer Shamera." Gwen teased as she gave her stuffed toy a hug.

Shamera looked at her and smiled. "I suppose you will little sister. I suppose you will." he said softly.

The conversation fell silent as everyone tucked into their breakfast of bacon, eggs, and freshly baked bread. Shamera lifted his head and looked at his mother, raised his eyebrows, blew his cheeks out nervously, stood up from the table and said "Okay, I will see you all at the Choosing. I need to help Mirabilis at the apothecary beforehand, she will be expecting me."

Shamera set off through the cobbled streets and the rows of single storey stone houses of the village. The apothecary was near to the market square, which was now getting busy with the hurly-burly of market life, and the stallholders making ready for the festival. All kinds of aromas filled the air, with the smells of freshly baked bread, flowers, and hogs being gently roasted over wood smoke. Shamera was nervously aware of people staring and discussing among themselves whether he would be the next apprentice and become the pride of Elms Hollow. "Good luck at the Choosing Shamera." someone shouted from a crowd. "Thank you, I think I'm going to need it!" he shouted back with a smile and continued on his way. "Make the village proud." Shouted another. Shamera smiled nervously and waved politely.

As he reached the apothecary's shop, he could see Mirabilis through the large front window. She appeared to be talking to a hooded figure. As Shamera opened the door, the shop bell rang out, announcing his entrance. He stood inside the doorway and was about to say good morning when a hooded figure hurried away out of the back door without looking back. Mirabilis turned and stood staring at Shamera, her wrinkled and weathered face even more deeply creased with a look of concern.

"Who was that? He seemed to be in a hurry."

"Erm… no one, it was no one." Stuttered Mirabilis. "I have to go out for a short while; you can mind the shop, can't you? I won't be long." Mirabilis quickly grabbed her bottle green summer cloak off the peg and hurried out of the door.

Shamera looked out of the window. He felt a little bewildered as he watched Mirabilis scurry down the main street. Her cloak flowing and fluttering behind her; she was also glancing nervously around as she hurried down the street. She was soon out of sight. Shamera turned from the window and thought to himself, this was odd behaviour; he had never seen Mirabilis acting so troubled.

"Whatever could the matter be which has her acting so strangely?" he muttered to himself. He hoped whatever the problem was, it would be sorted out swiftly and Mirabilis would return quickly, as he needed to get himself organised for the Choosing ceremony. He was also hoping to ask if Mirabilis had any last-minute advice which may give him an advantage over the other candidates.

Shamera wanted to keep his mind busy, so he pottered around dusting and rearranging large jars and bottles which were being displayed on shelves around the shop. Blue, green, purple and red, translucent bottles displaying a variety of coloured plants and strange objects steeping in the liquor. Plain bottles, fancy bottles with fancy glass stoppers, all adorned the shelves and cabinets. Clumps of dried herbs and plants hung down from the rafters, wicker baskets filled with a mixture of dried berries, aromatic leaves and dried fruits filled the shop with a heady, sweet aroma. In between dusting and rearranging some displays, he served the odd customer who came in to buy a healing potion of some description and wished him good luck at the Choosing.

He looked around the shop and thought it was looking a lot tidier, and the aroma of the scented oils and plant extracts appeared to be even more inviting. Shamera kept looking at the large ornamental timepiece hanging on the wall; he watched the slender, ornate hands as they leisurely turned about its face. Barely thirty minutes had passed, but it seemed like hours. He thought to himself how quiet the shop seemed for a festival day, with barely a handful of customers entering the shop. Time appeared to be passing by agonisingly slowly.

Bored with merely pottering about, he distracted himself by sitting for a while and read a large comprehensive book which contained all the secret ingredients and special mixes for the potions. As he sat reading the book, he could not help but contemplate what might happen at the Choosing. He was deep in thought when the shop door burst open, virtually taking the bell off its spring. Startled, he jumped up out of the chair. A stranger stood in the doorway; his face obscured by the dark brown hood of his cloak. He was breathing rapidly and sharply, with a sense of urgency in his voice, demanded to know. "Where is the apothecary named Mirabilis?"

Shrugging his shoulders, he replied, "I do not know. She…" before Shamera could say another word; the stranger turned around and took to his heels down the street.

"What is going on? This is not doing my nerves any good." He muttered to himself. He took a deep, chest expanding breath. The time for the Choosing was getting closer, nerves were setting in and thoughts were running wild inside his head. He looked at the clock again as another hour had gradually passed by; the shop door opened and in walked Mirabilis looking a little flustered. Her face was flushed, and she was panting.

"What's going on Mirabilis? A stranger came in looking for you. Did he find you? What did he want?" Probed Shamera, standing there with a furrowed brow, looking and feeling very confused.

"So many questions lad, anyway… it's nothing that needs to concern you, you need to be getting ready for the Choosing." replied Mirabilis quickly and calmly, trying to divert the conversation. "Not long now lad, you better be looking sharp and get yourself over there. I have already seen Verazslo roaming around the village; wandering around doing his usual conjuring tricks and entertaining everyone, getting them all excited."

"But what's with you and all this rushing around? And who were those people looking for you?"

Mirabilis looked calmly at Shamera and quietly said, "It was something I needed to take care of is all. It's all sorted now. You need to concern yourself with the task at hand; getting chosen. Everything is fine. Remember, during the Choosing, you need to think precisely before answering any of Verazslo's questions. Concentrate fully on any task you have to perform. Think carefully before rushing in. Now, you prove yourself the worthy candidate I know you to be."

"But…."

"But nothing. There's no more to be said on the matter. You need to focus on what YOU need to do; I will be there to watch you at the ceremony. Now go quickly and take your place." Mirabilis held out Shamera's summer cloak and helped him put it on.

"This is not the end of the matter; I know you're holding out on me." Shamera said as he made his way out of the door. He glanced back and said, "I know there is something you are not telling me." Shamera stood there looking at Mirabilis who shrugged and gave a slight smile through her tightly squeezed lips.

"If you show the same tenacity at the Choosing, Verazslo will have no option but to appoint you. Good luck lad. Off. You. Go. Trust. Your. Instincts." Mirabilis said as she punctuated every word, then leaned against the door frame as she watched Shamera for a while as he made his way down the street. She could not help a proud, motherly type smile forcing its way across her face. She had watched Shamera grow up from a small child to a young man.

The streets were full of people all enjoying the start of the festival. Shamera gradually made his way through the hordes of bustling people and down towards the market square. The noise levels were growing louder the closer he got. The scents of fresh bread, cooked meats, roasting nuts, and many other delicacies filled his nostrils. There were jugglers in extravagantly colourful costumes, juggling all manner of things, from large knives to flaming clubs. Traveling musicians playing different instruments added to the noise level as he made his way to the Choosing. He tried to relax but could not stop speculations about what was happening with Mirabilis from occupying his mind.

'Finally!' he thought as he entered the square. Glancing around, he saw the gathering of villagers, especially the large number of children being entertained by Verazslo. Who was meandering through the crowds, performing party tricks, conjuring up pyrotechnics which went whizzing and fizzing high into the air. He was also creating different flying creatures and colourful butterflies that would appear out of thin air, and small birds which flew out of his long beard and under his hat.

People cheered and patted Shamera on the back as he made his way through the crowd. He eventually made his way up the wooden steps to a loud roar from the delighted spectators. As he walked out on to the stage, the intensity of the cheering grew to a deafening level. He took his place on the stage with the five other apprehensive-looking hopefuls who had arrived a few moments before. Shamera nervously observed the hordes of people all looking towards the stage and pointing in his direction; now the realisation set in. His mouth dried as he tried to swallow, his stomach churned. It felt like it was performing cartwheels as he realised; the Choosing would soon begin.

He nervously paced around the stage, his eyes quickly flitting across the audience, looking for his family and Mirabilis. He would not hear them calling over the loud commotion of the crowd. His eyes were rapidly darting around the sea of faces. Some, he recognised but most he did not. He spotted his little sister sitting on the shoulders of their father. He could see they were trying to get closer to the front, but the vast throng of bodies impeded their progress. Shamera waved his hand high in the air to let them know he had spotted them. A small group of musicians tuning up their instruments for the start of the proceedings momentarily distracted him.

A loud booming voice from behind startled him. "ATTENTION ALL!!" shouted an enormous man in a bright yellow suit, holding a hefty megaphone to his mouth. "Verazslo will come up onto the stage and commence the Choosing. Will his next apprentice be among these six hopefuls? We will soon see." The man moved to the front of the stage and with gesticulating arms, as though trying to part the crowd, he bellowed again, "Make way, make way, let Verazslo through. Come on, give him room."

The deafening clamour became a mere whisper as trumpets sounded the approach of Verazslo the Sorcerer. Everyone watched and applauded eagerly as Verazslo gradually made his way through the crowd. The musicians played a fanfare, announcing his arrival to the stage. Verazslo, with the aid of his staff, trekked up the steps and onto the stage. He was still producing colourful butterflies and small birds, flashes of pyrotechnics exploding in the air. This whipped up the crowd again. His well-worn, multi-coloured robe swept along the wooden boards as he walked to the front of the stage.

The musicians played another fanfare as Verazslo paused for a moment, waving to the crowds. He stood at the front of the stage with a big grin, which was partially hidden behind his bushy grey beard. He listened to the sound of the whooping and clapping for a short while before raising his staff high in the air; paused for a few seconds before banging it down hard against the wooden boards three times. The commotion of the crowd dropped to a hush as Verazslo addressed them.

"Magic comes from nature, the lifeblood of our world, even from our universe; we should never use it for evil or personal gain." he bellowed. He turned to face the six nervous candidates who had formed themselves into a line across the stage. Verazslo stood looking at them for a short while before addressing them.

"You hopeful few will undergo a test of your worthiness; will one of you, this day, become my apprentice?" Verazslo walked along the line of aspiring pupils looking at each one in turn. It must have appeared to those watching as though he were peering into their very souls as he pondered and looked deep into their eyes.

"With this staff and this wand, you can have the power of sorcery; forget all you think you know. Use your instincts and intuition to show me…" Verazslo held a glass globe cupped in both of his hands. He held it in front of the first candidate and continued, "Make this glass globe glow." the first hopeful deliberated for a moment, held a hand over the globe and concentrated on making it glow. Unfortunately, there was not even a glimmer of a glow. "NO!" exclaimed Verazslo as he passed to the next contender.

"Make this glass globe glow." he asked again. The candidate, without hesitation, hovered his hand over the globe and, try as he might; he too failed to make it glow. "NO!" Verazslo continued along the row of candidates, each time declaring NO! As they each failed to make even the faintest flicker of light within the globe.

Shamera stood watching and tried to remain confident as Verazslo approached him and asked, "Can you make this globe glow?" Shamera looked at the globe. He poised his hand over the globe and scrunched his eyes shut. Concentrating as hard as he could, he imagined the globe glowing in Verazslo's hands. Shamera felt his hand getting warmer. He gradually opened his eyes a little to sneak a peek at the globe. His eyes shot wide open as he saw the globe glowing dimly. It might have been dim, but there was a glow within the globe!

Verazslo stared back straight into Shamera's blue eyes. It was barely a few seconds, but to Shamera it felt like minutes. Verazslo turned and looked towards the crowd, raised his staff into the air and banged it hard on the wooden boards, before exclaiming, "YES! At last, a candidate of potential worth." It took Shamera all of his willpower to contain his excitement; yet a broad grin forced itself across his face as the crowd erupted in whoops and whistles at the result.

"W-A-I-T!" shouted Verazslo as he repeatedly banged his staff on the wooden boards. "There are still two more tests to be completed."

The crowd plunged into silence as Verazslo handed Shamera his wand. He stared at the wand and considered all of its potential magic energy. His deep blue eyes opened wide as he carefully examined the object.

"Wow, this feels very smooth, even though it looks gnarly and crooked. You must have had it a long time."

He felt how comfortable it was, nestling in his hands. It measured about twelve inches long. It was heavier than he expected and made from twisted Ash; it appeared to have a golden grain which ran its full length. *'I cannot believe I am holding Verazslo's wand.'* He thought to himself. His heart was thumping with excitement.

Verazslo watched for a few moments as Shamera examined the wand. With a stern expression, he held Shamera's gaze. Then startled everyone, especially Shamera, when Verazslo shouted, "You have bested your opponents. You must now make them vanish. Use the wand and make them disappear; concentrate, think them gone and the wand will do the rest." Verazslo gestured with his hands as if to hurry him.

Shamera again peered down at the wand he was holding. Surprised and dumbfounded at this request, he looked towards the Sorcerer and asked. "Where will they go? Can I bring them back?"

The five unfortunates stood there, rooted to the spot. Verazslo had placed a spell on them and no one could move their feet. With fear etched upon their faces, they anxiously looked at each other and, in sheer panic, turned and stared straight at Shamera. Who looked anxiously at Verazslo; *'surely he did not mean it?'* He thought. Shamera looked back towards the extremely fearful competitors, who were desperately trying to move.

"Sorry, I err... I can't." he mumbled as he turned to face Verazslo.

"Do it or fail! Do you want to be the new apprentice or not?" reiterated Verazslo, again gesturing and pointing towards the unsuccessful candidates.

Shamera paused for a few seconds. He turned to face the fearful participants. Again, he looked down at the wand in his hand before raising it high into the air and shouted aloud.

"Magic comes from nature, the lifeblood of our world, even from our universe; we should use it only for the purposes of good; we should never use it for evil or personal gain!" he turned to Verazslo and offered him back the wand, saying aloud. "So be it... I have failed."

A large gasp boomed from the crowd as they watched Verazslo take back the wand. Verazslo took a deep breath and exhaled it slowly; his face was expressionless as he stood there gazing at the wand and looking back at Shamera. He said nothing as he turned his back on Shamera and faced the crowd. Verazslo stood and looked upon the faces of the expectant audience; his own face remained inscrutable as he thrust his staff high before bringing it down and hitting it hard against the stage three times. The chattering crowd were cut to silence. You could hear a pin drop as they all watched in anticipation as Verazslo raised the staff and the wand high over his head and shouted, "Test two...... Passed!"

An enormous roar erupted from the crowd. The other aspirants were no longer rooted to the spot and appeared to dance a little jig, their faces beaming as they realised nothing bad was going to befall them. Shamera's face could no longer hide the relief or the excitement, and after hearing the proclamation, he was ecstatic as he jumped up and punched the air with his fist. He was grinning from ear to ear as the other competitors came over to congratulate him, more out of relief than anything else.

Verazslo once again turned to the crowd and gradually raised his staff and his wand into the air and with a resounding voice bellowed, "S-i-l-e-n-c-e...." once again, a hush befell the crowd.

"We will hold here the third and final test tomorrow at noon." he exclaimed.

Verazslo looking out over the crowd; observed three men wearing dark-coloured cloaks with their hoods pulled up, they were forcing their way quickly through the crowd. He watched with concern as they hurtled up the steps and onto the stage. They approached Verazslo and at once exclaimed "You must come with us... NOW!"

One man whispered something to Verazslo, which caused him to spin around and look straight at Shamera. Verazslo's face appeared concerned as his eyes narrowed.

"What about the boy?" questioned Verazslo, nodding his head in Shamera's direction.

"There is no time... you must come with us now. Come there is no time to lose."

Verazslo turned to Shamera. "I'll see you tomorrow, here at noon. For your last challenge." He said in a half whisper. He turned away and quickly left with the mysterious hooded trio. Shamera watched as they scurried away through the crowd. A mystified look engrained itself upon his face as Verazslo and the three men quickly vanished into the thinning crowd.

Chapter 2

"What in the name of Stefremmus is happening? Who were those men?" one of the other hopefuls asked.

"I don't know." he replied. Shamera stood there, trying to make sense of what had happened. Was this part of the test he wondered?

The crowd of onlookers, surprised at the way they led Verazslo away, speculated on what was happening. Some people stood scrutinizing the stage, waiting to see if anything else might happen, while most of the crowd dispersed as everyone questioned each other about the events now unfolding.

"It's all part of the Choosing, it's all staged in order to get you excited." someone said.

"I heard a rumour Niniane is back and is looking for revenge." said another.

"Rubbish, she is long gone," replied the man he was talking to.

Mirabilis appeared as if out of thin air and took Shamera by the arm. "You must come with me." he said softly.

"Mirabilis… where did you come from?" remarked Shamera, surprised by her sudden presence.

"Where are we going? What is going on? Is this part of the Choosing?"

"No time for questions, young apprentice. We have to go from here with haste." Mirabilis stated with some urgency as she rapidly led Shamera through the crowd.

The other hopefuls looked at each other, totally mystified, before one of them smiled and proposed, "Let's go to the slaughtered lamb to commiserate." They all smiled, nodded at each other in agreement and set off for the Inn.

"Where are we going?" asked Shamera.

"First, we must stop by my shop and pick something up, and… well, you'll see when we get there."

They scurried through the crowded streets like a pair of urban rats, dodging in and around the people until they eventually reached the Apothecary. As they entered the shop, a hooded figure emerged out of the shadows from the far corner of the shop.

"Have you got it?" the stranger enquired.

"It's here... it's safe. It's in this secret drawer." Mirabilis walked over to a wall mounted display cabinet and started twisting and pulling at two decorative knobs adorning the cabinet, a secret drawer sprung open with a loud click and a puff of dust. Mirabilis reached into the draw and pulled out a small parcel, wrapped in what looked like soft dark leather. She handed the parcel to the hooded man and said, "Here it is... it must be taken to the Elvenii before the Blood Moon has waned. It cannot fall into the wrong hands." stated Mirabilis.

The hooded man took the parcel and carefully un-wrapped it. He held the object up to examine it against the light flooding in from the large shop window. It looked like a tear-drop shaped gem of purple crystal. "It's beautiful." said the man as he examined the shard. The purple colour of crystal radiated around the room as it reflected the sunlight in all directions.

"What is it?" asked Shamera.

"It is called the shard of Ellaria; it is ancient and is has great power." the man replied before gently wrapping it up again. The hooded man looked at Shamera. He could see a thousand questions written on his face.

"So, you are the new apprentice sorcerer?" he stated. The man turned to look at Mirabilis "What have you told him?"

"Nothing... he knows nothing." Mirabilis replied.

"I'm not the apprentice yet. There is still one more test and... what is it I don't I know? Mirabilis what is going on? Where is Verazslo, and who are you?" he asked inquisitively, turning towards the stranger. "Why do you hide in the shadows and cover your face under your hood?"

"You will have your answers in due course." The stranger gestured with his hands, palms down, to calm Shamera, who was looking a little worried.

"But first we-"

Another hooded stranger burst into the shop, the shop bell clanking its alarm as it bounced wildly upon its spring. The man stopped in the middle of the room, looked around the shop whilst gasping for breath. "Am I glad I have found you...

Who's this?" he said, panting and levelling his finger straight at Shamera.

"This is Shamera our new sorcerer's apprentice. It's okay." Mirabilis replied.

"I ran here as fast as I could. They're gone, Verazslo and the others. They've definitely disappeared! No message, no nothing." he said, still panting for breath and leaning heavily against a staff. The man came further into the shop; he too left his dark hood pulled up, obscuring his face.

"They left these in the inner sanctum." gasped the man whilst pulling out a scroll of paper and Verazslo's wand from deep inside his cloak pocket. "Shamera, you say, strange… this scroll has your name on it. Here, this is Verazslo's staff, too." he offered them to Mirabilis who took them and placed them on the countertop.

Shamera turned towards Mirabilis and raised his voice. "WHAT IS GOING ON! Disappeared where? Why? Who are you people? Why do you hide yourselves under your hoods? Mirabilis please." he pleaded; there was an obvious quiver in his voice and a pained expression on his face. Shamera tried to swallow, but his nervousness had made his throat dry.

"The lad needs to know; he needs to be told… He could be our best hope." stated Mirabilis, she looked over at the two hooded figures who both nodded in agreement.

"I could be the best hope for what? What's special about me?" Shamera enquired. He was feeling confused, desperately needing some answers. He watched inquisitively and nervously as one of the hooded men walked purposefully towards the door, gradually drew down the blind, locked and bolted the door. Mirabilis drew the blinds over the large shop window, turned and lit a small oil lamp which was standing on the countertop. The small oil lamp barely lit the room; the orange glow of the flame reflected in some of the glass bottles in the cabinets and appeared to make some of their contents glow with a strange iridescence.

"What we are about to tell you must go no further. Swear it!" Mirabilis said firmly.

"I swear." Shamera replied, shrugging his shoulders and throwing his hands palms up in the air.

Mirabilis picked up the scroll and handed it to Shamera. He looked at it as though it were about to bite him.

"Well... go on. Open it, it won't read itself lad." said Mirabilis.

Shamera broke the seal and unravelled the scroll.

"What does it say?" questioned Mirabilis.

"I can't read it." he replied bewildered, he examined both sides of the parchment, looked up at all three of them and with a mystified expression stated, "It's written in a strange language, I do not know what it says or what it means."

Shamera handed the parchment to Mirabilis who handed it to one of the hooded men, who looked the parchment over.

"How strange... they have addressed it to Shamera yet what is written within is unreadable. Look here, under Shamera's name. Three small runes... can either of you read them?" he enquired as he looked up at the others. Mirabilis took the scroll and examined the markings.

"These look like Elvenii runes. They have not used this type of runes for centuries. Maybe the Elvenii can tell you more when you get there."

"What do you mean... when '*I*' get there?"

Mirabilis looked at him and placed a hand gently on his shoulder.

"The Choosing was merely a formality; Verazslo has had his eye on you for some time as his apprentice. He was waiting until you were old enough. He could sense you have the gift of magic."

"Come lad... sit, it's time you were told." beckoned the one of the hooded men as he pulled up a chair for him to sit on. The others took a chair each and came and sat with Shamera who was feeling extremely apprehensive. The two hooded figures stood up and took off their hooded cloaks. Shamera, with his eyes wide open, leaned back and gripped his chair as the two men revealed who they were. He let out a little gasp. "Mystics."

He looked as though he'd seen a ghost. The older Mystic looked back and smiled. He was a man of about sixty years; he had a long narrow face with angular cheekbones and a square chin. His Almond-shaped eyes were a pale green, there was an eye shaped indentation on his forehead about an inch above his nose. His long wide nose hooked down towards his top lip; he had tucked his shoulder length grey hair back behind his rounded ears. His skin appeared leathery and weather-beaten. His companion was about half his age, slightly taller with wide muscular shoulders, powerful arms, and bared similar facial features.

"B-but... you're extinct... you were all wiped out centuries ago." he remarked.

"No, not quite. As a race, they decimated us during the dark times. They hunted our ancestors down and slaughtered them because of their gift, huh! gift... a curse more like. Those who could, fled to the mountains of Moldern where some of us still live and farm today. Our numbers are few, and sadly, most of us no longer possess the ability to read minds or see into the future. The Elvenii secured us land, and they help protect our homeland and keep out uninvited guests." he replied.

"My name is Agnar, and this is Lethron." he said, pointing towards his older friend,

"We are part of a group of people known as the Guild; we help protect these lands. We have many brothers who have joined us from many other races, towns, and villages like yours. We all have one goal in common and that is one of keeping the peace. We travel in secret throughout the land and meet with town and village elders, who are also part of the Guild. Verazslo is part of our Guild, as is Mirabilis." He listened intently as Lethron told his story.

"But why do you hide under your cloaks?"

"We are Mystics. They once persecuted us for our abilities. People feared us and so we prefer to remain anonymous and not let the same fate befall us again." Agnar explained.

"You need to take this shard and give it to Lord Salogel of the Elvenii; he will know what to do with it." Lethron said, holding the tightly wrapped parcel.

Shamera sensed the urgency and fear in his voice, "You must get it to him before the Blood Moon wanes, which is in three days' time. It must be in the hands of Lord Salogel and Lord Salogel alone, before the Blood Moon wanes. Failure to do so could mean the end of the peace we have enjoyed these five hundred years." stated Mirabilis.

"Me… why me? What makes me so vital?" He looked inquisitively at the three men as he waited for his answers.

"Wait a minute. Is this part of my test? This is part of the Choosing, isn't it?" He said with a slight look of relief on his face, sitting more erect, thinking he had seen through the ruse.

"No lad, this has nothing to do with the Choosing. This is serious. You wanted to know what all the fuss was about this morning; well, this is part of it." replied Mirabilis. She looked directly at Shamera; her expression was one of anguish as he continued to explain what was occurring. "Niniane, the dark sorceress, is back. Rumour has it she intends to take revenge and to take possession of these lands. She is reportedly massing an army of followers from nearby islands in the south. She rules by fear, enslaving and forcing these people to do her bidding… killing the families of anyone who disobeys her or refuses to fight for her. You are to be the next apprentice sorcerer; you have the magic within you. You must have felt something deep inside of you? This is your destiny, Shamera." Mirabilis recounted.

"I know I have always wanted to be the next apprentice, but I could never do magic." Shamera replied.

Mirabilis placed her right palm on Shamera's chest, "It is there… deep inside, you need to be shown how to find it and use it. That's what being an apprentice is all about." said Mirabilis.

"We need to find Verazslo and the others. You are perfect for taking this shard to Lord Salogel, and besides, no one would suspect a young lad travelling alone, an apothecary's assistant out herb collecting." Mirabilis said as she tried to reassure Shamera.

"What is so special about this shard?" Shamera inquired.

"It is supposed to have great power… Verazslo knew what power it holds. All we know is it cannot fall into the hands of Niniane. We have kept it safe and hidden all these hundreds of years, and it must remain safe." replied Agnar.

"Has it been in this shop all this time?" Shamera asked.

"No." replied Mirabilis, "It is entrusted to different people. We keep it moving secretly, so it is harder to locate."

"It's an enormous responsibility we're placing upon you, especially for someone so young. The future of our land could depend on it." said Lethron quietly as he stood up and placed his hand supportively around Shamera's shoulder.

"You will leave first thing in the morning; you will need to rest before your journey. You will need your wits about you. Niniane and her followers are out there. They will not be looking for a young boy travelling alone but remember... trust no one. Besides... Niniane is supposed to be in the south. You're heading north." said Mirabilis comfortingly.

Shamera thought for a while, and with a slight quiver in his voice, he said, "I won't let you down; I will deliver the shard before the Blood Moon."

"You are a brave lad, and you will make a great sorcerer one day; Verazslo has had his eye on you for a couple of years. He was waiting until you were old enough to be chosen. Here, take this backpack... there is a secret pouch at the bottom, here let me." said Mirabilis placing the shard and the scroll inside it.

"I have also placed sample bottles of various herbs and some empty collecting bottles in there, too. Remember your potion making experience, it may come in useful. You will also need to take this wand and staff. Take excellent care of them. I dare not think what might happen if these fell into the wrong hands." Mirabilis informed.

Agnar had been scratching away furiously with a pencil across a piece of brown wrapping paper he found on the countertop.

"Here Shamera, I have drawn you a map. You may find it useful." he said, passing Shamera the piece of paper.

"Thanks." Shamera replied as he studied the map. "This takes me through the Screaming Forest." he exclaimed suddenly. He looked up at the three of them with an incredibly concerned look on his face.

"Don't worry about that. Stay on the path. It is an enchanted path; do not stray from it for anything or anyone and you will be okay. Here, take this." Agnar reached behind his neck to unfasten a chain and removed an amulet suspended on the silver chain. He gave it to Shamera. It was silver and resembled a five-pointed snowflake. The tips of the points were rounded and had what looked like little recesses to enable it to hold something. At its centre was a red, ruby-like crystal. It had two other crystals, one blue and one green, attached at two of the points.

"This will offer you some extra protection through the forest. It's not complete. As you can see, three crystals are missing."

"What happened to them?"

"This amulet has many powers when complete, and as with all our powerful magic, we agreed to dismantle it and hide the crystals so peace would prevail. We kept some lesser powerful items, as did the Khul Dwarvian and the Elvenii."

Shamera placed the amulet around his neck and took hold of the staff; it was about five feet long, made of hickory and about two inches thick. Coffee coloured grain ran the full length of the staff. It had an ornate carved top of about six inches with a hollow centre. Shamera could feel the wear of the staff where hands had held and rubbed it smooth over the years.

The Elvenii will teach you how to use the wand and the staff properly. They used a lot of magic at one time, and I believe they still do, but they won't admit it. Verazslo will be back, and he will teach you everything you need to know to become a great sorcerer. Go home say nothing to your folks; especially about the Mystics, the fewer people who know about their business, the better and safer your journey will be. I will see your parents early tomorrow and tell them you went off on part of your training. We do not want to worry them now, do we?" Mirabilis queried.

"Erm... no, no I do not want them to worry. Is there any need to worry?"

"Not at all lad, not at all." Lethron said as he stood up.

"You are merely delivering those items to the Elvenii; it's not like you're going into battle." He continued. And with a wry smile, patted Shamera on the back reassuringly.

Shamera looked at the three of them standing in front of him, stood as tall as he could, drew a deep breath "I will get these items there." he said proudly. He knew this was an enormous responsibility they had placed on him; he turned and headed for the door.

"Allow me, young sorcerer." said Agnar as he unbolted the door, "Providence be with you lad." he continued as he opened the door. He stood in the doorway for a moment before turning around and taking one last look before heading home. The three men stood and looked at each other for a few seconds.

"I hope we have done the right thing. The shard cannot fall into Niniane's hands. He is so young." Agnar said with concern.

"What other choice do we have? We have to find out what happened to Verazslo." replied Lethron. His voice sounded heavy.

"He will be fine; he is a good lad… honest and hardworking… and besides he is the apprentice, and he has to do it; he'll get them there." Mirabilis remarked. Knowing the dangers which lay ahead and not fully informing Shamera of them made her heart weigh heavily with guilt.

"As long as Niniane or her men don't realise who he is or what he carries, he should be safe." Lethron replied hopefully.

"Why should they? He is merely a young apothecary's assistant, out gathering plants." Agnar stated.

"Don't underestimate Niniane; after all, everyone in the village has witnessed Shamera become the apprentice, and she has become stronger, according to our reports. She probably has spies everywhere." replied Mirabilis as she sauntered towards one of the cabinets.

"It is our custom, at times like this, to raise a glass of brandy. I have a special bottle of plum brandy put by if you would both like to join me in a glass, a toast to wish the lad well on his journey." Mirabilis held aloft a dark dusty red bottle. The cork squeaked and squealed as she gently twisted it up. It popped as she removed it from the bottle. She poured three glasses and gave one each to Agnar and Lethron. Mirabilis held her glass aloft as she toasted.

"To a safe and speedy journey, and may providence and wisdom be with you, Shamera."

They all raised their glasses and in unison repeated the toast aloud.

It was late afternoon when Shamera arrived home to a hero's welcome. His mum had laid the table with celebratory cakes, biscuits and freshly made fruit juices.

"Where have you been?" asked his mother excitedly. She then spotted the backpack and staff. "Are they, are they yours?" She continued; a proud smile beamed across her face.

This had taken Shamera completely by surprise. He stood looking at the table and then at his family. Little by little, he regathered his thoughts.

"Erm... not exactly. I had to pick these up from Mirabilis's shop."

His stomach dropped. How was he going to explain about the journey he was to embark on, without worrying his family? He had never been away from home before. Shamera took a deep breath, "I'll just take these up to my room. I cannot wait to get stuck into this feast."

He gave a strained smile and took his belongings to his room. He sat on the edge of his bed and took a deep breath. His heart was racing. The truth of the matter was, he had not anticipated the anxiety he was feeling about his journey. Nor about having to tell his family about it. Should he tell them about Verazslo or about Niniane? Would this worry them too much? His emotions were running wild. He cradled his head in his hands, trying to think straight. He listened to his heart thumping away; he knew he couldn't hide away in his room much longer. *'This is too conflicting for me to deal with right now. Happy to be chosen to be the next apprentice, and sad having to lie, or not tell my parents the whole truth.'* He thought to himself. He closed his eyes, sat up straight and ran his fingers through his hair, trying to calm himself before going back downstairs.

"Come on then, tell us all about it." His mother asked enthusiastically.

"Let the lad sit first." Remarked his father, pulling up a chair at the table.

"I'm sorry. I'm just excited for you."

Gwen sat eating some cake, his mother and father sat down at the table with expectant looks on their faces. They said nothing but stared at Shamera waiting for him to speak.

"What can I say? The morning dragged waiting for the Choosing, even working at the shop. Time appeared to stand still. Then I made my way to the Choosing, and it's all a bit of a blur. I keep piecing bits together, but nerves got the better of me, I think."

"And those things you brought home, are they for your training?" Asked his father.

"Not exactly." He replied hesitantly.

"What do you mean?" asked his mother.

Shamera paused, he agonised whether he should tell them everything. Then, without giving it another thought, replied, "I have to deliver them to the Elvenii, and they are to teach me to use the wand and staff in order to do magic." He swallowed hard and waited for their reply.

"You have to go to the Elvenii? I'm not sure I like that. It will take days to get there. That's not a journey for a young lad." she said worryingly.

"He's a young man; we should not stand in his way. This has been his dream for as long as I can remember." Said his father reassuringly.

Shamera looked at his father and just smiled.

"I know but... Well, come on then. This food won't eat itself." Said his mother with a slight break in her voice. She looked at Shamera. She knew a day like this would come, but like all mothers, it was a day she dreaded. Her child had grown up and now must leave home.

"So, when you come back home, you can magic me up my own unicorn." Gwen said as she finished her piece of cake.

"Well, we will have to see if I am good enough first." he smiled.

Shamera tucked into his celebratory food, he tried to look happy and excited whilst thoughts of Verazslo and Niniane invaded his mind.

"We are very proud of you son." said his mother with a teary eye.

"An apprentice sorcerer in the family, who would have thought?" Said his father.

His mother gazed at him, her eyes betraying a layer of concern. "Promise me something," she said, her voice steady yet tinged with an underlying worry.

He nodded stiffly, jerking his head a little. He locked his eyes upon her face.

"You won't do anything that will put you in danger, will you?"

"Leave the lad alone. He's all grown up. He has to make his own way in life. Stop fussing, he's going to be just fine."

"I'm his mother. It's my job to worry."

"It's okay mother, I don't think the Elvenii will put me in any danger."

"And what about the last apprentice? You said he blew himself up."

"Mother, stop worrying. I'll be fine." he said, trying to sound confident.

They all tucked into the hearty celebratory food. Shamera occasionally glancing up and looking around the table. Mixed emotions still troubled his thoughts. He did well to hide them.

"I will pack some of this up for your journey. You can get it out of the pantry in the morning."

"Thank you. I will be up and, on my way, very early. I will try not to disturb you. It shouldn't be too long before I am home again and do not worry. I will be just fine."

"Don't be silly, I want to say goodbye properly." said his mother.

"I would rather say my farewells now, if that's alright. I would feel much better about the journey and would be more settled about it."

"Perfectly fine, son." said his father standing up. He walked around the table and gave Shamera a strong fatherly hug.

"You take care son, don't trust strangers. And I wish you a speedy and safe journey."

"Thank you, father, I will be alright."

"I can't believe my son is all grown up. Send a message of your safe arrival when you get to Selvenora." A tear rolled down her face as she gave him a warm, loving hug.

"I will, mother, I promise."

Shamera then kneeled down, "Come here, you." he said to Gwen as he held his arms outstretched. Gwen ran into his open arms. "I will look after them while you are away." She whispered in his ear.

Shamera pulled away a little to get a better look at his sister, "You too are growing up quickly. You'd better be on your best behaviour while I am away, and then you just might get your unicorn." He cocked his head slightly to the right and smiled before giving her another hug.

Shamera did not sleep well; merely catching a few hours between restless thoughts of the adventure he was about to embark on. It was still dark when he rose. He wrote his mother a note; he wrote they were not to be concerned, and Mirabilis would come to see them to explain things in greater detail later that morning.

Shamera checked his backpack one last time. *'The shard, scroll, food and drink for the journey, all safely packed'*, he thought to himself. Verazslo's wand was safe in his cloak pocket. Shamera took hold of the staff, which was leaning against the wall, tiptoed out of the house and set off for Selvenora. He knew he had a long road ahead, and he was feeling proud at being trusted with this responsibility. As he reached the outskirts of the village, he stopped and turned to look back.

The village looked peaceful. The flickering flames of the streetlamps gave a warm, welcoming glow to the empty streets; the only sound came from the birds' early morning chorus. He knew his family would be concerned about his safe return; this made him a little anxious as he obviously did not want them to fret about him. His heart was already beating fast with the excitement and anticipation of the adventure which lay before him.

Chapter 3

As with all journeys, they start with one small step. Shamera looked at the road ahead. Taking a deep breath, he walked forward. Taking the first step on the biggest adventure of his life. *'This is it,'* he thought, *'the journey has begun.'* The moon was waning fast and soon it would be dawn, his favourite time of day. Shamera had been walking for about an hour when the sun broke the horizon. The early morning light added a delightful, warm, magical atmosphere to the valley.

As he reached Chuddar's Orchard, he could see the fruit trees were in full bloom and a myriad of colourful blossom adorned the branches. As he got closer, he noticed the sweet scent of the blossom gently wafting on the early morning breeze. He paused under the trees; drew a deep slow breath through his nostrils and filled his lungs with the fragrant air, held it for a few seconds before slowly breathing it out. His face lit up with a slight smile, which gradually grew larger as he gazed around at the beautiful landscape. This was his home, and therefore he loved the Sloendor Valley. A sharp breeze caught the blossom, sending a flurry of petals cascading down like a pink snowstorm.

'I can't stand here all day,' he thought as he reluctantly walked on down the road again. He had been walking for a couple of hours, admiring the landscape, when he noticed six riders on horseback heading down the track towards him. He dropped the staff into the dry ditch running along the side of the track.

As the horsemen drew closer, Shamera could see they were not slowing down. He stood back off the track to allow them to pass without himself being knocked down and trampled over. Abruptly, they drew to a halt. "You, boy!" shouted the man astride the lead horse. "How far to Elms Hollow?"

"Not far, a short distance down the road," he replied, pointing in the direction he had travelled from.

Shamera felt a little uneasy as these men loomed high above him. The horses were sweating and lathered heavily; the men had obviously been riding hard and for some time.

"What is your business there?" Shamera asked.

"None of yours," the lead horseman replied sarcastically.

Shamera looked down; these men did not appear friendly; he did not want to antagonise them.

"Who are you? And what are you doing out here?" another horseman asked.

"I am collecting herbs and plants; they have to be picked early in a morning, so they are at their best. I sell them at the apothecary." He replied.

"Then be about your business," the man on the lead horse said in a curt manner.

The man kicked into the flanks of his horse and rode off towards Elms Hollow with the others in close pursuit. Shamera watched them for a few moments before picking up the staff and starting on his way again. Something in his gut associated these rough-looking people with Niniane. He decided he would play safe and would go across the countryside and not stay on the main road; this would probably be the safer option.

It was not long before Shamera came upon a large field of tall maize. This would be the perfect place to head across the farmland, as the maize would offer protection and help to hide him from anyone looking down the road. As he walked through the field, he could not help wondering who those men were and what they wanted in Elms Hollow. He was also thinking about his family and if they would worry about what Mirabilis told them. He knew he must not dwell on these thoughts, as they would cloud his mind and slow him down.

He eventually came to the end of the maize fields; the main road was a long way out of sight. He decided he was going to avoid all the villages until reaching the Whinging Bridge.

Now potato fields lay in front of him. This made his trek a little slower as the undulating fields made him a little unsteady on his feet. He stopped and took the map out of his pocket and, after a quick study of it, he could see he was not far off the main route. He trudged his way across the fields, using the hedgerows for cover. He plodded across the fields until eventually he reached Two-Acre Pond. This was a place he knew well as he fished here regularly with his father. The sun was high in the sky and Shamera stopped to have a bit of lunch. He found some shade under a large old tree and sat with his back to its trunk. He tucked into some of his bread and cheese. He sat under the shade of the tree for about an hour, resting and looking around, when he caught sight of a purple and red flower with a long dark green stem and broad yellow leaves. He sat looking at it for a while, then realised it was a plant known as the Somnohypnos plant, also known locally as 'Dead Man Living'; the leaves made a very strong sleeping draft, especially when mixed with lavender. Shamera took out a collection bottle and placed a couple of its leaves in it. He looked around for a blue flower with a short fat green stem and dark shiny green leaves; he knew it would not be far as both plants usually grew close together. It was not long before he had found what he was looking for; this was the Radixo Exsomnii plant. Shamera carefully dug up the plant. For a small plant, it had large orange roots which grew deep into the ground. This is what Shamera was looking for. This was the antidote to the Dead Man Living.

After he had collected his samples, he packed up his things, had another quick look at his map, and set off again. He would have to head towards the Saxby Hills; this would take him close to the road once more. They could easily see him there. He kept scanning every inch of the countryside; he was even avoiding farmers tending their land. He did not want to have contact with anyone. The fewer people who knew where he was, the better.

It was mid-afternoon by the time Shamera reached Thistlewood Lane; this narrow dirt track led to a few farmsteads. Across the other side of the lane, and through a small copse, was the start of Saxby Hills. Shamera started along the track towards the main road; this was going to be the quickest route, and it appeared to be quiet. Farmers used this road to access the land, and it led nowhere else. It was not long before he was back on the main road again. High hedges and tall trees flanked Thistlewood lane and offered Shamera some protection from being spotted. Shamera was close to the end of the lane. He climbed a tree to see if the road ahead was clear. He could not be certain the riders were not followers of

Niniane, but he could not take a chance. He squeezed through a gap in the hedge and was climbing a suitable tree when he heard horses. Peering carefully around the tree, he saw six riders heading towards him along the main road. He quickly descended the tree and hid behind the hedge, pulling tall grasses in front of him to help camouflage his position. The riders drew close and stopped at the entrance to Thistlewood Lane.

"You two try down there," one man shouted with authority, "We'll carry on this way; we'll meet up at the other side of these hills in about two hours," he continued.

"He can't have got too far," another one said.

"Keep looking," said the first man again.

Two riders set off trotting down the Lane, and the others rode off towards the Whinging Bridge. He was now certain they were looking for him; he decided his best option was to change tactics; leave the track and go over the hill instead, as the riders could not follow him up the steep, rocky sides.

The climb was not as bad as he expected; he reached the top and hid in between two large boulders; he looked out towards the Whinging Bridge. He was looking for the riders or even dust-clouds in the distance which would show their whereabouts. Once he was down the other side of the hill, there would be very little cover in which he could hide. He decided he would rest here and make his way after dark. He contemplated how he was going to get to the bridge without being spotted. The daylight was fading fast as the sun slid quickly behind the jagged silhouette of the mountain range to the west. It was about two miles to the Whinging Bridge, so named because of the creaking and groaning sounds its wooden structure makes when horse-drawn carts are crossing it. It was going to be a full moon tonight; two more nights before the Blood Moon. The moonlight will help light the way, yet it should still be dark enough to hide should the need arise. However, there was a long way still to go, and he still had the 'Screaming Forest' to pass through.

As he walked down the hill, he recalled the stories he was told about the forest and of the creatures who lived in there. Creatures like Spriggans, mischievous little creatures which are normally harmless, but play tricks on the unsuspecting traveller.

Tree fairies: totally harmless little flying creatures that, as their name suggests, lived amongst the trees. Wild boars, which can be aggressive, feeding and living deep in the forest, but they usually steer clear of people. Boggart's: short fat and hairy creatures of human form, said to devour anyone who strays from the track and gets lost in the forest. Nighreag's; said to be ugly hags who can appear as beautiful women to lure the unsuspecting traveller to his death. They are also said to scream when someone is about to die. For this reason, the forest is not a safe place to be if you become lost. He placed his hand on his chest and felt the amulet reassuringly. *'I hope this works,'* he said to himself.

His mind was already playing tricks on him as some shadows looked like creatures hiding amongst the rocks and the bushes. He wondered where the horsemen could be. Were they close? The moon was rising higher in the dark velvet sky. The noises of the night appeared to be louder and stranger than normal. He kept telling himself everything was okay, and it was his imagination running wild. The moon was high in the clear night sky as the Whinging Bridge came into view. Looking at the bridge in the distance, its wooden structure seemed to glow as it bathed in the moonlight. It wasn't a wide bridge; it was merely wide enough for one cart at a time to cross, but it was the only crossing point for 10 miles in either direction. He scanned the roads and the surrounding countryside for any sign of the horsemen. He could not see any sign of them, but knew they were out there somewhere, somewhere in the dark. He carefully made his way towards the bridge. Through the stillness of the night, the babbling waters of the river ran under the bridge seemed somehow louder. He felt exposed out in the open. He carried on to the Inn about a mile down the road; there, he would see if they had a bed for the night. It was not long before he reached a fork in the road and the Inn. To the right, the road led to towards Handorth, a small hamlet about half-a-mile away, and then on to Khulderhern. To the left lay the road to Errinbar, and beyond there, the 'Screaming Forest'. Through the forest are the Venora foothills leading to the mountain range and the mountain entrance to Selvenora. The forest was at least a good day's walk away, so he decided he would rest at the 'Three-Legged Pony' Inn. He checked around the Inn to see if there were any horses tied up, there were none.

He crept over to the ditch at the other side of the road; he would leave Verazslo's staff hidden here. He did not want anyone to recognise it and ask questions about why it was in his possession. It was dark. He checked to see if anyone was around. He could not hear or see anyone and so he hid it in the undergrowth and carefully covered it with twigs and leaves; it will be safe here until morning, he thought to himself. He checked around again to see if anyone might have seen him hiding the staff... all was clear. He crossed back over the track and entered the establishment. He stood in the barroom and looked around for the innkeeper; the place was full of people drinking late into the night. The stringent aroma of stale ale and wet sawdust was strong. Silvery/grey plumes of pipe smoke floated up towards the ceiling looking like ghosts of the tobacco it once was. It hung in the air; stinging eyes as it danced along on the drafts of an old creaky building.

There was a loud chatter of conversation as people tried to talk above each other. The glowing embers of the log fire appeared warm and welcoming after being out in the cold night air.

"Excuse me sir," Shamera said politely as he approached a tall man wearing a dirty, once white apron.

"What can I do you for?" the innkeeper replied in a deep, gruff voice.

"I'm looking for a bed for the night. Would you have one spare?"

"Ask the wife. She's over there," he replied, pointing to a plump, red-haired lady behind the bar.

He walked over to the bar. As he did, a man stood up from a nearby table and bumped into him.

"Watch where you are going you clumsy oaf," the man shouted. The noise suddenly dimmed, and all eyes turned towards Shamera as the man again shouted, "You spilled my ale!"

"I am sorry sir," apologised Shamera.

"Well, what are you going to do about it?" he shouted again.

Before Shamera could say another word, the innkeepers' wife intervened, "The lad spilled nothing, and you're drunk... again. You need to go home to your wife... now... before she worries where you are," she insisted, as she stood between the man and Shamera.

"He spilled my ale, and I want another!" he shouted at her. A little of the ale mixed with his saliva ran down his chin, which he wiped away with his sleeve.

"You're drunk again Tarkis, you'll be getting no more ale tonight; and you'll not start any trouble in here either," she replied forcefully.

The inn keeper came up behind Tarkis grabbed him by his collar, raising him slightly off his heels. "I have told you before about shouting at my wife," he said as he marched the drunk towards the door. "Go home and sleep it off."

The noise level returned to normal as everyone downed more ale and blew more pipe smoke into the already tobacco laden air.

"Now lad, what can I do you for?" the innkeeper's wife enquired with a smile.

"I need a bed for the night if you have one, please?" he asked politely.

"I have one upstairs; it'll be noisy until this lot goes home though," she replied apologetically.

"I can cope with that." he said relieved.

The innkeeper's wife took him upstairs to show him to his room. "Sorry dearie, but this one's right above the bar," she said as she opened the door and with her hand gestured to him to enter the room. He entered the room and the innkeeper's wife followed. She went over to a small table next to the bed and lit a candle. The room was small with a single bed pushed into the far corner; a few wooden pegs were jutting out from the wall near the bed for clothes to hang from. A dirty, small square window looked out onto the road below. The raised muffled noises from the bar filtered up through the floorboards. He looked at her and said, "It's fine, it will do me for the one night."

"What brings you here at this time of night?" she asked.

"I am out collecting herbs and plants. I sell them to the apothecary at Elms Hollow. I didn't realise the time and before I knew it was getting dark," he replied.

"Hmmm," she uttered disbelievingly, through tight, narrow lips and raised eyebrows, then replied, "Visiting a girl, perhaps? Well, whatever the reason, a lad like you should not be out this late, and alone in these parts," she advised.

"You sound like my mother. That's the sort of thing she would say," he replied softly.

"Have you eaten tonight? I can rustle up some of my heart-warming soup?"

"Erm… thank you, yes please."

"And what about breakfast? Will you be requiring breakfast?"

"I need to be up really early, so no thank you."

"You cannot travel on an empty stomach," she said, tapping her own belly. "I'll make you a sandwich to take with you if you prefer?"

"Yes, that would be a good idea, thank you."

"How much do I owe?"

A wry smile crept across her face. "Four pennies for the room: two pennies for the soup and one penny for the sandwich."

Shamera took out his little leather money bag and paid her the seven pennies.

She stopped in the doorway, turned slightly to look back. "Your soup won't be long," she said as she closed the door.

He did not waste any time getting undressed and into bed. He wanted to rise early and be out before the sun came up. He lay with his head on his pillow for a while, his head full of thoughts of the journey ahead, the horsemen, and his family. After about ten minutes, there was a knock at the door. He quickly put on his shirt and sat up in the bed.

"Come in!" He shouted.

"It's only me with your soup, dearie," the innkeeper's wife replied. "Here, enjoy it while it's hot. I'll leave it here on the table."

"Thank you," he said, feeling and looking a little shy.

The innkeeper's wife smiled and left him to enjoy his soup. He tucked into one of the best bowls of soup he had eaten in a long while. It wasn't long after finishing his soup, he heard the late-night revellers leaving the Inn and making their way home. He heard a couple of people coming up the stairs and going to their rooms. He climbed back into bed and made himself comfortable. Now the place was quiet, he soon dropped off to sleep.

The sound of loud banging on the Inn door abruptly woke him.

"Open up!" shouted someone from the street as they banged loudly on the door once again. Shamera leaped out of bed and peered out of the window. It was still dark, but he could make out the silhouettes of three men sitting astride their horses and three horses without riders. "Open this door!" someone shouted again. He immediately got dressed and went to the top of the stairs. He heard the inn keeper unbolt and open the door.

"What do you think you are doing at this time of night?" the innkeeper exclaimed, displeased at being awakened so rudely.

"We are looking for a boy, an Ethaenian boy. Have you seen him? He may have passed this way," a man's voice asked curtly.

"Who are you? And what do you want with him?"

"That's no concern of yours. Have you seen an Ethaenian boy pass this way?" a man asked forcefully.

"We possibly had someone in here last night. What's he done?"

The three men pushed their way into the bar area. Shamera could see by the light of the innkeepers' lamp these were the same horsemen he came across earlier.

"Is he here?" the tallest of the three demanded.

Shamera's heart was beating hard and fast. He had to think rapidly. He noticed a small window at the end of the corridor. He tiptoed into his room, grabbed all of his belongings, and ran to the window.

"Search the rooms," he heard someone downstairs order.

He quickly and as quietly as he could, opened the window wide enough for him to climb through. He threw out his things out and climbed down, dropping as quietly as he could onto the roof of the woodshed and jumped to the ground. He found himself at the back of the Inn and scrambled into the dark undergrowth to find a hiding place.

Two of the men ran up the stairs with the inn keeper close behind. "Where do you think you are going?" the innkeeper shouted.

The inn keeper's wife stood firm at the top of the stairs, in front of the two men. "Here, who are you? And what do you think you are doing in my house?" she shouted.

"We're looking for an Ethaenian boy. He was here last night," one man replied.

"Yes, he rented this room," she said, pointing to the room.

The two men quickly opened the door and entered the room. Seeing it was empty, they searched it for any clues they could find.

"Where... is... he...?" The man's voice sounded very menacing. The inn keeper and his wife stood looking into the room from the doorway.

"I don't know," replied the innkeeper's wife. "The last time I saw him, he was in here. He's obviously left."

"Aarrgghhh! Do you know where he headed for?" the tall man asked, looking at the inn keeper menacingly.

"I didn't speak to him."

"Hold on a minute, if you had to unbolt the door from the inside, he must still be in here. Search the building," he ordered. The men set about searching the rest of the Inn. The rest of the guests came out of their rooms to see what the commotion was about. The ruffians searched the Inn in vain. One man noticed the open window.

"He's jumped; the little bugger must have heard us and scarpered. He can't be far."

"Out of the way..." the man said as they both pushed their way past the Innkeeper and his wife. The men ran down the stairs to search around the outside of the building. Shamera was hiding in some bushes, and heard the men come out of the Inn and join the others. "He's gone!" he heard one of them say.

"Gone where?" asked another.

"They said they don't know. Apparently, he must have heard us and jumped from a window."

"He can't have got far. Search the area. He has to be found. Niniane wants him captured, and quick. Find him and we find the crystal," he heard one say.

They lit a torch and searched around the Inn; they were beating the bushes with long sticks. He thought it would merely be a matter of time before they found him. He made himself as small as he could and kept still.

"Nothing!" cried one man. "He's had it on his toes. He won't have hung around here."

"You three ride towards Errinbar to see if you can pick up his trail, and we'll head for Khulderhern."

He watched from behind the bush as they split up and rode off. His heart felt as if it was going to explode. He waited; hiding in the bushes until he was sure the coast was clear before running across the road to collect the staff.

Chapter 4

Shamera walked in the shallow dry ditch at the left side of the road. This was so he could hide amongst the bushes if anyone came by. Shamera crouched down in the ditch and took out his map. Barely able to read it by moonlight, he could make out his destination lay straight ahead. To the left was Tussocks Bog and Lethron had written KEEP OUT and underlined it several times. He had no option but to continue along the road. As he walked, he muttered to himself, "Just deliver these items they said. It will be safe, they said. Niniane and her men are in the south, they said." He watched the moon slowly waning. It would be daylight soon, and someone could easily spot him now he was out in the open. He walked as fast as he could whilst waiting for the sun to come up. For the first time; he was not looking forward to the sunrise. All he could do was concentrate on getting off the road and not getting caught.

The morning had broken. Dawn brought with it the unwelcome light. Shamera knew he would no longer have the protection of the dark. He kept looking as far ahead and as far behind him as he could. He was feeling worried; he had never been in a situation like this before; he had nowhere to hide. For the first time, he felt alone. He could feel his heart beating in his chest.

There were barely a few bushes scattered along the roadside, offering little or no cover. To the right was open flatland, to his left a dangerous bog. Stories say people had gone into the bog for various reasons, very few came out. It was full of dangerous tracks leading into quicksand and slippery quags. He had been walking for about three hours when in the distance he saw a dust cloud heading towards him, horses… and they were getting closer. He looked for somewhere to hide. There was no cover anywhere, and the horses were getting closer and closer. Too late, the riders had spotted him and were closing in at a gallop. Shamera had no option but to run towards the bog, and hopefully lose them in there. He ran across the drenched grassland. Water soaked his feet. Tripping over something, he fell face first into the marshy grass. He scrambled to his feet, coughing and spluttering. His clothes were sodden and heavy. He did not stop to turn and see how close they were. Shamera darted straight through some bushes; his foot caught on a creeper lying low to the ground, sending him sprawling. He desperately scrambled to his feet and continued running. He could hear the horses as they galloped through wet marshland. They were very close. Finding himself on a dry patch of land, he bolted towards a group of trees. A short distance beyond those trees, he saw some thicker undergrowth and headed straight for it. He leaped between the trees and dived headlong into the undergrowth. Panting and gasping for breath, he crouched down as low as he could, pulling some of the undergrowth together in front of him for better concealment. The horses came thundering into a small clearing ahead of him.

"Can anyone see him?" someone yelled.

"No, not yet," came the reply.

"Split up. He has to be close by," one horseman ordered. "We have him trapped." he continued.

Shamera peered through the undergrowth and saw them set off in different directions; one of the horsemen was heading straight for him. Shamera watched and held his breath as the horse stopped close to the trees he had leaped between. *'Has he seen me?'* He thought. His instinct was to run, but fear rooted him to the spot.

"Come on!" the man shouted at his horse whilst kicking his heels into its flanks. "Come on... what's the matter with you?" No matter how hard the man kicked his heels, the horse refused to move forward. It appeared to be frightened of what lay ahead in the bog.

"Help me! Over here!" someone shouted desperately. "Quicksand! Help me! Over here!"

The horseman turned his horse and headed towards the cries for help. Shamera stayed exactly where he was and tried to catch his breath.

"Where are you?... keep shouting," someone yelled out.

All fell quiet.

"Urack! Where are you?... Urack!" shouted the others as they searched for their companion. Shamera heard one say,

"Let's get out of here, back the way we came… follow the hoof prints we know that's safe ground."

As the two remaining horsemen rode close to Shamera's hiding place, one of them asked, "Do you think the Ethaenian met the same fate?"

"Probably, if not, he soon will. This place is full of quicksand. He won't last long."

They followed their hoof prints back out of the bog. Shamera stayed hidden for what felt like an age before daring to stand up to see if they had really gone. Now shivering in his wet clothes. He cautiously crawled out of the undergrowth and carefully climbed a tree. As he climbed a fraction above the level of the tallest bushes, he could see the horsemen patrolling up and down the road, stopping occasionally and looking across into the bog. Carefully, he climbed down again; he decided he would try to wait it out for a while; but time was not on his side. He was shivering even more now; he jogged around the trees and occasionally jumped on the spot, slapping his arms against his body, trying to warm up. He waited a while before climbing the tree again. This time, he saw the other horsemen had joined them as they still patrolled the road. Wet through and shivering, he decided he would try to pick his way carefully further through the bog. Using the long staff, he poked at the ground in front of him, testing it for quicksand and soft mud. The ground was getting softer, and he was again ankle deep in water. As he poked his staff into the water-logged ground, it released a fowl smelling marsh gas. He was gagging on the smell of rotten eggs emanating from beneath his feet. Deeper into the bog he went, poking and prodding the ground before him. He was fearful he may step into quicksand or a slippery bottomless quag, and as there was no one here to save him, no one would ever learn of his fate. He eventually came across some dry ground, which appeared to wind its way through the bushes and trees.

He had been walking through the woods for a while when he came across an old wooden shack. He stopped and looked at it for a while, *'Who would live in here?'* he thought. Fearful it may be a Hag or something similar, he reached inside his shirt and took hold of his amulet; he wasn't sure if it would help but he grasped it tightly. As he approached the shack, a woman appeared, carrying a small pile of wood. The woman spotted Shamera, dropped the wood, and shouted at him. "Who are you? And what do you want here?"

"I mean you no harm. I am lost and merely trying to find my way out of this place." He replied, trying to inject some confidence into his voice.

"Who are you?" she asked again.

"My name is Shamera. I come from Elms Hollow. I am trying to make my way to Selvenora," he replied. "Who are you? Is this your home?" he continued.

"Come here, come closer," she beckoned him over with her thin spindly fingers.

Still grasping his amulet, he walked closer to the woman. As he got closer, he saw she was a Mystic; she was quite old and her face was thin and wrinkled; her eyes were a cloudy pale grey, her lips were thin and pinched together. Not sure of who she was or if she was indeed, some sort of changeling. Shamera grasped the amulet even tighter and had his staff ready to strike. The old woman appeared to look him over as he walked closer towards her.

"Hi… I am Shamera," he said nervously.

The woman did not speak but appeared to continue looking him up and down, and appeared to be sniffing the air, like an animal trying to catch a scent.

"Sorry, I might smell a bit. I fell over in the bog, and I probably smell like a wet dog on a hot summer's day," he said apologetically.

He thought it strange the woman had not spoken but stood looking at him through the clouded eyes of a blind person. He waved his staff in front of her face.

"My eyes maybe clouded but I see you; I have the gift to see with my mind's eye. I see more with my mind than my eyes ever could," she uttered. "What is it around your neck you clasp so tight?" she continued.

He looked down at his hand still clutching the amulet tightly. He let it go and looked up; the old woman's expression changed.

"How come you by that?" she exclaimed. "Who did you steal it from? Tell me! I will know if you lie." the old woman appeared to be agitated about something.

"I stole it from no one; it was given to me, two days ago. How are you able to see it? Your eyes... you appear to be blind."

"I don't need eyes to see. Like I said, I see you with my mind," she pointed her thin spindly finger to her forehead. "Who gave it to you... who?"

"I can't say. I promised not to tell anyone."

"Tell me, or I will set the hounds upon you. You will tell me, or you will die in this place, you'll not find your way out without my help... besides who am I going to tell?"

"It was a Mystic, his name was..."

"Well?" she said impatiently.

"His name was Agnar."

"Agnar, you say. You know him well?"

"Erm, no, we met but two days ago."

"Met two days ago, and he gives you a trinket like this."

"Yes, as I said; I did not steal it. I am not a thief," he said adamantly. "Anyway, you did not answer my questions. Who are you? And why do you live in this place?"

"My name is Elgrin, and I choose to live here. It provides me with all I need. Come inside and get out of those wet clothes. No one will harm you here, you have my word." she said as she turned and walked towards the door.

"What about the hounds?" he enquired.

"What hounds?" she said with a slight smile.

Shamera stood a while and thought his other choice would be to refuse her and try to find his own way out of the bog by himself. He was wet and cold. Shamera accepted her hospitality, and he reluctantly followed her in. The cabin was dimly lit; it smelled of pine, wood smoke, and best of all, freshly baked bread. Its only source of natural light was coming through one small window near the door. A small fire glowed in the hearth. The room was sparsely furnished with a rustic looking wooden bed in one corner, a table and two chairs sitting in the middle of the room. The sink and worktop were directly under the small window and had a couple of dead rabbits and a variety of freshly picked vegetables waiting to be cooked. On top of the table were some curious-looking objects, some looked like small bones with strange markings on them, and a clear oval crystal about the size of a goose egg sat on some dark blue cloth. The old lady picked up some of small logs and placed them on the fire.

"Take off those wet things and put this around you," she said, handing him a large blanket. "Don't be shy. You don't want to catch your death, do you?"

Shamera feeling embarrassed at undressing in front of the old woman he wrapped the blanket around him and took off his wet clothes. The old lady strung them across a line hanging above the fire to dry.

"Give me your right hand, young Ethaenian," she said, holding out her right hand.

Shamera looked at her suspiciously, Elgrin stood there holding out her right hand, he hesitantly offered his right hand. Elgrin took hold of it, clasped both her hands around his. Elgrin took a quick deep breath as her body appeared to stiffen up. She tilted her head over to the right before letting go of his hand and gave a little 'hmm'.

"What was that? What did you do?" Shamera enquired.

"You can tell a lot from someone's hands; your right hand is what we Mystics call your trait hand. You have narrow palms and long fingers; this tells me you are sensitive and connected to nature, you are receptive and caring. You also have inner magic, although you do not yet know it."

"What do you mean... inner magic?"

"Magic is born from the earth; it is all around us if you know where to look. Some people are born with the ability to develop it. And some people's destiny is to become a great sorcerer. But magic has a price if they do not do it for good... It will corrupt your heart and soul, it will turn them black."

Elgrin looked towards Shamera and pointed to the amulet and said, "Agnar, you say... gave you the trinket... two days ago you said."

"Yes,"

"Why would he give you that...? He knows it has virtually no power without all the stones."

Elgrin reached for a pitcher of water. "Are you thirsty? This is good clean water." She poured two glasses and gave one to Shamera, who looked at it with suspicion.

"It's safe, look," she said reassuringly and drank some of the water from her glass.

Shamera stared at her with a glazed, puzzled look and with an air of disappointment in his voice said, "Agnar said it would help protect me."

"Hmm... he didn't tell you about the missing stones then." She replied softly.

"Err... No... he forgot to mention them. What do they do?" he inquired and sipped his water again.

"Three different coloured stones fit into these spaces on the amulet," she explained whilst pointing to the recesses where the stones once sat. "When reunited, it can make the wearer invisible, or form a temporary shield around you, depending on their position on the amulet. They have been missing a long while; no one knows where they are. Maybe one day you will find them, maybe you won't. Who knows?"

"How come you know so much?" Shamera asked, feeling a little more at ease.

"I have lived a long time and learnt many things. You have a lot of learning to do yet, my young friend."

Shamera looked at Elgrin with furrowed brows; he thought a little, gave his head a little shake from side to side, and asked, "Can you help me get out of these bogs? I need to get to Selvenora as quickly as I can... it's very important."

"It's alright; you're safe here... those men chasing you will not get you in here," she replied comfortingly.

Shamera looked at her in astonishment, "How... how did you know?"

"I am a Mystic, a seer; I have the gift of foresight and vision through my all-seeing eye," she said as she touched her eye shaped markings on her forehead.

"There are very few of us left with the gift, and we are getting fewer and fewer. I live here because it is safe. People fear us... even amongst our own people, there are those who fear the gift. They do not understand... or refuse to understand. They believe it to be a curse. Although nowadays my visions are rare and are often quite vague," she explained. "Also, the runes informed me someone would be in danger this day and would pass this way." She pointed at the rune bones on the table.

"Oh, and as for Agnar... he's my son." She said with a smile.

"He's your son?" he replied, suddenly sitting upright, his forehead wrinkled as a surprised expression washed over his face.

"Yes, he visits me from time to time."

"You said you can read runes," Shamera thought carefully for a short while.

"Yes, why do you ask?"

Shamera lightly scratched the side of his face. He nervously asked, "Will you see if you can read these, please?" Shamera reached over for his bag and, after rummaging around the bottom, he took the scroll out from its hiding place. "Look... here," he said, pointing to the three rune markings as he placed the scroll in front of her.

She took the scroll and placed the crystal egg against her forehead and appeared to look at the scroll carefully. She ran her fingers lightly over the markings. "These are from an ancient Elvenii language long since dead, not used anymore. They say, '*Hand on heart,*' she said wisely.

"And what about the writing? Can you read this too... please?" he enquired.

"Hmm, let's see. *En'deler nobrothrim Selvenora numelthrail sh'an...* Open now, doorway to Selvenora, I come in peace," she said, reading it aloud. "This must be the password which gains you admission to Selvenora," she said with a quiet voice.

"Thank you," Shamera replied, holding his hand out for the return of the scroll.

"Can you tell me how to get out of this area safely?"

"What's your rush?"

"I cannot tell you; I really have to get to Selvenora as fast as I can," he replied.

"Won't be easy. You have a long way to go and a dangerous place this bog is," she informed him. "Those men are still out there looking for you. Rest here and have something to eat. You have plenty of time."

"You can see them?" he said, looking very surprised.

"I can... sense them."

"Do I safely make it to Selvenora?"

"Sorry, young one, I have had no vision of your future. I told you my visions are vague these days. I sense if you go now, they will find and capture you."

"So how long must I stay?"

"Long enough for your clothes to dry properly and to have something to eat. You need to keep your strength up; you still have a fair way to go."

Elgrin prepared some bread, meat, and cheese. It would have taken too long to prepare the rabbit stew that was waiting to be done.

"It's not much, but you are welcome to it. You can take some with you."

"Why are you helping me like this? You do not know me."

"You know my son, and if he needs your help, of course I am going to help you too. Now eat up, young one."

Shamera sat with his warm blanket wrapped around him and tucked into his meal. He didn't think he was as hungry as he was, and it tasted very good.

"Thank you. How kind of you. I think I'd better be on my way. I still have a long way to go."

He got up and checked to see if his clothes were dry. He kept the blanket wrapped around him whilst he dressed himself in his dry and very warm clothes.

"You need to take great care travelling through this place; there are many paths with terrible dangers that will lead to your death. There is but one path will give you safe passage." Elgrin informed. She picked up a long, thin whistle and blew it. Shamera looked bewildered, as it appeared not to emit any sound. It wasn't long before a four-legged animal ran into the room. It was the size of a Labrador dog, reddish fur, a flattened looking face with large floppy ears.

"This is Iston. He's a Bogthwart. I have known him for many years. He is good company. He knows the safe route out of here; he will lead you to safety." Elgrin said, as she tied some twine around his neck. "Don't let him go until you reach the dead oak tree. Lightning struck it many years ago. Its death marks safety at the end of the bog. When you get there, let him loose and he will find his way back."

She handed Shamera the twine and issued her warning again, "Do not let him go until you reach the oak tree, or we will lose you for certain." Elgrin placed a wrapped sandwich in his bag and handed it to Shamera. He took hold of his staff in his other hand and started out of the door. Elgrin followed him outside. Elgrin looked down at the Bogthwart and said softly, "Take him to the end of the bog; take him to the lightning tree."

Shamera wrapped the twine twice around his hand. He did not want to lose the Bogthwart and become lost; he heeded Elgrin's warning well. Elgrin stood and watched as the animal led Shamera down the path. The Bogthwart appeared eager to be away. As Shamera followed the Bogthwart, he noticed all the paths looked very much the same as the shadows from the trees and bushes cast over them. Shamera tried looking as far forward as he could to see if the end of the trail was in sight, but all he could see were trees, bushes, and bends in the path. Now and again between the trees and the bushes, he glimpsed the treacherous waters of the bog glistening in the sunlight. All the while he followed the Bogthwart, but a growing uncomfortable thought kept entering his mind, *'Can I trust this animal? Am I already lost?'* The path had lots of forks and different paths branching off through bushes and trees. He could see how easily you would become disorientated and lost.

Eventually, he came to the end of the path. A large oak tree stood before him; a lightning strike had split it down the middle. Never had he felt more pleased to see a charred, dead tree. He bent over and removed the twine from around the Bogthwart's neck. "Off you go, go home." he said, pointing back along the path.

The Bogthwart took off back down the path. He looked back and watched as the Bogthwart soon disappeared out of sight.

He had been walking for a few hours, stopping briefly to rest before finally reaching the Screaming Forest. The sun was setting. He stood on the track which led into the forest. The forest was massive; it was the largest one in the land. But if he was to deliver the shard before the blood moon set, he would have to travel through it. There was no other way. This would be a test of his courage. A large wooden sign by the side of the path read *Etlai Amasha Etrei Durai Arbormae* (*Beware the Blood Beast of the Woods*). "What! What's a Blood beast? That's a new one!" he exclaimed. *'No one ever said anything about a blood beast,'* he thought. He didn't like the sound of that, but there was no other way for him to go. He had to go through the forest; he took the wand from his pocket. "Light, let me have light!" he whispered forcefully, but nothing happened. "Damn this wand and sorcery, how do you get it to work?" he said aloud. Disappointingly, no matter how hard he tried, he could not conjure up any light. Feeling defeated and annoyed, he put the wand back into his pocket. He took the amulet from the inside of his shirt and wore it on the outside, hoping the limited power it had would ward off any creatures he may encounter. The moon was rising. Again, it would be a full moon, and this would offer some light, but he knew the deeper he went into the forest, the thicker the canopy of trees would be, and the less light would shine through. Shamera contemplated waiting until daybreak, but he knew time was short and he had to reach Selvenora soon.

Hesitantly, he started down the track leading into the forest. He walked cautiously along the path, trying not to let his imagination run away with him. His eyes were adjusting to the dark, eyes opened wide, he was scanning every inch of the trees and bushes. The crunch of twigs and leaves underfoot echoed in the darkness and announced his presence. His heart was racing. He held his staff at the ready. He was ready to strike out at anything which may threaten him. As he walked along the track, he could smell various scents like night jasmine, purpleberries and pine wafting up into the warm night air. He walked along, attempting to identify all the night-time scents, trying to distract his mind as best he could whilst his eyes and ears were still scanning for danger. He could see the moon shining through the trees and was glad of the light, as little as it was. The branches of the trees looked to be stretching out like gnarly hands and fingers as they reached upwards and over the track, forming a twisted arch stretching deep into the eerie darkness. He looked around. Shadows formed in the bushes along the track. He was becoming more afraid as he made his way deeper into the forest. The light breeze rustled the trees and undergrowth, which added to his already overactive imagination of creatures hiding in there.

Chapter 5

He had been walking for about an hour. Strange noises resonated in the dark, beyond the twisted, interwoven branches of the trees. A cold shiver ran down his spine. The hairs on the back of his neck stood on end. Movement in the bushes caught his eye. He turned to glimpse something hiding in the undergrowth. He stopped dead in his tracks.

A pair of bright red eyes were staring straight at him through the undergrowth. They disappeared back into the boscage as the sound of pounding footsteps reverberated through bushes, "Who-who is out there?"

The footsteps stopped, a loud terrifying screech thundered out of the night air; it sounded a short distance ahead of him. Every muscle in his body tensed up. His heart beat faster as he breathed more sharply. He looked back at the undergrowth, hoping whatever was hiding there had now gone.

The chattering of small nocturnal animals around the forest stopped. All fell silent. Panicked, his eyes scanned all around, the darkness hid well whatever was out there. The terrifying screech split the silence of the forest once more. This time, it came from behind him. He cautiously turned around. His heart was trying to pound its way out of his chest. He remembered about the banshee howling moments before someone dies. His mouth dried as he tried to swallow again, his heart beat harder than it had ever done before; he quickly scanned every inch of the visible forest. His eyes and head darting looking all around him. The bushes shook as something enormous appeared to force its way rapidly through the thick undergrowth. His eyes were now focused on the bushes to his left. *'what was it?'* he thought to himself; his eyes widened as the noise of the creature sounded ever closer. Fear clasped his heart tightly and froze him to the spot; his heart pounding rhythmically as though someone inside his chest was beating a large drum.

The noise stopped; everything fell silent again. Shamera's heart felt as though it had leaped into his mouth. His skin ran cold. He stood silently, waiting for the creature to appear.

Shamera looked all around, not knowing what he could do with the wand if the creature appeared before him. Everything remained silent; he waited a little longer, his eyes straining to see in the dark, his ears listening for the faintest sound. "Who's out there? Show yourself," he shouted with a quivering voice, "Show yourself… I am Shamera the sorcerer's apprentice, I am a powerful sorcerer," he bluffed, whilst holding his wand high as if showing it to whomever or whatever was out there and hoping nothing would call his bluff. The moonlight cast an array of strange, eerie shadows across the forest as it shone through the canopy and between the gnarly branches of the trees. He could feel eyes watching him from behind every bush and from deep inside the darkness. He did not like this, every fiber in his body was telling him to run.

Something started rapidly moving through the undergrowth towards him, the anticipation of danger again rooted him to the spot. He was gripped with terror; his heart was pounding and his whole body was physically shaking. With eyes wide open, Shamera was scanning the darkness but saw nothing but shadows. He wasn't sure whether they were all shadows, or whether something was hiding, could it be about to attack him? Thoughts of dread raced through his mind, as fear began to overwhelm his senses. His hand trembled as he took a tighter hold of the staff. He attempted to shout. His mouth and throat were dry, he tried to swallow but his mouth was too dry. The trepidation of something hiding, a terror lurking in the darkness was too much. He knew he had to go on, the responsibility of getting the shard to Lord Salogel was his, and his alone. He turned and ran, his legs felt heavy and sluggish. He had only ran a short distance when he tripped on something and fell headlong onto the ground. He rapidly got to his feet. He waited for a few moments while his eyes and ears scanned the darkness again for any dangers lurking there.

Tiny voices and high-pitched laughter were buzzing all around his head. He looked up slowly… "Spriggans!" he exclaimed.

Suddenly, he felt a sharp needle-like prick to his neck, as if being stung by an insect. He instinctively clasped that region of his neck with his open hand; he felt something sticking out, a small thin object. He placed his thumb and forefinger around it and pulled it out of his neck. It was a sleeping dart. He tried to look at what he had removed, but his eyes would not focus properly on the small object. He felt a strange cold sensation pass through his head and surged down his body to his feet. His knees buckled and gave way. He crumpled to the ground. He tried to move, but his body felt so heavy and cold. He lay there, his body felt paralysed. Fighting to stay awake, he felt his eyes closing. There was nothing he could do. He was out cold.

He gradually started to regain consciousness and tried to open his eyes; his eyelids felt very heavy. Straining, he forced them open, albeit slightly. He felt dizzy; his head felt like it was about to explode with the intense pain. He could sense he was sitting up, but he could not focus his eyes properly. Everything appeared a blur. He tried to move, but something was preventing him from getting up. His eyelids again became so heavy he could not stop them from closing; his head fell forward, and he passed out again.

He was awakened by having a pail of cold water thrown over his head; The cold water gave him a shock which took his breath away. He gave a sharp intake of breath and, along with air; he inhaled some of the water, which made him cough and splutter. Cold and wet, he looked up to see who did this to him. His eyes gradually regained a little focus. He could make out the shape of a man standing over him.

"Wake up!" The man shouted as he kicked the side of Shamera's legs.

Shamera shuddered and shook his head as he tried to clear his mind, and to shake off the water still running down his face. "Who are you?" He asked, still spluttering.

"It doesn't matter who I am Ethaenian, there is a handsome reward for your capture," the stranger replied.

He walked away and put the empty pail on the ground. He turned his head casually around and, looking back over his right shoulder, peered at Shamera for a few seconds before snidely saying, "Sorcerer's apprentice, huh!"

Shamera's vision was still a little blurred; he could make out a man in a long dark coat, long grey hair, and a short grey beard. He looked around the room; a shaft of light shone through the small dirty window which lit the dingy interior of the room. The remains of a log fire barely smouldering in the hearth added little heat to the room. Two rabbits and a large bird were hanging from a hook in the ceiling. The sink area was full of pots waiting to be washed. The air was stale with something like rotting cabbages, this turned his stomach.

He could see the man had tied him to sturdy wooden chair. On the wooden table in front of him were his bag, wand, and staff. He tried to get up, but he was bound by his hands and legs.

"Who are you and what do you want with me?" Shamera asked again, as he struggled to free himself from his bindings.

"Who I am is of no concern of yours. But by tonight, I will have a big reward, a large bag of gold, thanks to you."

"Reward... What reward?" Asked Shamera.

The stranger took Shamera's bag, wand, and staff and tied them together before hoisting them up to the ceiling.

"There we are sorcerer's apprentice. They are safely out of your reach," he said as he smiled sarcastically, showing his brown stained, and rotting teeth. "The reward from Niniane of course. She has plans for you my lad. I am to take you back to the edge of the forest tonight."

"What time is it? How long have I slept?"

He knew he had to escape, but how? He was losing time and needed to get to Selvenora by that night.

"You were out all night; it's middle morning, no more questions." The man snapped.

Whatever he had been darted with was now starting to wear off. His whole body ached, and he had a sharp stabbing pain across his forehead. Shamera now felt in fear of his life, he had run away from one terrifying event in the woods, straight into another. And now, he was to be taken to Niniane. He had failed to get the shard to Lord Salogel, and now she would get her hands on it. He started to tremble with fear, knowing that he had failed. He had let everyone down. His fear was making it difficult for him to concentrate, he sat wondering what he had done to deserve this and questioned whether he had done the right thing in attending the Choosing. He tried hard to regather his thoughts, his saving grace was that he was alive, and he had to stay that way. He knew he had to stop feeling sorry for himself and had to think of a way get out of this situation.

He looked up at his bag. 'How am I going to get from there?' he asked himself. Shamera kept looking around the room for inspiration, but there was nothing obvious.

Fear was starting to be replaced by anger. Unlike being in the woods, in the dark, where he could see nothing. He could see the threat before him, it was just a man. He would have to use his cunning, remain calm and think clearly.

"I am thirsty & hungry." Said Shamera.

"You'll have to wait; I have to go out for a short while." Replied the man.

"Where are you going? How long are you going to leave me here for?" Shamera was concerned not merely for his safety, but he had to be with the Elvenii before the blood moon that night.

"I told you, no more questions," the man scolded whilst checking the rope which bound Shamera securely to the chair. He walked over to the sink and picked up a dirty wooden tumbler, filled it full of water from an old wooden bucket sitting next to the sink. He slapped the tumbler on the table in front of Shamera, splashing some of the water onto the table.

"That's disgusting, and what's floating on the top?" He thought he was about to throw up at the mere thought of drinking from the beaker. The man looked at the tumbler and, with his fingers, fished out the floating green object and flicked it onto the floor.

"There… it's gone, it's all there is. Drink it, don't drink it, it's all the same for me. I won't be long; you can make yourself at home," he said with forced laugh, "This place is being watched, so I wouldn't try to escape if I were you. You wouldn't want to run into the beast now. Would you?" He continued, with a menacing smile and another short, forced laugh.

The man left; Shamera could hear the door being locked. He spent the next half hour trying to free his bindings, but the knots were strongly tied, and they held fast. He sat there frightened at the fate which lay ahead of him; his breathing increased, and his heart started to race once more. Fear once more clasped his heart, 'How am I going to escape and get to Selvenora in time?'

He questioned himself. He knew time was not on his side. He could not fail; he knew he had to escape. But how? He looked around the room. His belongings were being held aloft out of his reach. He thought about trying to break the chair, but it was well built and strong. Nothing was coming to mind; he was feeling very helpless and alone. He sat contemplating his fate. What was Niniane going to do to him?

He looked down at the dirty wooden tumbler once more; his mouth was dry, and he was very thirsty but still could not bring himself to drink the water. It felt like he had been tied to the chair for quite a long time, his arms and legs were now feeling numb. Shamera's ears pricked up as he heard the key being placed in the lock. The door opened. He held his breath. The man had come back; he was alone? Shamera breathed a temporary sigh of relief to see his captor was alone; he still had time to come up with a plan of escape, but what?

The man locked the door; then placed the key in his waistcoat pocket. He looked over at Shamera and grinned, "So, you're still here, then? A couple of hours not long enough for you to escape?"

Shamera looked at the man and pleaded, "Please untie me. I cannot go anywhere... you have locked the door, and you have the key. You have trussed me up like this for hours. My legs feel dead, and I ache all over. Please!" Shamera pleased.

"You haven't touched your water, and you said you were thirsty." He said with a sarcastic tone.

"I cannot drink out of this. It's disgusting." A thought entered his head. "Untie me and I can make myself useful. I am thirsty and hungry. You must be hungry too? I will clean your pots and cook us both something to eat. You know Ethaenians are very good cooks. And besides, where can I go? You have locked the door, and you have the key."

The man stood there for a moment, looking at the pile of dirty pots in the sink, and glanced a look at Shamera.

"Come on... untie me," Shamera pleaded again.

"I am a bit hungry." He said as he licked his lips, "I have the key and I will keep it in my pocket. Try anything stupid and I will batter you. They did not specify the state of your condition for the reward," he stated as he took a knife from his pocket and cut the bindings.

Shamera massaged both wrists where the rope had bound tightly around them. He stood up, rubbing both his legs from top to bottom to help his circulation.

"I need some hot water to clean with."

"Fires gone out... use what's in the barrel." He said, pointing to a water butt.

"I will need a fire to cook on."

"Then you make it!" The man said curtly.

The man sat on the chair watching Shamera set about making the fire; he swept the old ashes to one side of the hearth, placed small kindling down with some larger logs on top. The man threw him some macche-sticks to light the fire with. He lit the smaller kindling and left the fire to get going. He cleared the sink area and set about washing the pots in cold water. It wasn't long before he had finished. He now turned his attention to cooking.

"I can make you a large pot of rabbit stew. It will last you a few days. Get one down for me; and I will need some vegetables, and some lavender too."

The man said nothing as he rose from his chair and took down one rabbit, he picked up some carrots, an onion, and a turnip out of a cupboard. He pulled off a sprig of lavender he had hanging from the wall. The man watched Shamera intently as he prepared the ingredients for the stew. He placed everything in a large iron cooking vessel. He placed it on the pot crane. This was a large black metal bracket which swung out from the side of the fireplace and held the cooking pot in front of the fire.

"Do you have any herbs?" Shamera enquired.

"No, you'll have to make do with what you have," the man replied in a very abrupt manner. He sat at the table carefully watching Shamera's every move.

"I have two cooking herbs in my pack if you would pass them to me."

"What... are you trying to trick me?"

"No, of course not... we use them all the time. You can get them for me; I will eat one to show you they are harmless. It's what we regularly use, it's what makes our food taste great. And besides, I don't fancy being battered."

The man looked at him for a while and glanced up at the bag suspended from the ceiling.

"You stand over there, any funny stuff, and I will beat you to a pulp."

Shamera went and stood in the furthest corner as the man lowered the bag.

"There are two jars. I need them both, please."

The man reached in the bag and took out both pots and placed them on the table; he hoisted the bag back up out of reach. Then sat back in his chair. Shamera was hoping the man hadn't recognised the plants. He did not want to get battered, or worse. This would be his only chance to get free of his captor.

"Go on, you eat some before you put any in that stew."

Shamera took at the jars, unscrewed them. He took the large pieces of root, chewed one of them, and swallowed. He showed his empty mouth to the man; he ate some more for good measure.

"You need but a small amount, as they are very strong and can easily ruin a good stew."

Shamera hoped the man would not make him eat any of the leaves, as he did not quite know how quickly the antidote would work. Shamera chopped up all the leaves with the lavender and placed them in the pot. He stirred the pot of stew as it boiled and bubbled in front of the fire.

"It's practically ready." Shamera said as he retrieved two bowls from the draining area of the sink.

Shamera ladled out two bowls of the stew and set them both down on the table. He hoped he had eaten all of the antidote and hoped that it would be enough.

"You eat first," said the man cautiously.

Shamera closed his eyes as he ate the first spoonful, 'please let the antidote work,' he prayed to himself.

"It tastes okay but would have been much better if you had some decent herbs around here. Go on, tuck in… it won't kill you," Shamera said as he took another small spoonful.

The man picked up his bowl and ate the stew with vigour. "Not bad," the man said with his mouthful. "Not bad at all."

Shamera did not eat anymore, but watched the man eat his bowl of stew. The man put the bowl to his lips and drank the last of the liquor at the bottom of his bowl. He plonked his bowl down onto the table before giving a hearty belch. He stared straight at Shamera; his face became expressionless as he continued to stare at Shamera. The man's head dropped forward, and his body followed it. His head landed with a large thump on the table, his arms hanging limply by his sides. Shamera looked on as the man lay there motionless; he then poked him with his spoon. The man did not move; so, he poked him again, this time a little harder… still no movement, to make certain he cracked him hard over the head with the spoon… not a murmur. The man was out for the count.

"Who's going to batter who?" He said triumphantly and gave a little fist pump. Shamera untied the rope holding his belongings and lowered them to the ground. He held his breath as he checked the lining at the bottom of the sack; it felt like the shard was still there; he took it out to check it. He felt a massive sense of relief as he filled his lungs with air, puffed out his cheeks, and blew it out slowly. He cautiously went over to the man. He stood looking at him for a few seconds with a puzzled expression.

"Who… who are you?" whispered Shamera curiously.

The man lay sprawled across the table, totally immobilised. Shamera poked him again to make sure he was still unconscious before searching the man's pockets. He found the key and unlocked the door. He gingerly went outside; he scanned his eyes all around. 'Is it safe?', 'is the thing still watching me? What was it he heard last night that made him run fear for his life?' These thoughts ran through his mind as he turned back, closed, and locked the door. He hung the key on a nail that was sticking out of the door. Shamera was not sure of the direction he should head in. He ran down the path leading from the house. It appeared to lead deeper into the forest. Shamera wanted to get as far from this place as he could.

The forest became gloomier as dark clouds hid the view of the sun. As he ventured further into the forest, the light lessened as the canopy became denser. The forest looked like the early evening; the path was gloomily lit as barely a flicker of sunlight managed leach through the canopy.

He saw a shadowy figure was approaching from the other direction. He stopped and watched as the figure drew closer and closer. Shamera gripped his staff, his heart again beating fast as the figure approached. "Hello stranger," the figure greeted in a soft female voice. "What brings you through this forest alone? Something important it must be if you venture through here by yourself," she continued.

"Who are you?" Shamera asked.

"I am no one important," the woman said as she stood in front of him. She carefully removed her hood. The woman looked quite old with her dark brown weathered skin and a wrinkled face; she had long straggly grey hair which fell past her shoulders. Her eyes appeared dark and piercing, yet her voice was soft and young sounding.

"They filled these forests with danger. Why would someone so young risk travelling through them?" she asked as she walked calmly around him.

"Your direction leads to the hills and there is nothing of importance there... Ahh, wait, are you going to see the Elvenii? You won't get there that way... the great entrance has not been opened in hundreds of years," she said.

"No," he replied. "I am off to collect the berries of the Nocterium plant. They grow on the hillside. We can only collect them at night and solely during a full moon. They are going to be used to make a fever remedy," he quickly replied. "Anyway, it can't be safe for a woman to travel through this forest, either, and if there is nothing in that direction but the hills, where did you come from?" he asked curiously.

"Oh, I live round about young man. I am used to these forests and all who lives in it; it holds no fear for me."

"Are you a banshee?" He asked nervously, not taking his eyes off her.

"Would you like me to be one?" she said teasingly, pointing a long slender finger at him.

"NO! I was merely asking." he said, forcing a slight smile.

"No... I am not a Banshee, and I mean you no harm," she said with a comforting chuckle.

"Who are you?" he asked.

"I'm merely an old woman who lives in this forest. Tell me, you wouldn't have anything to eat in that sack of yours, would you?"

He reached into his bag and pulled out some bread and cheese and offered it to the woman.

"Thank you. Will you share it with me? My name is Zelda."

"No thank you, you can have it," he replied, holding it out offering it to her. "Go on, please take it. I have plenty left."

The old woman took the food, looked straight into his eyes. "You look like a nice person, if it is the entrance you seek, you won't find it along this path. This path eventually leads away and deeper into the forest. A bit further down this path there is a folk, take the left path, it will lead where you seek. But beware the beast; it follows you through the forest," she said quietly, "Do not stray from the path. Do not stop until you reach the clearing."

"What beast?" he asked, as an incredible ear-piercing scream tore through the forest. Shamera spun around to the direction he had come from to see if he could see anything behind him. The fear he felt last night came rushing back. His skin had goosebumps and an icy shiver ran down his back. With his heart pumping he turned back to ask more questions. The woman had vanished. He quickly looked all around him. Not a sign of her anywhere, "Zelda!" He called out but received no reply. "Zelda where are you?" he yelled.

He glanced around; he was once more alone. Without hesitation, he picked his backpack up, slung it over his shoulder and ran down the path as fast as he could. Zelda's warning of the beast and the scream of a large creature hastened his pace. From out of nowhere, thousands of fireflies appeared and lit the way along the track. "Where did this lot come from?" he whispered to himself. A soft voice echoed from the woods, "For your kindness… Now run."

He ran along the path as the fireflies illuminated his way. It seemed like he had been running for ages when suddenly he found himself in a clearing outside the forest. He ran to the middle of it and stopped. He looked back; the fireflies had disappeared as quickly as they had appeared. The forest again looked dark and uninviting.

'*What was the beast Zelda warned was following him?*' He thought to himself. '*Would it follow him out of the forest, perhaps?*' These thoughts filled his head as he stood staring at the forest. He turned towards the foothills and quickly walked away from the forest as fast as he could until he reached the bottom of the rocky slopes about an hour later.

Feeling quite anxious, he made his way up the rocky foothill until he came to a small plateau. Exhausted, he sat for a while to gather his thoughts and to catch his breath. The comfortless chill of the late afternoon air made the hairs on his arms stand on end; he looked up at the clear sky and knew it was going to get colder. He decided he would rest here for a short while. He gathered a pile of dry wood for a fire; he started by making a circle of stones in which to contain the fire, placing the smaller twigs and some dried leaves at the bottom. He placed some of the larger pieces of wood on top. The fire would keep him warm. It should also hopefully keep any beasts at bay. The old woman's warning was still haunting him. He then realised he had nothing to light the fire with; he sat and thought for a couple of minutes. He placed his hands inside his pockets to warm them. He felt something in his pocket; he pulled out the wand, '*I wonder,*' he thought. He recalled what Verazslo had said at the Choosing; think it and the wand will do the rest. '*well it hasn't worked so far*', he thought. Shamera pointed the wand at the pile of sticks and thought 'burn'… nothing happened. He tried again and again and again, still nothing happened. "What sort of useless sorcerer am I? I can't even make a basic fire," he said out loud. It was getting colder as the sun started setting; he looked up once more at the sky and thought, '*it's going to be another cold night.*'

He sat looking at the pile of sticks, and at the wand he was still holding. "You're as useless as those sticks. If the beast shows up now, what use are you to me?" he said to the wand, as though it could understand him. He sat there and imagined a nice roaring fire to keep him warm. "Burn," he said again despairingly. Shamera stared at the wood. Not a flicker. He continued staring into the pile of wood as though hypnotised by it. After a few seconds, a small yellow flame suddenly appeared under the sticks; Shamera startled by what he had witnessed, quickly knelt and gently blew into the flame and dry sticks. Soon he had his warming fire going. "How did I do that?" he blurted, it mystified him as he toasted himself next to the fire, and sat up straight and smiled with a small sense of achievement.

He looked at the wand again and thought he would need a lot more practice before he could call himself anything like a sorcerer. As he sat on a rock and warmed himself by the fire, he wondered what else he could do with the wand. He looked at a small rock close to his feet, pointed the wand at it and said, "rise… rise into the air," nothing happened. He concentrated as hard as he could, yet the rock stayed firmly on the ground. "Vanish!" he shouted whilst flicking the wand at the rock, again nothing. Shamera was becoming frustrated he could not get the wand to work. *'How am I ever going to learn how to use this useless twig and become a sorcerer?'* he thought. He pointed the wand quickly and randomly at the rocks while again shouting things like vanish, disappear, & evaporate. He looked at the wand; his shoulders sank as he exhaled frustrated, *'why will you not work for me?'* he thought to himself. He sat quietly contemplating the journey ahead; and stared deeply into the fire as the flames danced, and the sparks flew upwards as the wood crackled and split as it burned. The flames seemed to have a mesmerising effect as he sat staring at them. He recalled how he started the fire. He had imagined the fire in his head, said burn and the fire started. He looked at the small rock again and imagined it floating in the air and pointed the wand at it and said "Rise," after a few seconds, the rock shook a little before it lifted a short way into the air. Amazed at what he has done, he broke his concentration, and the rock fell back to the ground. He tried it again, this time he held it up slightly longer before the rock fell back down.

The fire was now well established, the flames dancing in the breeze. He placed the last of the wood on to burn. He took the last of his food out of his backpack. This made him think again of the woman and who or what she might have been. Since she did not harm or threaten him but gave him a warning of the beast, he thought she was merely an old, friendly woman. But he could not get his head around how or why she vanished. He tucked into the last of his bread and cheese and drank some of his water to wash it down. Feeling satisfied and nicely warmed through, he put the fire out by kicking dirt onto it. He continued up to the Selvernorian gateway. A cold chill ran down his spine as he witnessed another ear-splitting shriek burst the tranquility of the early evening. He could not tell from which direction the sound came from as it echoed around hills. Once inside the entrance, he would be safe, he thought. He looked down the hillside to make sure nothing was following him; the sun was low over the hilltop and cast a dark shadow on this side of the hill. Onward and upward, he quickly climbed until he reached a much larger plateau.

Chapter 6

The entrance to the Elvenii homeland stood about three hundred yards straight ahead, partially lit by the setting sun peering through a gap in the hills. The rocky entrance looked like a giant; majestic cathedral carved straight out of the side of the mountain. Shamera looked behind him and down the hill again, checking nothing was following. Especially the creature, whatever it was. He picked up the pace as the sun was setting fast; he scrambled up the rocky outcrop, his feet sometimes slipping on the loose stones and rocks. He finally reached the pathway, which zig-zagged its way up the hill leading to the giant doorway. Dwarfed by the size of the doors, He looked up at them in humbled amazement.

These impressive giant iron doors have protected the Elvenii homeland for centuries, the doors were adorned with figures in battle and of the Elvenii warriors of long ago. No one ever breached these doors during the dark times of war. They looked like they had not been opened in a very long time.

The Elvenii Homeland lay beyond those doors. He looked up at the inscription above the door which read; *En'darain Atish'an* which, when translated, says *'Enter this place in peace'*. Once again, the ear-piercing shriek shattered the silence. He quickly raised the wand and quietly spoke; "*En'deleron nibrothrim Selvenora nemalethrai sh'an.*" He waited with bated breath, but nothing happened. He said it in plain language. "Open now doorway to Selvenora. I come in peace." Still, nothing happened. The doors remained firmly closed. Shamera took off his backpack and took out the scroll; he tried to remember what the Mystic had told him. He looked at the runes and remembered they said, '*hand on heart.*' He stood before the doors and placed his hand over his heart and repeated the words again, "*En'deleron nibrothrim Selvenora nemalethrai sh'an.*" The doors remained firmly closed. *'What am I doing wrong?'* he thought to himself. Once again, the ear-piercing screech shattered the silence. It seemed to be closer. He stood back and looked at the doors; he looked at the carvings and one caught his attention. An Elvenii elder, depicted standing with his right hand over his heart. He moved closer for a better look; the hand looked to be recessed. He stood looking at it for a short while. *'Could it be that simple?'* He thought to himself. He quickly placed his hand over the recessed hand of the elder and again said aloud, *En'deleron nibrothrim Selvenora nemalethrai sh'an.*

He held his breath... the large black iron doors creaked and groaned as they slowly opened outwards. Dust and particles of rust had lain undisturbed for many years slowly rained down like a waterfall between the doors. The cascading dust sparkled in the evening light as it slowly drifted downwards. The noise of the giant doors echoed loudly through the darkness of the dark void which lay ahead, as though to warn him to turn back and not to enter this protected place. Shamera put away the scroll... slowly and gingerly he entered into the darkness. The smell of damp and fusty air was evident, this place had not been aired for many years. As if by magic, a torch which was hanging on the wall to his right suddenly sparked into life and burst into flames. The flickering yellowy, orange light offered some relief to the darkness. He walked over and took the torch down from its holder. His footsteps echoed on the stone tiled floor as he cautiously ventured further into the unknown. The large iron doors behind him creaked and groaned once more as they closed, once more sealing the entrance with a loud metallic clunk, which resonated all around him. He held the torch high in front of him as he nervously walked down the middle of what looked like an enormous hall. Through the dim light he could make out life-size statues of Elvenii elders, which had been carved meticulously out of white granite, and each set into their own alcove along both walls. The statues appeared to watch at him as he proceeded along the hall. His eyes were slowly adjusting to the poor light. He stopped and looked about him; six beautifully carved stone columns appeared to be placed evenly along the length of the hall. The columns rose high and appeared to support a beautiful ornate vaulted ceiling. Ahead, a deeper darkness beckoned. He continued forward. A large stone staircase lay before him, it loomed out of the murky shadows and curved upwards into even more darkness.

With his eyes opened wide and cautiously looking all around him, Shamera walked towards the staircase when he suddenly stopped in his tracks... Something large was scurrying behind him. Was it a large rat perhaps? He shivered as the chill of the cold air brushed across his skin. He had barely walked a few paces more before he froze to the spot. He heard the scurrying noise again, this time it was much closer. It sounded like large claws scratching on the stone floor, and it was getting even closer. Run! screeched a voice in his head, but Shamera couldn't move. His legs were rooted to the spot. He turned around slowly, raising the torch high in front of him to illuminate as much of the room as he could. A pair of orange eyes were slowly advancing out of the shadows. In front of him stood a Vark, an oversized dog-like creature with huge eyes, long razor-sharp teeth, and long claws. Its short black fur was the perfect camouflage for hiding and ambushing its prey in the dead of night. It stood there looking at him, saliva dripping from its formidable deadly teeth, as it snarled and growled. Shamera was rooted with fear. All he could do for the moment was to stare straight back at it. The Vark took a slow, cautious step forward towards Shamera, who, out of pure instinct thrust the torch towards its face. The Vark quickly took a couple of steps backwards; Shamera looked around for an escape route. There was nothing but the staircase. The Vark started slowly circling around him. He kept thrusting his torch towards it, trying to keep it at bay. Shamera's heart was beating hard as he looked around the dark hall for any way out. The stone staircase offered retreat. He noticed some of the statues were holding long spears. He slowly made his way over to one of them, closely followed by the snarling Vark. Shamera tugged at the spear until it was loose, but he could not pull it away from the statue. He held the torch to see what was holding it; he noticed the spear was placed through the grip of the statue's hand. He would have to thread it up and out of the statue's hand. He looked towards the Vark, who was edging its way even closer. Shamera sprang forward, and he shouted as loud as he could whilst thrusting the flaming torch towards the Vark's face. Sparks flew upwards which made it retreat a little further. He quickly placed his staff against the statue and, as fast as he could, he lifted the spear up and out of the statue's hand.

He slowly bent down to pick up his staff, which had fallen to the floor. The Vark Suddenly lunged forward from out of the dark. Startled by this, Shamera shouted "aarrgghhh!" as he thrust both his hands forward, the torch and staff in one hand and the spear in the other. The Vark got a little too close to the point of the spear which nicked its left shoulder. The Vark gave a yelp, jumped back and retreated hastily. Shamera stood up quickly and moved towards the staircase. The Vark was quicker, it was now standing between him and the staircase. The Vark leapt up towards his face. Shamera twisted away sideways to avoid those gnashing teeth. The Vark snapped at him, narrowly missing his face but it managed to grab a hold of his backpack. The weight of the Vark pulled him to the ground, he was now lying on his back, helpless. The Vark had a strong hold and would not let go, it was snarling and tugging hard. It was pulling Shamera backwards along the stone floor. Shamera flung both arms repeatedly backwards over his head; the torch hit the floor close to the Vark, sparks flew everywhere, startled it let go of his backpack. Shamera quickly scrambled to his feet and ran towards the stairs. Again, the Vark was too quick and stood before him on the stairs cutting off his retreat. Shamera took a deep breath and let out an almighty scream, "aarrgghhh!" and ran towards the snarling Vark, which retreated up a few of the steps. He stopped and looked at the creature, *'What do I have to do to get past it?'* he thought.

The Vark leapt into the air again towards his face, startled by this Shamera fell backwards whilst pointing the spear towards the creature. He hit the floor again with a loud thump; the Vark let out an ear-piercing scream, Shamera felt the spear being pulled backwards and out of his grip. Quickly getting to his feet, he held the torch towards the Vark, which was still lying on the ground. He could see the spear had impaled its chest. The Vark lay motionless; he walked towards it and poked it with his staff. The vanquished creature lay there… dead. He took a deep breath of relief as he looked at his hands, which were trembling. He did not feel good about what he had done, but knew it was either him or the creature. He shuddered as he thought of what could have happened had he not found the spear. He hurriedly turned and headed towards the stairs.

Shamera warily climbed the winding staircase. The sound of his footsteps on the stone steps echoed as he strode up into the darkness. The flame from the torch cast eerie shadows which danced on the walls as he ascended further towards the top. The stairs appeared to go on and on, winding their way ever upwards into the darkness. He stopped to catch his breath for a short while before climbing on once more. The flame flickered and danced, blown about by small gentle gusts of wind. Shamera knew he must be close to the top. He continued upwards and as he did; the gusts of wind became stronger, and the torch struggled to stay alight. As he looked up the stairway, he could see what looked like an arched porch, an exit perhaps. His goal in sight, now spurred him on to climb the last of the steps with a little more enthusiasm. As he reached the arched porch-way, a sharp gust of wind finally blew the flame out. He placed the smouldering torch on the floor. He turned to look back down the stairs, but all he could see was the blinding darkness and the emptiness of the stairs he had ascended. Shamera walked through the doorway. He found himself once more on the outside. Steps carved out of the mountainside led him again upwards. This time, the light of the moon illuminated them. The crystals within the dark granite steps sparkled like diamonds in the moonlight, showing his way up. *'Not more steps,'* he said to himself despairingly. He was already feeling drained. Urged on by his quest to get the shard to the Elvenii, he once again trudged upwards. It wasn't long before the steps led him down the hillside. *'At last!'* he thought. He was relieved to be starting his descent. The light of the moon illuminated the narrow pass he was descending into. As he rounded a sharp bend, the narrow pass opened out, revealing a beautiful valley below, delicately lit by the moonlight.

A lake appeared as if by magic as he rounded the turn. In the stillness of the night, the lake looked like a seamless flat sheet of glass. The moon illuminated the valley floor and shone its light across the lake, giving it an eerie silver sheen as if it were made from unicorn blood. Hardly a sound rang out from the emptiness which surrounded the lake. It was eerily quiet; the lake was lined with tall slender pine trees. Small night flowers flourished in the moonlight as they grew along the grassy embankments. The scent of purpleberry flowers wafted upward into the night air. The idyllic scene was so beautiful it practically took his breath away. As Shamera descended lower towards the valley floor, he again paused for a while to admire the beauty of the vista. His words could not express the cascading emotions he was feeling at the tranquillity of the scene before him, and which reminded him of his favourite views back home.

Not being disturbed by wind or rain, the picturesque view was as still and as restful as the caverns of the Khul Mountain. As he listened attentively, he heard a solitary crow cawing somewhere in the distance; he could also hear the night bees buzzing energetically as they fed and collected the pollen from the purpleberry flowers. He was soon down on the valley floor and could see faint lights in the distance, *'Selvenora!'* he thought to himself… not far to go now. He had one last look around before heading off towards the lights.

Knowing his goal was in sight spurred him on again, and he picked up the pace. He could see the moon was changing colour and would continue to do so until it became blood red. It was low in the sky and shone silvery pink, it was only a matter of time before it became blood red.

He had to get the shard to Lord Salogel. Looking again into the distance, he noticed something moving; it appeared to be heading straight for him. He strained his eyes to see better in the moonlight… horsemen, and they were heading straight for him. As they drew closer, he could see there were about twenty riders. He hoped these were friendly.

As the riders drew closer, he saw they were wearing what looked like silver armour which glistened in the moonlight. Long red capes fluttered behind them as they galloped. He could see they were all well-armed with a long spear and a sword which was strapped to the horses' flanks. Their helmets sported a headdress, a plume, a long white ponytail made from horsehair which also flowed behind them as they rode quickly towards him. Shamera stopped walking and watched in anticipation as they drew near. He took a deep breath and allowed himself a small smile as he saw one rider was holding the banner of Selvenora and realised he was safe, and he had made it. The riders slowed down as they approached him and stopped a few yards in front of him... one rider kick on and slowly approached Him.

"Who and what are you? And how did you gain entrance to our lands?" he enquired whilst looking down from his chestnut-coloured horse and pointing his spear towards him. He looked at the magnificent beast, breath misting from its nostrils in the night air. He looked up at the majestic figure sat astride this beautiful beast. He faltered for a few seconds before answering him nervously and quickly. "I am an Ethaenian, and my name is Shamera. I am the sorcerer's new apprentice; I came through the large iron gates at the foot of the hill. I have journeyed for three days to see Lord Salogel before the Blood moon... I must see him. It is of great importance, and you are?"

"Slow down, my young friend, take a breath... I am Derrell, captain of the Selvernorian guard. No one has come through those gates in hundreds of years. How were you able to do so?" Enquired Derrell.

"I entered through the doors in peace, using the password... and I come unarmed. I am the sorcerer's apprentice; it is very important I speak with Lord Salogel before the blood moon... please," pleaded Shamera, barely taking time to breathe.

"Remove your cloak and empty your bag on the ground." Derrell commanded.

Shamera looked up at Derrell, took a deep breath and exhaled sharply whilst shaking his head slightly in disbelief. He quickly removed his cloak and carefully emptied the contents of his bag on the ground.

"I do not have a weapon; this is all I have... please take me to Lord Salogel quickly." Implored Shamera again. He looked up at the moon, which was deepening in colour.

"Put your belongings back, hand me your bag and staff. You will ride with Derrell." He said, as he waved his hand and beckoned Derrell over.

Shamera passed up his bag and staff to Derrell, went over and reached up to Derrell who offered out his gauntleted arm. Shamera took a tight grip as he pulled him up onto his horse.

"Hold on tight Ethaenian I wouldn't want you to fall off." Said Derrell with a little laugh.

Shamera threw his arms around Derrell and clung on as hard as he could. The Selvernorian guard set off at a gallop back towards the lights of Selvenora.

He kept a tight hold as they galloped across the valley towards another set of hills. Soon they reached the outer limits of Selvenora, the entrance of which was through a large, gated doorway carved out of the rock.

"Open the gates." Derrell ordered loudly.

Two large iron gates guarded the front of what looked like an old medieval gatehouse. The gates comprising a latticed grille made of interwoven strong metal bars. Large spikes of iron hung down menacingly at the bottom of the gates, which when the gate was closed, fitted neatly into holes in the stone floor. The large black gates creaked and groaned as they rubbed their way between the stone grooves cut into the walls which guided the gates as they were raised on their heavy chains. With the gates raised, the horsemen started their way into the stronghold. The iron horseshoes clattered and sparked on the hard-cobbled stone surface. The noise echoed around the courtyard, which was surrounded by three large buildings. Large flaming torches illuminated the courtyard and two blazing braziers with their metal frames glowing invitingly as the night grew colder. The horsemen stopped outside the tallest of the buildings, which stood right in front of them. Several guards, again dressed in silver armour and armed with a long spear and a sword, placed themselves on either side of the stone steps leading into the building, as though forming a welcoming guard.

Shamera looked up at the star-studded sky once more and saw the moon rising higher, it was starting to redden, time was running out. Derrell escorted Shamera up the steps and through the large double oak doors and into the building. The building opened into a large white marbled hall. Shamera looked around the room in amazement. The hall was it was lit by several large, mirrored candle sconces attached to the walls and a large crystal chandelier hung centrally overhead suspended by four gold-coloured chains. As Shamera looked around the room, he saw several carved, full-size statues of Elvenii warriors with two on either side of a flight of marbled stairs. Several large vases of fresh flowers adorned the hall, filling the air with a fresh clean fragrance, while a carved marble fountain in the centre of the hall added a feeling of serenity with the gentle sound of trickling water.

Derrell came halfway down the stairs and beckoned to Shamera to follow him. Shamera thought to himself *'What is it with these people and stairs,'* as they ascended the marble staircase. Shamera and Derrell entered through another pair of large oak doors, which led into yet another large, marbled hall. The doors appeared to make no sound as they effortlessly swung open on their large iron hinges.

"Wait here." Derrell said as he headed off up yet another flight of stairs carrying Shamera's effects.

Shamera looked around the sparsely decorated room; a white marbled floor delicately inlaid with black marble depicting Elvenii designs the craftsmanship of which was exquisite. A couple of marbled benches with silky red cushioned seats were placed along two of the walls. A rectangular marble table stood in the centre of the room; long white flowing net curtains in front of a large, open window, fluttered in the night breeze.

"They surely love their stairs and marble," he said to himself in a low voice.

"We do indeed." A soft female voice replied from behind him.

Shamera spun around to see a young woman of a similar age standing there. She was about an inch shorter than him. Long black hair flowed halfway down her back. Her emerald, green eyes stood out next to her pale complexion. He could not help thinking how beautiful she looked.

"Where did you spring from?" He asked nervously.

"Whispers of a stranger in our midst are spreading fast. We don't get many strangers visiting our land uninvited. I had to come and see for myself who you were." She said, whilst looking him up and down. She appeared to be examining Shamera closely as she walked slowly around him. She stopped in front of him and smiled sweetly.

Shamera's face reddened a little as he stood there feeling slightly embarrassed. This did not go unnoticed by Elithrin.

"Well, at least you have nice ears." She said with a sparkle in her eye and a cheeky smile.

"My, erm... my name is Shamera. I am an Ethaenian... and you are?" He asked, then coughed nervously.

"Oh dear, how rude, please forgive me. I am Elithrin, daughter of Lord Salogel."

Shamera's eyes widened as he realised who he was in the presence of. He gave another little cough to clear his throat, stood up straight, before giving a courteous nod of his head. "My Lady, please forgive me. I did not realise who you were." He said shyly.

"That's alright, there's nothing to forgive. Please, relax. We are a lot more informal with our visitors these days. We like them to feel welcome and at ease, this is now our way of life, we are more open and not as closed off as we once were, since the dark times we strive to cultivate peace in all areas of our lives.

"If that's the case, why do you still have an army?"

"Purely for defensive purposes, or in order to help others should they ask for it. We do not interfere with other nations; they don't interfere with us. What brings you to our land?" Elithrin replied softly.

"I am here for an audience with your father."

She slowly walked a little closer to him. He blushed even more. She peered straight into his striking blue eyes, "They are a gorgeous colour."

Shamera started fidgeting, shifting his weight from one foot to another. His mouth was dry, and his heart felt as though it was beating in his throat. He had never felt so uneasy and nervous. Elithrin smiled at his uneasiness and took a step back. "So, you are here to see my father."

"Erm... yes," he stuttered. "I am the new sorcerer's apprentice, and I must see your father urgently... what is keeping Derrell?" He said glancing around the room, trying to avoid further eye contact.

"You are Verazslo's new apprentice." She said with a look of surprise.

Derrell reappeared at the top of the stairs; and made his way quickly back down. As he walked over to them, he stopped and gave a courteous court bow to Elithrin who slowly bowed back in acknowledgement.

"I am to take you straight to the council of five. You will follow me?" Derrell said with an air of authority.

Derrell led Shamera up the staircase, down a long corridor, which turned left towards a single large oak door. Derrell knocked twice; the door appeared to open by itself. Upon entering the room, five Elvenii sitting around a large circular table, greeted him. Upon the table lay his belongings.

"Come... sit." Said the person sat in the middle.

He looked around the room; to the left was a large open window with fine silky white curtains that fluttered in the slight breeze. Against the right wall were two busts of Elvenii elders mounted upon carved marble columns. He slowly walked over to the table and sat opposite the Elvenii. They introduced themselves, starting with the one sat in the middle.

"I am Lord Salogel, leader of the Elvenii." He said, looking straight at Shamera, before placing his right hand over his chest and giving a little nod.

The others introduced themselves.

"I am Revilo," he said, placing his right hand gently over his chest.

"I am Nehpets," said the second, placing his hand over his chest in a similar manner.

"And I am Alegna," smiled the third, before placing her hand over her chest.

"And I am Einnor." Placing his hand in a similar manner.

"We are the council of five. Why do you bring us Verazslo's effects? This is most curious? Is he alright?" asked Lord Salogel as he pointed at the bundle.

"They asked me to bring them along with this crystal shard; I was told you would know what to do with them. And you would teach me how to use the wand and staff. I was told had to get them here before the blood moon, which is tonight... soon in fact." Shamera replied, hardly taking time to breathe, and pointing to the shard on the table. He was becoming slightly anxious and fidgety.

The other four Elvenii turned and looked at Lord Salogel, they then looked straight at Shamera.

"You said, they. Who are they?" Asked Salogel.

"Mirabilis and two Mystics. They said it was imperative I got them here before the blood moon, and you would know what to do with them."

"We have not joined the crystal and the staff together in roughly four hundred years. Why now does Verazslo send this child with them?" Nehpets asked, looking mystified.

"CHILD!" Shamera blurted out. He took a deep breath and looked straight at Nehpets. "Didn't you listen? It wasn't Verazslo who sent me; it was Mirabilis and two Mystics. Apparently, the dark sorceress, Niniane, has kidnapped Verazslo." He said excitedly.

The other four council members started chatting amongst themselves when Alegna looked straight at Shamera and said, "Niniane! NO! She has been long gone, her magic stripped, and she was banished from our lands. We've heard nothing about her since; if she were back, we would know."

Lord Salogel slowly raised his right hand as if to ask for silence. Everyone stopped talking. Lord Salogel looked deep into Shamera's eyes before saying, "Verazslo would not have left these things behind without good reason; if indeed, he has been taken captive, he would not want to be taken with them still in his possession. And why now would he entrust the shard of Ellaria to this young man?"

"I am his new apprentice."

Lord Salogel looked at him and paused for a while. "You're Verazslo's new apprentice?"

Shamera took a deep breath, "Yes, and all I know is Verazslo is missing, assumed kidnapped. Verazslo left these for me. Mirabilis and the Mystics said I had to get these and the shard to you, before the blood moon. They said you would know what to do with them. They also said you would teach me what I needed to know in order to use the wand. The moon is practically blood red. I have made it in time, I hope."

"Verazslo has placed a great burden upon you. How do we know if you are up to the task? How do we know this is not some sort of ruse to have the staff for your own ends?" Alegna asked.

Shamera stood up, placed both hands on the marble tabletop, and leaned slightly forward. He took another deep breath and with conviction said, "I have travelled three days to get here; I have been chased by Niniane's horsemen, travelled through Tussocks Bog, and survived. Spriggans have darted me, I was kidnapped by heaven knows who he was in the Screaming Forest, and I escaped. I have trekked all the way here. I even came through the great gates at the foot of the hills. Something no one has done in hundreds of years, apparently. Killed a Vark in the great hall, and you don't think I am up to the task!" Shamera paused for breath and looked at each council member in turn.

He was about to continue when Lord Salogel looked at him, smiled and said, "Please… sit, you certainly have spirit, and it would appear your journey here was obviously not an easy one. What you ask is difficult for us to consider. We removed the crystal from the staff for a very good reason all those years ago. When fully restored, the staff has the potential for great evil as well as for good. Verazslo thought it was too much power for any one person to wield and so, we dismantled it, and the crystal was hidden."

"Yes, you have somehow found the shard and have concocted this story to deceive us. We cannot reunite the staff on this so-called apprentice's say so. Where's the proof?" Alegna demanded.

"I am not 'so called' I am his apprentice. Lord Salogel please, believe me," he pleaded.

Lord Salogel looked at Shamera and sat back in his chair. "Alegna is right. What you ask is too great without proof. I am sorry but…" A loud knock interrupted the meeting. The door flew open. A guard hurriedly entered the room and approached the table; he stood next to Shamera, looked down at him and then looked at Lord Salogel.

"Members of this council, please accept my sincere apologies for my discourteous entrance. I have ridden hard to get back here with urgent news, it cannot wait. The rumours of Niniane's return… are true. Niniane… she's back." The guard gasped.

Chapter 7

Lord Salogel's eyes widened as a concerned expression crossed his face. "Thank you, you may leave us." Lord Salogel nodded politely to the guard, who gave a nod in return. The guard turned and left the room, quietly. The council members looked panicked as they chatted amongst themselves; Lord Salogel turned to them and spoke quietly in their native tongue. Shamera tried to listen but could not understand what was being said. There was a lot of gesticulating and what appeared to be arguing going on; and now and again it would fall silent, with one of the council members glancing at Shamera before speaking again.

The commotion stopped, Lord Salogel looked at Shamera, stood up and said "Most of the council feel Verazslo has placed great trust and faith in you. Therefore, we shall perform the healing ceremony and once again reunite the crystal with the staff. Be warned, young one; for what we are about to do has the potential to unleash great power. It will have to be handled carefully and cautiously. Give this council your word of honour as apprentice to Verazslo that you will never use it for anything other than good. Your word will be bound to the staff during the ceremony. Break your word and it will have grave consequences for you." Stated Lord Salogel.

Shamera placed his right hand across his heart and replied humbly. "You have my word, Lord Salogel; I will let none of you, this council, or Verazslo down."

"Come, we need to go to the 'Kuu-Luna'. The moon is virtually aligned and full-blooded. If we are to do this, we must do this now," Lord Salogel stated with a sense of purpose. He led the way through the large window, which led out onto a very large balcony. At the far end, a large stone altar with a smaller stone block in front of it. To its right, a tall flat surfaced stone, at least twice the height of Shamera, it had a narrow slit about two-thirds of the way up. The slit was hardly wide enough to slip your hand in sideways. Lord Salogel took the staff and placed the crystal within the ornate section of it. He placed the staff into a hole in the centre of a small square stone on the floor. There was a silent eeriness as the red moon illuminated the balcony as it passed slowly through the night sky.

"Shamera come, stand here. Hold on to the staff with your right hand and hold aloft the wand in your left hand. Whatever happens, do not let go of the staff or drop the wand." Instructed Lord Salogel.

The other four council members took position a few feet behind Shamera and held each other's hands; Lord Salogel took his position behind the larger altar. The moon was moving behind the large standing stone; Shamera gripped the staff and wand tightly in anticipation of what was about to happen. As the moon aligned with the narrow slit, a shaft of red light shone through it and hit upon the crystal. Lord Salogel raised both hands into the air and recited something in the Elvenii ancient tongue, which was repeated by the other four.

After a few moments, the crystal in the staff erupted with a bright purple light. It shone with a brilliant luminance which became brighter and brighter... so bright, in fact, Shamera had to close his eyes tightly. A bright beam of purple light discharged from the crystal and connected with the wand. Shamera's body stiffened up as a surge of energy appeared to flow through his body. His face grimaced as his teeth clenched tightly together. He let out a painful shriek as his body was filling with the charge from the staff and the wand. The beam of light from the blood moon broke. The moon had passed by the slit in the stone. The crystal slowly dimmed. Everything went dark. Shamera fell to the ground. He started writhing in pain. Lord Salogel and the others ran over and helped Shamera to his feet.

"Come Shamera, you need to rest. Your body will feel drained." They helped Shamera inside.

"What happened? My body feels strange, my legs... they feel so weak."

"Sit here. I will get someone to prepare a room for you." Lord Salogel said reassuringly.

Shamera sat on the bench near to the window, his whole-body aching and tingling from head to toe, wondering what had happened to him.

"Hello again, Shamera," said a familiar, soft female voice. He looked up to see Elithrin standing in front of him.

"Are you able to walk?" Elithrin asked.

"Put your arm around me. Do not worry, I am stronger than I look. Your room is not far."

Elithrin escorted him down the corridor to his room.

"Here we are." Elithrin helped him into his room and sat him on the edge of the bed; it was quite a basic room with the bed opposite the window. On the right wall stood an ornate carved wooden wardrobe. Near to the left wall was a small white marble-topped table with a washbowl and jug upon it. Shamera lay back on the bed, not knowing quite what was wrong. He felt woozy and lightheaded. Every muscle in his body was burning with a pain he had never experienced before. He did not know it yet, but his body had gone through the quickening. He lay there a while, trying to make sense of it all. Shamera made himself as comfortable as he could on the bed. His body felt heavy, and every movement was an effort. Elithrin left him to rest. He fell asleep almost instantly.

Voices outside his window woke him. He slowly sat up, expecting his body to still ache. Amazed and relieved, he noticed there was not a single ache or pain. In fact, his body felt different somehow. He could not put his finger on it, but he felt more invigorated. He sat on the edge of his bed trying to remember what happened the night before, but all he could remember was a bright purple light, and a surging pain which passed right through his body. He stood up and went over to the washbowl and splashed water on his face. He looked deeply into the mirror and stared at himself. He wasn't sure what had changed; he looked the same as he always did. Yet he felt a little different somehow.

There was a soft knock at the door. "Come in."

The door opened and Elithrin entered the room carrying a silver platter upon which was a selection of fruit, bread, and cheese, and a glass of milk. Over her right shoulder, draped some white garments.

"I have brought you breakfast. I thought you might be hungry after your Quickening."

"Quickening?"

"My father will explain. Eat something, you will need to keep your strength up, my father will expect you soon, he is keen to start your training as soon as possible, you'll need to put these on," she said handing him a long white robe.

"What are these?"

"Training robes, of course. My father will be out in the gardens," she said, pointing outside. Elithrin left the room and Shamera sat on the bed and tucked into the food. He was hungrier than he thought. Once he had finished, he donned the robes and went in search of the gardens and Lord Salogel. Shamera walked through a set of French windows which lead outside.

"Good morning, young man. I trust you slept well?" a voice asked, coming from behind him.

Shamera turned around to see Lord Salogel walking up towards him, holding the staff and the wand.

"I see you dress appropriately for today's lessons." He was also in similar white robes.

"May I ask a question?" Shamera asked politely.

"Yes, of course?"

"What's the Quickening? Elithrin mentioned it when she brought me breakfast."

"Putting it simply, it is the paring of the wand and staff to a sorcerer using the power of the blood moon." He explained.

"What does it do? Last night I could barely move because of the pain and this morning I feel great."

"I will reveal all in good time. Let's not run before we can walk."

The sun was still low in the sky as Lord Salogel walked with Shamera through the water garden. Small fountains of water gently trickled into various pools of water; intermittent fine jets of water shot upwards from under the surface of the pools. Lily pads in full bloom adorned the surface of the water. Small birds chattered from the trees, and some flew down to drink from the pools. This gave a feeling of calm and tranquillity in the area. They continued into the walled garden of contemplation. Their long white robes flowed gently in the slight breeze of the early morning.

They entered the walled garden; it was long and narrow. A single blossom tree stood roughly in the centre. Along the south wall was a variety of colourful border plants growing amongst boulders and large stones were carefully placed there. Along the wall, ivy cascaded down, virtually concealing the bricks. There were two small stone benches along the north wall; short, well-tended grass lay underfoot.

"A person... no matter how hard he may try, cannot hope to know his true destiny. Like everyone, you must live and learn in order to grow. And so, it will be for you young one. The acorn at the fullness of its life becomes the oak. You are that acorn... as you learn, so you will grow, and in time you will grow to be a great sorcerer for the good of all. There are many things in our lives which are beyond our control. However, it is possible to take accountability for your own state of mind and to control it for the better." Instructed Salogel.

He continued, "Meditation is a means of transforming your mind, and with regular meditation and patience, you will focus your mind and profoundly energise it in all its states. We see the world as but pieces of the whole; we see the sun, the moon, the tree, the grass, the flower," Lord Salogel said as he walked around the garden, pointing them out. "These are but the various pieces of nature, our world, our universe. These pieces form the soul of our world, a world that holds a deeper power in which we all exist, and it is accessible to those of us who know how to harness it. The act of seeing and the thing looked upon, the seer and the objects, will become one. You need to be at one with all around you in order to harness its power. Elvenii beliefs are respect for life and the natural world. This is essential. By living simply, one can stand in harmony with other creatures and learn to appreciate the interconnectedness of all life. The simplicity of life involves developing openness to our environment and relating to the world with awareness and responsive perception. It also enables us to enjoy, without possessing, and mutually benefiting each other."

Shamera tried to understand the meaning of it all, but for now confusion ruled his brain as he tried hard to process and put it into a meaning he could understand. Lord Salogel could see by the pained expression upon Shamera's face; he did not fully comprehend the meaning, but knew, in time, Shamera will come to understand it all. Lord Salogel looked at Shamera smiled slightly and said, "To put it another way, we use our natural states of being and our senses to help us relay our spiritual or internal feelings into emotions, and it is these emotions we must harness. Your senses are the receptors for your emotions and your mind must be the reflector. The wand and staff merely focus and amplify this power."

"Magic is not something you choose to do... the time, and the person has to be right. There has to be a spark within you. Magic has to be felt. It needs to emanate from your soul, from your emotions, and from what you feel in your heart."

Shamera stood there with a sense of pride, listening intently; he was finally going to be an apprentice sorcerer.

"I can teach you to build on the natural forces, to absorb them and to do some rudimentary skills. It will be up to Verazslo to teach you the real magic and how to use it. Here, hold the wand in your less dominant hand. Close your eyes... what do you feel?"

Shamera stood there holding the wand, trying to feel something. No matter how hard he tried, he felt nothing different.

"I don't think I feel any different. What am I supposed to feel?"

"Don't think it!... Feel it! Magic isn't something you think about doing. It comes from your innermost self. You must feel it, sense it, want it to happen. The wand and staff are merely tools to focus the magic through; they help to amplify your energy... the energy you take from the force of nature."

Again, Shamera tried to feel something different. He held his breath and strained intensely, trying to feel something.

"Okay, stop. For your magic to work, you must become one with the universe. Stand comfortably upright with feet apart. Let your wand arm hang loosely by your side, here take the staff, and lightly rest it on the ground in front of you. Close your eyes... feel the warm glow of the sun on your body. Imagine there is a golden ball of light above your head. This is the energy of the universe. Breathe in slowly and deeply to strengthen your internal energy. Feel the energy as it passes down through your head and into your body."

Shamera stood, following the instructions. He relaxed and concentrated on Lord Salogel's words as he repeated the instructions again.

"Yes, I can feel it." Shamera said excitedly.

"Good, let it fill your body with warmth, feel it course down through your body." Lord Salogel said softly.

Shamera opened his eyes. "Wow, I could really feel it!"

Lord Salogel looked at him with a look of irritation. "Did I ask you to open your eyes and break your concentration?"

"No, but…"

"No buts, do it again and concentrate. Listen to me and follow my instructions."

"Close your eyes again… feel again the warm glow of the sun on your body. Now, once again, see there is a golden ball of light above your head. You have done it once. It should be easier to do it again. Once you can see the light above your head, tap the staff gently on the ground."

He concentrated once more. After a couple of minutes, a slight smile appeared on his face. He slowly lifted the staff and gently tapped the ground with it.

"Good, now visualise a ball of white light below your. feet, this energy is held within the earth. Feel it, imagine it getting stronger, and as the feeling strengthens, it will naturally enter your body. Do not be afraid of it, accept it."

He again concentrated on feeling the energy. After another couple of minutes, he once again lifted the staff and gently tapped the ground with it.

"Very good Shamera, visualise this energy flowing upwards through your body to meet the golden light, pull the golden light down and the white light up. Concentrate and pull these energies deep into your body." Lord Salogel watched in anticipation.

He concentrated on Lord Salogel's voice, "Nothing's happening," he cried. "I don't think I can do it."

"Do not think of what you cannot do. Visualise these energies in your mind and let them happen." Lord Salogel said firmly.

"Feel the energy above your head and feel the energy below your feet. Now bring them together within your body." Lord Salogel continued, in a much softer virtually hypnotic voice.

"Feel both energies coming together and spreading throughout your body like the branches of a tree, feel the golden energy flow towards the white ball of energy, visualise them blending together. Visualise your energy, drawing strength from the blending of these two natural energies. Feel it Shamera…. feel it." Lord Salogel softly encouraged.

As Lord Salogel finished speaking, he noticed the crystal shard in the staff glowed; it was merely a faint glow. But it was a positive glow none the less.

"That's it Shamera." Lord Salogel cheered, as a smile crept across his lips.

"Feel those energies blend, and as they do, feel how they grow stronger within you." His voice was soft as he urged him towards success.

Shamera stood there and concentrated with all his might. He could feel a warm glow growing within him. Suddenly, he took a sharp intake of breath, opened his eyes, and looked at the crystal on the staff, which glowed brighter. Smiling, he looked at Lord Salogel for confirmation of his success.

"Don't think this is it. The crystal needs to shine far brighter." Lord Salogel stated, not wanting Shamera to let up on his efforts. "Now, let's start again."

They practiced late into the afternoon without a break. Lord Salogel felt pleased with Shamera's determination and progress and offered words of encouragement for tomorrow's lessons. The sun was getting much lower in the sky and Lord Salogel suggested they called it a day, and to get some well-earned rest.

"Enough for today, young one. Rest and we'll take it up again tomorrow. This should become second nature to you. You need to summon these energies effortlessly and speedily without thinking about it." Lord Salogel said.

Shamera looked at Lord Salogel and nodded. He felt drained and yet exhilarated at the same time. *'Becoming a sorcerer will not be easy,'* he thought to himself. They both set off back through the garden; Elithrin was waiting for them with a jug of cold water and a platter of freshly picked fruit. The three of them sat under the shade of a tree and rested for a while. Lord Salogel stood up and excused himself. "I have some things to attend to. Elithrin, will you take care of our young apprentice?"

"Of course, father." She replied.

When her father was out of sight, Elithrin looked at Shamera, smiled and enquired, "Well... how did you get on?"

"I think I did alright. Your father kept me at it for hours. I didn't think we would ever stop." he replied.

"Close your eyes," said Elithrin as she rose to her feet and stood behind him.

"Close your eyes. This will help relax you and enable you to concentrate better. Sit, relax, and trust in me."

Elithrin placed both of her hands on either side of his head. As she gently laid the palms of her hand upon his head, he felt a warm sensation emanating from her hands. He soon felt all his tension leave his body; he sat with his eyes closed as every muscle in his body suddenly relaxed.

"Wow..." he exclaimed.

"Shhh..." she replied.

Elithrin appeared before him in a white room filled with flowing white fabric. He opened his eyes.

"What was that?" he questioned.

"Shhh.... Close your eyes and let it happen." Elithrin quietly whispered.

He once again closed his eyes, and, as if by magic, she once again appeared before him in the room. Fine white translucent net like material gently flowed all around them. Elithrin spoke to him. "We are here and yet we are nowhere, and we are still under the tree."

"How are you doing this? It seems so real." said Shamera as he looked around the space he appeared to be occupying.

"I'm merely helping you to open up your mind and show you what is possible. You have the gift of magic within you, and I can feel it. The quickening has released some of it. Open yourself up and feel your energy. You are a very special person, Shamera."

He felt a warm glow within him. As he slowly opened his eyes, he was once again sitting under the tree. She was sitting beside him; she gently smiled as they sat gazing at each other for a few moments.

"Did you feel it?" she asked.

"Oh, I felt something." he replied with a smile. Realising what he had said. He was grinning from ear to ear. He blushed, got up and stuttered, "I better, erm, go, and erm, rest."

Elithrin smiled sweetly as he stood up and quickly walked back inside to hide his embarrassment. He made his way back to his room, stood the staff against the wall, and placed the wand on the table. He sat on the edge of his bed and reflected on what he had been doing all day, but his mind kept wandering back to Elithrin. And how did she do what she did? *'Come on... concentrate,'* he said to himself. He lay back on his bed, made himself comfortable, placed both hands behind his head, supported by his pillow. His eyes were becoming heavy; he was fighting a losing battle to stay awake.

He woke early; the sun was about to rise. As he looked out of the window, his thoughts turned to home and his favourite spot in the Thornbeck Meadow. He wished he was home right now with his family; he had never been away from home this long before and was missing them greatly. He hoped everything was well back in Elms Hollow and hoped to be back there soon. He turned away from the window feeling a little saddened; He sat for a while, contemplating on what he may do this day when, there was a knock at the door.

"Come in."

Elithrin entered with his breakfast. She placed it on the table and turned to face Shamera.

"How are you feeling this morning?" she enquired; a soft smile lit up her face.

"Drained and a little homesick. I'm missing my family," he sighed.

"I imagine they are missing you just as much, but you have a job to do, a destiny to fulfil. Come... sit in this chair."

He stood and slowly walked over to her and sat down. Elithrin stood behind him and again placed her palms gently against his head, as she did the previous day.

"Let these thoughts go for now. This is not the time for distractions." She whispered softly whispered.

He felt a warm glow emanate from her hands and travel down his body.

"Concentrate on the task ahead. Clear your mind of distractions. Know you are going to be a great sorcerer. You can master this. Be at peace with yourself; be as one with all things."

He felt his body totally relax. "You are fantastic at this."

"You can be too; you need to open up your mind and accept your destiny."

"You make it sound so simple."

"The Elvenii believe respect for life and the natural world is essential. By living simply, you can be in harmony with other creatures and learn to appreciate the interconnectedness of all life. The simplicity of life involves developing openness to our environment and relating to the world with awareness and responsive perception. It also enables us to enjoy things without possessing them, and we mutually benefit each other and harness the surrounding energy."

Shamera sat there and pondered Elithrin's words while she moved her hands from his head to his shoulders. She gently patted his shoulders.

"I feel very relaxed and, somehow, energised."

"It's time for breakfast, after which, you need to find father. Remember to open up and accept the surrounding energy. Do not think about it. Know you can do it." She instructed.

She left him to eat his breakfast in peace, and to contemplate her words and what today's lesson would bring. Shamera ate heartily and went in search of Lord Salogel who was waiting for him outside by the water garden.

"Good morning." Shamera said with renewed vigour and a soft smile.

"And a good morning to you, too. Are you ready to move to the next step?"

He smiled and nodded as they continued their way into the walled garden to continue his training.

"Today we are going to do something a little different. Today you can allow your mind's eye, your third eye, to see outside of yourself whilst keeping your eyes shut."

Shamera reflected on what Elithrin had told him earlier. It prepared him to relax and let whatever he needed to, happen naturally.

"Through the power of your mind and using the layers of your aura, I want you to connect to the surrounding environment. Close your eyes and breathe deeply and slowly. Your aura is connected around you, and it is also connected to the environment you now occupy, and therefore you are connected to the environment."

Shamera stood there and breathed deeply. He tried to relax and let things happen, but he felt nothing.

"Can you feel and see your aura yet?" Lord Salogel asked quietly.

Shamera concentrated harder. This made him scrunch his eyes even tighter. His head tilted to his left; he rotated his head as though looking over his right shoulder.

"I think so; I can see a pale, glowing light. Yes, it's a pale blue glowing light." He exclaimed.

Lord Salogel looked at Shamera in astonishment and allowed himself a slight smile. No one had ever connected so quickly before.

"Concentrate and make the light brighter." Lord Salogel said firmly.

"I can see a light all around me, its blue and shimmering."

"You have come a long way and quickly in two days; Verazslo was wise in choosing you. This is the true nature of seeing and reflects your abilities. With practice and determination, you will see what is all around you without using your eyes. Seeing with your mind."

"Like a Mystic, you mean?" Shamera asked inquisitively.

"They see things differently, but yes. Like the Mystics."

With his eyes still closed, Shamera was moving his hands over his arms as though trying to touch and feel his aura.

"Keep your eyes closed and try to see."

He focused his mind; he cocked his head slightly to the right.

"I think I can see something, but I can't quite make it out."

"Stop thinking about it. Do not force it. Relax and let it happen."

His shoulders tipped forward, and his head dropped. The release of his body's tension as he relaxed felt good. He concentrated as hard as he could. "I can see… I can see a faint outline; you're standing in front of me with your arms outstretched sideways."

"Very good." Lord Salogel stated as he quietly and slowly crept around the back of him.

"I can see you going around the back of me. It is very faint, but I am sure of where you are." He said with confidence.

"Very good indeed. I am amazed you have picked this up so swiftly. You definitely have magic within you. With practice, the images will become clearer."

Shamera felt very proud of what he had accomplished. They practiced some more over the next couple of hours.

"Okay, enough for now. We will try to do some levitation and some simple things with the staff and the wand after we have had some refreshments." Lord Salogel stated.

Shamera thought to himself, *'At last, real magic'*. He was excited about learning to use the wand and staff he had carried with him all this way. They both walked back into the water garden where they sat peacefully, ate, and drank some berry juice. It was hard for him to contain his excitement. At last, he was learning some magic.

After about thirty minutes had passed, Lord Salogel stood up, "It's time to practise some more."

Again, they peacefully walked back into the walled garden.

"I want you to hold the wand in your right hand and the staff in your less dominant left hand. Close your eyes and bring in the energies as you did yesterday."

Shamera stood there and concentrated. Lord Salogel stood looking at the shard, waiting to see if it would glow. After a short while, Shamera could feel the energy growing inside of him. The crystal glowed, barely noticeable, then it steadily grew brighter.

"Keep concentrating and open your eyes."

As he opened his eyes, the shard dimmed.

"You must not let what you see distract you; you must be able to hold those energies within you at all times. Now, with your eyes open, bring back those energies. You will need to concentrate harder."

He focused on a boulder in the flowerbed as he tried to bring the energies back into his body. He did it; the shard was glowing again.

"Good, that's good." Lord Salogel praised. "Point your wand at the boulder and think of it rising into the air."

He pointed the wand at the boulder. The boulder trembled as though it was being shaken by an invisible hand. Slowly, the boulder rose about a foot in the air; amazed at what he had done, he turned to look at Lord Salogel. As he did, the boulder slammed back down.

"No... you must not break concentration." Lord Salogel scolded.

"Sorry, I..."

"Try again." Lord Salogel insisted.

Shamera concentrated on the boulder; he pointed his wand and imagined it rising. The boulder didn't shake as much this time as it rose steadily into the air, to all of about three feet.

"Now move it, place it near to those pink flowers, on the left."

He concentrated as the boulder moved to the left, as it hovered over the pink flowers he momentarily lost concentration, and the boulder dropped and crushed the flowers. He spun around to Lord Salogel who stood there with a disapproving look on his face, shaking his head.

"I'm sorry... I must have lost concentration again; I didn't mean to crush the flowers."

Lord Salogel pursed his lips together and shook his head in disbelief. For the rest of the afternoon, he had Shamera lifting and lowering the boulder all over the garden; by the end, Shamera could lift the boulder at least ten feet into the air with little effort.

"Okay, it is getting late. Time for one final task, a true test of your concentration. I want you to raise the boulder into the air and have it hover over your head," he said with a large smile.

"What!" Shamera exclaimed.

"You heard me raise the boulder and have it hover above your head. This will be a true test of your ability and concentration."

"You are joking, right?"

"I never joke; now... do as I ask." He insisted.

Shamera pointed the wand at the boulder and focused intensely as it rose into the air, it moved upwards and forward to hover over his head. Unwavering, he stood looking up at the muddy bottom of the boulder hovering a few feet above his head. He held it there for about a minute, which felt more like ten.

"Okay, enough for today. You must be hungry? Go get something to eat and drink; rest well, and tomorrow we will go over what you have already learnt and move on to making fire and other simple feats of magic."

Shamera moved it back to its original resting place amongst the flowers. That night, Shamera did not sleep well. He kept thinking about what he did that day. He was keen to learn more, and even though he did not sleep well, he was up early. He went to sit outside in the early morning sun. It was not long before Lord Salogel joined him. Both once again headed for the walled garden of contemplation. Lord Salogel schooled him even harder today, going over all he had learned in the last two days. By lunchtime, Shamera was getting better at summoning the energies and could quickly move the boulder around the garden without crushing the flowers. He learnt how to make fire, how to make rudimentary energy balls, which he could shoot from his hands in order to incapacitate an enemy. He learnt a couple of rudimentary protection spells. Lord Salogel called him a natural sorcerer. They both caught sight of an Elvenii soldier stood at the entrance to the garden. He was standing bolt upright, his highly polished armour glistened brightly in the sun. Lord Salogel went over to speak with him. They stood there talking for a while; the soldier took one step backwards and saluted by bringing his right fist up to the left side of his chest. Lord Salogel walked slowly back. Shamera could see by his expression something was wrong.

"We are going to cut short your training, Niniane and her armies have invaded in the south, we are sending some troops to support the men we already have stationed there, we are also sending riders to the Dwarves to ask for their help too."

"My home is in the south. How far are they from the Sloendor Valley and Elms Hollow?" He asked with concern.

"A way off yet, lad. We may need to expedite your training. The staff is not at its full potential, and as your powers are nowhere near their fullest, you are going to need help. I was hoping this day would not come, or at least not yet. You will have to go to the valley of the pig farmers. A good day's ride from here. There you must seek the dragon slayer."

"Dragon slayer?"

"Yes, a dragon slayer. Tell him you need a dragon's heart string, a fresh one. I will give you a parchment with a spell written on it. You must place the staff on the ground, place the dragon's heart string along its length, and then recite the spell. The dragon's heart string will bind with the staff and give it its full potential. Once you have completed this, you must immediately return here." Lord Salogel instructed.

"How do I get to the valley?"

"I will send you with three of our best riders; they will take you there, wait for you and bring you back. They will see you safe."

"But what about my family? I thought I would be seeing them soon?"

"We need to get you as prepared as we can before we are able to try and rescue Verazslo, and, with the two of you leading our armies, we can defeat this sorceress once and for all. This is something you have to do. You are the apprentice, after-all. We will evacuate towns and villages as we need to. We will keep your family safe; I promise."

Shamera stood there for a while, trying to process the information. All he could think about was his family back in Elms Hollow. The realisation of the invasion and his village could be in danger was now hitting home.

"Shamera, I know you are worried. But there is nothing you can achieve back home. The best thing you can do is to continue to get stronger as a sorcerer; and improve our chances. I will send an out-rider to inform your family you are well. But your training has not yet finished." He said reassuringly.

"I'm not sure I am cut out for this; it's getting all too much. It's all too soon," he said, his voice was quiet and concerned.

"Get changed. I am going to call a council gathering and I want you there, too. I will send for you when it's time. It's time to become the person Verazslo saw in you."

Shamera went back to his room, his head filled with thoughts of home and his family. He sat on the edge of his bed, leaning forward and cradling his head in his hands. He questioned himself, *'What strange journey have I become entangled in? What have I let myself in for? There is so much to learn and so much practice. Am I up to it?'* A gentle knock interrupted his thoughts.

"Who is it?" The door slowly opened. "It is me, Elithrin. I thought you might like some company; I have heard my father calling the council together and heard him talking of an invasion by the dark sorceress."

"Your father wants me to go on some quest for a dragon's heart string. I have to go to the valley of the pig farmers, of all places."

"Ah yes, about a day's ride from here. I have been there. It was a couple of years ago. I can't exactly remember why, but I went with my father on business." She said, tying to comfort him.

There was a more determined knock at the door, and in walked Lord Salogel.

"It's time for the council meeting."

Elithrin looked at her father and glanced a look at Shamera. Her facial expression said all that needed to be said. Her concern for Shamera was obvious; she said nothing and casually left the room. Lord Salogel and Shamera headed for the council chamber. They spoke not a word between them. They arrived at the chamber and Lord Salogel pushed open the heavy wooden door and they both entered. The council sat around the white marble table chatting amongst themselves. Lord Salogel and Shamera sat in the two unoccupied seats. Silence befell the room as they waited for Lord Salogel to address them.

"As you are all aware, we have confirmed the Dark Sorceress has invaded in the south. We need to prepare and send more troops to meet her invading army and to evacuate any villages in danger. I have sent riders to inform and to seek help from the other nations. We need to unite the nations; no one army is big enough to defeat the sorceress. For those who don't know, Shamera is going on a short journey to get a dragon's heart string and after successfully powering the staff, he is to come back here for more basic instruction. Hopefully, by the time of his return, the Mystic Shaman Korell will be here to help with his training." Lord Salogel announced.

Einnor looked up, sadness and fear written on his face. He looked around the room, took a deep breath and stated, "These are times I thought we would never experience again. A dark cloud hangs heavily over our lands today."

Lord Salogel nodded in agreement, he turned to Shamera, "I have arranged riders to take you as far as the Hog Roast Inn. There you will meet up with the dragon slayer; I have it on good authority he is a frequent visitor to the Inn. The men will wait for you there and when you have completed your task, they will bring you safely back. You will leave after breakfast tomorrow. I suggest you get an early night, as it will be a full day's journey." Lord Salogel turned to face the council. "Has anyone got anything else to add?"

Einnor looked at Shamera, and at Lord Salogel. His face this time was totally expressionless. "No offence lad, but how can he go up against the dark sorceress? He can barely make fire. The sorceress is powerful… Does no one know where Verazslo is and how we can rescue him?" he asked Lord Salogel.

"I have every faith in Shamera; Verazslo has had his eye on this lad for quite some time and intimated he will be a powerful sorcerer. We have people searching for Verazslo. We know roughly where he is being held prisoner, but currently we do not know the exact whereabouts." Lord Salogel replied.

Chapter 8

Shamera awoke to the bright rays of the sun bursting through the white, flowing curtains. He had barely slept at all, thinking about his journey and what might lie ahead and how was he going to gain a dragon's heart string. Surely, they did not expect him to fight a dragon. Elithrin once again brought him his breakfast. As she entered the room, she smiled at him and placed the large silver tray full of fresh fruit, toasted bread, and milk carefully on the table.

"Good morning, Shamera, I've brought you your breakfast and also I have prepared some food for your journey."

"Thank you, but I don't think I can eat much this morning." There was a nervous undertone to his voice as he gingerly sat up in bed, holding the bed sheet close to his chest.

"You will be fine; father has chosen three of his best soldiers to escort you there and back," Elithrin said comfortingly.

"Well, it can't be any harder than my journey here, I suppose," he said, exhaling a large breath.

Elithrin removed a special brooch from her dress and pinned it on his shirt, which was hanging on the back of the door. "For good luck," she said with a smile, then stood at the foot of his bed.

Shamera blushed a little and thanked her for her kindness. The door opened again and Lord Salogel entered the room.

"I'm sorry. I hope I am not disturbing anything?" He said as he looked at them both. Elithrin jumped back a little, and Shamera blushed again.

"Of course not father, I was wishing him luck on his quest." Elithrin smiled at Shamera and left the room, closing the door softly behind her.

"You look a little warm, are you alright?" Lord Salogel teased.

"Erm, yes… a little apprehensive about the journey is all." He replied with a slight stutter.

Lord Salogel smiled slightly as he pulled some folded parchment from his pocket. He looked at the parchment and glanced at Shamera for a few seconds.

"You have come a long way. I would even go as far as saying you are a natural, but you still have a lot further to go before you can become a fully-fledged sorcerer. It looks like someone else has great faith in you already," he said, pointing to the brooch.

"It's for good luck." Shamera said embarrassingly, trying to avoid eye contact.

"You must have impressed Elithrin a lot for her to give you her Ordriel... this jewel would not have been given lightly. But for now, we must concentrate on the task at hand. When complete, this staff can yield great power. On this parchment, is the enchantment needed to complete this task. Verazslo himself wrote it." Lord Salogel handed the parchment over to Shamera who inspected it closely.

"What do I need to do?" He asked inquisitively.

"Lay the staff on the ground and lay the heart string along the length of the staff. Hold the wand over the staff, summon the energies, and recite the words on the parchment. That's all you need to do. Concentrate on what you are doing and believe in the words. Once it is done the staff will be fully charged once again. I also have this; it's a small book of magic. Verazslo left it here for apprentice training. There are but a few incantations, some you may find useful. Remember your training before attempting any of them. Bring forth the energies and concentrate."

Shamera took the book out of its velvety pouch; the book was bound in soft dark leather with two crossed keys above an open eye embossed into the cover. He thumbed through the yellowing parchment. It even smelled old as he examined the book with obvious excitement.

"What is the meaning of the symbols on the cover?"

"The keys represent unlocking the mind. The eye represents your mind's eye and vision."

Shamera nodded his head as he further examined the pages of the book.

"Once you have dressed and packed everything you need, make your way to the courtyard. Your escort will wait for you there. Good luck and stay safe. Your destiny awaits."

Lord Salogel left Shamera to dress and finish his packing, which, whilst experiencing feelings of nervousness and excitement, the packing did not take long. Once packed, he grabbed a slice toasted bread, which he wedged between his teeth. Picked up the staff and his backpack and set off for the courtyard.

Three Elvenii soldiers were already mounted upon their horses and were waiting patiently for him. They were wearing their everyday clothes, and not the armour he was used to seeing them in. A fourth riderless horse stood saddled and waiting. He slowly descended the steps, looking warily at the fourth horse, said, "What's this?"

"This is your horse; you have ridden before, haven't you?" One of the soldiers asked.

"Erm. No, never. The only time I have been on one of these things, I was sitting behind one of your men. Clinging on tightly so I did not fall off. I did not like it," he replied nervously.

"Well, this should be fun; you'll have to learn to ride on the way." Said another disbelievingly.

"My name is Vesryn. I am in charge today. This is Hethoral, and this is Theronas," he said, introducing everyone.

"Hi, I am Shamera," he replied.

"Give me your staff. It will be safer with me. You will need both hands for the reins. Come on, get mounted, we have a lot of ground to cover." Vesryn said, taking the staff from him.

Shamera tried mounting the horse, but the horse kept moving sideways. He at last got one foot in the stirrup but could not lift himself up onto the horse's back. The three Elvenii tried hard to hide their amusement at Shamera's failure to mount his horse.

"It's not as easy as I thought," he said, embarrassed at not been able to mount properly.

"Go stand on the plinth and mount from there," Vesryn said whilst shunting Shamera's horse with his.

Shamera stood on the plinth, which was about three feet high, it gave him a better height from which to mount the horse.

Finally, he anxiously sat upon it. Vesryn gave him some quick instructions on riding and how to hold the reins lightly. They set off at a walk across the stone courtyard. Iron horseshoes clanking against the stone ground as they set off in search of a dragon's heart string. This was a strange experience for him, having never ridden before. He shook his head in disbelief and hung on to the saddle horn for dear life. They were soon out of the courtyard and heading for the valley of the pig farmers. Vesryn rode next to Shamera and instructed him further in horsemanship.

"You're riding out of rhythm. Feel the horse come up and you rise with it. Your backside will appreciate it too," he instructed, and gave a little smile.

Shamera soon found the rhythm and found the ride a lot more comfortable.

"Also, be gentle with the reins. Don't hold them tightly or suddenly pull on them. They gently steer the horse in the direction you want to go. If you wish, you can hold on to the horn in front of you until you gain more confidence."

Shamera lightly held the reins but took Vesryn's advice and held the horn firmly. They picked up the pace a little and trotted.

"Whaooo!" blurted Shamera, panicking, "Too fast, I'll fall off."

Vesryn rode next to him again, reassuring him if he relaxes in the saddle and keeps his feet in the stirrups, he will be fine at this speed. They kept this pace up for a couple of hours, Shamera feeling quite the horseman, was a lot more relaxed and had let go of the horn and was lightly holding the reins as instructed. He was readily enjoying the ride and the countryside.

A snake lying in the grass near the road suddenly rose and hissed, spooking his horse. The horse reared up, flexing its two front legs in the air. Both the horse and Shamera were balancing on the horses' back two hooves, one wrong move, and both could easily fall. Shamera instinctively hung tightly onto the saddle horn for dear life and held his feet firmly in the stirrups. The horse neighed loudly, as it put all four legs back on the ground, the horse took off up the road at full gallop.

"Oh Shhhhitt," Shamera shouted as he flew past the others. The other three looked at each other and, without a word being spoken, kicked into their horses' flanks and set off at a full gallop after him.

"Hold on Shamera," Vesryn shouted in hot pursuit, his horse kicking up dust as they galloped after him.

Shamera was bouncing around in the saddle like a ragdoll. He was holding on with all his might as his horse refused to slow down.

Shamera tried to shout for help, but his mouth and throat were too dry. Panic stricken and in fear for his life, he clung on hard to the horn with both hands, his legs squeezing hard into the horses' flanks.

"Hold on! we're coming." Shouted Vesryn as he urged his horse go quicken.

Vesryn and Hethoral were closing fast and were drawing up to either side of Shamera's frightened horse. Shamera was clinging on for dear life. Hethoral moved closer to him and leaned over to grab the reins which were loosely hanging around the horse's neck. Vesryn's first attempt missed, he lined himself up again. This time he grabbed the reins near to the horse's bridal.

"Whoa, whoa, steady… steady," he shouted as they pulled up.

"Are you alright?" Hethoral asked.

"What… what the hell happened? It... it just took off! It's trying to kill me," he spluttered. His experience had unnerved him greatly and he dismounted as fast as he could. His legs practically gave way as he tried to walk, he felt wobbly and looked for somewhere to sit.

"Look, he's got jelly legs," laughed Theronas.

"You did well to stay in the saddle," Vesryn said, trying to hold back the laughter.

"I thought you said you couldn't ride?" Theronas teased.

"Enough." Vesryn said, still chuckling to himself. "We'll take a break here."

"Is it going to keep doing that?" He asked, disgruntled. "Well, is it?"

"I'm surprised it did it at all. These horses are all well-schooled." Vesryn replied.

"Well, this one needs to go back to school," he rebutted.

Hethoral still having a little snigger, took all the horses by their reigns and led them into the shade of a couple of trees.

"Shamera, sit here and get your breath back." Vesryn said, pointing to a spot underneath a tree.

He sat with his back against the tree trunk. His body felt as though it was still bouncing around on the horse. He sat there for a short while, gathering his thoughts. He looked up at Vesryn. "It just took off… I couldn't stop it."

"That was the funniest thing I've seen in a while; you surely bounce well. Anyway, no harm done, you're safe," Vesryn replied, desperately trying not to laugh.

"Well, I'm glad you all found it funny."

"We are merely trying to lighten the mood; you had a scary experience… A lesser person would have unseated and had a very nasty fall. But you… you hung on in there, you did very well, very well indeed," Vesryn said softly.

Theronas brought Shamera some water and sat down beside him. "Here, drink this; we still have a long way to go. You can ride my horse the rest of the way. He doesn't spook, and in fact… he eats snakes for breakfast," he smiled.

"Fine, thank you. But, if you don't mind, I'd rather walk," he said before glugging the water.

"The best thing you can do right now is get back in the saddle, or you may never get back in one again. You have had a nasty shock. We have all been there when we first learnt to ride, and some of us even fell out of the saddle, some of us more than once. My backside still has the bruises all these years later, but we were all encouraged to get back on the horse straight away to conquer our fear. You need to do the same. Try not to dwell on what might have been. Might have been's never happened. Sit and rest a while and let the experience subside." Theronas gently patted Shamera on his shoulder and rose to his feet and went to join the others.

Shamera said nothing, but thought about what Theronas had told him? They had rested for about thirty minutes when Vesryn shouted, "Okay, time to mount up. Come Shamera we need to go if we are to be there before the sun goes down."

Shamera looked at him, his eyes widened as he realised, he had to get back on a horse.

"Come Shamera, take my horse." Theronas shouted.

He reluctantly stood up and went over towards Theronas.

"Come, let me help you up. You will be fine, I promise."

Reluctantly, and with fear in his eyes, he got back into the saddle.

"Well done lad," Vesryn said encouragingly.

They all set off once more. The journey had taken all day; and Shamera was very pleased to see the village and the rest of the journey had been uneventful. Weary from their journey, they finally reached the outskirts of the village. The sun had set behind the tall distant mountains of Khuldehern; the air was becoming colder as they rode down the main street. They arrived at the Hog Roast Inn. Shamera dismounted first. He could not wait to get out of the saddle. Stretching up slowly, he raised his arms high into the air and made a circular rotation of his head and neck. Every muscle in his body ached, especially his backside.

"You three go ahead, I'll see to the horses," Vesryn said as he took hold of all the reins and led the horses towards the Inn's stables.

Hethoral pushed the door open, and the three of them stepped inside. They had stepped into a warm room which felt much better and more inviting than the cold chill of the night air they left outside. The smell of ale and roasting pig filled the room.

"I'm starving," Shamera remarked as he sniffed the air. The room was quiet, with six people sitting at various tables eating and drinking. They headed towards the innkeeper; he was a short, balding man with a dirty white apron wrapped around quite a large, rounded belly.

"By the size of his stomach, it looks like the food must be good here," Hethoral whispered whilst smiling and nodding in the innkeeper's direction.

"Do you need a room?" the innkeeper asked.

"Yes, please. We'll be sharing if you have a room big enough?" Theronas asked.

The Inn keeper shook his head slowly. "I'm sorry, but we have two double rooms you can have."

"Well, it'll have to do," sighed Theronas.

"Tell me, inn keeper, do you know the whereabouts of the dragon Slayer?" Hethoral enquired.

The Inn keeper turned and pointed towards a man sat quietly in one corner, his hat and the shadows obscuring his face.

They walked over to the man; he sat staring at them as they approached him.

"What can I do for you fine, gentlemen?" The man asked.

"The innkeeper says you're the dragon Slayer."

"It's a living," the man replied.

"May we sit? We have a proposition for you," Hethoral asked.

The man said nothing but gestured with his hand toward the empty seats. Hethoral reached over and pulled the unlit candles towards him and lit them. From the light of the candles, they could see many years of dragon slaying had taken its toll on the man. His hands bore the scars of battle, half a finger was missing from the third finger of his left hand. His face weathered and leathery looking, a long scar starting under his right eye and finishing down towards his jaw, a battle scar awarded to him from a dragon who got too close.

"So, what can I do for you?" the Slayer asked.

"I am Theronas, this is Hethoral, and the one coming in is Vesryn, and this is Shamera. He is the new apprentice sorcerer. And you are?"

"I'm known locally as the Slayer. You can call me… the Slayer," he replied somewhat sarcastically.

"I supposed you have heard the dark sorceress is back and massing an army on our shores?"

"Yes, bad news travels fast. So, what need have you of me?"

"We need you to take Shamera on a quest for a dragon's heart string," Vesryn said.

"You want me to take him on a quest to kill a dragon?" he questioned.

"Hang on… nobody said anything about dragon hunting or that I was to go on such a mission."

The Slayer stared at Shamera and glanced at the soldiers. His brow furrowed as he thought to himself. Shamera sat there looking at all four of them with a worried expression creeping across his face.

"And how much is this worth to you?" He asked inquisitively.

Vesryn pulled a small leather purse from inside his coat, shook it gently. The sound of gold coins rattled within. He softly tossed it to the Slayer. He caught it in his right hand. He slowly unfastened the draw strings and emptied some coins into his hand.

"This is handsome payment; there must be some urgency to this?"

"We are to accompany you, to keep the young lad safe," Vesryn said firmly.

"No… if I am to do this, I go alone. Stealth is of the essence; I cannot have you all banging and clanking around and scaring off the quarry," he replied.

"Not acceptable, besides we are Elvenii soldiers. We do not bang or clank around. We need to ensure the safety of the lad," Theronas exclaimed.

"Apprentice Sorcerer, you say, can you do magic?" the Slayer asked whilst looking him over.

"I can do a little. Lord Salogel has been training me," Shamera replied.

"A little!" He exclaimed. "What use is a little?"

"Look, it is important he gets the dragon's heart string, and soon. We are going to need all the help we can get against the sorceress," Vesryn said with a sterner tone in his voice.

The Slayer looked at Shamera again and weighed the purse of coins he was holding. He inhaled deeply and exhaled slowly.

"He has to come along, you say. It's not open for debate; he comes alone, fear not he will be safe with me. Besides, he can do a little magic. Maybe it's me who should be worried," he said as he smiled at Shamera.

"No!"

"Look, I'm not taking you all. We need to be stealthy. Besides, the dragon I have been tracking recently is old; it shouldn't put up too much of a fight."

"And what say do I get in all of this?" Shamera asked.

"None," Vesryn replied. "Okay, but you better make sure he is safe at all times, or you will have us to answer to."

"How dangerous is this going to be?" Shamera asked with concern.

Everyone appeared to ignore him.

"I have been hunting dragons all my life. He'll be safe; besides you haven't told me why you want its heart string?"

"All you need to know is Shamera needs it," Vesryn stated firmly.

"Fine, keep your shirt on," he replied, holding both hands in front of him, as though holding back Vesryn.

"Hang on!! Will someone please answer my question?" Shamera asserted.

"It won't be dangerous for you, so long as you do as I say, and all will be well. And don't get in my way," the Slayer stated adamantly.

"We should eat." Hethoral said.

"You should. He needs to rest. It will be a long day tomorrow. Meet me down here shortly after sunrise. Don't be late, I will not wait," he said as he stood up and set off for his room.

"Inn keeper!" shouted Hethoral and beckoned him over with a hand gesture.

"Can we have 4 meals and water to drink, please?" Hethoral asked politely.

"Water?" the innkeeper asked.

"Yes, water, we are Elvenii soldiers. We do not drink ale," Hethoral replied firmly.

"I'm not a soldier, I'll have the ale please,"

"You'll have water," Vesryn insisted. "Be up early and alert tomorrow,"

Shamera gave a loud, deep gasp for Vesryn to hear his disappointment. After their meal, the four of them asked to be shown to their rooms. The inn keeper's wife escorted them up the creaky wooden staircase and along a bare corridor, her meagre candle barely lighting the way. The corridor was wood-panelled with 2 sets of doors on either side of it. She stopped opposite one room; the candle was flickering, making eerie shadows on the walls as her breath caught the flame. As she pushed the door open, its old rusty hinges creaked and groaned. She entered the room and lit the candles which stood upon a table. The room was as plain as they come. The bare boards creaked beneath their feet as Shamera and Vesryn entered the room. Two beds lay side by side with barely a gap between them. A small table with the candles and a washbowl stood against the opposite wall to the beds. A small dusty square window was the entire supply of natural light, and it was home to a large, dusty spider's web. The large spider lay dead and mummified on the windowsill.

"I'll show the other room to you two now," she said, leaving the room and closing the door behind her.

Vesryn walked over to the door to lock it. Vesryn's face fell in disappointment as he discovered it merely had a small rusty latch.

"Well, at least the door screeching will let us know if someone tries to break in." Vesryn remarked with a slight sigh and a sarcastic tone.

Shamera laid the staff and the wand between the two beds, and his bag on the other side of his bed. He sat on the edge of the bed, looking out of the dusty window at the barely visible moon. Shamera moved the candle closer to his side of the table, took the book of magic out of his backpack, and read through it. After about an hour, Vesryn looked over at him, and with gentle reassurance, spoke. "Don't worry about tomorrow, lad. You will be fine. Now get ready for bed. You have a big day ahead of you."

The next day, Vesryn opened his eyes slowly to see Shamera was already up and dressed and quietly packing his backpack.

"What are you doing?" Vesryn yawned sleepily, gave a large stretch and yawned again.

"I couldn't sleep. I kept thinking about the dragon. So, I have been going through what I must do and have been practicing the enchantment should we get a heart string."

Vesryn turned to look out of the window. "It'll be sun up soon. Go see if you can rustle up some breakfast. I'll join you shortly," he said, giving a large yawn and stretching his arms above his head once again.

Shamera opened the door to a chorus of squeaks and creaks from its hinges and went in search of some breakfast. To his surprise, the Slayer was already up and sitting at the table eating his breakfast.

"I've ordered you all breakfast, bacon, eggs, sausages, and toast," the Slayer said as he took another large mouthful of sausage and egg.

"Vesryn is getting up and will be down soon," Shamera replied as he sat down and waited for his breakfast to be served.

"We'll be heading out to Aysgarth woods. It's a large wood, and I have tracked the dragon there. Albeit an old dragon, but it has still been making itself a nuisance, taking pigs and other livestock."

Shamera didn't say another word. He sat quietly and ate his breakfast. It was not long before Vesryn and the others came downstairs and joined them. The Slayer watched them as they approached the table.

"Before you even ask, no, you are not coming along. And don't even think of following us. I will know if you do," the Slayer insisted.

"I could follow you merely a few feet away and you would never know Slayer, a tracker and dragon killer you might be, but we Elvenii soldiers are like ghosts... invisible when we need to be."

"I would know," he said confidently.

"How big is this dragon?" Shamera enquired, trying to stop the bickering.

"It's hardly a four-clawed dragon, and old. You will have nothing to fear as long as you do exactly what I say," the Slayer remarked.

"You can put a protection enchantment on the Slayers' armour and shield. Be warned it will not last long as the dragon's flames will constantly weaken the enchantment," Vesryn said as he slightly raised his eyebrows and nodded towards Shamera.

"You can do that?" asked the Slayer.

"I don't know. I have never tried it before. How will I know it has worked?" Shamera replied, looking quite surprised.

"Well, if he doesn't get cooked, it worked," smiled Vesryn whilst smiling at the Slayer.

The Slayer shook his head in disbelief.

"I've taken the liberty of saddling a horse for you; I've tied it up outside next to mine," the Slayer said.

Shamera looked at Vesryn with trepidation.

"You'll be fine, have you all you need?" Vesryn asked.

"I think so, wand, staff, and backpack" Shamera reeled off his list.

"Right lad, time to be heading off," the Slayer said, standing up from the table and letting out a very loud burp.

Shamera and the Slayer headed for the door.

"Good luck to the both of you!" Shouted Vesryn.

"And don't be following behind, I can track ghosts too!" the Slayer shouted back as they walked through the doorway and headed to the stables.

They mounted up and Shamera followed the Slayer; he was quietly hoping they would not be riding for long as he was worried about the horse bolting again and he was still aching from yesterday's journey.

"You have not said how far we have to go?" Shamera questioned.

"It's particularly a couple of hour's ride to the hills, we will be on foot the rest of the way," he replied.

Shamera contemplated facing the dragon. He did not know what to expect and feared they would end up being a roasted dragon's dinner. Not a lot was said between them as they travelled towards Aysgarth woods, Shamera thinking about what might lay ahead, the Slayer looking at the countryside and the ground observing for any tracks or signs of dragons.

"Look, over there, Aysgarth hills, the woods are on the other side of them," the Slayer shouted.

Shamera's heart beat a little faster, as he realised, they were close.

"Once we get to those hills, we will be on foot the rest of the way," he shouted again.

They were not huge hills, but they were very loose sided slate, which were no good for horses to climb.

"We'll tie the horses up here," the Slayer said, pointing to a tree.

"Once we get to the woods, you do everything and anything I say without question, do I make myself clear?"

"Yes," he quivered.

"I mean it; never ask why... just do exactly as I say when I say it. And maybe you will live through this."

"Oh great, you're really building my confidence."

"You'll be fine."

The Slayer, changed into his dragon scale armour, medium and small scales from the dragons he had hunted and killed. Dwarves had carefully tailored them into long pants, body armour and gauntlets. A large dragon's scale formed the basis of his shield, which was further furnished with dragons' teeth.

"The dwarves made these for me; the dwarves have great Smithing skills," said the Slayer proudly, "Now, how about this magic spell?" he asked.

"I'm not sure how good it will be, but I will do my best," Shamera replied apprehensively. The Slayer took his shield down, which was tied to the saddle. Shamera opened his book, raised his wand, closed his eyes, and tried to remember all Lord Salogel had taught him. He felt the energy rising within him as he imagined the Slayer being protected from the dragon's flames by the shield and dragon armour. He recited the incantation from the book. A bright blue light briefly engulfed the Slayer's armoured carapace and his shield. It appeared to gradually fade away as it encased his body and shield.

"Was that it?" the Slayer asked. He appeared to be disappointed there was not more to it.

"I think so," Shamera replied, obviously never having performed this spell before.

"Well, we'll soon see, won't we?" the Slayer said, heading off up the side of the hill.

"It says here the dragon's flames will weaken the spell, so you had better not take too long and kill it quickly," Shamera added before placing the book back into his backpack.

They climbed the loose black slate which appeared to be tinged with purple. For every five steps they made forward, they seemed to slip back two. The hill had a strange metallic odour and was void of any plant life. Not even moss grew here. It was harder going than it first looked. Eventually, they scrambled their way to the top. Both panting from the strenuous climb up the hill; they looked down towards the woods. Suddenly, a heart-wrenching, ear-piercing shriek echoed through the woods below.

"Come my lad, the hunt is on," the Slayer said eagerly, slipping and sliding his way quickly down the hill.

Going down was definitely easier, he thought, sliding through the loose slate underfoot whilst trying his best to stay upright. Shamera used the staff to help him maintain his balance; it would be a painful fall if he lost balance, he thought. Finally, they reached the bottom of the hill and onto firmer ground. A wide stream laid a few metres ahead; large bluish grey steppingstones showed the route they should take. The Slayer was the first to the stones and hurriedly forded the stream, promptly followed by Shamera not wanting to be left behind.

"Why are we hunting this particular dragon?" Shamera asked.

"This is an old female dragon, it has moved into the area because of the easy pickings, mainly due to the large pig farms in the area, but it has been known to take people who get in its way."

The Slayer moved slowly through the woods, paying close attention to the floor of the wood which was covered in fallen leaves, twigs, and plants, examining everything for any signs of disturbance.

"We are looking for any signs animals have run through here escaping our quarry. These signs will give us a direction to the dragon's whereabouts," the Slayer whispered.

The ground looked like any other woodland ground, Shamera thought as he tried to see what the Slayer was trying to convey.

"Look… here," he whispered, beckoning Shamera over.

"See how these twigs have broken, look the sap is still wet. These have recently been broken, but unfortunately not by our dragon. There is not enough damage to the area. Nor by any fleeing animal, again, they would have stirred up the ground more," he explained.

They ventured further into the woods methodically searching area looking for any signs of the dragon. It was not long before they came across some. The dragon had been sharpening its claws, leaving large deep scratches down the length of some trees. These deep, long wounds in the trees gave the dragon's presence away, as some of these scratches were freshly made. The Slayer pointed out the pale colour of the wood were the bark had been stripped back. The exposed wood had not oxidised, and the sap was still sticky.

The Slayer looked all around, his eyes penetrating deep into the woods, his ears listening for any signs of danger. Slowly he made his way through the woods quietly and carefully, with Shamera following closely behind, mimicking all the Slayer's moves. They heard the noise of something large moving in the undergrowth ahead and to their right side. Shamera quickly turned towards the sound of something large, very large, and it was rushing through the undergrowth towards them. The dragon Slayer drew his sword and softly whispered, "Oh, we have you now, dragon."

Chapter 9

The Slayer edged his way slowly and warily towards the direction of the sound; they soon found themselves in a large clearing. Shamera looked at all the fallen trees. The sound stopped... "It may have gone to ground," the Slayer whispered.

They both looked around for any sign of the dragon. The scorched and fallen trees looked like a heavy force had felled them. Charred tree trunks split and fractured lay rotting in the clearing. These had not been felled recently, as many were decaying and mosses had made themselves at home on the dead, rotten wood. A few large boulders lay strewn across the clearing, which were also covered in varying shades of green moss and lichen. The Slayer pointed to a pile of human bones which lay partly covered by the undergrowth.

"Look... that was probably a Slayer, it must have been a very formidable dragon. That would explain these beaten up and charred trees," said the Slayer whilst all the time looking around the wood for any sign of the dragon.

Shamera looked at the bones, and a cold shiver ran down his back. "Aren't you scared?" he whispered.

"There will be plenty of time to be scared later. You best keep your wits about you... dragons can be sneaky buggers."

The sound of something large was again making its way through the trees and undergrowth; the crashing noise was getting faster and faster; it was coming straight towards them. The Slayer pointed his sword towards the noise and held tightly onto his shield; he focused on the sound and told Shamera to take cover behind a large tree. He did not hesitate. He quickly took cover and nervously watched as whatever was coming was now almost upon them.

"Don't use any of your spells or magic on the dragon. You'll probably piss it off and make my job even harder," he laughed.

Branches snapped and leaves rained down like giant green and yellow snowflakes as the dragon crashed through the tops of the trees as it propelled itself straight up into the sky. The Slayer and Shamera scanned the skies with keen eyes, trying to spot the beast. The Dragon swooped down from out of the direction of the sun. At the last minute, the Slayer caught sight of the dragon and in the nick of time too, the dragon started raining fire down upon him. He quickly raised his shield to protect himself from being burned to a crisp. The stench of the dragon's breath as it rained fire down made him heave. The shield and its magic did their job well as it deflected the flames all around him. The flames set the small bushes and undergrowth alight. He knew the shield's magic would not last long against the dragon's intense flames, he was hoping for a swift victory. He could already feel his armour warming up. "Can you take its fire away?" he shouted to Shamera, "At least it will give me a greater chance of slaying this beast quickly."

"I will try," he shouted back.

The Dragon swooped down again, laying another trail of evil smelling fire; the Slayer raised his shield whilst choking on the vile odour. As the dragon flew by it lunged and clawed at the shield, sending the Slayer sprawling across the burning ground. Tightly grasping the shield and lance, the Slayer rose to his feet. Feeling slightly stunned and shaken from the fall, he staggered out of the flaming undergrowth, shook his head to regather his senses. "You'll have to do better, dragon!" The Slayer shouted. He knew he could not last long if the dragon kept breathing his fire upon him.

Shamera observing from behind a large tree held his wand aloft. He could feel the energy bubbling up inside him; and imagined the dragon without its fire, and before he could utter a single word, immediately a heavy downpour of rain started and yet the sky was still blue.

"Rain! What use is rain?" he shouted, mystified at Shamera's choice of spell.

The magic rain started extinguishing the fires in the trees and bushes; plumes of acrid smoke rose from the smouldering fires, the Slayer's eyes stung and watered, the smoke was catching the back of his throat and made him cough.

"Whose side are you on? You're supposed to help me, not the bloody dragon," he spluttered. Still coughing, he ran towards the large tree where he had left his battle axe resting against it. The dragon made another terrifying strafing attack on the Slayer. The dragon's fire was again unsuccessful in harming him, the shield once again offered the protection of its magic. The rain was soaking everything, offering a small yet helpful added defence. As the dragon flew passed; he quickly raised the battle axe, with both hands over his head, and with all the strength he could muster, hurled the axe at the dragon.

A blood-curdling shriek echoed through the trees as the axe cut deep into the dragon's left side just above its front leg. The dragon landed on the ground barely a few yards from the Slayer. The smell of the dragon's breath, coupled with the smouldering shrubbery permeating the air was becoming too much to bear.

"What the hell have you been eating? This has got to be the worse dragon's breath I have ever smelled." He shouted at the dragon.

The dragon strained to breathe fire, but the magical rain had doused his flames too. Smoke merely bellowed from the dragon's nostrils and mouth. The dragon, furious and in pain, swished its tail at the Slayer, glancing him a stiff blow which sent him reeling and sliding across the wet muddy ground. The dragon started using the scales on its tail as a colossal cutting weapon, slashing at the Slayer. These scales were sharp. The dragon's tail sliced through the bushes and small thin trees like a hot knife through butter.

Shamera, from the relative safety of a large tree, watched the Slayer skip and bound around the clearing, skilfully avoiding the dragon's tail. With the agility of a dancer, he spun and ran around the clearing, clutching his sword in one hand and his lance in the other. The dragon flung his tail around repeatedly at him; he dodged around the clearing, ducking behind tree stumps and rocks to avoid being struck. The Slayer ran from behind a large rock and took shelter behind a fallen tree trunk, hoping to gain a slight positional advantage. The dragon saw him; it turned its body slightly and brought its tail down with such force; it smashed the rotten trunk into a thousand tiny pieces sending him once again, sprawling across the ground. Shamera, still hiding behind the tree, could see the Slayer was tiring, and his wet armour was weighing him down. The dragon turned to face his adversary; the Slayer, still a little stunned, picked up his sword and lance before advancing wearily towards the dragon. The dragon used its front right leg to claw at the Slayer. The dragon with the axe still embedded in its thigh limped forward, snarling, and snorting, its claws were mere inches away from shredding the Slayers flesh. He used his sword to parry the claws away from making contact. The clang of steel against the hard-impenetrable scales of the dragon rang out with every blow; the muscles in his arms were burning from the constant swinging of his sword. After several minutes of attempting to cut the dragon with his sword and trying to pierce the dragon with his spear, he lost his temper. "Aarrgghhh! I **WILL** kill you," the Slayer cried as he swung his weapon, desperately trying to find a weak spot in which to vanquish the beast. He was angry and frustrated at not being able to get close enough to strike a killer blow.

"For an old dragon, you surely are a worthy opponent," he remarked.

Shamera watched as even with the Slayers' axe still buried deep into its flesh, the dragon gained the upper hand. The dragon advanced, roaring and snapping its large deadly teeth at the Slayer; he was being driven backwards. He stumbled over his shield which was lying on the ground. He quickly picked himself and the shield up from the ground. The dragon again lashed out with its deadly claws, both adversaries locked in a battle for their lives. The dragon glanced its claws across the Slayers' shield with such force the Slayer could not hold on to it; the dragon had sent the shield flying into the smouldering undergrowth and propelled the Slayer sprawling to the ground at the same time. The Slayer quickly rose to his feet, he staggered and around; his legs giving way beneath him. Somehow, he stood firm as he used the sharp point of his lance to poke up at the face of the dragon. The dragon roared as it flinched instinctively away as the point of the lance that neared its head. The dragon attacked once more, snarling and clawing at him. Its right front leg hit the side of the Slayers' body, which sent him flying, knocking him to the ground once more. The dragon quickly moved forward and stood over the Slayers prone body; it looked straight down at him. The Slayer, exhausted, lay on his back and was totally helpless. Exhausted, he looked up at the dragon, who was still staring down at him, their eyes locked upon each other. The dragon's upper lip lifted as it snarled, exposing its deadly jagged teeth. The Slayer was gasping for air as he choked on the acrid air and the dragon's foul odorous breath; he accepted his fate and awaited death to claim him.

He looked up at the dragon; saliva dripping from its large murderous teeth, the rain ran down the dragon's head and cascaded like a small waterfall falling upon him. The dragon fixed its large yellow eyes on the Slayer who lay sprawled before him, beaten. The dragon opened its mouth and slowly lowered its head towards him. "Make it quick, dragon!" he shouted through gritted teeth, awaiting his demise.

The dragon's body stiffened up, it yelped in great pain and jerked its head upwards. It turned to see a very large boulder had landed on its tail, pinning it to the spot. The Dragon jerked upwards again, trying to free itself and revealed its softer under belly; the Slayer summoned up what little strength he had left, quickly grabbed his lance, and thrust it upwards between its scales, piercing deep into the dragon's chest. The dragon gave an ear-piercing scream as the lance penetrated between its scales and deep into its flesh. The dragon reeled in pain; the Slayer rolled away and stood up, and with his last ounce of strength, took hold of the lance again and drove it even deeper into the dragon's heart. The dragon fell forward with a large splash on the waterlogged ground; the Slayer drew his sword, held it aloft, and drove it deep into its skull. The dragon was dead. The rain stopped falling. The Slayer fell to his knees, exhausted and gasping for air. Shamera reappeared from behind the tree and came down to see if he needed any help. As he did, he did not take his eyes off the dragon for one second. "Is it dead?" he asked.

"Yes, it's dead," he replied. Breathless, he held his face skywards with his mouth wide open, catching the last drops of rain falling from the leaves of the trees to quench his thirst. "Oh... and thank you," he said, still trying to catch his breath, "That boulder was a nice touch; I thought he had me for sure."

"My powers are still somewhat limited; but luckily, I had been practicing levitating boulders," he replied proudly.

The two of them stood there looking at the dragon as it lay there motionless. Shamera turned to the Slayer and asked, "How do we get the dragon's heart strings? Are you going to… have to, cut it open?" he asked squeamishly.

"Yes, WE are going to cut it open, unless you can magic it out of there," he said sarcastically.

"Erm… I'm not sure I can." He replied. The colour drained from his face as he felt his stomach churning.

"Oh, a great warrior you are! Can your sorcery at least turn the beast over onto its back?" He said wearily.

He lifted his wand, concentrated hard, the dragon rose in the air and turned over before crashing back to the ground with mud splashing everywhere. The dragon's head fell sideways as if turning towards them. The dragon let out a deep groan. Shamera was quickly on his toes and ran for the trees. The Slayer stood there laughing.

"It's okay; it's the dragon is letting out its last breath. You dropped it pretty hard," he said with a grin which reached from ear to ear.

Shamera cautiously made his way back towards the dragon, not taking his eyes off it for one moment.

"We can feast on dragon meat tonight. You will never have tasted such a sweet flavoursome meat. You would think it would be as tough as old boots, no, it's very tender," he said as he raised the tips of his fingers to his lips and appeared to kiss them, "Lift the scales so I can get my sword in there to cut it open," he instructed.

Shamera sheepishly lifted the dragon's scales. He turned his head away; and screwed his eyes tightly together as the Slayer cut open the dragon. The sound of the sword cutting through the dragon's flesh turned Shamera's stomach; he thought he was going to throw up, but somehow, he held it together.

"There… I'm done. You can open your eyes now, young sorcerer," he said, with a wry smile.

Shamera gingerly turned to look at the Slayer, who was standing there with blooded hands, holding a long yellowy white heart string. Shamera's face contorted with repulsion as he stated, "I hope you're going to wash that, and your hands,"

Shamera searched through his backpack. He pulled out a piece of parchment.

"Found it!" he exclaimed.

He scrutinised the piece of parchment carefully, reading every detail before placing the staff on the ground. He asked the Slayer to place the dragon's heart string upon the length of the staff. He held his wand aloft and read the words on the parchment.

"Tamina ten'oio thisia uroloki hoon wit amin wandiff en' maranwe. Parf amin lakilea thar goth rim amin; amin am I' chil en' I' istar, his neuro. Mak amin beleg in I' templa. Amin naa tualle; Parf amin maranwe en' I' iant mens'."

Translated, it says, *"Forge forever this dragon's heartstring with my staff of destiny. Grant me victory against my foes; I am the heir of the wizard, his successor. Make me strong in the magical arts. I am your servant; grant me my destiny of the old ways."*

They both looked upon the staff lying on the wet, leafy ground as a small breeze rustled through the trees and across their faces. The air around them felt as though it was becoming charged with static. They felt the hairs on their necks and arms rise up. The staff radiated with an iridescent orange glow. They looked up at each other in anticipation, expressions of amazement on their faces. The glow became brighter and brighter until they could no longer look upon it. In an explosion of bright white light, all fell silent. The light disappeared, leaving them both rubbing their eyes. They glanced down at the staff, the dragon's heartstring had vanished. Shamera's face lit up with elation. He had done it. The incantation worked. Shamera expecting the staff to be hot, cautiously stretched out his left hand as he bent down to pick it up. As his fingers drew slowly towards the staff, he couldn't feel any heat radiating from it.

"It's cold!" he exclaimed.

"What did you expect?" the Slayer replied.

"No… I mean, it's freezing. With that amount of bright light, I thought it might be hot."

The Slayer slowly reached out and touched the staff. "Wow, it is cold, icy cold. Now what? Do some magic with it," he said, encouraging Shamera to try something.

"I had better not. Lord Salogel instructed me not to use it; he said he would know if I tried." He replied.

"I would try it to see if it works... what if it doesn't?"

"And what happens if I cannot control it? I could kill us both."

"In that case, we should head back to the tavern; we should be able to make it before dark."

The Slayer cut off a few very large chunks of meat, wrapped them up, and placed them in a cloth bag. They set off back through the woods.

"We'll go this way; it should be quicker," the Slayer said, pointing along another path trodden through the woods.

They did not speak but followed the path for a short while. There was a loud CRACK. As they looked at each other, something rapidly propelled them upwards. They found themselves trapped within a rope net suspended from a tree. Struggling to get free, Shamera dropped the staff through the netting.

"NO!" Shamera exclaimed, still struggling to free himself.

"STOP... stop struggling; I'm trying to reach for my knife."

Shamera stopped struggling and tried to see if he could spot the staff on the ground; the pair of them were helpless to do anything, slowly spinning about four feet off the ground. The Slayer reached for his knife and was about to cut the rope when a band of five freebooters came out of the woods brandishing weapons.

"Well, what do we have here?" one of them said as he walked over and picked up the staff.

"Leave it alone, that belongs to me." Shamera shouted.

"This is a fine staff indeed," the freebooter replied as he walked around with the staff as though it was a walking aid.

"Cut us loose," Shamera demanded.

"Drop your knife," another freebooter shouted, as he poked the Slayer with his sword.

"Do you know who I am?" The Slayer shouted.

"Oh look, a dragon Slayer," replied the first freebooter.

"What about some magic?" the Slayer whispered to Shamera.

"They have the staff, and my wand is in my backpack," Shamera whispered back.

"Do not let them know who you are or what they have; it looks like they don't know what it is," the Slayer whispered again.

"Drop the knife and we will lower you down," shouted another freebooter.

The freebooters started whooping and laughing, slapping the net with their swords and clubs and spinning the net around even faster to disorient their captives.

After a short while and assessing their predicament; the Slayer dropped his knife. A Freebooter picked it up and went over to the rope anchoring the net, he held his sword aloft.

"NO!" shouted the Slayer, but before he could say another word, the freebooter cut through the rope with one swipe of his sword. The pair of them came crashing down. The gang rushed forward, unravelled the net, and held their swords against the Slayer and Shamera.

"Your stuff, give me that bag, I'll take the shield too." Ordered a rather stout man with a long ginger beard, pointing his sword at them.

"No, you can't have it," Shamera said, clutching her backpack tightly.

"Look, we don't want to hurt you. But we will, if you don't do as we say. Snib… tie them up."

The gang dragged the backpack from Shamera and all the belongings from the Slayer.

"We should get a tidy sum for this lot," the shortest of the gang said, his eyes wide open with greed.

Once stripped of their belongings, Snib tied them both tightly to a tree whilst the rest of the gang rummaged through their ill-got gains.

"What do we have here? look at what I have found," the shortest one said, holding the wand aloft in one hand and the book of spells in the other. The leader of the gang rushed over and held out his hand and motioned with his fingers to be given the items. He looked at the wand and the book. He looked over at Shamera and smiled.

"This isn't a fancy walking staff; this is a magician's staff and wand," he began waving the wand around, flicking it towards the trees, he turned to one of his men pointed the wand at him said, "I turn you into a toad," he flicked the wand. To the relief of the freebooter, nothing happened. Whilst the leader was busy trying to perform magic, the Slayer whispered to Shamera "Whatever you do, do not let them know who you are or what you need them for. Trust me."

"How do I make this work?" the leader of the gang snarled at Shamera.

"Bring it here and let me show you," Shamera replied.

"Do I look stupid? Just tell me how it works."

"You need to possess magic or it's merely a stick to you," Shamera said, trying to free his bonds.

"Do you possess magic?"

"No, if I did, I would have used it to free us from that net." Shamera said, shrugging his shoulders.

"So, why have you got them?"

"We are to deliver them to someone called Krell. He's a Mystic."

"A Mystic… freaks. Well, he won't be getting these. C'mon men, let's get out of here before someone comes."

The gang casually turned away to walk back through the woods when one of them turned and shouted, "You'd better pray there are no more dragons around here," he laughed, and walked away.

"Come on, let's go. We do not want to be around here when it gets dark." another one shouted.

"Are there more dragons?" Shamera asked.

"I wouldn't have thought so. They are very territorial."

"How are we going to get our things back? I need those to defeat the dark sorceress. I cannot go back to the Elvenii and tell them I have lost the staff and the wand… and the book of spells," Shamera said as he tried once again to free himself.

"They are not the brightest of people. We need to free ourselves first, and I will track them down. We'll find the scum."

They both struggled for quite a while, trying to free themselves, but the ropes held firm. They were making their arms and wrists sore from struggling. They had been there for quite a while; the sun was setting; the woods were becoming darker. Shamera was getting quite worried.

"Looks like we will be here for the night," the Slayer remarked.

"No, we cannot. We need to find them and get our things back... HELP! HELP!" He struggled even harder to break free.

"Save your breath. No one will venture into these woods at night. They'll be too afraid of the dragon. No one will know we have slain it."

"Great! Some apprentice sorcerers I'm turning out to be."

They tried again to free their bonds, but it was in vain. The rope held firm. Night-time was upon them, and the woods were dark and eerie. All they could do was to sit there and hope either someone would pass by their way, or the soldiers would come looking for them once they realised, they were missing. The noises from the woods appeared louder and stranger in the dark. The Slayer tried to reassure Shamera by telling him there are no dangerous animals in these woods, and someone would find them in the morning. The moon was high in the night sky and barely visible through the canopy.

"It's getting cold." Shamera remarked.

"It's a good job this isn't winter. We would freeze to death for sure."

"Is that meant to reassure me?"

"Well..." the Slayer started, but before he could say anther word Shamera shouted.

"HELP! Over here, HELP!"

"Don't waste your breath."

"No, look, there is a light over there. Look, it's moving. We're saved. HELP! We're over here. This way, we're over here," Shamera shouted as he watched the torchlight getting closer.

"We're saved, someone is coming," Shamera said with excitement and relief.

"Let's hope it's not another robber," the Slayer said sarcastically.

"No, it can't be... do you think it could be?" Shamera sounded concerned.

The stranger was virtually upon them. They could see a silhouette of a person holding a torch high and to the right.

"Well, if it isn't the young sorcerer and the ghost tracker. What are you two doing down there?" a familiar voice said.

"Hethoral, am I glad to see you," Shamera said, feeling quite relieved they had been found.

"Please cut us loose. My wrists hurt, my body aches," Shamera pleaded.

"What happened to you two heroes?" Hethoral asked.

"They have robbed us. Five bandits with swords trapped us in a net. They have taken everything; we have to get it back," Shamera recounted frantically.

"First things first, I need to get you two safely back to the Inn," Hethoral replied.

"But what about our things? I must get them back," Shamera pleaded.

"There were five freebooters, they trapped us in a net snare, and there was nothing we could do. The staff fell through the net, and he could not reach his wand in his backpack. They were on us straight away," the Slayer explained sheepishly, embarrassed at being trapped and robbed.

"It's too dark to do anything right now. Let's get back and sort things out," Hethoral stated.

"But.."

"But nothing, we cannot do anything at this moment in time, let's get you both back before something else goes wrong."

Hethoral led the way with his torch held high. It was not long before they were out of the woods. The full moon lit their path back to the hills and scrambling back up the slate hill and to their horses. No one said a word as they headed back to the Inn. All Shamera could think was he had let everyone down and how was he to get his belongings back. The sun was coming up as they reached the village, cold and tired. Shamera thought of nothing else but how he could explain losing the staff and the book Salogel had entrusted to him. At last, they reached the Inn. They both hoped the fire was still burning, at least they could get warm.

"I'll take care of the horses; you two go inside and warm your bones," said Hethoral.

Shamera and the Slayer sheepishly entered the Inn. Shamera was very nervous at what consequences awaited him. Vesryn and Theronas sat waiting for them to arrive; awkwardly Shamera approached them and sat down. The Slayer sat uncomfortably at the next table. The Slayer cocked his head to one side, his brow furrowed in thought, and spoke.

"How did you know where to find us? And why only one of you?"

"We are Elvenii soldiers," Vesryn said, staring straight at him.

"That's not in dispute, and it has been puzzling me all the way back. If you thought us lost or worse, I suspect all three of you would come looking. Yet you appeared to know exactly where we were."

Shamera peered at the Slayer and at Vesryn in turn. "You knew where we were all this time?" Shamera asked.

"Not all the time," Vesryn said, being evasive in his answers.

"What do you mean?" Shamera asked again.

"You said you would keep the lad safe. Huh... worked out well, didn't it?" Vesryn alleged.

"I kept him safe... from the dragon. He got the heart string and did his magic. The trap was well hidden, and I wasn't looking for traps. And you haven't answered my question. How did you know where to look?" the Slayer asked in reply.

"Tell them Vesryn put them out of their misery. The lad looks worried sick," Theronas insisted.

"Well, five not so intelligent muttonheads came in here peddling some rather interesting items. So, we relieved them of the items, and, after a little persuasion, they told us where you were," Vesryn said, grinning from ear to ear.

"Persuasion... you hung them from their feet and threatened to disembowel them slowly," Theronas added with a smile.

"So, you have all of our things?" questioned Shamera eagerly, letting out a loud gasp of relief.

"You have been very lucky. If those idiots went the other way or didn't stop here, who knows what might have happened? You have been very lucky indeed. I knew we should have gone along," Vesryn said sternly.

"You, Slayer, your things are over there," Vesryn said, pointing towards a bundle near the fire.

"Shamera, you can have breakfast first. Then we need to get back. If you need to, you can sleep on your horse. I'll look after these until we get back. You need to do better than this if our hopes are to rely on you." Vesryn said disappointedly.

Vesryn did not look happy; he understood the importance of the responsibility placed upon Shamera. He had to learn and learn quickly if he was to stand any chance of defeating the dark sorceress.

Chapter 10

"Captain of the Guard, three riders are approaching," the lookout shouted from the tall tower.

"Can you see who it is?" the Captain of the Guard replied.

"It looks like that Ethaenian and the escorts."

"That Ethaenian is the apprentice sorcerer, and your future may depend on him," the captain said with authority.

"Yes sir, I meant no offence towards him."

"Open the gates," the captain shouted.

The heavy iron gates rose slowly as the chains clanked and groaned around the creaky cogs. The gate was lowered as soon as the riders passed through. As they dismounted, a guard took hold of the horses' reins and stated that Shamera's presence was required in the council room upon his return.

"You best go see why you are required. Sounds important," Vesryn said.

"I need to rest," Shamera pleaded.

"You can rest later, best go and don't say a word of being robbed, we'll keep that between the four of us." Vesryn added as he handed Shamera his belongings and his staff.

"Thank you, I don't think I could face Lord Salogel if he knew," Shamera said as he gave a sigh of relief.

Shamera set off for the council room; he hoped Lord Salogel hadn't been informed of the incident. *'How could he?'* he thought to himself. His stomach churned at the mere thought of having to explain it all to him. He reached the council room and knocked on the heavy wooden door, and waited for a reply. There was no reply, so he knocked again, a little louder this time. After a few seconds of silence, he slowly opened the door. He looked around the empty room. It puzzled him to see the room empty, yet they summoned him to go there. Shamera slowly entered the room and softly shouted, "Hello…"

No one answered back; Shamera was about to leave when in walked Lord Salogel and a Mystic.

"Ah, Shamera, I heard you were back. This is Krell. He is a Mystic Shaman."

"Hello Shamera," said Krell as he offered his outstretched hand in friendship.

"I sense I am not the first Mystic you have come across."

"Err, no," Shamera replied. He could not help but to stare at his third eye, which was closed but had a definite eyelid which appeared to move slightly. Krell looked at Shamera and smiled slightly.

"I see the staff has got its dragon's heart string. I feel its power," Krell exclaimed, holding his arm forward, palm towards the staff.

"Come, please both of you sit. I assume the journey was a success if Krell can feel its energy." Lord Salogel said.

"Are you here to show me how to use it?"

"Not exactly," Krell replied cautiously.

"What do you mean, not exactly?"

"This is now a powerful weapon, but on its own it is still not enough to defeat the dark sorceress. And I do not mean to insult your progress, or your current abilities. But you are still very inexperienced, the sorceress is very experienced and powerful. There is evidence of another powerful weapon." Krell paused.

"What is this other weapon?" Shamera asked.

"We do not know what it is, but it goes back further than the war between all nations."

"Okay, where is it located?"

"We know roughly where it is," Lord Salogel said unconvincingly.

"So, there is another powerful weapon, but you don't know what it is, or where it is. And how do you think I can help?"

"We do not know what it is, that's true. That information has been lost to time. All we have is this old parchment to tell us where roughly it is." Krell recounted.

"So where roughly is it?" Shamera asked inquisitively.

"That's the problem."

"Problem?" Shamera raised his shoulders incredulously.

"It's... well, all we know is it's no longer, erm, in this realm," Krell spluttered, having difficulty getting his words out.

"Can't you send riders to find it?" puzzled Shamera.

"No, it has to be you who retrieves it."

"Not another journey," Shamera scoffed.

"Yes, I am afraid it is. But, it will be a journey like no other. Only people touched by magic can make this journey." Lord Salogel explained.

"I'm thinking, all I'm going to be doing is going on journeys for everyone," Shamera replied, shaking his head.

"I can understand why you say that. But, these are troublesome times, and it is not how we expected things to turn out. I am sorry most of this seems to have fallen on your shoulders, but... with Verazslo not here, it falls to you, the apprentice sorcerer," Lord Salogel reminded Shamera.

"So, where is this other weapon?" Shamera asked.

"You are going to travel through a portal to a place called Engla Land," Krell advised.

"Portal... Engla Land?" Shamera looked both concerned and curious.

"Yes, you alone must undergo the journey. There is no magic in this land, well, none we know of, not since people called Druids existed. They used to visit here in the very distant past. We are not sure how the portals came to be, but we know a couple still exist," Krell explained.

"Portals?" Shamera looked confused.

"Transdimensional shifting; look at it as an energy gateway between our two worlds," Krell tried to explain.

"Energy gateway... trans di... whatever, doesn't sound safe," Shamera replied.

"Not to worry, it is perfectly safe, as long as you are touched with magic," reassured Krell.

"You need to travel to Engla Land, take this parchment to the gatekeeper and have it translated. We think it is a coded plan showing the whereabouts of the weapon. Hopefully, by the time you return, we will have found where they are keeping Verazslo and can mount a rescue," Lord Salogel explained.

"How will I find this gatekeeper?" Shamera asked.

"We can open the portal and send messages to the gatekeeper, but we cannot travel through it. It would appear inanimate objects can pass between our realms easily. But people need to have magic within them." Krell enlightened Shamera.

"But you two have magic. Why can't you go?"

"My gift is a genetic trait, not magic." explained Krell.

"And I need to be here to coordinate our armies and speak with the other nations leaders, we need them to agree to fight with us." Lord Salogel explained.

"And where is this Engla Land?"

"That, my young friend, is a very good question. The answer to which I do not have. All I know is whoever erected the stone circles connected the portal to Engla land, and only those touched by magic can travel through, Verazslo travelled through the portal many, many years ago." Krell said with a sigh.

Shamera sat there trying to get his head around what he had been told. He closed his eyes and inhaled deeply. He shook his head in disbelief at what he was about to say, "If I do this, I want my family evacuating here. I need to know they will be safe."

"You have my word. I will send for them tomorrow. I will have them brought here and we will look after them," Lord Salogel said reassuringly.

Shamera slowly took a deep breath. He was feeling exhausted from the journey and could not properly process the information. He sat and closed his eyes, contemplating his situation.

"I can feel your anxiety and confusion; this is a lot to be placed upon your young and inexperienced shoulders. You will find as you grow nothing is ever straightforward and very little ever goes as planned," Krell said, trying to reassure Shamera.

"You need to rest after your journey. This is a lot to take in, we will talk again later," Lord Salogel suggested.

Shamera stood up and slowly walked over to the door. He turned to look at Lord Salogel and Krell, both nodded to him with a comforting smile. He calmly made his way to his room whilst trying to make sense of the information he had received. He eventually reached his room and flopped onto his bed. He laid there trying to contemplate the meanings of portals, trans-dimensional realms. What is Engla Land? Why him? What have I got myself into? These questions flew around his mind like a whirlwind, sending his emotions into turmoil. He laid on his bed and fell exhaustedly into a deep dreamless sleep. He had been asleep about six hours when there was a loud knock on the door. Shamera woke up with a jolt, rubbed his eyes and shouted, "come in."

Krell entered the room.

"I have come to see how you are and to enlighten you; I felt your confusion and emotion earlier. I thought it better to let you rest first."

"This is too much for me to take in; I don't know if I am up to it?" Shamera's face looked pained; his eyes squinted as he scrunched up his face.

"I truly understand… I can feel your emotions and your anxiety. Will you let me try to ease them?" Krell's voice was soft and reassuring.

"I'm not sure I am up to this? Everyone is expecting too much of me." His doubt and fear echoed in his voice.

"I am a Mystic Shaman; I can see certain events in the future. I have seen you grow up. I have seen you become a great sorcerer. I passed this information to Verazslo, who also had his eye on you for a while now. And between us, we have watched your enthusiasm working for Mirabilis and learning all about becoming an apothecary. What you have embarked on is a journey of surprise and amazement few will ever witness. However, the reappearance of the dark sorceress was unexpected and has caused chaos everywhere in the land. I had a vision. In said vision, I saw you would be our saviour. You are the one to bring us all together to defeat her."

"Did your vision say how I will defeat her?"

"No, it does not work like that. I have visions and they have to be interpreted, deciphered; I sometimes see people in my visions as I have seen you. Sometimes they are like a series of pictures and their meanings have to be thought about."

"It's a pity you did not see the sorceress coming," Shamera said with slight sarcasm.

"The sorceress is strong and can currently block all foresight. I have been trying to read her but without success. Let me help you straighten your thoughts; I sense they are all over the place, disorganised, not logical. You will think more openly afterwards. You have my word."

Shamera sat there; his lips pursed. Krell was right, his thoughts were a mess.

"What do I need to do?" he asked as he closed his eyes and dropped his shoulders, relaxing them.

"Come, sit in this chair," Krell beckoned him over.

Shamera sat in the chair. Krell put the other chair in front of Shamera and sat down.

"Sit and relax, close your eyes. Take a deep breath and open your mind to me. Don't fight it. It may feel strange, but please go along with it. It makes things easier."

He sat with his eyes closed and tried to relax his body. Krell closed his eyes; he regulated his breathing to match that of Shamera's. They were both breathing in harmony. Krell slowly opened his third eye. As he probed into Shamera's mind, his eye glimmered with a soft golden light. Shamera felt a little lightheaded. He saw pictures inside his mind; the pictures appeared to be flying around his head like a flock of frightened birds. They appeared to be sorting themselves into some sort of order. He recognised pictures of his distant past, home, his family, and his recent quest for the dragon's heart string. The pictures slowed down as Shamera relaxed. They faded and disappeared. The light-headedness had passed, and he was feeling much calmer and at ease. Shamera opened his eyes to see the Mystics' eye still open and glowing with a golden hue.

"Whooaa!" Shamera blurted out, slapping a hand over his mouth, this broke the Mystics' concentration. His eye stopped glowing and it slowly closed.

"Sorry. I am really sorry. I did not mean to shout out like that. It's... well, I was not expecting that," Shamera apologised profusely, and feeling very ashamed, he hung his head down low.

Krell smiled and nodded understandingly. "How do you feel now?"

"Embarrassed." he replied, his face was bright red.

"Think nothing of it. I'm sure it was a bit of a shock if you have seen nothing like it before." Krell smiled. He understood Shamera meant nothing by it.

"I feel settled. Thank you for whatever you did."

"Don't look for answers that can't be given. Let those answers come to you in time. You have chosen a path to walk. This is your destiny. Accept it, embrace it, and agree all experiences are lessons in life. Learn from them. Do not fear the things you have no control over. They are going to happen anyway and worrying needlessly about them will not stop them from happening. Instead, look at what you can do to make it a more positive experience and keep on moving forward. I have seen you will become a great sorcerer. Use it to your advantage."

"So, if I go on this journey to this other realm, I must succeed, as one day I will be a great sorcerer," Shamera smiled.

"Sort of. It does not mean you will succeed in this journey's outcome. You may not find what you seek. But you will return."

Shamera felt much better, and more focused. A gentle knock on the door interrupted them.

"Come in," Shamera and Krell shouted simultaneously.

In walked Elithrin. "Sorry, I did not know you were busy," she said, apologising to them both.

"It's okay, Krell was telling me he has seen my future and I will become a great sorcerer."

Elithrin looked at Krell and telepathically said, *"You can't say that! You do not know for definite, that is only one possible outcome."*

"I am merely giving him the confidence he needs to achieve his next goal. He doubts himself and we need him," Krell replied.

"Are you okay?" Shamera asked Elithrin as she appeared to be deep in thought.

"Yes, yes, of course. I was not expecting you to be busy. It took me by surprise," she replied with an endearing smile.

"Father would like to see you," Elithrin continued.

"Come, let's all see what he wants," Krell requested as he stood up and walked towards the door.

As they walked, Krell spoke again to Elithrin, telepathically.

"This is a confused young man; I sense he has feelings for you, and you for him. A distraction he cannot afford at this time. This journey he must undertake is of the utmost

importance. He needs to be strong, but you need to be stronger for his sake. This journey is not without risk. We need him to concentrate and not to be distracted by anything. I have not lied to him, I merely boosted his confidence is all."

"Yes, I do have feelings for him. I too want him to succeed, I know I cannot let my feelings interfere and for them to be a distraction for him. And I don't want you filling his head with falsehoods. He probably feels invincible, which puts him in even greater danger." Elithrin was obviously very concerned for his safety.

"Worry not; I will explain to him he is not invincible," comforted Krell.

They reached the council chamber, and Elithrin opened the door for them.

"I will leave you both here," Elithrin said as she looked at Shamera and blushed.

Krell and Shamera entered the room. As they did, Krell whispered, "I think she likes you."

"What?" blushed Shamera, who felt quite uncomfortable.

"Don't worry, it'll be our little secret from Lord Salogel," Krell whispered again. This time he had a slight mischievous smile lighting up his face.

"Are you alright?" Lord Salogel enquired of Shamera.

"Erm, yes, I'm fine," Shamera replied quietly.

"You look a little uncomfortable. Anyway, we need to go over your next mission. There is very little information to go on, but what we have, we need you to be clear about. Are you sure you are alright? You look a little red in the face." Lord Salogel asked.

"Probably a result of our mind link," Krell quickly interrupted, trying to save Shamera's blushes.

"Whatever," Lord Salogel replied, frowning and slowly shaking his head disbelievingly.

"Shamera, these are indeed strange times, and if we are to defeat the sorceress, we need all the weapons we have at our disposal. Therefore, we need you to travel to this realm called Engla Land and retrieve this other weapon. All we have is this parchment from the Mystics; unfortunately, no one here knows how to read it, the ability has been lost down the centuries. It may be an ancient Engla Land language of the people called the Druids." Lord Salogel said, as he handed the parchment to Shamera.

"I sent a message through the portal stones last night to the gatekeeper in Engla Land. He will expect you tonight. He will help you decipher the parchment and, hopefully, lead you to the weapon," Krell added.

"So, let me get this clear. I have a letter no one can read; I'm going to a place you know not where. To find a weapon that no one knows what it is," Shamera remarked. "Not a lot to go on, is it?" he continued, shaking his head despairingly.

"I have faith in you. We both do." Lord Salogel said reassuringly.

"This is ridiculous. It could take me forever to find this weapon, while I am in this place searching, Niniane could have already conquered our lands," Shamera said, shaking his head.

"Hopefully that will not be the case. Give yourself four weeks, if you have not found it by then... come home and we will have to rethink our strategies." Lord Salogel replied.

For the rest of the day, Shamera did not venture out of his room. He laid there thinking of the mysterious journey he was about to undergo. What and where was this strange land? How was he going to find a weapon no one knew what it was, or where it was? He surely had more questions than answers. It was early evening when Lord Salogel and Krell came to his room.

"It's time, time to go," Krell said quietly as he stood at the foot of the bed.

"Where are we going? Where is this portal?" Shamera replied as he lightly scratched his head.

"To the stone rings in the woods next to the silver lake," Lord Salogel replied.

"I've seen them, the night I came here. I was coming down the side of the mountain pass," Shamera said as he remembered his journey.

"Yes, you will have done; you can get a good view of the lake from the pass," Lord Salogel's words were soft, and Shamera detected slight unease in his voice.

"Don't worry; I will do my best to find and bring back this weapon, whatever it may be," Shamera tried to reassure them, but he felt he was the one who needed to be reassured. He did not want to let anyone down, as he was more than aware of the great responsibility he had on his young shoulders. He had come close to losing the staff and wand. He did not want to make such mistake again. Shamera picked up his backpack and placed his wand safely in it. Krell handed him the parchment, which he also placed in his backpack. They headed off for the courtyard, where an escort was waiting for them. He noticed Vesryn sat upon his horse with Hethoral and Theronas close by. This time they were dressed in their silver armour, their headdresses with their horsehair plumes wafting in the breeze. Their lances held erect, proud smiles upon their faces.

"You don't think we would miss escorting you on your greatest journey yet did you? Oh, and don't go galloping off again, will you?" Vesryn joked.

Lord Salogel and Krell mounted their horses whilst Shamera went over to the plinth to mount his. "It won't bolt again, will it?" Shamera asked nervously.

"If it does, this time you're on your own." Hethoral joked.

"I suppose you think you're all funny." He replied smiling sarcastically.

They all set off for the stone circle. Once outside of the gate, they set off at a steady trot.

"I forgot to ask how this portal works." Shamera asked Krell.

"There is an incantation which opens up the trans-dimensional portal and links the two realms." he replied.

"And, what then?"

"Then... poof, you are trans-dimensionally transported there. I assume."

"Poof! you assume. You surely know how to reassure someone." Shamera exclaimed.

"I don't know how else to explain it. One minute you're here, the next you're not."

It was not long before they reached the stone circle, which stood in a clearing in the wood. It comprised a ring of twenty roughly honed and weathered standing stones, each around ten feet tall. The stones were a light grey colour and covered in all kinds of lichen. They looked like they had been there for a very long time. They all dismounted and slowly approached the stone circle. Shamera noticed how quiet it was. The moon illuminating the clearing made it appear a little mysterious.

"This is the incantation you must recite from the centre of the stones, recite it with your wand held high," Krell said as he passed Shamera a torn piece of parchment. "Keep it safe. You will need it to get back," he continued.

"Have you got everything?" Lord Salogel asked.

"Yes, I have checked twice to make sure. There will be someone there waiting for me, yes?" His voice was full of nerves; he did not know what was going to happen or where he was going.

"You must try and bring back the weapon Shamera, but do not spend too much time looking for it if you feel it to be lost. If it is lost, so be it. The gate keeper will be waiting for you, and he will help you as best he can. Good luck, my friend," Lord Salogel said as Shamera walked over to the stone rings. Shamera said nothing as he slowly and cautiously walked into the centre of the stone ring. Shamera glanced back nervously, "Good luck, sorcerer," Vesryn shouted.

Shamera slowly raised up his arm and looked up to the heavens as he quietly recited the magic chant. An electrical charge appeared to jump across the stones, which quickly intensified. A ball of blue light surrounded Shamera. As this happened, he felt a sudden jolt forward, as though being pushed from behind. A bright flash of light made him quickly scrunch his eyes together. He felt an abrupt stop and suddenly fell forward onto the hard-grassy ground. He lay there for a while, trying to gather his thoughts and to stop his head from spinning. He tried to stand up; he felt very dizzy as the blood rushed around his head; he stumbled forward again. He gradually got up onto his knees and removed his backpack and placed it next to him. He knelt there for a few seconds more with his eyes closed, supporting his head in his hands. He wished he could stop the spinning feeling whooshing around the inside of his head.

Shamera eventually opened his eyes slowly and looked around. He could see an orange sun setting against the dark blue sky and reddish-purple clouds. He was kneeling within a ring of very large, tall, grey standing stones. They appeared similar to the ones he was standing amongst a moment ago. He closed his eyes again; his heart was thumping and his head still spinning. He shook his head and gradually opened his eyes again. *'What happened? Where am I?'* He thought to himself, looking around and trying to gather his thoughts.

"Welcome to England, Shamera, is it?" a soft male voice said from behind him.

Shamera spun around on his knees. Before him stood a man in a long, dark coat. Although the light was failing, he could just about make out the man. He was about 30 years old, average build and height for a human. He looked at the man's pale pink skin; he noticed his small, rounded ears. Shamera stared at him with uncertainty. "Who? Who are you"? he enquired.

"I've been expecting you. You are the young sorcerer, I hope," the man replied softly.

"Who are you exactly? Is this Engla Land?" Shamera asked again.

"Engla Land, yes, but it has not been called that for centuries. It is called England these days. Come on, it'll be dark soon. I'll explain everything when we get back to my house."

The man offered his outstretched hand and gently helped him up to his feet. Shamera again shook his head slightly, still feeling the effects of the teleportation, he was still a little unsteady on his feet. They walked slowly along the path to the man's car; the man took a bunch of keys out of his pocket and pointed them towards his car; the car made a loud beep and the orange indicators flashed twice. Shamera jumped back. *'What was this magic?'* He thought. The man chuckled at Shamera's expression and said, "There are many wondrous things in this world, things you've probably never seen, nor will again I imagine. Come... don't be afraid. I'm here to help," the man said reassuringly. "This is called a car, a motor car; it's a means of transport in this world," he explained.

"This world?" Shamera asked, "What do you mean... This world?"

"Apparently porting can leave you a little disorientated. Everything will soon become clear," the man said with a slight reassuring smile.

The man opened car the door, as he did the interior light came on, Shamera took another slight step backwards, his eyes quickly scanned the car, he took a couple of steps forward and tapped the car with his hand. He looked at the man again and peered into the car; the man smiled and with his hand gestured to him to get inside. Shamera hesitated and cautiously got into the car. The man closed the door and went around the other side and got in.

Shamera looked over to the man and again asked, "You said 'this world'... where exactly am I?"

"It's perfectly fine, relax, and enjoy the ride, I'll explain everything when we get home, you will feel a little disorientated, but it will soon pass," replied the man as he placed the key in the ignition and turned the engine over. The noise of the engine startled Shamera and, with both hands, he tightly grasped the edges of his seat. The man again chuckled to himself and spoke. "You'd better buckle up my brave warrior," as he pointed to the seatbelt. "Look... pull on the strap next to you," he said as he showed what to do with his own seatbelt. Shamera pulled the seatbelt around him and clicked it firmly into the fastener. The man turned on the headlights which lit up the area in front of the car.

"Wow!" gasped Shamera. He asked, "Are you a sorcerer?"

The man smiled and said, "Let's get home... have something to eat and drink and I'll explain all."

The man put the car into gear and drove off; it was merely a journey of a few miles to Salisbury and wouldn't take long to get there. Shamera kept peering out of the car window to see where he was and to see what other strange things may be lurking out there. They soon arrived at the man's house. The man parked the car, turned off the engine and got out; he went around to the passenger's side and opened the door for Shamera.

"We're here," he said as he leaned into the car and unfastened Shamera's seatbelt.

"Come on, let's go inside and have a nice cup of tea. I will explain everything to you."

Shamera got out of the car and looked around at the street; it was lit by tall slender streetlights partially hidden amongst the tall trees. He also noticed there were lots of cars parked down the street.

"Has everyone got one of these carriages?"

"Not everyone... but many get around in a car. You will find many differences here than what you are used to in your world."

The man walked over to the door and put his key in the lock and opened the door. He turned to Shamera and, with his hand he beckoned him over and they both went into the house. The man turned on the lights, which startled Shamera a little; he looked up at the bulb in amazement.

"What magic puts the sun in a bottle?" Shamera enquired.

The man looked at him and smiled whist gently shaking his head. Shamera had lots of questions running around his head. As he entered the house, he inhaled long and slow. A citrusy aroma from the air freshener made him think of the orchards near his village. He curiously looked all around him. It reminded him of home, but this house contained many things which looked strange to him. They walked through the hallway and entered the kitchen. Shamera's eyes darted about, looking around the room, and some items in the kitchen looked strange to him.

"Please sit," said the man, pointing to a chair.

The man switched the kettle on, took two mugs out of a cupboard and asked, "Tea or coffee?"

"What's coffee?" Shamera replied.

"Tea." smiled the man.

Shamera sat there, bewildered. This was a strange place filled with curious items and new kinds of magic. The man finished making the tea and sat at the table opposite Shamera. He pushed the mug in front of Shamera, raised his mug and with a smile said "cheers," and took a sip. Shamera picked up his tea, looked curiously at the hot brown liquid, sniffed at it, and took a slow sip. Shamera took a second sip; it tasted quite nice, he thought to himself.

"This isn't nettle tea... but it tastes quite nice," he said.

"No... it's made from tea-leaves, a special bush grown purely for this purpose," he replied.

"Where am I?" asked Shamera.

"England."

"Where's England?"

"I am supposed to be in Engla Land."

"You are, like I said, that is an ancient name we no longer use. It's complicated, you have used the stone rings to transport here. To another dimension. England."

The man tried to explain this world and Shamera's world were connected via a trans-dimensional portal, which were the stone rings. It had linked them for many hundreds of years, but certain people could use the portal... those who are touched by magic. Shamera sat and tried to make sense of this whilst sipping his tea.

"So... people have been travelling between each of our worlds?" Shamera enquired.

"Not everyone, like I said, merely those touched by magic. However, your magic here will be very limited. You will be able activate the portal to get back home. That's probably about it, I would think. I'm not sure," he explained.

"But we speak the same language," Shamera said with a confused look.

"People have travelled back and forth through the portals for hundreds, maybe thousands, of years. Therefore, we have this common language... English," replied the man.

"Why have I never heard of this before?" Shamera asked.

"I have kept the portal a secret. We have not used them for a long time. We agreed it after the wars in your world it would merely be known to those who needed to know. And they were to be used purely under exceptional circumstances. We passed messages between the realms this being the easiest way for all who need to, to keep in touch," the man explained.

"Keep in touch with whom? Are there more from my world here?" Shamera asked.

"There have been those who have visited here, but none for a long time."

"So, who are you?"

"I am called Remy… Remy Limners."

"Are you a great sorcerer?" Shamera asked excitedly.

"No… I'm more of a gatekeeper to our realms. I have never held any magic powers… I could never perform any magic. I own a business dealing in old, rare books and documents in this world. Which brings me to the subject of the parchment which I hope you have brought with you?"

Shamera looked at Remy for a short while, as if deciding whether he could trust him. He opened his backpack and took out a folded parchment. Reluctantly he handed it to Remy who the carefully opened it and placed it flat on the table. Remy studied the parchment for a while before looking up at Shamera with a puzzled expression.

"I don't recognise these words, but they could be Welsh." pondered Remy as he attempted to speak them aloud.

"Che gwruthyl chalenj Gwagyon huder, Tre war Venyd," slowly spoke Remy.

"Welsh, what's Welsh?" enquired Shamera looking a little confused.

"It's a language spoken by some people who live in a country called Wales. It's not too far away from here, around 160 miles. It borders England, but why would this be written in Welsh?" Remy replied as he folded his arms across his chest and rested his chin on his right fist. Shamera glanced at Remy. It meant absolutely nothing to him and felt none the wiser.

"You cannot read it? I was told it could be Druid," Shamera asked.

"No, it's definitely not Druid. I'll have to decipher it. So… how come it's in Welsh?" he repeated, his face slightly contorted, and forehead wrinkled in deep thought.

Remy stood up and went into another room; he soon appeared again carrying a silver-grey rectangular slim box. Shamera looked on in astonishment as Remy lifted the lid, and the screen lit up.

"What magic is this?" Shamera asked, as he stared intently at the device.

138

"It is not magic; it's called a laptop… a computer. It can perform many wondrous things and has access to a wealth of knowledge… Thinking about it, I suppose it is magical." Remy looked at the parchment and typed the words into the laptop's search engine.

"Well… it's not Welsh. It's Cornish… Another language of this world, it's not commonly spoken these days, although some people do still speak it," Remy replied and looking even more puzzled.

Remy kept typing and writing on his notepad the English translation. Shamera said nothing but watched on attentively.

"Hmmm," murmured Remy, as he read the results.

"Do you know what is says?" Shamera asked eagerly.

"Not all of it… not yet, but it says something about a challenge, and a cave… But what's this Tre war Venyd? There are these numbers and rune symbols," Remy rested his right elbow on the table, took a deep breath, held it for a second before slowly breathing it out, whilst at the same time ponderously tapping his right forefinger on his chin.

"What challenge? A cave?" started Shamera, Remy interrupted.

"I think I have an idea."

Remy kept staring between the screen and the parchment, his eyes squinted as he contemplated the meanings. He shook his head in disappointment, but no matter how hard he tried, he had, for now, hit a brick wall.

"We need to go into the town centre tomorrow; my book shop might have what we need to shed some more light on the subject," said Remy, as he slowly closed the laptop and gave a little sigh.

"Are you hungry?" Remy asked.

"Yes, I could eat something."

"Do you like pizza?"

"What's pizza?"

"Pizza… it's a thin bread base, with a tomato sauce, meat, cheese. Not overly healthy but tastes very good."

"I'm not sure what all that is but is sounds good to me. I'll try it." Shamera said with a smile.

Remy picked up his mobile phone, took a leaflet out of a draw and ordered a large meat feast pizza, chips, and a large bottle of cola. Shamera looked puzzled as Remy spoke into the little black box.

"I see you look confused. This is what we call a mobile phone. It allows us to speak with people over great distances."

They sat for a while as Remy tried to explain more about England and the world, and the stone rings which had transported him. Shamera listened attentively but found it hard to comprehend what was being revealed to him. This land was a great deal stranger than the one he left.

'Ding-Dong' sounded the doorbell. Shamera was a little startled by the chime.

"It's okay, it's the doorbell... pizzas are here."

Remy answered the door; spoke to someone and came back carrying a large brown package and a bottle of black liquid. He placed it on the table, took out a couple of plates from the cupboard and tore off pieces of paper from the kitchen roll. Whilst un-wrapping the parcel, he looked at Shamera and said, "You're in for a bit of a treat." Remy placed equal amounts of pizza and chips on the plates before pouring two glasses of cola. Shamera sniffed the pizza, picked up a slice, and bit off a small piece. His eyes widened as he chewed and tasted his first slice of pizza.

"Hmmm, this is good," remarked Shamera.

After he ate his first piece of pizza, he picked up his cola and looked at the bubbles fizzing away in the glass. Feeling a little thirsty, he guzzled about half a glass.

"Burp! excuse me... Burp!" Shamera looked at Remy, raised his eyebrows slightly and gave a little smile from behind his hand which was covering his mouth.

"Sorry... what is this drink?" Shamera asked, holding it up.

"Cola (laughed Remy). It's quite fizzy; I suggest you sip it slowly."

Both of them sat and finished their pizza and chips. When they had finished, Remy suggested they get an early night, as they could have a long day ahead of them tomorrow.

"It was delicious, absolutely a new experience for me. Thank you," Shamera said gratefully.

"My pleasure. I'll show you to your room. I'm sure it will be comfortable enough for you,"

Remy led the way upstairs. "This is the toilet and bathroom. The back room here is your bedroom," he said, pointing them both out.

"This is the light switch; flick it down to turn the light on and up to turn the light off." Shamera looked at the switch, and at the light, he looked and Remy and nodded his head.

"Good night Shamera," Remy said softly as he left the room and closed the door.

Shamera couldn't help himself. He switched the light off… and turned it on, off, and on again. He smiled to himself as though he had invented it himself. Shamera slept well that night in the soft bed. A couple of pigeons cooing outside his window woke him early. He sat up in bed and looked around the unfamiliar room; disorientated, he tried to remember where he was. '*Engla land*', he said to himself, suddenly remembering. A very familiar aroma filled his nostrils; he quickly got dressed and went downstairs. Remy had risen early and started cooking breakfast. Shamera stood in the doorway to the kitchen, closed his eyes and inhaled deeply again and said, "Bacon," Remy turned to see Shamera standing there with a broad smile on his face.

"You know what bacon is?" Remy replied.

"Yes, my mother cooks it," Shamera stood there for a while with a slightly sad expression as he thought of home and his family.

"Please, sit; we have bacon, eggs, sausages, mushrooms, and toast," Remy said whilst pointing to a chair.

Shamera tucked into his breakfast and started thinking of his world and his home and wished he were there right now, with his family. He hoped he would soon be back home and would see familiar faces once again. After they had eaten breakfast, Remy poured them both a cup of tea.

"Well… that filled a gap," Remy stated. "We had better get cracking; we have a lot of books to look through," Remy stood up and put the dirty dishes on the side near the sink.

"Here, you'd better wear this; it's called a beanie hat. Your ears…" Remy said apologetically, pointing at them, and gave a little smile before remarking. "They are not normal for here. Best keep them covered. We don't want people thinking you're a Vulcan."

"A Vulcan?"

"Never mind... it would take too long to explain. I suggest you keep your hat over your ears."

It was a short drive into the town centre and, although it was a Saturday morning, Remy parked close to his shop. They approached the bookshop; it wasn't anything out of the ordinary, and it looked like many other shops on the street. It had a bottle green wooden bay window with a large glass pane displaying various books. A bottle green wooden door encompassing a large, frosted window, written on the glass in gold lettering, was the name of the bookshop *Wizdom Books*. As they entered the shop, Shamera faced row upon row of shelves, every one full of books of all sizes and colours. Remy locked the door behind them.

"We need to go down to the basement. It's where I keep all the specialist reference books," Remy stated as he pointed to a door.

Remy unlocked the door and switched on the light to the basement. He descended the wooden stairs and Shamera followed close behind. The basement had a typical woody, earthy scent of historic papers and old books. Remy filled the basement with shelves jam-packed with books, documents, and scrolls, most of which looked ancient. A single bare light bulb hanging from a dirty white cord in the middle of the ceiling lit the room. Remy was confident the books and documents down here would help with translating the parchment. Shamera stood looking around the room, feeling quite daunted about the job in hand. He felt, not being from this realm, he could not be much help. Remy looked around before selecting a couple of books and scrolls from off the shelves and placed them down on the table; he sat down and opened his laptop.

Shamera sat looking through the books, not really knowing what he was looking for. Remy scanned through one book, mumbling to himself and scribbling his findings in his notebook. Shamera started look around the room as if looking for something else to do, he stood up and walked over to a row of very large books. He stood for a moment looking at a large reddish-brown leather-bound book as he stared at the symbol on the spine of a book. His eyes lit up, he recognised the symbol embossed on it.

"I know this symbol," said Shamera pointing it out to Remy, a gold Celtic pentagram with two dragons entwined within it.

He carefully took the book from the shelf and handed it to Remy.

"Where do you know this symbol from? This book is about King Arthur," Remy stated.

"I'm sure Verazslo had one very much like it on his robe," Shamera replied as he shut his eyes and tried to see Verazslo's robe in his mind. Shamera smiled and nodded as an image of the robe entered his head.

"Yes... Yes, I remember. It was this symbol he had on his robe," smiled Shamera.

Remy looked through the book; the pages were thicker than normal and appeared to be made of different parchments and vellum. They were ancient and well worn; the pages contained hieroglyphs, cyphers, runes, and different alphabets. Someone had made notes in the margins, and they had underlined some words and hieroglyphs. Evidently, an attempt to decipher the mysterious contents of the book. The time seemed to pass slowly for Shamera who looked on as Remy cross-referenced the books which lay open in front of him and wrote and rewrote his findings. Remy glanced at Shamera, and saying nothing, he stood up and took a smaller book from the shelf; he handed it to Shamera.

"Here you go," Remy said as he handed Shamera the book.

"This is a book on the Arthurian legend... King Arthur, it will help you understand the period we are looking at in English history."

Shamera sat and looked at the book. It showed many artefacts associated with King Arthur and Merlin. Shamera looked up and said, "I'd like to take this sword, Excalibur, back home. Its powers would prove valuable in defeating Niniane," Shamera stated.

"If it ever existed," Remy replied.

"What do you mean?"

"Well, there's a lot of myth and folklore associated with the history of King Arthur. We will have to filter fact from fiction," Remy said.

Shamera looked a little deflated as he read the book again. Mumbling to himself again, Remy put the large book to one side and unrolled a scroll. The scroll contained a list of runic writings and a list of their meanings. Finally, after about two hours, Remy looked up at Shamera and smiled.

"I think I've got it... well, roughly," smiled Remy.

"Look... this is what I have so far," Remy exclaimed, excited at his discoveries.

The Ogham stone starts your journey at Tre war Venyd. Take what lies beneath to Maria Gritun, the dead Roman, who conceals more than he knows. In a weathered rock is the place the laid-back Nilrem, you will need you to prove yourself worthy before the next step.'

"What is it?"

"A riddle, a clue telling us what we need to do. We need to decipher the riddle,"

Remy let out a little sigh as he pondered the riddle. It had been a good few hours of researching and he was feeling a little tired.

"Ogham is a type of ancient Celtic rune writing..." Remy paused, looked up at Shamera and smiled. He had a light-bulb moment.

"Of course," exclaimed Remy.

"Look here, in this book. Tre war Venyd is Cornish for Tintagel, Maria Gritun must be Latin. Hence the reference to the dead Roman. I think it's an anagram too. Hmmm..." Remy tapped away at his keyboard and searched the internet for an anagram solver and typed in Maria Gritun.

"Well, it's not Latin itself, but this result says Magni Arturi," he said, typing this into the search engine.

"Yes!" he exclaimed.

"It is Latin... Magni Arturi is 'Arthur the Great'... King Arthur," Remy was smiling from ear to ear.

"Wait here, I need to go upstairs," Remy rose to his feet and ran upstairs; Shamera could hear him rummaging around. Remy ran back down with a book on Cornwall. He quickly thumbed a few pages.

"Here it is a map of Tintagel."

Remy opened out the map on the table, after looking at it for a couple of minutes, Remy exclaimed.

"Of course!!... Look here," Remy pointed to a part of the coastline "Merlin's Cave... that must be the weathered rock... and the laid-back Nilrem is Merlin spelt backwards," Remy said excitedly, he picked up his notebook and examined his notes, he looked even more closely at the map.

"What is this Ogham stone? I can't see it on the map" Remy shook his head slightly and mumbled something as he sat down and started reading the large book again. He quickly read a few more pages. He cried out. "Eureka! Got it! The stone lies near the river Camlann, described in Arthurian legend where the battle took place between Arthur and his nephew Mordred. We need to start there," Remy said, looking rather pleased with himself. He had finally cracked it.

Remy closed the books and rolled up the scrolls and left them neatly on the table.

"We need to go home and pack. We're off to Cornwall," Remy said enthusiastically.

The main street was busy with people going about their daily business, totally unaware there was a stranger from another world walking amongst them. Remy suggested they pay a visit to the local charity shop to get Shamera some more clothes so he could blend in even better and have a fresh change of clothes. Their little shopping spree finished, they headed off home and prepared to head for Cornwall.

Chapter 11

Remy and Shamera arrived at the *'Sword in the Stone.'* It was a bed-and-breakfast establishment Remy had booked for a few days. Shamera was unpacking his new clothes when there was a knock on the door. He opened the door to find Remy standing there with a map and a large book in his hands.

"Come in."

"I picked up this leaflet in the reception area. Apparently, there is an information centre nearby, it has lots of information about King Arthur and Tintagel Castle. I think we should pay it a visit and see what information they do have, it could help us, in our quest." Remy suggested.

"Right now?" Shamera asked.

"There's no time like the present." Remy replied.

Shamera put on his beanie hat, grabbed his backpack and they both set off in search of the information centre. It was not long before they found it; it looked bigger than Remy had imagined it to be. He parked the car, and they both made their way into the centre. Banners and posters adorned the entrance, showing pictures of the Knights of Camelot, King Arthur, and Merlin. As they moved further through the centre, there were lots of glass cabinets displaying objects and other archaeological findings from local excavations. A large display showed a young girl with a sword almost as tall as her, stating she had found Excalibur. It read; *'On September 7th, 2017, a seven-year-old girl was thought to have found a 4ft sword in the same lake where King Arthur's Excalibur was said to have been returned to the 'Lady of the Lake' by his loyal friend Bedivere. The girl from Doncaster was paddling waist deep in Dozmary Pool on Bodmin Moor when she came across the sword while on a family holiday.'*

"Hmmm, I don't think it's what we are currently after, look how old and rusty it looks. It's also in the wrong location." Remy stated.

"Well, it looks like this part of the tale is true, and if she has it... we need to get it, don't we?" Asked Shamera.

"I don't think that is what we are looking for, be we will keep it in mind." Remy replied.

They kept walking around the exhibition, checking out the other exhibits. Shamera wondered over to a glass cabinet. He swung around to Remy, beckoned him over, and whispered excitedly. "Look... in here."

Remy looked at the photographs in the cabinet.

"Is this the stone we are looking for?" Shamera asked, pointing to a display.

The cabinet showed photographs of the Ogham stone lying next to the river. A typed notice stated the worn inscription on the stone referred to 'Magni Arturi' Latin for 'Arthur the Great'. Shamera pointed towards a broad golden arm bracelet. It was about six inches wide; a large white semi-precious stone was set in the centre of the bracelet. Two engraved dragons entwined themselves around the stone. Another typed notice called it 'Merlin's Cuff' once believed to belong to Merlin the Magician.

"Look... it says archaeologists found this under the stone a year ago." Remy whispered.

"Can't we take it?" Shamera asked.

"NO!... it's probably alarmed, and there are security cameras everywhere. They would arrest us for theft. No... we cannot steal it." Remy's heart sank as he realised, they were too late and someone else had already found it. It was so close and yet out of reach to them.

"What are alarms and cameras?" Shamera asked as he looked around, not knowing what he was looking for.

"Don't make it obvious. Look behind you at the device attached to the wall... that is a camera it watches everything and records your likeness," Remy tried to explain.

Shamera slowly turned and, as best as he could without making it too obvious, he raised his eyes upwards to see what was there. He turned back to Remy and whispered. "But it's the thing we have come for, the thing we need; we cannot go without it... wait, I have an idea."

Shamera took his backpack off and rummaged around inside. He took hold of his wand, and whilst still concealed inside his bag, he mumbled something.

"What are you doing?" Remy asked nervously.

Shamera took his hand out of his bag and fastened it back up quickly; he looked at Remy and with a slight smile and a look of achievement said, "We need to go... now!" He whispered, putting his backpack back on.

Shamera turned and headed for the exit. Remy looked puzzled but followed Shamera out of the centre. Shamera said nothing as he walked hurriedly back towards the car. Remy unlocked it, and they both got in.

"Are you going to tell me what that was all about?" Remy asked curiously.

Shamera smiled as he slowly opened his backpack and reached inside. He gradually withdrew his hand. Remy's eyes widened and his jaw dropped in disbelief as he saw Merlin's cuff in Shamera's hand.

"How?... How the hell did you manage that?" Remy exclaimed.

Shamera shrugged his shoulders, smiled, "You said my magic would be limited, I thought I would give it a go... and it worked," he said with a smile.

Remy slowly drove out of the car park so as not to draw any attention to them. He drove them straight back to the *'Sword in the Stone.'* They parked up and went directly to Remy's room. Once in the room, Remy couldn't wait for Shamera to take the Cuff out of the backpack. Remy held his hands out his hands, they were shaking in anticipation of holding something which once belonged to Merlin. Shamera gently placed the cuff in his hands. Remy carefully examined the object; it was surely substantial, he thought as he felt the weight of it. He examined the jewel and the engraving. "It looks like the genuine article. You do realise we have just broken the law, and we could go to prison for this?"

"My world needs this, I am sorry, but we cannot take it back."

"We need to take it to Merlin's cave as soon as possible; we don't want the police knocking on our door."

"Is that bad?"

"Yes! They could lock us up in prison if they caught us with this. They must have noticed it missing by now." Remy stated anxiously.

Remy took out his laptop and searched for tide times. "The only way we can gain access to the cave is at low tide." Remy stated.

Remy let out a slight sigh. "The tides are not favourable for a couple of days yet."

"What do we do in the meantime?" Shamera asked.

"Keep our heads down, do some quiet sightseeing until we can access the cave safely." Remy replied.

Remy once again examined the cuff. He took off his jacket, rolled up his sleeve, and placed the cuff on his arm. Holding his arm in front of him, he rolled his arm back and forth, admiring the artefact.

"I wonder if Merlin really wore this. Apart from a couple of small dents and scratches, it's in remarkably good condition." uttered Remy.

"Can I have a look, please?" Shamera asked.

Remy carefully removed the cuff from his arm and handed it to Shamera.

"Wow... it's beautiful. It surely looks worthy enough to be worn by a great sorcerer," Shamera stated as he appreciated its beauty.

"Okay, we need to put it somewhere safe." Suggested Remy.

"There is a hole in the wall in my room; there is a white grate in front of it... I put my wand in there to keep it safe; I'm sure this cuff will fit in there too."

They went to Shamera's room to check out the potential hiding place. Shamera took off the grate and Remy carefully placed the cuff into the space. Shamera replaced the grate, and they both sat on the edge of the bed and said nothing for a couple of minutes.

"I think we should eat out tonight. It will get us away from here. There's a pub we passed earlier '*The Smugglers Inn*', I noticed they do bar meals." Suggested Remy.

Shamera put his beanie hat on and they both went in search of the pub. They had driven for about fifteen minutes before they reached the pub. It was a sixteenth century inn, white plastered walls with black wooden beams. Topped with a straw thatched roof. Remy parked the car, and they went into the pub. It was still quite early, and the pub was quiet. It was bright and airy, with round wooden tables in the restaurant area. The aroma of freshly cooked food wafted in the air as they sat down at a table. There was a large TV attached to the wall opposite them; Someone had already switched it on, but the sound was down low. Remy picked up a menu and gave it to Shamera.

"If you're not sure what some meals are, let me know and I'll tell you what it is."

"They do pizza," said Shamera with a smile.

"Well, if you fancy another, that's fine." Said Remy.

"Do they do that drink we had, too?"

"Cola... yes, I will get us both one of those, too." He chuckled.

Remy stood up and went to the bar to order the food. He returned with the drinks, some cutlery, and napkins. They both sat sipping their drinks and stared at the TV.

"Who's for pizza?" a lady asked, carrying two plates of food.

"Me," Shamera exclaimed excitedly.

"Scampi and chips for you then," she said, placing the meal in front of Remy.

"I hope you both enjoy your meals," said the lady as she smiled and walked away.

They had eaten half their meal when a news flash appeared on the TV. The news flash read: *"Ancient artefact stolen from the Cornwall Information Centre."* Remy went over to the TV and turned the volume up barely enough to hear the news reader say, "Earlier today, someone stole a valuable artefact from the Cornwall Information Centre. The artefact was a wide gold bracelet... pictured here, known locally as Merlin's Cuff. It is a priceless artefact. The police have released this portion of a video of a man seen close to the display cabinet before the artefact went missing." The time lapse video showed Remy looking at the Cuff and other exhibits before walking away from the cabinet and leaving the centre. It also showed him driving away in his car, alone.

"Police are eager to speak to this man; The police do not suspect the man of stealing the artefact, but he could provide the police with valuable information," the newsreader said.

Remy turned to look at Shamera. Remy was looking very puzzled; he traipsed back over to the table and sat down.

"This is not good! But why aren't you on the video? You were stood there, right next to me… and you're not even visible in the car." Whispered Remy.

"I don't know." Shamera said as he shrugged his shoulders.

Remy looked around to see if anyone was looking in their direction. Luckily, The pub was nearly empty at this time, and the few that were sat eating had not seen the news flash. They quickly finished their meals and left the pub. Remy drove about halfway home. He pulled the car over in a lay-by.

"I need to think," said Remy.

"The police are looking for me. I can't understand why you were not in the videos, and it showed only me… did you use any other magic?" asked Remy.

He looked at Remy, shook his head, "The only magic I used was to get the Cuff; I wasn't sure it would work."

"Well… it did, and now the police are looking for me and so will the whole of Cornwall," Remy sat thinking a while, and stated. "I will have to go to the police before they find me. They have no proof I had anything to do with stealing the Cuff. The video showed me looking around the centre… apparently alone."

"What will they do to you?" Shamera asked.

"Nothing I hope… besides, they don't have any evidence of me stealing it." Remy said reassuringly.

He drove back to the 'Sword in the Stone.'

"You go back to your room Shamera, speak to no one and wait for my return. I'm going to look for the police station. I don't know how long I am going to be but wait in your room until I return."

Shamera went back to his room, and Remy drove off in search of the police station. He stopped a woman walking her dog; and asked for directions to the police station. When she finished giving him the directions, Remy thanked her and drove off. He quickly found the police station and parked up in the police car park. He sat in the car for a few moments, thinking about what he was going to say and wondering what evidence they may have. His heart was pounding fast and hard, whilst thoughts of prison ran wild in his head. *'It's no good, It's time to face the music.'* he thought. As calmly as he could, Remy walked into the police station and approached the main desk. The desk sergeant looked up from his paperwork and watched as Remy approached.

"Hello, I have just seen myself on the news; apparently I'm the person you want to see regarding the information centre incident." stated Remy.

"Ah right... Please take a seat Mr.?"

"Limners, Remy Limners."

"Please take a seat. Mr. Limners and I will get the officer dealing with this incident." said the desk sergeant.

Remy sat with his hands on his lap and waited with bated breath for the police officer to appear. It was not long before the sergeant reappeared with another police officer who approached Remy.

"Mr. Limners, would you please come with me?" He politely asked.

The officer was carrying a brown folder and a CD. He took Remy to an interview room and offered him a seat. The room was very bare, a small black table and two chairs sat in the centre of the room. A small silver coloured camera was fixed to the wall opposite Remy. Under the camera was a small TV screen, which was currently blank. The officer sat himself opposite Remy.

"Thank you for coming in, Mr. Limners. My name is Officer Cooper, and before we proceed, I must inform you. You are not under arrest at this time. This is an informal and voluntary meeting which you are free to leave at any time. But, I do have to caution you. You do not have to say anything, but it may harm your defence if you do not mention when questioned something which you may later rely on in court. Anything you do say may be given in evidence." stated the officer.

"Court... I have done nothing wrong." Remy stated with concern.

"It's merely a caution, sir, nothing to worry about." Officer Cooper replied as he opened his folder.

"Can you tell me you full name and address please sir?"

"Remy Limners, 36 Carlton Lane, Salisbury."

The officer wrote his name and address in his notebook.

"What is your business in Cornwall, sir?"

"I am here on a short break, purely pleasure. Apart from being suspected of stealing a rare artefact that is."

"Speaking of which, can you tell me anything about the missing artefact, sir?"

"I'm sorry... no. I visited the centre for a short while. I looked around at the various exhibits. I remember looking at the gold bracelet, and thinking how beautiful it looked, and wondered if it really did belong to Merlin."

"Did you notice anyone acting strange? Anyone out of the ordinary?"

Remy appeared to think for a few seconds before pressing his lips together, shaking his head and answering, "No, nothing. I was concentrating on the exhibits... sorry."

"We have the video showing you close to the artefact before it apparently vanished."

"Vanished?" Remy said disbelievingly.

The officer placed the disc into the side of the TV, pointing the remote towards the TV he played the recoding.

"This time lapse video shows you were the last person near the artefact before it vanishes."

They both watched the video. It showed Remy on his own. Looking around the exhibits, there was no sign of Shamera in the recording at all. It showed Remy looking at the display cabinet with the golden cuff visible over his right shoulder. It showed him walking away, but his body covered the view of the Cuff. The next frame showed the cabinet, with the Cuff now missing.

"It was still there when I left, or at least I thought it was. As you can see, I walked away, I did not touch the cabinet."

"How do you explain its disappearance, sir?"

Remy took a deep breath, paused, and replied, "Apart from magic, I can't... all I know is I didn't take it... Do I need a solicitor?"

"Not unless you feel you need one, sir; this is an informal interview. You're merely helping us with our enquiries. Do you need a solicitor present, sir?"

"No... But I don't see how I can help you. The video distinctly shows me looking at the display unit with my hands in my pockets. You can see the cuff over my right shoulder, and there I am, walking away and not stealing it. I can't explain how shortly after it had vanished."

"We have to explore all avenues of enquiry, sir. But as you can see, one minute it's there, then it's not, and you were the closest person to the exhibit at that time. Where are you staying in Cornwall, sir?"

"The *'Sword in the Stone'* bed-and-breakfast."

"Ah yes, I know it well. Would you object to us accompanying you there and searching your room? Merely to satisfy ourselves and to eliminate you from our enquiries."

"Not at all officers. I suppose you would also like to search my car, too. It's parked outside."

"Thank you for your understanding, sir. If you can wait here, I will be back shortly."

The officer collected all his notes and left the room. About ten minutes passed before he and another officer re-entered the room.

"Right, sir, shall we proceed?"

The two officers accompanied Remy to his vehicle and searched for it. After a good search of the vehicle, the officers looked at each other. "There's nothing here." stated officer Cooper.

"What did you expect?" Remy stated whilst gesturing with his hands.

"We're sorry, sir, but we need to do our duty." said the second officer.

"There's one more thing before we go. May I hold on to your mobile phone until we arrive at your lodgings?"

"Why?"

"It's another formality, sir." Stated Officer Cooper.

"I have nothing to hide here." Remy stated, handing the phone over.

"We will follow you, sir. Please drive carefully."

Remy drove back to the *'Sword in the Stone'* with the police close behind. On arrival, the officers accompanied Remy to his room. They made a thorough search and again found nothing.

"Thank you for your cooperation, sir. We can, for the time being, state, you are no longer a person of interest to us. However, should you remember anything that may help us, or, other information come to light, we may need to speak to you again." Stated officer Cooper.

Both officers left the room, Remy waited until he was sure the officers had gone before knocking on Shamera's door. Shamera opened the door slowly, not knowing who was there; he smiled with a great sense of relief when he saw Remy.

"Come in… You were gone quite a while," said Shamera smiling and motioning with his hand.

"What happened?"

"They questioned me for a while, showed me the video. I still can't understand why you were not on the recoding. They searched my car, and my room. Obviously, they found nothing and had to let me go. They are not stupid, because they found nothing on me; they will probably follow me for a while to see if I might have hidden it somewhere else. They cannot see us together until we can complete the task in a couple of days. If they get a hold of you, how would we explain that away?"

For the next two days, Remy and Shamera went out sightseeing separately, visiting all around Cornwall. Especially noting Merlin's cave and how best to get to it. Although Remy did not see any police officers or anyone obviously following him, he felt he was being watched. It was the morning the tide would be out; giving them access to the cave during daylight. Remy woke early and went to knock on Shamera's door. Sleepy eyed Shamera opened the door to see who was there.

"Come in." He yawned.

"We have a couple of hours before the tide is fully out. You need to take the cuff to the cave, and I will join you there once I'm sure the police are not following me."

Shamera yawned and nodded in agreement.

"I will go out an hour before you. If I am being followed, I will lead them away and you will have a clear run to the cave, and you will hopefully find out what needs to be done."

"Okay, I'll get ready and see you at the cave later."

"Good luck Shamera... today's the day." Grinned Remy.

He walked over to the door and was about to open it. He turned back. "If you see me speaking to anyone, you pretend you do not know me. Do not acknowledge or speak to me until we are alone in the cave. It's the safest way, as no one has to know about you, especially the police, and I'd like to keep it that way." Remy instructed.

He opened the door and sauntered back to his own room. His plan was to walk through Tintagel Castle and down the wooden steps leading to Merlin's cave. This way, if someone was following him, he should be able to notice them in the open spaces of the castle. Remy picked up the map of Tintagel Castle and looked through the window to see what sort of morning it was. The blue sun-drenched sky stretched out into the distance with a few small white fluffy clouds which appeared to be hovering gently in the windless sky. Birds softly sang in the surrounding trees. *'It's going to be a very nice day,'* he thought to himself. He grabbed his car keys and set out for the castle.

He spotted the aptly named 'King Arthur's Car Park.' He pulled in and parked up. He bought his ticket and displayed it on the dashboard. A large wooden sun-bleached signpost pointed the way to the Castle. He looked around and noticed there were a lot people around at this time of the day; he tried to keep track of who was around him and where they were going. He finally reached the castle; he stopped to pay his entrance fee. He took this opportunity to have another look around. It appeared to be all clear. As he entered the castle, he felt a cold shiver run down his spine. He had the feeling he had some sort of connection to the place, but he knew he had never visited here before, not even as a child. *'Strange'* he thought. He continued walking along the paths and the countless steps which meandered through the internal slopes of the Castle, stopping at various viewpoints he carefully observed who was around. Were the police really following him or was his mind playing tricks now the important day was here? He was feeling paranoid and uneasy.

He slowly made his way to the steep wooden steps leading down to Merlin's Cave, he paused again at the top, and had a good look around. He looked to the skies as he heard the seagulls above him squawking as they glided effortlessly on the wind. As he listened, they seemed to give him the 'all-clear'. Confident no one was following him, he descended the wooden steps. The steps appeared to go on and on as they wound down the side of the cliff. A good ten minutes had passed as he finally neared the bottom. To his right, he saw the valley stream ending into a small waterfall cascading down onto the beach. He took some time to watch the waterfall and again looking to see if anyone had followed him. Assured he was not being followed, he made his way across the cove to the cave. As he reached the chalk cliffs, he noticed, carved into the rock near the entrance to Merlin's Cave, was the sleeping face of the Great Sorcerer, Merlin. As Remy looked at the carving, a cold, tingling sensation travelled down his spine again. He sensed this place had a special meaning. He approached the cave where history and legend combined. The atmosphere felt electric the closer he got to the cave entrance.

As he reached the mouth of the cave, he looked around and shouted for Shamera.

"Shamera... Are you here?" he called out.

Shamera walked out of the mouth of the cave to greet Remy.

"I've been here but a short while, I've had a look around and as far as I can see this is merely a cave, there's nothing special here, well nothing I could see," Shamera said, sounding a little disappointed.

The salty smell of the sea and the aroma of drying seaweed filled the cave. The cave floor comprised of large wet boulders, rocks, and green slippery seaweed. This made it very tricky walking in the cave. The lower parts of the cave walls were stained with a green hue and worn from the effects of the tides repeatedly coming in and out. The cave was cold, and a firm breeze circulated around them. The cave was dark and, as yet held no clues what they needed to do next. Remy took a torch out of his pocket. They looked around the cave carefully, but nothing stood out to them. It looked like any other cave. They carefully walked further in, Remy stopped, and shone his torchlight trying to illuminate as much of the cave as possible, looking for any clue which may be present.

"Hello!" Remy called out; his voice echoed around the walls of the empty cave.

"Merlin… are you here?" Shamera yelled, again all that replied was the repeated echo of his voice reverberating around the cave.

"We are in the correct cave, aren't we?" Shamera asked.

"Yes, did you not see the carving in the rock outside? We are obviously missing something... Let me see the cuff, please."

Shamera took the cuff out of his backpack and handed it to Remy. He examined the cuff again; he held it aloft and called out. "Merlin… we have brought the gift." Again, nothing happened.

"What are we missing?" questioned Remy.

As he handled the cuff, he felt a small static charge which caused the hairs on his arms to stand on end. Shamera and Remy stood looking at each other, pondering what to do. Shamera looked at the cuff; a moment of inspiration entered his head. An expression of realisation beamed across his face. He looked straight at Remy.

"It's a cuff… a bracelet... It's supposed to be worn. Put it on, and see if it helps."

Remy placed the cuff onto his right arm; a tingle, like a static charge shot up his arm. They both looked at the bracelet, they noticed the white stone was glowing. Remy cautiously touched it. Instantly, a blinding white light filled the cave, causing them to shield their eyes. The light faded. They found themselves in what appeared to be another cave. It was a slightly smaller cave, dry, and did not smell of the sea. Two flaming torches lit the interior; it wasn't a bright light but enough to see the whole cave. A sweet, perfumed scent of incense filled the air. The floor was a reddish colour and resembled hardened clay. From out of nowhere a knight clad in shiny silver armour appeared before them. The visor of the helmet was down obscuring any view of his face, both hands one placed on top of the other rested upon the pommel of the sword which stood upright on the ground before him. The knight stood there motionless, looking like a giant chess piece. They both looked at each other in total amazement.

"Where did that come from?" Shamera asked.

"Hello," said Remy cautiously as he slowly approached the knight.

"You are required to take a test of worthiness before you can proceed." The knight replied.

"Who are you?" asked Remy, slowly edging closer to the knight.

Remy was standing straight in front it; the knight did not move at all. Remy slowly stretched out his hand to touch it. Remy was astonished to see his hand had passed straight through, although it appeared to be solid, clearly it was not. He slowly walked around the knight, slowly waving his hand through its body.

"What is it? It looks to be there yet has no substance?" Shamera asked curiously.

"It looks like some sort of advanced hologram, I can walk right around it... it looks solid and real, but my hand can pass right through." Remy stated as he hesitantly and slowly withdrew to stand next to Shamera again.

"You are required to take a test of worthiness before you can proceed." The knight repeated.

"Test... what test?" asked Shamera.

The knight turned to his right and raised his arm, one finger slowly raised within the gauntlet, and pointed to a stone table. The knight remained stationary as Remy and Shamera walked over to the table. On it were three grey pewter mugs. They looked ancient and worn, as though they had been well used. Each one had a different engraving on it. The knight spoke again. "In order to pass this test, you must give me Merlin's cup. You can pick up but one cup, and the cup you touch, is the cup you choose. You can leave, or you can choose wisely, but, beware, a failure to do so and I will trap you here for evermore." He warned.

They both inspected the cups and were careful not to touch any of them. All three had engravings. One had a single dragon engraved upon it, another had two entwined dragons breathing fire at each other, and the last one had a Celtic Pentagram with two dragons below it.

Remy looked at the cuff he was wearing which had two dragons engrave on it, but they were not breathing fire.

"Damn... I thought this was it." Whispered Remy.

Shamera turned to look at the knight, who had returned to its original position. He looked at Remy and, with a slight sideways motion of his head towards the knight, asked. "Is it real or not?"

"I'm not sure; I've seen nothing like it before. It surely can't be real if I can pass my hand through it. Either way, we need to progress. We need to choose the right cup."

"Do you know which one it is?" asked Shamera.

Remy shook his head and replied, "No... but obviously it must have something to do with a dragon... as they are engraved on all the cups. But which one? I wish I had my books here to help... well, at least we have a two-to-one guess if all else fails."

"I do not know about this... this is your world." Stated Shamera.

"This isn't my world either... nothing like this happens in my world." Remy replied firmly. "Hmm... come on... which one?" said Remy, with a pained expression on his face.

"Have you chosen yet?" asked the knight impatiently.

"No, not yet. Give me a minute." Snapped Remy.

"The sands of time run short. Choose quickly but choose wisely." The knight replied.

Remy pulled his sleeves up, as though to help him concentrate more. He slowly reached out as if choosing a cup. He changed his mind and reached out for another. As he did, he noticed a slight tingle from the cuff. He withdrew his hand. "I have an idea." Starting from left to right, he slowly reached out, observing if he got another tingle from the Cuff. As he reached the final right-hand cup, he again received a slight tingle.

"I do not know which to choose, but as I reach for this one, I get a slight tingle in my right arm. I think it's from the Cuff. I don't want to get it wrong or all we have done so far is for naught, and it will trap us here for ever."

Remy's face looked saddened; He looked at Shamera who stood looking back with a blank expression. Shamera closed his eyes, took a deep breath, and said, "Go with your gut feeling."

"Wait... do you have your wand?" Remy asked.

Shamera took off his backpack and took out his wand.

"See if your magic works in here. Can you use magic to identify the correct cup?"

"Is it allowed?"

"Well... you're a worthy sorcerer in your realm, aren't you? And it didn't say we couldn't use magic, did it?"

"I'm simply an apprentice, but I cannot remember it saying anything about magic."

"Your magic must count for something, right?"

Shamera took the wand out of his backpack and held it in front of him. The wand appeared to vibrate as his hand shook with nervously, his heart beat faster in anticipation. Shamera took a deep breath, closed his eyes and whilst slowly passing the wand over the cups, whispered, "Show me Merlin's cup... make the cup known to me."

Shamera slowly opened his eyes, and they both stared at the cups. They both looked at each other in amazement as one cup gradually moved slightly forward. Remy smiled and stated. "This must be the one. It's the same one I got the tingle from."

Remy took a deep breath; he hoped this was the right choice. With a trembling hand, he slowly picked up the cup with the two dragons breathing fire. They both walked slowly over to the knight. Remy slowly offered it up to the knight. He held out his gauntlet clad hand and Remy handed over the cup.

"You have chosen wisely; this is Merlin's cup." Stated the knight.

"If you please Sir knight... what is so special about this cup?" Remy respectfully asked.

"Merlin was about to be executed by Vortigern. These two dragons represent Ice and Fire. Merlin's first prediction was the Fire Dragon would defeat the Ice Dragon. This came to pass, and Vortigern, good to his word, allowed Merlin to live. Merlin adopted the fighting dragons as his symbol from that day forth," the knight replied in a measured, yet humble, voice.

The knight and the cup vanished before their eyes. This made them both jump back slightly; they looked around the cavern to see they were on their own again. Remy was about to call out when another blinding flash of white light filled the cavern, causing them both to once again tightly close their eyes, whilst quickly dropping their heads forward.

Adjusting to the cavern's dim light, they slowly reopened their eyes, they saw the figure of an old man slowly approaching them. The old man slowly shuffled his way across the cavern, struggling to walk with his old, arthritic joints. He was dressed in long brown rags; long white hair flowed down his back, whilst a long white beard hung down to his belly. An old and weathered face looked straight at them. It took a few seconds for him to realise that the two of them were standing there. Even though they were standing before his eyes, and larger than life, the old man could not comprehend it straight away. Before either of them could speak, the old man shouted at them slowly and deliberately. "Who are you? How did you enter here?"

Remy and Shamera looked at each other; could this really be Merlin standing before them? Remy saw the shock register on the old mans face.

"Well!... Answer me." The old man said with a stern, gravelly voice.

"We mean you no harm. My name is Remy, and this is Shamera."

"Well, how did you enter this place?" The old man repeated, standing right in front of them. His eyes appeared dull and bereft of life. He squinted as he suspiciously looked them up and down.

"What is this place? Where are we?" Asked Remy.

"Have you come to free me?" Said the old man in a soft, yet croaky voice. There was fear in his voice, but also curiosity about who they were. The three of them stood looking at each other for a few moments before Shamera spoke.

"We are looking for someone called Merlin, would that be you?"

"Merlin, what would you want with him?" Said the old man, apprehensively.

"It's a little complicated to explain. I have been sent on a quest, a quest to find a weapon. A powerful weapon, the map and the clues led us here. To you, if indeed you are Merlin." He said softly.

"Map? What map? Weapons are dangerous, why would you seek such a thing?"

"We had a map; we think it was written hundreds of years ago by people called Druids. Have you heard of them? We are in search of a powerful weapon, one that was hidden somewhere here hundreds of years ago. We need it to help defeat Niniane, the evil sorceress who is trying to conquer my world."

The old man shuffled around as though in deep thought, yet there was a look of suspicious confusion on his face.

"Niniane... evil sorceress, hmm." Said Merlin as he continued shuffling around. He stopped, pondering for a moment. "Your world... You said your world. Where is your world?"

"I'm not quite sure where it is, in relation to this one. It's far away. All I know is that there is supposed to be a powerful weapon hidden here, one we need to take back so we can defeat her. Are you able to help us?" Pleaded Shamera.

"Hmmm, curious. And what is this weapon of which you speak?" Asked the old man. His eyes were narrowed, and his face scrunched up, as though trying to see Shamera more clearly.

"Excuse me." Asked Remy politely, "Are you... Merlin?"

"And, if I am?"

"Then we are hoping that you can help us find what it is we are looking for. Help Shamera back in his world, help him to defeat this sorceress."

The old man paused for a few seconds, "I am he, I am Merlin. But I am not sure of how I can help you. I do not know of any weapon." His face looked sad.

Remy's eyes fixed on Merlin. "Oh. My. God. Is it really you? I can't believe it's really you? I have a bookshop full of stories about you and King Arthur. They have always been my favourite books. It was because of those books that we were able to find you. I always thought they were folklore, a myth. This is absolutely incredible." Remy's jaw almost hit the floor, his mouth opened wide, and before he could hide it, a large smile lit up his face.

"There is always an element of truth in any myth. Have you... have you come to free me at long last?" Merlin's eyes welled up, "I have not spoken to another living person in hundreds of years. You are real? This is not another of Nimue's cruelties?" Merlin's voiced cracked as he fought back the tears.

"Yes, we are real. If we can, we will get you out of here, I would really like to hear your stories. I never thought I would meet Merlin, Emrys. The greatest sorcerer of all time." Remy said comfortingly,

"You flatter me, if I were the greatest, I would not have ended up in here, would I? I am too old, my bones ache. Too many years of living in this cave has taken its toll on my body. My mind is willing, but the flesh is weak. Come, I need to sit." He scurried over to an old table and sat down next to it.

"Sir, I am sorry to pester you. But do you know of the weapon we seek?" Shamera said apologetically.

"Weapon? There's no weapon here, lad. Only me, and I've been trapped in here ever since she tricked me." Merlin replied, shaking his head.

"She… Who's she? Who tricked you?" Shamera asked.

"If you free me from this servitude, I will tell you all about it. Please do not leave me here. If you have the means, then please take me with you." He pleaded. His voice was one of desperation.

"This is all very well, but how do we get out of here?" Remy asked with a heavy sigh, realising they too could be trapped.

"Only someone with magic can enter here. One or both of you have magic." Merlin replied curiously.

Merlin shuffled around again; his head bowed in deep thought. He would pause, mumble to himself again before once more shuffling around. He stopped and turned around and shuffled his way back. He looked at both Remy and Shamera before speaking.

"The years would appear to have taken a toll on my mind; it would seem I'm not as sharp as I used to be. How did you two get past the guardian knight and get in here?"

"We picked your cup as a test of wisdom, and we had this," said Remy as he pointed out the gold cuff.

Merlin stood and stared for a few seconds at the gold cuff on Remy's arm. He shuffled slightly forward and gave a slight whimper, "You have it… you have come to free me, at last."

Merlin outstretched both his hands, which were unsteady because of a tremor he had developed after years of captivity. Slowly, he ran his trembling fingers over the cuff and looked at Remy and said in a quiet voice. "You must give it to me; I can use it to get all of us out of this wretched place."

"But what about the weapon?" Asked Shamera.

"There is no weapon. There is only me." Merlin replied in a quiet, apologetic tone.

Remy and Shamera looked at each other, wondering what to do. Remy shook his head slightly as he removed the cuff from his arm. He turned to Shamera. "Well, the clue said take the gift to Merlin."

He handed the cuff to Merlin. Cradling it caringly in his hands he gazed upon the golden object with teary eyes. With a trembling hand, he placed the cuff on his own arm. A tear fell from his right eye and ran down his cheek as he realised he was going to be free of his imprisonment at last.

"I will need your wand too, my lad," Merlin said with renewed enthusiasm in his voice.

"How did…"

"It is sticking out of your pocket, and I can feel its magical powers."

Shamera slowly removed the wand from his pocket.

"I hope we don't end up trapped in here," Shamera said to Remy as he reluctantly handed the wand to Merlin.

"Why would I leave my rescuers trapped?" Merlin replied with conviction.

"Before we get out of, wherever here is, there are some things you need to know, Merlin. Things have changed quite a lot in the world."

Merlin nodded his head. "I know… yet another one of Nimue's torments. I have a giant crystal ball in which I could see the outside world. I can see it, but never could I be part of it." He said with contempt. "I have seen many nations rise, thrive, and fall. I have seen many men fall senselessly in battles around the world. I have seen this country and its many wondrous inventions come along through the ages and yet I remained trapped in here." The sadness in his voice was clear;

but there was hatred in there too. Nimue had used and tricked him, and, for this reason he could never forgive her.

"Are you ready?" Asked Merlin.

Remy looked at Shamera, nodded and spoke. "Yes, we are ready."

Merlin waved the wand over the cuff, pressed the glowing white stone. There was a bright shimmering light, and a loud crackle filled the air.

The smell of the sea and seaweed let them know they were back in Cornwall, back in the original Merlin's cave. Both Shamera and Remy assisted Merlin carefully over the slippery rocks and out of the cave. The bright daylight made Merlin squint and close his eyes.

"It seems so bright." Merlin said covering his eyes with his hand. Merlin looked around whilst shielding his eyes with his hand; tears of joy ran down his cheeks as he could not believe he was free.

"What a beautiful bright day, and the joy of feeling the warmth of the sun and salty breeze upon my face once more." Merlin said through teary eyes.

"Come, we must get Merlin home. I don't want the police to find us all together. This I could not explain away, and they may hold you two captive for a long while, not being of this world." Remy hastened.

"To be held captive again, I could not bear it. Let's get to shelter and safety." Merlin said as he tried to walk quickly away from the cave. But the years of being trapped in the cave had paid a toll on his body. The effort on his stiff joints and weak muscles was almost unbearable. Merlin fell forward onto the soft sand. Remy and Shamera quickly helped him back to his feet. A small party of people approached on their way to the cave. They looked at Merlin, stood there in his brown rags, and being supported by two men.

"We've found Merlin." Remy said with a wry smile as they assisted Merlin to walk.

"Why did you have to tell them?" Shamera asked.

"Because they will not believe it. They will think we have found merely a homeless person near the cave."

"Can you make us invisible?" Shamera asked Merlin.

"Sorry, this I cannot do." Merlin replied apologetically. He was struggling to walk on the sand and needed their help to hold him up. They slowly made their way to the car. People looked on but did not really take much notice as they were used to seeing homeless people around the town centre.

Chapter 12

Merlin stayed with Remy and Shamera for a week while he regained more of his strength. Both Remy and Shamera updated Merlin on the current times and the changes which had happened in England, and what was happening back in The Second Realm. Remy even found some suitable clothes from a local charity shop which Merlin was very grateful for. And in exchange for their help and kindness, Merlin helped Shamera develop some of his magical abilities; Shamera was obviously very keen to learn and was very attentive to Merlin's teachings.

"In the cave when we first met, you said that someone had trapped you there. How? What happened?" Enquired Shamera.

"It happened such a long time ago. There was a young girl, her name was Nimue. She was my… so-called true love." Merlin replied, his voice was full of animosity.

"What did you do to upset her?" Remy asked with a smile, trying to lighten the situation.

"I met and fell in love with her when she was sixteen. I was a few years her elder. She used to accompany me on my journeys across the land. When I look back on it, she didn't care for me at all; she traded her so-called love for lessons in sorcery. Nimue was a quick learner. After several years, when she had learned enough, she turned against me, I never knew why. I had never done anything but to love her, I never thought she would betray me like she did. She used one of my own spells to trick me and imprison me in here." Recounted Merlin angrily.

"What happened to her?" asked Remy.

"I'm not sure; I have had no contact with the outside world for many hundreds of years."

"Hundreds of years? Why are you not dead?" asked Remy, disbelievingly.

"She cursed me with immortality. Another one of Nimue's bitter cruelties."

"I wish I was a fast learner; I need to be able to defeat Niniane, the evil sorceress."

"You have come on well. It has barely been a week, yet you are mastering your magic well. You will become a great sorcerer in time." Merlin stated.

"I do not have time; unfortunately. I have to get back to my world. I came here in search of a great weapon, it was supposed to be here. A week has passed, and I am no further on, and back home, Niniane is warring with the peoples of my realm." Shamera replied with a pained expression.

Merlin looked at Shamera for a short while, as though looking deep within him. He lowered his head and pondered a while; he took a slow deep breath and spoke.

"There is a weapon which might help... Excalibur! We need to retrieve Excalibur from the Sacred Earth Temple; it was King Arthur's sword." Merlin stated.

"I have read about a sword in a building we visited. What's special about this sword?" Shamera asked.

"It is a magical sword with an unbreakable blade, fashioned by an Avalonian elf smith, and tempered in the breath and flames of a dragon. It can cut through armour and can easily cleave a man in two. Also hidden within the pommel is the Triskelia."

"Triskelia?"

"The Triskelia is a Celtic symbol of three conjoined spirals. The Druids charged it with magical powers. I see the amulet you wear around your neck is missing some items." Merlin said in a tantalising manner.

"How do you know about this amulet? It is from my realm."

"I do not know how it got to your realm, but it once belonged to me." he explained.

"Is that Triskelia thing part of this? What does it do?" Shamera inquired eagerly, whilst lifting the amulet forwards.

"What it does, I will teach you in good time. Be patient, young sorcerer, one step at a time."

"But the sword has already been found. There was a display showing a young girl finding it in erm... Dozmary, a lake, near here. Remember Remy, in the place we went to get the cuff." Shamera stated, looking a little confused.

"Yes, I remember. There was a photograph of her holding it; it was as tall as the girl."

"Fear not. Whatever was found, it will not have been Excalibur." Merlin replied with a knowing smile.

"How can you be so sure, Merlin? They trapped you in a cave for a very long time." Shamera asked.

"When King Arthur died, *Sir Bedivere* returned Excalibur to the Lady of the Lake. But soon after, Nimue found out about it and wanted it for herself. Before she could lay claim to it, I moved it for safety. It resides in a cavern known to the Old Religion as the Sacred Earth Temple, an ancient oracle of knowledge and learning which is hidden deep inside the Tor. I placed an enchanted gate at the entrance so no one but me could gain access and steal Excalibur."

"So, it is well hidden?" Shamera smiled with relief.

"Yes, only I can retrieve it."

"So, what are we waiting for? We need to get it and get back to my world." Shamera said excitedly.

"First, I need the waters from the Chalice Spring, and later we need a night of a full moon to open the veiled door."

"Water, we have water here." Shamera said as he stood up and turned on a tap.

"No, my young sorcerer, we must first invoke the help of the nine daughters, the Sisterhood of Avalon. They were the original ring of the Tors' summit. These nine maidens are experts in healing; they healed King Arthur when he was once close to death. They and only they can reveal the Chalice Well."

"Ah, the place where Joseph of Arimathea washed the Holy Grail in a puddle, and which turned that simple puddle into a flowing spring of healing waters." Said Remy, he remembered reading it in one of his books.

"Correct, my learned friend, you know of this. Well, I need those waters to heal my bones and my weakened body. All those years held captive in that cave have left me weak, and all my joints are very stiff and painful."

"The moon will be full tomorrow night." stated Remy.

"Then we need to be ready." Merlin replied.

"Be ready for what? What do we need to do?" asked Shamera.

"We need to go visit the Faerie woods of *Ynys Afallon*. They are close to the Tor. There, we must leave a motive offering and recite an invocation before climbing to the summit. It's a simple offering of apples, berries, and wine to show the Faeries of the wood we come with honest intentions, as the Sisterhood also protects and looks after them." Merlin explained.

They spent the rest of the day preparing for tomorrow's adventure. Merlin meditated for a couple of hours before retiring to bed. The next day, Merlin stated he needed to meditate again and would need quiet and solitude to do so.

"Shamera and I will go out and get the wine, berries, and apples; you can remain here and meditate." Remy suggested.

"Acceptable." Merlin replied.

"We are close to the Tor and will not need to set off until mid-afternoon."

Remy took Shamera out to the shops and left Merlin to his meditation. After a couple of hours of wandering around the shops, they headed back home. For the rest of the day, Merlin taught Shamera some more magic, while Remy planned the route he would take to the Tor.

Shamera kept watching the hands of the clock move slowly around its face, eager to get Excalibur and return home. Remy read the paper. It seemed like an age, but it was now time to head off for the Tor.

"Okay it's time to set off." Remy informed them.

"About time." Shamera said, eager to set off.

After a thankfully uneventful drive, they arrived at their destination. Parked the car and walked towards the Tor. The three of them stood at the wooden gate, blocking the path leading to the base of the Tor. A warm breeze blew towards them; Shamera looked up to see white, fluffy clouds gently moving over the silhouetted tower on the top of the hill. Remy turned to look at a map and some brief facts informing visitors of the Tors' history. Shamera and Merlin also took a momentary look at the map before Merlin shook his head and scoffed. "These people know nothing of its history."

They entered through the wooden gate and headed for the Faerie wood. They walked along a foot trodden grass path before entering the wood. It was a small wood, overgrown with nettles, bushes, and high grasses. As they moved through the wood, the birds twittered loudly as though to announce their presence. The light wind rustled through the leaves of the trees, tall nettles danced along the path in the breeze. Shamera felt a strange presence within the woods, but try as he might to see them, the Faeries remained hidden. It was not long before they stood before two large, old and gnarly oak trees.

"This is the place." Merlin declared.

Remy placed his bag on the floor. He took out the berries, apples, and wine while Merlin arranged some rocks to form a makeshift altar. Merlin placed the food at the base of the altar and poured the wine over the rocks and the food. He cupped his hands in front of him and closed his eyes.

"Faeries of *Ynys Afallon* we offer this token in praise and respect of your reverence. Gog and Magog, the benevolent giants, watch over us, keeping evil at bay as we enter the Sacred Earth Temple of *Ynys Witrin*. May I ever bless the druids and the old religion as they watch over mother earth? I, Emrys, give my word to uphold the old ways for the good of humanity, as I have always sworn to do."

The breeze stopped, and the leaves became motionless. The tall nettles were unruffled and stood motionless. Even the birds fell eerily silent; Merlin turned to the others and suggested they leave the woods quietly and quickly, as their offering had been accepted. As they left the woods, the breeze once more gently blew, and the birds sang again. Remy looked back into the woods, hoping to see the faeries, but it disappointed him to merely see the trees and their leaves gently swaying in the breeze.

With this part of the adventure completed, they headed towards the Tor. It stood before them, rising enigmatically towards the heavens. Climbing the winding paths and steps leading to the summit, an electrical charge filled the air, which made the hairs on their arms and necks stand up on end. The breeze became a little stronger the higher up they walked; it was becoming more difficult for Merlin as the steps became a little steeper. Both Remy and Shamera assisted Merlin to carry on. Finally, they reached the top; the breeze had become a blustery wind, as it swept across the Tor. The three of them stood in silence as their eyes took in the panorama, which stretched towards the horizon. Merlin looked around. His heart felt a little heavy, and with a tear in his eye, said, "This view brings back so many memories. There have surely been some changes made to the landscape I once knew; a lot of the land has now been built upon. However, much does remain the same."

"What do you mean?" Asked Lemy.

"All the small settlements have gone; a lot of the countryside is now these large red brick houses."

It was late and most of the visitors were making their way down the winding path. Remy suggested they took shelter under the tower's arch. Remy had a good look around the arch and pulled out a brochure and began commenting on its history.

"This is all that remains of a fourteenth-century church which was dedicated to Saint Michael. Apparently, the church ended in 1539 when Henry VIII dissolved the monasteries. It was a replacement for an earlier church which was destroyed by an earthquake in 1275." He read out loud.

"Earthquake! It was no earthquake which destroyed the original church." Merlin replied firmly.

"What do you mean?" Remy asked.

"This is a very sacred and spiritual place; there is a veil which separates our world from that of the dead. The veil here is very thin, Nimue knew it, and it was she who tried to break the veil and bring forth an army of the dead. The magic I placed over the Sacred earth temple and with the help of the Sisterhood was all that stopped the veil from tearing and the dead roaming and ravaging the land as Nimue's unstoppable army. It was the dead trying to get out of the underworld which caused the Tor to shake and brought down the church." Merlin recounted.

The three watched as the last of the visitors left the Tor. They waited long enough for people to reach the bottom and the full moon to rise before Merlin stood up and moved to the right of the ruins.

"This is the site of the original ring which once stood here. For your safety, you two will stand over there and stay quiet. The Sisterhood protects the entrance and has instructions solely to allow me access."

Merlin raised his arms towards the moon, and in a loud voice, he said.

"The ritual offering in the Faerie woods of *Ynys Afallon* has been made and accepted. Let the Sisterhood of Avalon come forth and open Merlin's gate. I, Merlin, demand entrance to the Sacred Temple and the healing waters from the Sacred Chalice Well. The nine maidens, I summon you again to form the ring. Come forth to aid and help me heal."

The wind had reduced to a soft breeze, slowly one by one, the maidens appeared like glowing ghosts forming a circle around Merlin. At Merlin's feet, a large puddle of water appeared to bubble up from the ground. He knelt, cupped his hands, and scooped up some of the water and drank it. He slowly rubbed his wet hands over his face and beard. He scooped up a second handful, and this time poured it over his head and again wiped his face and beard with his wet hands. He gradually rose to his feet; a bright white light surrounded the nine maidens who appeared to glow a pale blue as they outstretched their arms sideways, they all started to gradually sink into the ground. After barely a couple of minutes, Merlin and the maidens rose out of the ground again. The maidens gently lowered their arms by their sides and stopped glowing.

Shamera and Remy looked on in amazement as Merlin stood there dressed in white robes and holding a brown hessian sack.

"Thank you, maidens of Avalon, for your kind help. Rest peacefully once more until your help is required again," Merlin said with gratitude.

Gradually, one by one, the maidens slowly disappeared and left Merlin standing in the evening moonlight. Shamera and Remy made their way over to Merlin. As they drew near, they could see he was looking a lot younger and moved more spritely.

"Well, that's not something you see every day." Remy stated.

"Did you get the weapon?" Shamera said eagerly.

"I retrieved what needed to be retrieved. The night air is getting chilly, we had better make our way back down." Merlin replied, still clutching his mysterious bag of items.

Merlin, rejuvenated by the waters, led the way down the hill whilst still clutching tightly to his bundle.

"Wow, the old man can move now." Remy exclaimed.

It was much easier going down the Tor, and they soon reached the bottom. Leading the way, Merlin headed back to the car, his path illuminated by the light of the full moon. Merlin, still clutching the sack, suggested they did not open it until they were safely home. Merlin sat tightly clutching his sack. Eventually, they arrived back home and went straight into the house. Remy locked and bolted the door. Shamera was eager to see what Merlin had brought, especially to lay his eyes on Excalibur. Merlin placed the sack on the table and impatiently, Shamera blurted out, "Well, can we see what you have? Hopefully, there is something in there to help us defeat the dark sorceress."

Merlin un-wrapped the cords which bound the sack and teasingly placed his hand inside. He pulled out the sword. Shamera's eyes lit up as Merlin carefully drew the sword from its scabbard and handed it to Shamera.

"Be very careful. It is extremely sharp." Merlin warned.

As Shamera held the sword, he thought how a sword of this size could, weigh so little. The sword was about three and a half feet long with a red leather-bound hilt. It had an embossed gold pommel with the crest of Arthur Pendragon, which was a gold crown above a gold silhouette of a dragon on each side of the pommel. The sword felt well balanced in his hand. The makers had etched the very shiny silver blade with dragons near to the golden coloured guard.

"What do these words say on the blade? I cannot read them?"

"This reads 'Take me up' and on the other side it says, 'Cast me away'. Take the sword up against your enemies, once victorious, cast it back whence it came." Merlin explained.

Shamera thought the sword looked every bit as good as he expected. Shamera handed the sword back to Merlin, who carefully placed it back in its scabbard. Merlin pulled out a dagger from the sack; offering it to Shamera he explained, "Arthur also bore this dagger called Carnwennan. This was also given to Arthur by me, it too has been forged in the fire and the magical breath of a dragon, I placed a spell on the Carnwennan so it would shroud the wielder in shadow so he could approach unseen and slay his enemies from behind."

"Be very careful. This blade is so sharp, Arthur split the witch Orddu in half with a single stroke, or so he told me. These two are battle tested and worthy weapons for any man to wield."

"Hopefully these will help slay the evil sorceress once and for all." Shamera whispered, examining the knife.

Shamera gave the knife back to Merlin. He pulled a large, pointed hat with a wide brim from the sack. Made from brown, aged leather with a reddish and gold feather stuck in a thin leather band.

"What does this do?"

"Nothing, this is my old hat." Merlin laughed as he placed the hat on his head.

"It's very fetching." laughed Remy.

"When can we get these back into my world?" Shamera inquired eagerly. He could not wait to get back to his world, as he felt he had already been away far too long.

"Soon, tomorrow night, in fact." Remy responded positively.

"Why tomorrow night? Why not tomorrow day?" Shamera reacted.

"Be calm Shamera, one more day will not hurt. We don't want people watching, and there are lots of people visiting Stonehenge during the day. It is better we wait for the cover of darkness." Said Remy.

"I'm sorry, but I don't know what's happening back home. She could have attacked my village or taken over the country by now."

"There is one more weapon you can take with you." Merlin informed.

"What weapon? I thought you had nothing left in your sack."

Both Remy and Shamera looked at Merlin, waiting for his answer with bated breath. Merlin looked at them both for a few seconds before blurting out, "Me, of course. You need help, and if this sorceress is as powerful as you say, you will need my help. What little it is." Merlin answered back.

Shamera's jaw hit the floor at this news; he looked at Remy and grinned from ear to ear. "Really? She will have no chance now." Shamera burst out loud; he punched the air with his fist before continuing, "I can't wait to see the expression on Lord

Salogel's face when I turn up with you and these weapons. I feel a lot more confident."

"Don't get too cocky. If she is as powerful as you say, victory will not come easy. So, young sorcerer, tell me more about this dark sorceress." Merlin replied.

"I'm not sure what I can tell you. She came to our lands a long time ago, before our dark times. A time of war between the Elvenii, Dwarves, Horsemen of Mirropus, the Mystics, and us Ethaenians. Some say it was she who started it, pitting one against another. She waited until the war was at its peak. She tried to capture Verazslo back then. There were also some other magical items she tried to steal for herself. Magic was stronger in those days, and Verazslo was a lot younger. He eventually defeated her and could have killed her, but he showed mercy, and she fled. We heard nothing of her until recently when she came back with an army attacking our land. We think she has captured Verazslo and is looking for his staff, and the crystal of Ellaria."

"You think Verazslo will still be alive?" Merlin asked.

"Yes, the Elvenii say she will need him alive to show how powerful she has become, and for him to watch helplessly as she conquers our lands and enslaves us all, using that to get what she really wants... the crystal."

"I think she will keep him alive, merely to humiliate him. She sounds like a nasty piece of work; sounds like someone I once knew in this realm." Merlin recounted.

"Who was that?" Shamera asked.

"Nimue, I have already told you about her." The contempt in his voice was obvious, anyway let's not dwell on her." He continued.

"So, tell me about these Druids." Shamera enquired, changing the subject. He could see the anger in Merlin's face.

"The druids, well, where do I start? Druids are a spiritual people, followers of the old religion. They promote harmony, connection, and reverence for the natural world, including natural magic. I considered them members of the learned class among the ancient Celts. They acted as priests, teachers, seers, and healers. They used natural elements to heal, with the aid of plants and herbs."

"I could be a druid. I am learning magic, and Mirabilis is teaching me about herbs and plants for healing." Shamera said excitedly.

Merlin looked at Shamera and thought for a while, before commenting, "I'm sure you could be. I wonder if they have ever travelled to your realm in the past. It's a possibility, I suppose."

"They must have done. How else would Lord Salogel and the Mystic seer know about them? And the map, it helped us find you."

For the rest of the day, Merlin instructed Shamera on some more simple magic spells and meditation to help improve his abilities. Merlin had Shamera practicing into the early evening, Shamera wanted to learn as much as he could.

"Do you think I could defeat the dark sorceress?" Shamera asked.

"Not by yourself no, you will need the help of your Verazslo and I. If she is as powerful as you say you will need to practise hard and have your wits about you. She has had many years to practise and hone her skills; where as you… you have had hardly any time at all." Merlin replied.

The next day, Merlin taught Shamera more magic and made him go over what he had already learned. The time flew by.

"I'm sorry to interrupt, but it's time to go. There will not be time to send a message through the portal to announce your arrival, so once on the other side, you will have to make your own way." said Remy.

"Okay, it's not a problem. I know where to go." Shamera exclaimed excitedly. He was finally going home.

"I wish I was going with you two." Remy said with sadness in his voice, although he had not known them for very long. His heart felt heavy at seeing them having to leave.

"I wish you could come too. It has been great getting to know you. Maybe when this is all over, I could come back, and you could show me more of this world." Shamera responded as he hurriedly packed his backpack.

"Yes, that would be good; you will always be welcome back."

Merlin and Shamera were all packed; it was getting dark and time to set off. They were about to set off when there was a loud knock at the door. The three of them looked at each other in puzzlement.

"Who can this be?" questioned Remy, as he stood up and went to answer the door.

"Who is it?" Remy shouted through the door.

"Can you open up, please? It's the police." Said the voice from the other side of the door.

Remy reluctantly opened the door but left the safety chain on. "Police, what do you want here?"

"Please open the door, sir; we have a warrant to search these premises." Said a tall thin police officer.

"Search my house, but why?"

"Please open the door sir and I can explain everything as these four officers carry out the search." insisted the police officer.

"Erm, alright, but I will have to close the door to take the chain off." Remy closed the door and looked towards the kitchen; fear written all over his face. Merlin stood there, smiling.

"All is well. Let them in." Merlin whispered as he walked back into the kitchen.

Remy opened the door to the police. "Can I see your search warrant, please?"

The police officer waved a piece of paper in front of Remy. "These officers will conduct the search and I will ask you some questions. Shall we?" the officer instructed, whilst gesturing with his hand for Remy to head towards the kitchen. The police officer closed the door and followed Remy towards the kitchen. When Remy entered the kitchen, both Merlin and Shamera were not there. One police officer searched the front room whilst another one searched the kitchen, two went upstairs.

"What are you looking for?" Remy asked, looking around and wondering where Merlin and Shamera were hiding.

"The Cornish police interviewed you regarding the theft of a gold bracelet. We are merely following that up." The officer replied, and before he could say anything else, Merlin suddenly appeared behind the police officers with his finger poised to press the stone on his gold cuff. Remy's eyes widened in horror.

179

As the officer turned to see what Remy was staring at, Merlin pressed the stone. The police suddenly vanished, all of them.

"What have you done to them?" Remy exclaimed, as he looked around the room to see if they definitely had disappeared.

"They'll be fine. Let them try to explain that." Merlin replied with a chuckle.

"What have you done? They are the police; They will arrest me for sure."

"Worry not. They have not been harmed. I transported them to somewhere else; about a mile away would be the maximum."

"Oh no, I wish you had not done that. I will have a lot of explaining to do when they get back." He said, despairingly.

Shamera suddenly reappeared. "Wow, that one I must learn."

"Come, we'd better get going before they come back. Mind you, I would like to see the expressions on their faces round about now." Remy gave a little smile. He grabbed his keys and headed for the door. He looked up and down the street for any sign of the police. The coast was clear. The three of them set off for Stonehenge. Remy drove as fast as he dared without drawing attention to himself; it was not long when they arrived at their destination.

"I will drop you two off here. The pathway to the Henge is there. I will need to get back and deal with those police officers, as I'm sure they will pay me another visit. And they won't be happy. Good luck to the both of you and I hope everything works out well. Until we meet again, take care."

"We will. You take care and I hope all goes well for you too. Thank you for all your help. I will be forever in your debt." Shamera replied, as he and Merlin quickly headed towards the path.

They both stood there for a few moments as they watched Remy drive off back home.

"Let's get this done and get back home." Shamera stated as he pulled his wand and parchment from his pocket.

They hurriedly walked along the path to the centre of the stones. Merlin looked around and said, "These have changed little in all these years. They are missing a few of the lintel stones, but the rest appear pretty much as I remember them."

"You know about these stones?"

"Yes, they were around in my time, but I did not know they were a portal to another land."

"I have not known about them long, there is a small stone ring near to where I live, most of the stones there have fallen over. Merlin, come stand close to me."

Shamera held his wand aloft and read the incantation out loud. And, as before, an electrical charge built up and jumped across the stones. Rapidly intensifying with a ball of blue light encompassing them both. They both felt an immediate jolt forward, a bright flash of light made them quickly close their eyes tight. Instantly, they both fell forward onto their knees.

"Don't get up too soon," Shamera advised Merlin. "The effects will wear off soon, but you'll feel dizzy for a few moments yet."

They both knelt there for a few moments until the effects of the teleportation wore off.

"We need to get to Selvenora as quickly as we can; it's going to be a long walk."

"Let me have your wand a moment."

Merlin took the wand and held it skywards; red and purple balls of light fired off into the night sky, which exploded into a myriad of smaller red and purple balls which lit up the night sky. "Should get someone's attention." Merlin proclaimed proudly.

"Something else I need to learn." Shamera blurted excitedly.

Shamera led the way towards Selvenora; periodically, Merlin would set off another pyrotechnic display, which exploded brightly in the night sky. They had not been walking long before they saw horsemen heading towards them.

"I hope this is the Elvenii," Shamera stated, straining his eyes. "It's okay Merlin, I can see them… we're okay."

"Are they knights? They look like knights" Merlin enquired as he saw the soldiers in their suits of armour.

"No, they are Elvenii soldiers."

The horsemen drew closer; Shamera looked to see if he could recognise anyone, but it was too dark. As the horsemen approached, Shamera blurted out, "Vesryn!" Merlin, not knowing who they were, had his finger poised once more on the cuff's crystal.

"It's okay Merlin, you can relax. We are amongst friends."

"Shamera, welcome back." Vesryn replied.

The Elvenii soldiers pulled up in front of them. "Who's your friend? I assume he is a friend." Vesryn enquired.

"Yes, he is a very good friend. This is Merlin. Where are the others?"

"They will be back in Selvenora; your display put the citadel on alert. We were out on patrol when we saw your signal. Come, climb aboard and we'll get you back."

Shamera and Merlin were quickly on their way; soon they were in front of the citadel's gates.

"Open the gate, Shamera has returned." Vesryn shouted.

The gate groaned and creaked as it rose to allow them to enter. As they rode into the courtyard, Elvenii soldiers in their polished silver armour and headgear lined the stairway leading into the building.

"This really reminds me of the knights-of-the-round-table." Merlin's heart lifted as he remembered.

"Shamera, please take your friend to the council chamber and we will alert Lord Salogel of your arrival." Vesryn requested and walked up the stairs to find Lord Salogel.

Merlin followed Shamera to the council chamber, his eyes darting around at the beautifully carved marble statues adorning the hall and corridors. They eventually reached the council chamber; Shamera knocked on the large wooden door. There was no answer, so they entered the room and sat at the white marble table. It was not long before Lord Salogel and Krell burst into the room. Both Shamera and Merlin looked up in surprise.

"They informed us of your arrival; we were not sure if you would complete your quest. Did you find what you went for? And who is this?" Lord Salogel asked as he walked over to greet them both.

"Is my family here?" Shamera asked eagerly.

"Not yet. Your village is not in danger, and they did not want to leave right away. We have a patrol nearby who will give advance notice should the situation change. They sent their love and hoped you were safe and fulfilling your apprenticeship." Lord Salogel replied, being as comforting as he could.

Shamera's face could not hide the disappointment his heart was feeling. "I was hoping to see them, I hoped they would be here." He sighed.

"You will see them soon, I promise. Did you find what you went for?"

"I think so. I have brought a sword and a knife."

"A sword and a knife!" Krell spouted out. "Sorry, please finish." Krell said apologetically as he gave Merlin a little embarrassed sideways glance and a diminutive shrug of his shoulders. He was embarrassed at his little outburst. Merlin smiled understandingly.

"Yes, I have brought a sword and a knife. These are not ordinary weapons. I will let Merlin explain about them. And this leads me on to…"

Merlin stood up in anticipation of his introduction. "I am Merlin, once sorcerer and confidant to King Arthur of Camelot," he said, introducing himself whilst placing his right hand over the area of his heart and giving a little court bow.

"Sorcerer?" Lord Salogel exclaimed in surprise. "How can we trust you are here to help us and join in league with Niniane?" He continued, in a cautious tone.

"He has helped me with my magic and…"

"Please Shamera, let him speak for himself." Interrupted Lord Salogel.

Merlin looked at Shamera and gave him a reassuring smile and a nod. He turned to Krell, "I am Merlin. A spell had me trapped in a cave for many years by my once companion, lover, and pupil. Once she had learnt all she could, she tricked me and trapped me in a cave, until Shamera and his friend set me free. Nimue was her name, and from the information I have gleaned from Shamera, I believe your Niniane, and my Nimue are one and the same. If this is true, I have a score to settle, and settle it I will."

Krell looked straight at Merlin. "I cannot read you."

Merlin smiled and said, "You are a seer, are you not? You can penetrate and read minds."

"You are familiar with Mystics. Have you come across us before?" Krell asked.

"No, not your kind. Druid seers, different people. People with your ability, but they lack the third eye, which I undoubtedly see you have. I have over the years, developed the ability to block access to my mind. If it makes you feel happier, I will grant you access."

"It's late, we are all tired and we should let our guests rest and continue this in the morning." Lord Salogel proposed.

Krell nodded in agreement. "I would like to see these weapons before we retire, if I may." he continued.

"I will reveal them tomorrow. We should rest." Merlin expressed, still tightly clutching his hessian sack.

"Very well," Lord Salogel replied. "You can have the room, next to Shamera." he continued.

"Come Merlin, I will show you where your room is." Shamera offered.

The next morning came quickly as Shamera slept very well that night. He was up and dressed when a recognisable soft knock sounded at the door. "Come in."

Elithrin entered the room, carrying a large platter of fruit and a jug of water. She carefully placed it on the table and poured some water. She turned gently to face Shamera; a soft smile appeared on her face, she felt relieved he had come back safely.

"Well, what was Engla Land like?" Her eyes widened in expectation of hearing lots of wondrous tales. She walked over and sat on the edge of the bed and softly patted the space next to her, encouraging him to sit by her side.

"I don't know where to start. There was so much that is different and marvellous. Things called cars, horseless carriages, they move extremely quickly. Rooms with lights you turn on with a switch on the wall. The light looks like a small sun inside of a glass globe, many times brighter than a candle. It's like night turns back into day. Pizza, oh, you must try pizza…"

Elithrin listened intently as he filled her ears with tales of Engla land and the people living there. A knock at the door interrupted them.

"Come in." Shamera called out.

The door opened and Merlin walked in. "Oh, sorry, I did not know you were entertaining." Merlin exclaimed apologetically.

"Come in, come in, this is Elithrin, Lord Salogel's daughter. Elithrin this is Merlin, a great sorcerer from Engla land." Shamera replied, standing up to introduce everyone.

Merlin politely smiled and gave a slight nod of his head. "I'm not sure I'm a great sorcerer. Shamera flatters me."

"You are too modest, Merlin." he turned to Elithrin and smiled. "He truly is a great sorcerer. I have learnt from him."

There was a knock on the door. It was an Elvenii soldier.

"They requested you and Merlin to attend the council chamber; please take whatever weapons you have brought back form Engla Land and Lord Salogel and the rest council will see you there." He reported.

"I will see you both later, and you can tell me more about this fascinating world you came from Merlin. I want to hear all about it." Elithrin said excitedly. She smiled at Shamera as she left the room, followed by the soldier.

"We had better not keep them waiting," Shamera said as he held the door open for Merlin.

"I will get my sack from my room and you can show me the way."

Merlin retrieved the sack from his room and they made their way to the council chamber. When they arrived, they found two soldiers guarding the entrance. As they reached the door, the soldiers opened the door for them and closed it again. Lord Salogel and Krell sat towards the middle of the table, with the council of five sitting on either side.

"Come in, please join us," Lord Salogel said as he beckoned them closer.

Shamera and Merlin headed towards the two remaining empty seats.

"Please sit." Said Lord Salogel.

The other members of the council introduced themselves.

"I am Revilo."

"I am Nehpets."

"And I am Alegna."

"And I am Einnor. And along with Lord Salogel, we are the council of five." His voice was tinged with a little distrust.

Lord Salogel looked at Merlin and asked, "Please introduce yourself and tell us more about who you are."

Merlin looked around the table. He felt a little uncomfortable being put on the spot; he remained seated, paused slightly to gather his thoughts. He then said, "To tell you all about me would take longer than any of us have," he smiled. "Plainly and quickly, my name is Emrys. Merlin. I was born in a place called Wales. A country of my realm, I was sorcerer and confidante for a great and noble king, Arthur Pendragon was his name. I served King Arthur in the court of Camelot. After the death of this great king and after many years of teaching someone called Nimue, in lessons of magic, she tricked me and imprisoned me in a cave. Until Shamera and Remy recently rescued me. I retrieved Excalibur and Carnwennan, the great weapons of King Arthur."

Krell shook his head. "A sword and a knife. What use are they against Niniane?"

"By themselves, very little. Although they are magical weapons, I can wield them, or, I can present them to another worthy, true, and noble person. However, you have a far greater weapon here." said Merlin.

"This person is delusional, a sword and a knife. Niniane will reign victorious over us," Einnor blurted out as he stood up and pointed towards Merlin. "We had a great sorcerer. She overpowered him, what makes you so special?" Einnor continued.

Merlin said nothing as he quietly slipped his left hand into his right sleeve. Suddenly, Einnor vanished. The room fell silent as everyone looked at each quite puzzled. Shamera dropped his head and could not help smiling at what had happened. Lord Salogel noticed this and quietly asked, "Did you do this, Shamera? Have you come on so much?"

"It was not the lad, it was me. His whining was becoming bothersome. He is not harmed and merely transported to the garden, it was one way of answering his question, just a small demonstration."

"Please do not do that again." Lord Salogel requested.

"I am sorry." Merlin had a look of genuine remorse for his actions as he nodded slightly and lowered his eyes. Einnor burst into the room and was about to sound off when Lord Salogel rose to his feet and, in a stout voice, asserted. "Let it be a warning to you Einnor, we are here to hear what Shamera, and Merlin, have to tell us. You will have time to have your say when they have had theirs. Now, please take your seat again. I'm sorry Merlin, please continue."

"Where was I? Ah yes. The sword Excalibur can cut through the toughest armour, the knife can slice a man or beast in half. Both are made from sky iron, and forged in the breath and fire of a magical dragon. And there is this." Merlin stood and pulled his right sleeve up to reveal his gold cuff, "This made your man vanish. It can do many things. Shamera is becoming a great sorcerer and under my tutelage and that of Verazslo, he will become even greater than the both of us. If Niniane is Nimue, I should be the one to defeat her, especially for the way she betrayed me."

"I would like to see this sword of yours cut through our Elvenii armour. I believe there is no finer armour anywhere." Said Lord Salogel.

Merlin reached into his sack and pulled out the sword, drew it from its scabbard, and handed it carefully to Lord Salogel.

"Please, be careful. It is extremely sharp." Warned Merlin.

The long thin blade glinted in the light. Lord Salogel carefully examined the weapon.

"The detail on the sword is exquisite, and it is so light, lighter than any sword I have ever held. I can't believe this sword can stand up to battle, let alone cut through our armour as you proclaim."

"I assure you, it will do as I have stated."

"GUARD!" Lord Salogel shouted.

The two guards quickly entered the room, with their swords drawn, expecting trouble.

"Stand down. All is well; I need your body armour," Lord Salogel requested, pointing Excalibur at one of the guards.

The guard removed his body armour and walked over to Lord Salogel and presented it to him. Lord Salogel placed the armour on the table. He ordered the guard to hit it with the blade of his sword as hard as he could. Merlin and Shamera moved out of the way as the guard swung his sword at the body armour with all his might. It sent the armour sprawling across the room. He went and retrieved it and examined it as he brought it back. There was a slight dent where the blade made contact. Lord Salogel measured up for a swing with Excalibur. He slowly drew the sword back, keeping his eye on the armour. He quickly swung the sword down as hard as he could, sending the armour flying across the room once more. Lord Salogel made a slight gesture for the guard to retrieve it. On examination of the armour again, merely a slight dent was visible.

"I thought you said it could cut through the toughest armour. It has done no more damage than his sword." Lord Salogel looked quite disappointed.

"I also said, only I can wield the sword. Unless I present it to one of pure of heart." Merlin held his hand out to be given back the sword.

"Does this mean I am not pure of heart?" Asked lord Salogel, looking a little disappointed.

"No, not at all. It just means that I have not properly presented it to you for you to use. Its magic remains with me."

Lord Salogel nodded slightly as he now understood why it did not cut through the armour. He laid the sword over both of his hands and offered it back to Merlin, replacing the armour on the table. Without hesitation, Merlin swung the sword at the armour. The sword cut all the way through the armour as though they made it from butter. The council let out a loud gasp on seeing the armour cut through so easily.

"Very impressive," Krell piped up, "What else do you have in your armoury?"

"I have a few tricks up my sleeve," he said, tilting his head towards Shamera and gave him a little wink. "Between Shamera and I, I'm sure we can find and rescue your sorcerer. The three of us will be a formidable force and will be able defeat this

Niniane and give her what she deserves." Merlin placed Excalibur back in the sack and sat down.

"What she deserves? What do you mean?" asked Einnor sheepishly, hoping not to be transported again.

"To have her magic removed and imprisoned as I was."

"Can you remove her magic?" Lord Salogel asked.

"Not exactly, but I can place a bracelet on her wrist, no one other than a chosen sorcerer can remove."

"So, what happens now?" Lord Salogel enquired of Merlin.

"Whilst you organise your armies and locate your sorcerer, I will teach Shamera in the art of sorcery in both casting spells and defending against them."

"Niniane is still amassing her forces in the south. A black walled fortress defends her, guarded by an army of forced labour and a growing army comprised of Trolls and men. We will have the leaders of the Mystics, Dwarves, Dragonborn and the Formorians attending a war council in two days' time, and I would like you and Shamera to also attend."

Chapter 13

Merlin and Shamera started practicing early in the garden of contemplation. Merlin knew they did not have long and needed Shamera to be as ready as he could in the little time they had. Merlin made Shamera repeat all the things he had previously learnt from Lord Salogel and what he had learnt from Merlin himself whilst in England.

"Okay, take a break, come and sit." Merlin said, pointing to the bench.

"Nimue… sorry, Niniane will undoubtably have Mage Enchanters; a band of people she will have taught to do simple but deadly magic. With training, mages can manipulate the basic elements, such as conjuring flames and firing energy bursts. They will also be able to make charms, transmutation spells and, of course, killing spells."

"But how will they have got the ability to use magic? I thought it had to be within you naturally?"

"She can give them a charm, one that allows them to connect to the veil which shields this world from the one dead inhabit and enables them to draw power from it."

"And how do we defeat them?"

"It should not be too difficult for someone like you; but you will have to be very careful and be skilful in your defensive work."

"Defensive work?"

"We will do this next. I will fire small energy bursts at you, and you will defend against them. Defensive work is mostly a matter of anticipating the spell about to be cast by your adversary. You need nimble footwork and a swift reaction with your wand to avoid or deflect it."

"How do you do that? It does not sound easy." Shamera looked a little concerned.

"Concentration, concentration, concentration. You must expect what's coming and counter it. Come on, back to work."

Merlin positioned Shamera about twenty paces in front of him. "I will fire a small energy burst at you and you deflect them using your magic. Don't forget… concentrate."

Merlin formed an energy sphere in the palm of his hand and shot it towards Shamera, who waved his wand at it. But, the energy ball hit him in the centre of his chest and delivered a small electric shock. "Ouch!" he cried as another energy sphere headed his way.

"Ouch!" Several more times, Merlin fired his energy spheres, and everyone hit its mark. This was making Shamera quite angry, and he threw his wand to the floor.

"This is not working, and those balls hurt." Shamera shouted.

"Wait here." Merlin ordered as he walked away. He returned with two soldiers.

"Apparently this is Folmon and Arvad. Watch closely." Merlin stated.

Merlin asked the two soldiers to draw their swords and safely, but forcefully, attack each other. The soldiers nodded to each other and began attacking and defending the blows aimed at each other. Merlin explained, "An experienced swordsman can quickly expect a move and, without thinking about it, counter the strike. The same holds true for spell casting and defence against it. Okay, thank you. Please stop a moment." Merlin said as he beckoned them over. "How are you able to anticipate one another's strikes?" Merlin asked.

"Lots of practice and watching your opponent for a telltale sign of what he is going to do next." Folmon replied.

"What do you mean?" Shamera asked.

"Watch, Folmon prepare to come at me with a right sided head blow."

Folmon made a slight movement. "Freeze!" called out Arvad. "What did you see?"

"A slight twitch." Shamera replied with a slight shrug of his shoulders.

Arvad shook his head. "This is what I saw; his left heel raised slightly off the ground; he pointed his left toes inwards. His right shoulder rolled backward and his hand holding the sword rose upwards and to the right. This told me a strike was coming to my left side." he explained.

"Wow, you saw all that quickly." Shamera said, looking very impressed.

"If you do not see the clues and anticipate what is coming… you're dead." Arvad stated as he placed his sword back into its scabbard.

"I think I understand."

"Thank you for your help. You may return to your duties; I would not want you to get into any bother on my account." Merlin said as he nodded thankfully.

"Okay, so we will do this again, and this time you will move solely your body. So be nimble of foot." Merlin smiled teasingly.

Again, Merlin positioned himself about twenty paces away and prepared to fire an energy ball. The ball shot towards Shamera; he quickly twisted his body to the left as the ball passed by very close. He turned back to Merlin, pleased with what he had done when an energy ball hit him square in the chest.

"What did I say? CONCENTRATE!"

Merlin let fly another energy ball. Shamera moved sideways to his right but kept eye contact with Merlin. Shamera jumped up as a ball landed at his feet. Merlin was relentless as he fired energy balls at his head, feet, and chest. For about five minutes, Shamera danced around and dodged all the energy balls Merlin fired at him.

"Very good. Now do it with the wand and you do not move. Your wand is your shield. Use it wisely."

Shamera pulled his wand from his waistband and held it out in front of him, imagining a shield at its tip. Again, Merlin fired an energy ball straight at him, chest height, and with a deft flick of the wand, deflected it to his left. His eyes lit up at his achievement. Merlin fired another, and another, at his head, feet, and chest. Shamera deflecting everyone, Merlin speeded up, firing several, one straight after another in quick succession. Shamera defended well against them, deflecting them to the left and right with the odd one being deflected straight upwards. However, the last one hit his hand, knocking the wand from his grasp. Merlin fired a few more directly at his feet, which made Shamera dance around like a demented cat on hot tiles trying to avoid them. Merlin ceased fire and burst out laughing, "Well done lad, which goes to show if you lose your wand, you can still survive some spells. Let's take a break and have something to eat and drink, and we can look at some disarming techniques later."

Merlin and Shamera headed back to the main building for refreshments.

"Merlin, how were you able to fire off so many energy balls so quickly?"

"Through practice, lots of practice. You need to do things without hesitation. Your magic needs to be second nature to you."

Shamera thought about what Merlin had said. He would have to put in a lot of practice to react with the agility and speed he would need to defeat Niniane. After lunch and a meditation session to help Shamera focus, they returned to training.

"Disarming your opponent is an important tactic, as it means they can no longer cast spells against you and they become vulnerable. There are a couple of ways to disarm your opponent; the first is a direct spell, the second way is to rebound the spell they fired back to the attacker. For this session, you will need your wand and your staff. From now on, you do not go anywhere without both."

"Wow, this feels like it is getting really serious." He thought to himself, But, accidentally said it aloud. He felt a slight flutter of excitement in his stomach.

"Sorcery is not something you do lightly. It should always be serious. Your wand and staff need to become a natural extension of yourself. Let them become part of you." Merlin responded.

"Sorry, I didn't mean it like it sounded; I meant the situation not the training." Shamera said apologetically.

"Yes, by the sound of things, we need to be on our guard at all times. Especially you. You will be seen as a threat to Niniane, and she will want the staff to increase her powers. We cannot let it happen. Hopefully she does not know about me, and that's our advantage, for now."

Shamera's head dropped slightly as he contemplated his responsibilities to the situation he found himself to be in. Shamera slowly lifted his head and looked straight at Merlin and, with increased determination, said in response, "Right, what do I need to do?"

"We will start with the harder one first. This one involves using your staff. Keep the staff in front of you; you can have it in the air or resting on the ground. I will try to disarm you; you will use the staff's power to form an energy barrier and with a forward momentum of the staff, try to bounce the spell straight back at me disarming me with my own spell." Merlin rolled and flexed his shoulders, "Are you ready?"

Shamera did not say a word; he looked straight at Merlin and nodded to confirm he was ready. Merlin flicked his wand; Shamera pushed the staff forward. Unfortunately, he was too slow. His staff flew out of his hand and landed some five paces behind him.

"I said this was the harder one. It will take a lot of practice and anticipation to get it right. Pick up your staff and let's try again." Merlin said, trying to be as encouraging as he could. Shamera tried a few more times without success, "Keep a clear mind and do not get angry with yourself or you will never achieve it. Keep calm, keep focused, and keep your mind open." Merlin encouraged.

They practiced late into the afternoon. Shamera deflected the spell twice but did not manage to send it back and disarm Merlin. Instead, one spell could be seen ricocheting off the back wall as the other spell hit the tree branch, scattering some of its leaves. Shamera spent a lot of time chasing his staff as Merlin kept sending it spinning through the air. Shamera lifted his right hand and held it palm forward to halt Merlin from sending another spell. Merlin watched as Shamera drew a deep breath and closed his eyes; he stood for a couple of minutes before he turned his hand palm upwards and, curling his fingers, beckoned with his fingers for Merlin to continue. Shamera was trying to visualise Merlin and could see him as an outline of energy oscillating in the distance. Merlin fired his disarming spell. This time Shamera could see it as a small ball of quivering energy heading towards him. This time, he thrust the staff down on the ground and towards Merlin; his aim was slightly off, but he blocked the spell and shot it back towards Merlin. The spell went whizzing past Merlin's right elbow and sparked impressively as it hit the wall behind him. Merlin fired another; again, Shamera could see the quivering energy ball heading towards him. He thrust the staff forwards again. This time, it was a direct hit, and Merlin's wand was sent flying.

"Well done," Merlin gasped as he looked around to see where his wand had landed. "Now, do it again."

Shamera's aim was improving as he knocked the wand from Merlin's grasp with increased tenacity. With Shamera's confidence growing, he opened his eyes; he could no longer see the energy balls but could anticipate them and he either blocked them or sent them successfully back to disarm Merlin. After a few hours of practice, Shamera was improving beyond all expectations.

"Okay, Shamera, we'll call it a day." Merlin stated as he walked over to Shamera. "What made you close your eyes earlier, and what could you see?"

"I don't know what made me think to do it, I knew I had to close my eyes, and in my mind, I could see you as an outline of wavy lines and I could see the spells coming towards me as a ball of pulsating energy which made them easier to hit back." He said vaguely, as he tried to understand it himself.

"You are a natural," Merlin smirked. "You have picked this up a lot faster than I thought you would. You really are destined for greatness."

Shamera looked slightly embarrassed at the compliment Merlin had given him. But, allowed himself a little wry smile.

"So, from now on, you can call me Shamera the Great." he said, raising his eyebrows and grinning as he turned away. Merlin gave him a friendly tap on the back of his head. "Don't get cocky lad, you have merely started down the path of your destiny. You have a great deal still to learn."

They walked back to the main building. Shamera was feeling exhausted after the amount of concentration and training he had done, so he went straight to his room.

The next day, they summoned Shamera and Merlin to the council chamber, as all the leaders were now in attendance.

Shamera walked with Merlin along the corridors he had traversed many times, but this time, it felt different. His stomach was doing cartwheels, it felt like a thousand butterflies were fluttering all at once. "This could be a council of war and I might have to play a part of it." Shamera said. His voice quivered.

"War, a small three letter word, yet has giant consequences; it has the potential to destroy everything. War tears people apart, even those who were once close. The victims of war are constantly wracked with regret, pain and guilt." Merlin expressed with sadness in his voice.

They reached the large wooden doors, which were again opened by two soldiers guarding them. This time, they had drawn swords. The room was noisy with chatter as everyone was trying to add their opinions about what should happen and by whom. Shamera's eyes were drawn straight to Artos, the Dwarf leader. He had never seen a dwarf in the flesh before. Long copper coloured unkempt hair flowed from beneath his silver and gold war helmet, two thin plats of hair one on either side of his head were barely visible. His reddish brown, matted beard hung down to his chest. He sat there taking long draws on his very lengthy thin stemmed clay pipe. He was blowing the smoke out of the side of his mouth without removing his pipe. A large double-edged war axe lay at his feet. Lord Salogel observed them standing there. He beckoned them both over, and pointed to two vacant seats. Shamera and Merlin took their places amongst the war council. All fell silent as all eyes appeared to be on Shamera and Merlin. This left Shamera feeling very uncomfortable, and he fidgeted awkwardly in his chair.

"Which one is Shamera?" Artos blurted out in a gruff voice, then coughed a little on his smoke.

"I am," Shamera replied, slightly raising his hand, and with a slight nervous crackle to his voice.

"Why he's merely a child," Artos barked, "And who's he?" he said, holding the bowl and pointing his pipestem towards Merlin.

Merlin rose to his feet, looked around the room quickly. He looked straight at Artos and, in a calm voice, said, "I am

Merlin; I am a sorcerer from another land. I have been tutoring Shamera, who, despite being young of age, is progressing in his craft remarkably quickly."

As Merlin sat down, Lord Salogel leaned forward in his chair and responded, "We are not here to discuss Shamera. We are here to discuss a combined army. To bring all our forces to bear on Niniane and her army that threatens all our freedoms."

"We are but simple farmers; we do not have soldiers or warriors. We would be lambs to the slaughter." Piped up Aglym. By the outline of his third eye, Shamera knew he was a Mystic, but there were a couple of races he had not encountered before.

"You can still hold an axe or fire a bow; some of you still have seeing powers I have heard; they would be very useful. We too are a peaceful people... but, as the leader of the Ethaenian's I can say we will not idly stand by and watch our people become slaves to this evil person." Shegeth Vaga argued.

"We will not be led by the Elvenii." Artos blurted out.

"Nor we." shouted Urok Vimear, who had long straight hair which touched his shoulders. A broad forehead, narrow eyes and a short but straight nose with wide flared nostrils. When he shouted, his open mouth showed off his yellowish shovel-shaped teeth.

"Who will sit at the head of the table? Not the Elvenii." Artos snapped.

"Or the Dwarves." Shouted the Formorian.

"Absolutely not the Mystics." Bellowed Hisstor, a man with short, well-groomed golden blonde hair. chiselled facial features, with prominent brow ridges and green eyes. And a well kempt beard which was studded with different coloured glass beads that were woven into it.

The meeting was getting a little out of hand with everyone trying to shout over the top of everyone else. Merlin stood up and shouted, "WAIT!" Everyone stopped bickering and looked at Merlin. "What if no one sat at the head of the table? What if we had a round table? No one can sit at the head of the table... as there won't be one."

"Explain more, please," Lord Salogel asked. He was curious about what Merlin meant.

"We have a round table with segments divided equally. Everyone has the same space. No one can sit at the head of the table because there isn't one. Everyone who sits around the table has an equal say, and a majority vote which everyone signs up to, will carry any voted decision."

"That might work." Artos stated whilst drawing deeply on his pipe.

"A very good idea, Merlin, one we should adopt." Lord Salogel said softly, as he slowly rose from his chair.

"Well, it worked for King Arthur." Merlin whispered to himself.

"If everyone agrees, I will have our carpenters make one immediately," Lord Salogel enquired, hoping this would stop the bickering and allow them to work out a plan together.

"There's no need to wait. If you grant me permission, I can solve the problem right now." Merlin said eagerly. He hoped the demonstration of magic might quell the bickering and lead to more constructive matters.

"Erm, yes, of course, what do you need?" Lord Salogel replied, not really knowing what was going to happen next.

Merlin stood up and moved his chair back a couple of feet. "If everyone can move back, I wouldn't want anyone to get hurt." Merlin pulled his wand from his sleeve and made horizontal circular movements with it. Everyone quickly moved back. Merlin whispered an incantation and immediately a large wooden table appeared in front of them. The table was indeed equally portioned with deep red segments, separated by gold-coloured lines.

Everyone looked very intrigued at the large round table occupying the space where the marble rectangular table once stood.

"Please, everybody, take a seat around the table, and as you sit, please tell the table your name." Merlin instructed.

Everyone looked at each other with puzzled expressions and wondered why they needed to inform the table of their names. Artos wondered who would be the first to do it, and to see what would happen.

"Come now, quickly, before the magic wears off." Merlin insisted. He pulled his seat closer to the table, sat down, and called out his name. His name appeared in gold writing around the bottom edge of what would be his segment of the table. Shamera followed suit and looked on in wonder as he saw his name written on his segment of the table. One by one, they all did the same, and, like Merlin's name, theirs appeared in gold too.

"As I don't know you all, can we introduce ourselves so we can all become better acquainted? I will start if this okay with everyone?" Shamera asked politely, and after looking around and seeing a few nods of consent, he continued, "I am Shamera, an Ethaenian, and I am Verazslo's apprentice."

"I am Merlin, from the court of King Arthur. I am a sorcerer, and I am teaching Shamera in the absence of Verazslo." Merlin recounted proudly.

"I have never heard of this King Arthur; from where do you hail?" Aglym enquired, as he looked suspiciously at Merlin. Years of persecution had made a lot of the Mystics very suspicious of anyone they did not know.

"I can vouch for him, and from where he hails, he is the one from Engla Land." Lord Salogel responded.

Aglym looked at Lord Salogel for a few seconds and nodded in agreement towards Lord Salogel, and continued, "I am Aglym, Mystic leader."

"You know who I am, Shamera; I am Lord Salogel of the Elvenii." Lord Salogel smiled.

"Urok Vimear, leader of the Formorians."

"Shegeth Vaga, I speak on behalf of the Ethaenians."

"Aglym, Mystic."

"Hisstor, leader of the Dragonborn."

As the meeting progressed, feelings were being hurt, patience was being tested, and blood was going to be spilled if it continued down this path. They littered the discussions with innuendos and defensive posturing. The feelings of mistrust and obvious fear flowed through each of them as the exchange of insults grew.

"The Mystics are cowards." Urok Vimear shouted.

"We were never strong to begin with; we dislike conflict and so remained neutral in the wars. And yet, we were still persecuted for our abilities, hunted down like wild animals. And you wonder why we distrust people. We are not cowards... this would be a big mistake to think we are." Aglym stated through gritted teeth in an effort to remain calm. His knuckles were turning white as he clenched his fists hard.

"Arguing amongst ourselves is pointless. The real enemy is out there, and she will stop at nothing to conquer us all. We need to stand together, and not start doing her job for her. We have enjoyed five hundred years of peace and may it continue for another five hundred years at least. But the time has come to put any mistrust behind us. We must unite to save our lands." Lord Salogel urged.

"Lord Salogel is right. The greatest mistake anyone can ever make are when you merely see things through the eyes of your own wants and desires. To better yourselves, you need to want to make life better for others and for your own people. You must see things from their perspective, too. You do not know me or what my history might be. I'll tell you stories about me later; I've made mistakes too, some big ones. I can get angry; I can feel vengeful and hatred. I'll show you my past darkness. But now is not the time, now is the time to work together." Merlin interjected.

Eventually they calmed down and all agreed they had to work together to defeat Niniane's invasion, as one army would be neither big enough nor strong enough to defeat her on their own. Lord Salogel produced a map and unrolled it onto the table. "From what we know, she is holed up down here," he said, pointing to a southern region. "She has formed a fortress in this valley. As you can see, mountains surround it, and this is the only way in and out of the valley."

"So, what do you propose we do?" Shegeth Vaga asked.

"We will have to draw her out somehow?" Lord Salogel replied.

"Well, she will be after Shamera and the crystal. She will need it to increase her powers. And she will eventually want to kill both Shamera and Verazslo, as they will be a threat to her." Merlin replied.

"So, you're saying Verazslo is already dead?" Shamera jumped in.

"I don't think so; she will use Verazslo to get to you, for now she needs him alive." Merlin reassured Shamera.

"We have to find him and rescue him." Shamera blurted.

"We have people out everywhere trying to locate his whereabouts. Once we know where he is we will rescue him." Lord Salogel said supportively.

"With three sorcerers fighting her, she will have no chance." Artos stated, as he chuckled as he looked around the table.

"Do not underestimate her; she is very cunning and will stop at nothing to get what she wants." Merlin said.

"Our fates appear to be woven together; the road ahead will be a deadly one. Verazslo has done much for the Dwarves in the past and, therefore, we are in his debt. You can count on our battle axes to protect you, Shamera. We will find Verazslo and free him from her evil clutches." Artos said proudly.

"We will offer our swords also, to protect these little warriors." laughed Urok Vimear.

"I'll show you little warriors; I'll cleave your skull in two." Said Aglym. Seeing this as a challenge, he immediately picked up his axe.

"Be calm. Be calm. What you lack in height, you positively make up for it in guts, my little friend. I meant no offence, but purely to lighten the situation. You dwarves are strange folk, no sense of humour." Urok Vimear smiled.

"Lighten it without insulting dwarves, and there is nothing wrong with our sense of humour." Aglym put down his axe and resumed his seat. The meeting went on until the early evening, while trying to come up with a strategy which would be agreeable with all parties.

"Come now, please. Let's all remain civil and respectful of each other." Lord Salogel pleaded before continuing, "From the information we have, she is hauled up and too well protected. She sends out scouting and raiding parties of Trolls and Orcs. We are intercepting them as best as we can, but we have limited numbers in the south. Based upon this information we estimate Niniane has raised a force comprising around ten thousand Orc's and Trolls, all infantries. A slave army of men of around three thousand. They split this into approximately one thousand cavalry and two thousand infantrymen. Therefore, we need all of you to help to form a formidable force against her. There is one major trading route that leads north until they reach Tres-Shellon. Here, the route splits and becomes three potential routes." Lord Salogel informed them.

"Hmm, we need to make her split her forces up and lure them out to meet them on our terms." Artos said, puffing thoughtfully on his pipe before continuing, "If we can lure some of them to Treonia they will have to pass through the Hellvelyn pass. We can attack them on three sides. They won't know what hit them."

Lord Salogel ran his finger over the map towards Treonia. He traced his finger backwards a short distance before tapping his finger three times on the map, raised his head and nodded in agreement before speaking.

"This witch does not know what Shamera looks like... does she?" Lord Salogel said, looking over at Shamera.

"What are you thinking?" Asked Aglym

"We need to split her forces up. So, what if they see Shamera in different places? Three Shamera's each with a staff. She will have to capture all of them to get the real one, in order to get her hands on the real staff. Hopefully, she will split her forces. She will know it is an obvious deception, and this is why I'm hoping she will send a small army after each of them. Hopefully, the lure of capturing the lad and the staff will be too strong for her to resist." Lord Salogel replied.

"Wow, this is a big risk, and what about the counterfeit Shamera's?" Asked a very concerned Shegeth Vaga.

"We can use Mystics. We need three capable of using projection. They can project themselves as Shamera. They can leave their fake staff in a place easily found; they can then disappear into the crowds. Hopefully, once they find the staff, they will take it back to Niniane to check its authenticity."

"You do not instil me with confidence, Lord Salogel. You seem to hope for a lot. I think you rely too much on luck." Urok said disdainfully.

"If anyone has a better idea, please bring it forward." Replied Lord Salogel.

No one said anything. Blank looks and shaking of heads is all they managed, no one had a better suggestion. Urok stared at the map for a short while, looked up at Lord Salogel and spoke. "This could work, if we can get them to come through the Hellvelyn pass. The granite cliffs would be to our right and they are a sheer face of granite; there would be no threats to our right flank. The craggy rocks to the left would be a great place for your Elvenii archers and the Dwarves to attack from and hit their right flank, and the Elvenii Cavalry can hit them head-on, and we Horsemen can hit them from the rear. They wouldn't stand a chance."

"How will you hit them from the rear? They would have to come straight passed you." Artos asked.

"There is a forest here. Look here, on the other side of the gorge, Hazelwood Forest. Our horses are well trained and silent. We can hide in there and once they have passed; we can quietly follow them into the gorge from a distance. Once we hear the battle has started, we will attack. Make sure your archers know who the enemy is when we ride in." Replied Urok.

"I propose we set up camp at Shu-Fray. It would be a march of approximately five days for us to get there. We could use this as our staging area before moving to Treonia, and hopefully luring them to us through the Hellvelyn pass. Does anyone have any objections to this?" Asked Lord Salogel.

"What about us?" Shamera questioned. "Surely Merlin and I can prove useful. And what about the Mystics?"

"I mean no disrespect, young one, but you are barely a novice and…"

"I have Merlin as my tutor. He is the greatest sorcerer of his realm." He said forcefully, interrupting Urok.

"There's always room for a couple of sorcerers, you may need the help of the Mystics, too. Do not be narrow-minded. Others around this table can play a major part in defeating this monster." Aglym retorted, as the arguing started again.

Merlin rose to his feet and held out his right hand. Merlin looked at his open hand, it burst into flames. This took everyone by surprise, and they stopped talking and stared at Merlin and his burning hand. Merlin looked around the table at everyone's astounded expressions. He smiled, blew on his hand, and extinguished the flames.

"Now that I have your attention, we must utilise all our strengths. You may, in time, defeat her armies, but you will not defeat her with your armies. She is powerful, and only magic can defeat her. The Mystics have the power of foresight, yes?"

"Only some of us." Aglym said apologetically.

"No matter, you will still prove invaluable, and as far as Shamera is concerned, he may be a novice, but I would not want to get on the wrong side of him. His powers grow quickly. If we successfully cut off the head of the snake, the body will die." Merlin looked around the table as everyone looked at each other.

"You are absolutely correct; we will all have parts to play. The head of the snake… I presume you mean Niniane? How do you propose to take the head off that particular snake?" Artos asked politely.

"I do not yet know, but it will take a lot of cunning. I find this hard to say but we may have to use Shamera and his staff as bait to draw her out." Merlin replied.

Urok shook his head from side to side. "Decisive action is what's needed. Our armies will crush her and drive her from our shores."

"Urok, have you not been listening? We need to stop gesturing our positions and work closer with each other and defeat this monster once and for all." Artos stated as he held his pipe by its bowl and pointed its stem towards Urok.

"How long will it take for the rest of you to gather your horsemen and rally at Shu-Fray?" Lord Salogel interjected.

"We can meet you there on the seventh day." Urok replied confidently.

"We still have to find where Verazslo is being held captive. We need to rescue him." Said Shamera.

"Yes, of course, we have not forgotten about Verazslo. I am confident we will soon have news of his whereabouts. I have dispatched riders searching, asking questions. We'll find him." Lord Salogel replied reassuringly.

A loud knock at the door interrupted the proceedings.

"Enter." Shouted Lord Salogel.

A messenger entered the room, amazed to see a large round table in the middle of the room he stood there staring at for a couple of seconds before Lord Salogel asked, "What can we do for you?"

"Erm… sorry sir, can I have a private word with you on a matter most urgent?"

Lord Salogel stood up from the table and approached the messenger. The messenger took a rolled-up scroll from his bag and showed it to Lord Salogel; who nodded and thanked the messenger. The messenger left the room. Lord Salogel stood there looking at the scroll for a couple of moments before slowly making his way back to the table.

"We have found Verazslo's location. He is being held in a fortified building in Eldermar."

"So, she has moved from the south." Aglym said as he took a long draw on his pipe.

"Great!" Exclaimed Shamera. "When do we rescue him?" he continued.

"It's not that simple. We can't just walk up to the place and ask for him back." Lord Salogel replied. His saddened face said it all.

"What's wrong? He's alright, isn't he?" Shamera questioned.

"He's alive, but apparently very weak." Lord Salogel answered.

"So, let's go get him. Your army with Merlin and me should be more than enough." Shamera said anxiously.

"As I said, it's not going to be simple. He will be heavily guarded. It's obviously a trap, with Verazslo as the bait. She's hoping you will try to rescue him. She will have then captured you both. She cannot have your staff, or the crystal… or else we are all lost. Her powers would be too great."

Merlin looked over at Shamera pacing up and down. His face looked pained as a thousand thoughts and ideas ran through his head.

"What if one person was to sneak in to rescue Verazslo?" Merlin asked.

"What are you saying?" Lord Salogel replied inquisitively.

"They will expect an army and Shamera to rescue him. I will go with two of your men who can escort me to this place. I can sneak in there and rescue him. I can transport us both out of the building, and with an appropriate diversion, we can make good our escape." Merlin proposed.

"What if they capture you?" Lord Salogel asked.

"If there is any danger of me being captured, I will transport myself out, and look for another way to rescue Verazslo."

The room fell silent as Lord Salogel thought about Merlin's plan.

"Are you sure you can do this?" Lord Salogel asked, whilst rubbing his chin with his thumb and forefinger.

"I cannot say it will work for certain, but it's better than a full-on assault where many will die."

"I cannot ask you to do this Merlin, it is a very perilous undertaking."

"This is why I am volunteering. I think it stands a good chance, as they will not be expecting me."

Lord Salogel thought hard as he strained his eyes over the map.

"This can work to our advantage... look, Shu-fray is here, Eldermar is there and Treonia is there. If we let slip, we intend to attack Eldermar from Treonia. We can set our trap in the canyon as planned. Hopefully, they won't expect an ambush because they'll think we will centre our attention towards attacking Eldermar. It will also divert their eyes away from Merlin's sneaky rescue, as they may also put a defensive placement on their side of the river. We know she has spies operating in the area, so an overheard drunken conversation between a couple of soldiers should easily make its way back to her ears." Lord Salogel exhaled loudly, allowed himself a large smile as he looked around the table.

"That's all well and good, but how do we get to the snake and lop off its head?" Artos asked, whilst taking an extra-large draw on his pipe.

"One thing at a time, my friend, let's get our Verazslo back. It will really irritate Niniane. Hopefully, she will make a mistake and we can take advantage of it." Lord Salogel replied.

"How can we help?" Aglym asked.

"Do you still practice projection?" Artos asked inquisitively.

"Projection, we have not practiced this in my lifetime. There may be a few who still can."

"What is Projection?" Asked Shamera.

"Physical reality exists of time, space, and matter. We project our combined thoughts outward into the atmosphere, creating an experience and a simulation of the physical world. Essentially, we create and transform our thoughts into a fake reality, an illusion. We used this technique to evade those who hunted us." Aglym explained.

"I might be able to use you. It might come in handy if we can find a couple of your people still able to do this." Merlin said, as he lowered his head, thinking. His fingers tapped speedily on the table.

"Yes, it could come in very handy. How long can it be maintained for?" Lord Salogel asked.

"I don't think it was long, maybe a minute or two. Long enough to evade the hunters and make good an escape. I know the more who joined in the projection, the better the illusion."

"You will obviously need my help." Said a female voice from near the door.

Everyone turned to see who spoke. There was no one there.

"Who spoke? Show yourself." commanded Lord Salogel.

To their amazement, an old woman appeared, she was standing near the door. A hooded cloak hid her face.

"Who are you? And what's more… how did you get past my guards and gain entry here?" Lord Salogel asked abruptly.

"I see you made it here safely, Shamera." The old lady said as she made her way towards the table.

"Elgrin… is that you?" Shamera asked curiously.

The old lady removed her hood. "Yes Shamera, it is me."

"Another Mystic." Cried Urok.

"It's okay everyone, I know this lady. She saved me when I became lost in Tussocks Bog."

"I have been here for a while, yet none of you noticed me. I am Elgrin, a Mystic seer."

Aglym slowly rose to his feet and walked over to her. "I thought you were…"

"Where what?" she replied.

"Dead?" he said in a whisper.
"I did not want my powers to endanger the rest of you, so I went to live in solitude. One other knew where I lived until my path crossed with Shamera's. I knew I had to make my way here today, as you will need my help if you are to rescue this Verazslo."
"Elgrin, Aglym, we need to get together after this meeting. We can hopefully help each other. If you're willing, you can accompany me to rescue Verazslo, and your projection ability will come in very handy." Merlin, said with a grin.
"We would be honoured to assist you in rescuing Verazslo." Replied Elgrin.
"I will arrange for a couple of my soldiers to drunkenly brag about our attack on Eldermar from Treonia. Shamera will travel south with an army of my best soldiers and the Dwarves. Urok and the Horsemen will meet us there on the seventh day along with the Dragonborn. Merlin, Aglym and two soldiers will travel to Eldermar and hopefully rescue Verazslo. Are we all agreed?" Asked Salogel.
"Lord Salogel, who will be leading your men?" Asked Merlin.
"Derrell, an excellent soldier. Why do you ask?"
"I need to see and speak with him, I have something for him."
"I have just sent for him, I need to go over some things with him. He should not be long. Ah, here he is. Derrell, Merlin would like a word with you, he has something for you. When you have finished with Merlin I need to go over some details with you."
Derrell gave a court bow to Lord Salogel, "What do you want see me about?"
"Give me you hand." Instructed Merlin as he held out his.
Derrell looked puzzled but offered his hand to Merlin. Merlin held his hand and looked deep into Derrell's eyes, "I sense you are pure of heart, a loyal and worthy subject of Lord Salogel's."
"I am a Elvenii, we live by such a code. What is your interest?" Derrell appeared puzzled.

"You will be leading your army, I want you to have this." Said Merlin as he revealed Excalibur.

"I cannot accept this, it is too precious." Derrell was taken aback by Merlin's generosity.

"You will be in more in need of it than I. If you promise to return it to me when you have no further need of it, it is yours. This inscription reads Take me up, and on the other side it says, Cast me away. You are only to take it up against your enemies. When they have been defeated you cast it away by returning it to me."

"If you believe I should the one to wield such a magnificent weapon, then I will not protest but thank you for your trust" Derrell stepped forward and held out his hand once more.

"Be warned, this sword can only be used for good, there are grave consequences for anyone using it for any other reason." Said Merlin holding Derrell's gaze.

"You have my word, Merlin. It shall be returned to you."

"I give you this sword, Excalibur, to uphold truth and justice." said Merlin as he presented it to Derrell.

Chapter 14

They were two days into the trek to Treonia. The sun was blazing in the featureless blue sky, as the three hundred troops marched in the midday heat. The ground was baked hard and cracked, dry crumbling sandstone rocks littered the landscape. The wind whistled as a sudden gust of wind whipped up hot the dirt. Shamera got a mouthful of dust, he took hold of his canteen and drank a mouthful of warm water.

He watched as a dust devil swirled to the left of the column. The heat appeared to shimmer in the distance distorting the features of the land. The Elvenii soldiers moved as one well-trained cohesive unit as they marched through the heat. The cavalry guarded the flanks with proud heads held high as their heavily armoured horses glinted in the rays of the sun, their armour clinking and clanking as they walked. The ground was parched and hard underfoot. Shamera wondered how the Elvenii coped under their gleaming armour; he was finding it hot and uncomfortable in his normal clothes.

From out of the shimmering distortion, there was an attack. It was an ambush. Hundreds of men and Orcs came running forward from a cleverly concealed trench hidden behind some boulders. The enemy were upon them quickly, shouting and screaming in a wild frenzy. The enemies' screams were incoherent yet blood curdling.

"Shield wall!" Derrell shouted with urgency. Immediately the Elvenii soldiers quickly spread out and formed a close defensive wall with their shields.

"Long Spears!" The Elvenii soldiers quickly stood behind the shield wall, their long spears held out in front of the shields to protect them from the charge. There was no time for the Elvenii archers to react and rain down their arrows of death on the advancing enemy; the front line was quickly engaged in battle. By sheer numbers, the enemy broke through the front line. The battle had begun in earnest. Shamera's stomach suddenly sank with fear; his heart was pounding hard in his chest; the confusion of the battle temporarily froze his thoughts.

Shamera looked around as he made his way to the left of the Elvenii army, trying hard not to get trampled on in the melee which was raging all around him. An Orc was making its way towards him, its sword held high, ready to strike. Shamera looked on in sheer panic as fear gripped his heart and rooted him to the spot. Abruptly the Orc stopped in its tracks, a look of surprise and pain washed over its face. It looked down at its chest. Six inches of an Elvenii sword was protruding outwards and dripping with green Orc blood. The sword was withdrawn, and the Orc fell face down, motionless.

"Get yourself to safety over there," an Elvenii soldier said as he pointed to some long grass. Shamera tried to focus. This was his first real battle and although scared witless, he knew he had to be involved somehow.

A strong breeze blew across the battlefield and dust choked the air, making fighting more difficult. The battlefield was a cloud of dust and dirt, kicked up from the ground, which had baked under a persistent sun. It was a hot summer's day, and their highly polished Elvenii armour was light, yet very strong. It gave them good protection from the blows of the enemy's clubs and swords. The sun, like their adversary was relentless, sweat ran down from their foreheads, which stung their eyes like a thousand small sharp needles piercing into them.

Shamera anxiously looked all around; all he could see was the anarchy of the melee. Defenders and attackers, both fighting for survival, standing firm amidst a sea of organised chaos and brutal violence. Swords and spears clashing and clanking all around him, ear-piercing screams as sharp steel met and ripped through flesh. He spotted another Orc rushing towards him; the creature was huge and grotesque with its weapon held, ready to strike. Its wrinkled face stared straight at him; its expression was one of pure hatred which conveyed the evil within its soulless black eyes. Shamera held out his hands instinctively, pulsing from his fingertips was an energy ball, a bright light of flickering and swirling colours of amber and gold. He held it carefully between his hands, before sending it flying at the Orc; it struck the Orc clean in the chest; the force of the energy ball sent the beast sprawling backwards across the battlefield.

The sound of the cries from the wounded and dying was hard to bear. Deafening cries and screams made the blood course strongly through his veins. The Elvenii pressed forward as best they could; pain from wounds made barely noticeable by the adrenaline coursing through their bodies. Shamera tried to find a vantage point, somewhere higher, somewhere from which he could try to help win this skirmish. The ground was slippery with the spilled blood from vanquished foe and friends alike. Shamera noticed a high grassy mound; he made his way towards it, trying to keep his feet steady on the slimy ground of congealing blood. With his staff in his right hand, he was using it to swipe the enemy out of his way and into the deadly swords of the Elvenii; he dodged passed flailing blades which narrowly missed him, awkwardly he maneuvered himself over dead bodies and hacked off body parts until he made it to the mound. He looked around at the battle in full swing; he had never witnessed such carnage; it was now all too real, and he was in the thick of it. Shamera knew he could not let fear overcome him. He held his staff under his left arm and sent more energy balls flying into the advancing enemy's lines. Picking off as many of the enemy as he could, he fired his energy balls, sending man and Orcs reeling. An enemy spear came screaming down and pierced the ground in front of him. *'Time to move,'* he thought to himself as he retreated from the mound. He positioned himself to the side of battle and again fired energy balls into the enemy. Blood-stained swords danced with deadly accuracy as the Elvenii cut a sway through the enemy's line. Their barely armoured bodies were no match for this well-trained army.

"They're retreating," a loud cry came from the front.

Obscure cries of 'Forward' and 'After them' came from the lifted voices of the Dwarves. The screams from injured men and beasts howled terrifyingly across the body strewn battlefield. A loud horn sounded the regroup, everyone stopped chasing the enemy and fell back to form a defensive line in case they were charged upon again. This time the archers stood ready; their well-trained eyes scanning the terrain for any signs of another attack. The unpleasant smell from the spilled blood and entrails contaminated the air. The iron and coppery tang of blood left a disgusting metallic taste at the back of his throat. He made his way towards Derrell who stood amidst a sea of blood-stained ground. The encounter had barely lasted about twenty minutes, yet bodies of the enemy numbered in the hundreds, luckily the numbers of dead amongst the well-trained army of the Elvenii and Dwarves numbered only fifty-two.

"Is that it? Is it over?" Shamera questioned anxiously and trying hard not to vomit.

"We need to be alert, now we know they are here. They could attack again at any moment, and we do not know their true strength in number."

Shamera looked all about him; shocked by the carnage, he saw the soldiers tending the wounded and forming burial parties. Death hawks soared and circle above them eagerly awaiting a hearty meal.

"How do you do this? Are you not overcome with fear?" Shamera asked.

"On the battleground, your heart and thoughts can become gripped with fear. If that happens, you become an ineffective fighter. You need to learn to use fear to your advantage. The biggest battle is inside of us. This is where fear is transformed into a friend from an adversary. Accept the fear; do not give in to it, let it heighten your senses, and use it to your advantage," Derrell calmly glanced around and looked back at Shamera before continuing. "This field has seen five hundred years of peace and now we lay to rest the cold bodies of our friends. The enemy, Orc, and Troll alike have no empathy, no remorse; they kill on command of the evil sorceress. The men she has bewitched and forced to do her bidding. I do not think the men really want to; she is truly evil to use people like this." Derrell tried to explain as he observed the aftermath.

As Shamera looked across the battlefield, he saw Elvenii soldiers grasping their bloody wounds and wrapping bandages around them, whilst others silently slipped away beyond the vale. Their souls now to walk amongst their ancestors.

"Bury our heroes well; we don't want those scavengers feeding on them," Derrell shouted whilst pointing skywards at the death hawks.

"What about the enemy's corpses?" asked a soldier.

"Stack them in piles... and fire them," Derrell said as he turned away and walked over to the archers.

As Derrell approached, the archer looked at him and saluted by placing his right clenched fist across his chest.

"What do you see?" Derrell enquired of him.

"Nothing, sir. There is no movement out there. They are probably waiting to ambush us again in those hills."

"My thoughts exactly," Derrell stated as he pulled out his map. "If we head east, we can reach Thashona by nightfall, and we can continue the rest of the way by river raft."

Derrell walked back to Shamera and asked if there was some magic he knew to help the wounded. "Sorry Derrell, I wish I could help them. Merlin would be able to, I'm sure, if he were here."

"Okay, we rest here for a while until the clearing up has been completed. Make sure everyone has had enough water and make sure their canteens are full for the rest of the journey. The badly wounded can ride on the wagons."

Shamera signalled for the supply wagon to be brought forward and carried out Derrell's request. Whilst helping with the wounded, Shamera's thoughts once again turned to the enemy. How many had fallen this day? How many remained and could fight in the next battle? At last, it was time to start on the journey to Thashona. Derrell climbed up onto the wagon. He slowly removed his helmet as he looked over the newly dug graves. He stood there quietly for a few moments in silent contemplation, and shouted, "Turn to face our fallen," he raised his head up high and recited,

I am proud of the way you stand and fight,
Protecting this land by day and by night,
My Elvenii warriors, who bravely stood fast,
Sleep now in restful peace, with ancestor's past,
  Your attitude to life, and the Elvenii way,
  Your love and your valour will fill my days.
  Now I must be away with a heavy heart,
  Remembering you always, whilst we are apart.

The army clenched their right fists and beat them seven times upon their chests. This was their way to honour their fallen comrades. Derrell shouted for the enemy pyres to be lit.

"At least their ashes will help fertilise the land, something good from something bad. I want three riders to go ahead of us and make sure the enemy is not waiting for us again. You will report back every couple of hours." Derrell requested.

They were soon on their way again, this time more cautiously. It was early evening when finally, they made it to Thashona and set up camp for the night. The next morning, everyone was up early and loaded everything on the rafts and several small boats that they had acquired. There were going to be at least three sections of white water to traverse. They weren't dangerous sections, but tricky, nonetheless. They should be able to navigate them successfully, with a bit of luck.

Shamera had been rafting with his father, but nothing like this. He looked in amazement as he saw the flotilla of rafts and small boats winding their way quietly down the river.

No one made a sound, as they did not want to draw any unnecessary attention to themselves. The cool air had a pleasing freshness about it, pleasantly scented with the plants and trees growing along the banks. Along the river, large dragonflies danced wildly in the sun, their translucent wings sparkling as the sunlight reflected off them. With his senses being heightened after the last ambush, every noise seemed to be louder, the birds, animals, even the sound of the river all seemed to want to give their position away.

The archers had positioned themselves on every third raft and were standing back-to-back so they could help protect the convoy by observing both banks. They had been travelling for a few hours before they reached the first section of rapids.

"Hold on, this is going to be a little bumpy." Someone shouted from the raft in front.

Shamera held onto a rope, which was holding down some of the cargo. The raft entered the rapids. They were not dangerous but were still strong enough to overturn a raft, if not careful. The soldiers carefully steered the raft through the rapids trying to avoid the rocks. Water splashed up and hit Shamera in the face. The water felt icy; he did not fancy falling in the river so he held on even tighter.

The noise of the water became even louder as the raft bounced around in the turbulent white water. Shamera looked ahead; it looked like the river was boiling. Sunlit mist rose from the river as the water crashed energetically against the rocks. It had been two or three minutes but felt much longer as the raft traversed the rapids. He was clinging on tightly and hoping not to fall off the raft into the river.

Eventually, everyone came out of the rapids unharmed; all rafts and boats resumed a steady course down the river once more. For a day and a half, they travelled down the river, stopping long enough to eat and to exercise the horses. Everyone was on the lookout for an ambush, but luckily, none came.

"We've arrived!" He heard a voice call out. All the rafts and boats headed towards the right riverbank. Efficiently and quickly, everything was unloaded, and they were soon on their way again. It did not take them long to get to the staging area. Some of the Formorian Horsemen, and the Dragonborn were already there waiting for them. Derrell ordered everyone to make camp. He saw Urok Vimear sitting astride his horse and went over to investigate why he was here.

"Urok, I thought you were going to be positioned in the Hazelwood Forest."

"Yes, my men are there, positioned in the forest, they will hide themselves effectively. They are all well trained, they will attack when the battle commences."

"How many of you are there?"

"Three hundred, all ready to battle, and about one hundred of us here. I see you ran into a little trouble." Urok said as he spotted the wounded.

"Yes, we were ambushed a couple of days ago by a small force of men and Orcs. They were waiting for us, somehow, they found out our route. It was a very well-prepared ambush."

"It might have been an advance raiding party who spotted you and set up the ambush."

"Perhaps. But we soon sent them on their way with a very bloody nose. Strangely, we ran into nothing else. Maybe they were an advance raiding party." Said Derrell, looking around him at this impressive-looking ambush of his own.

"I have sent scouts through the pass; they have reported nothing yet." Urok said, slightly disappointed.

"Hopefully, last night my men should have let slip our plan to attack Eldermar tomorrow night with an army of three hundred soldiers. If all goes to plan, we can expect them to come through the pass sometime tomorrow and try to catch us off-guard and attack us from the rear. And, when we do not show up at Eldermar, Niniane will hopefully think they have killed us all, leaving Merlin and the Mystics free to rescue Verazslo."

A Formorian out-rider came racing out of the canyon, Urok spotted him, kicked into his horses' flanks, and rode to meet him. Derrell watched as they talked for a while before Urok came riding back and dismounted.

"My rider said there is a large contingent of Troll and Orc heading this way, about three thousand strong. They are all on foot and should be here by mid-morning tomorrow."

"Three to one in their favour. This will be an interesting battle." Derrell said smiling.

"What is there to smile about?"

"We have the element of surprise. They are all foot soldiers. We have cavalry and archers. What is there not to smile about?"

"The first strike has to be a good one. Using the men I have here, we can ride to meet them in the canyon. We will walk our horses towards them and send arrow after arrow into them. When they get close enough, we will canter away, letting them chase us until we reach your archers. Your archers need to hit them again, hard and fast."

"You sound a little worried Urok, they are only Orc and Troll. Big hard fighters, yes, but little brain and no battle tactics. Well, we have a few hours to prepare. We should eat and rest the men." Suggested Derrell.

Large fires illuminated the camp. Enormous cooking pots of food bubbled away next to them, filling the evening air with the aroma of Elvenii stew. The men sat around the fires eating, drinking, and sharpening their weapons, whilst also bragging about how many of the enemy they would kill in the inevitable battle. This was more of a way of boosting their morale, than just a boastful blood lust. Once their bellies were full and weapons taken care of, they tried to get as much sleep as they could. They would have to be up early in the morning to set their trap. Guards patrolled the outer perimeter of the camp, making sure their sleeping friends were safe to do so.

For some of them, morning came far too early. An Elvenii soldier blew his trumpet to signal time to rise and prepare for battle.

Derrell eventually had all the men gather around. Both he and Urok stood on the back of a wagon and faced the troops. Derrell took a moment as he looked around at the assembled men.

"I see fear amongst some of you. On your faces. In your eyes. Yes, the enemy will outnumber us, but this time when we go into battle, we do not fight amongst ourselves. In this battle we stand firm together, shoulder to shoulder, Dwarves, Formorian, Dragonborn and Elvenii standing firm, together. This day will be our day. Know that victory will be ours. Shamera, Hisstor, come, stand up here with me, you too Artos my Dwarvian friend," They scrambled up onto the back of the wagon and faced the assembled men, Derrell looked at them and smiled proudly, then continued his speech, "Together we fight as friends, together we will rid this land of tyranny and together we will rebuild the damage inflicted upon our lands. We will not let this enemy destroy our homelands, we will not become slaves to this evil witch, and we will not forsake our friends and allies. while we fight this battle, hopefully our sorcerer Verazslo is being rescued, this will give us a great advantage in the coming days. We have Shamera and Merlin too. Archers, I know of your skill with a bow. We may also need your skill with swords, too. Infantry, your fight will be the most demanding, when you feel you are tiring you will fall back to the rear and rest while those at the rear will advance and rotate forward to relieve you, this way we can keep fresh troops at the head of the battle. You all know what to do… so to your positions, everyone." Cries of victory and the waving of swords spread through the gathered crowd.

"Formorians… mount up and follow me. We go to meet them first. Let's show everyone how we shower the enemy with death." Urok called out.

"Battle axes ready, my friends. No one gets past us Dwarves this day." Artos shouted, waving his battle-axe above his head.

"Dragonborn, let us show them why we are called the Dragonborn, let our swords run with the enemies' blood." Hisstor shouted.

"And I will be… well… somewhere, hopefully doing something." Shamera said unconvincingly.

Derrell shook his head and smiled at Shamera.

"Shamera, I want you with my archers. They can look after you in the rocks, and from there you can see what's happening and help us in any way you can. We are going to need it." Derrell said reassuringly.

Shamera nodded. He remembered the ambush on his way here, and it instilled fear in his heart once again. His breathing became rapid, his mouth was as dry as the earth they stood upon. This was going to be a much bigger battle. He nervously looked around for the leader of the archers.

"Shamera, remember what I said, the biggest battle we face on the battlefield is the one which is inside of us. Accept your fear and use it to your advantage. Now go, take your place with the archers." Instructed Derrell.

Urok and the Horsemen galloped off into the canyon to meet the enemy head on. Urok noticed a cloud of dust rising upwards in the distance. It was not long before they saw a hoard of Orcs in the advancing towards them. The horsemen stopped and formed three lines across the canyon. Their bows at the ready, they sauntered their horses forward to meet the oncoming foe.

The enemy was a lot closer and were coming into the range of their arrows. The horsemen continued slowly advancing. Urok gave the order to rapidly fire their arrows into the enemy's ranks. The horsemen continued slowly progressing and firing their arrows into the advancing Orcs. The twang of bowstrings and the whoosh of arrows filled the air, as they flew straight and true with deadly, and devastating accuracy. In that first volley about eighty Orcs fell to the ground, those behind not stopping; trampled over the fallen. If the arrows had not killed them, they certainly died underfoot of their so-called comrades.

The Orcs charged towards them, screaming and grunting, their weapons flailing about their heads, ready to strike.

"One more attack the we lead them into the ambush." shouted Urok. The horsemen let them get close enough before turning and riding away to a safer distance, stopped; and turned to face the enemy again. Again, rapidly and with great accuracy, their arrows flew into the oncoming ranks of Orcs and Trolls. Once again, they let them get close enough before turning and riding away, drawing them closer into the trap.

With their arrows nocked, the Elvenii archers stood ready behind the rocks on the hillside, waiting for the command to 'loose' their deadly arrows.

The Elvenii watched as the horsemen sped past. The enemy was now in range of their arrows. "LOOSE!" came the command. Bow strings twanged as arrows fizzed through the air before raining down on the advancing enemy. Elvenii arrows screamed down from the slopes of the canyon like a vast black cloud. Volley after volley rained down on the enemy. Some of the Orcs scrambled up the rocks towards the archers. The Dwarves came out of hiding, and, with battle axes and swords drawn, attacked the Orcs. This provided excellent protection for the archers who were still raining arrows down into the canyon. The archers stopped volleying as the Elvenii and Dragonborn infantry moved forward, it was time for them to engage the enemy.

Shamera's mind was as much a battlefield as the melee he was watching. He swallowed his fear, saying to himself, Fear is natural and will keep me alive.

He stood up from the cover of the rocks and fired his energy balls down into the enemy's ranks, sending Orcs and trolls sprawling onto the canyon floor disrupting their attack. Watching the battle unfolding below, his fear turned to anger. Anger at having to fight in another battle when he should be with Elithrin and learning his craft as an apprentice. He fired his energy balls as fast as he could make them, taking his anger out on the Orcs and Trolls. He wished he could do more, he did not want to let his comrades down, he tried his best and hoped it was enough.

The enemy were, however, unrelenting, picking themselves up and advancing once again. *Derrell* was a true warrior, fighting with intelligence, and strength. Unlike the Orc enemy, who fought with strength and very little intelligence. A sword fight is supposed to have rules, a moral code, and have a perception of fair play. Not to the Orcs, they just tried to bulldoze their way forward. They had little in the way of technique, they were uncoordinated as they swung their clubs and swords wildly. Yet, it was deadly all the same. With the chaos of battle disguising any sense of victory for them, the Orcs and Trolls battled head-on relentlessly, in the belief they'd be the ones who would be victorious this day. The Elvenii and Dragonborn infantry were better skilled, but the sheer numbers of the Orcs and their relentless attacking made victory harder to attain.

The canyon was littered with death and destruction, both dead and wounded fighters lay scattered across the floor of the canyon. The battle was underway when the Formorian horsemen struck the enemy from the rear. The canyon, which merely ten minutes ago was quiet and carried but a gentle breeze through it, was loud and thunderous, with the sounds of combat. Metal clanking against metal, heavy clubs meeting armour and flesh, arrows fizzing through the air. Loud screams as sharp steel once again ripped through flesh and bone. The sound and carnage should have been enough to destroy the courage within the enemy, but onwards they persisted.

The Orcs were now fighting on three fronts, but they still battled on strongly. Some of the Dragonborn and Elvenii infantry succumbed to the exhaustion of battle and could no longer defend themselves effectively. They were ordered to the rear to rest, to be replaced by the fresher Dragonborn and Elvenii infantry, who were soon engaged in the battle. Derrell wielded Excalibur with grace. The sword cut a sway through everything in its path. The air was again thick with the iron and coppery tang of spilled blood.

Shamera from his vantage point amongst the rocks, was also becoming weary from the battle. Using magic was taking its toll on him. His energy balls were getting weaker and much less effective. He had to stop and rest for a short while. He looked down towards the carnage, there was a call for the infantry to fall back. As the infantry withdrew, Shamera had an idea. He raised his staff and banged it hard on the rocks in front of him. He pushed the staff forwards with a short, sharp movement towards the sheer granite cliffs. A purple beam of light shone from the staff's jewel and exploded in a bright, blinding light as it hit the granite. The cliffs rumbled and shook, the overhanging rocks crumbled and fell into the canyon, narrowing it by about half. The remaining Orcs had to funnel through the narrowing, making the archers' task easier to pick them off. Now it was the turn of the cavalry to attack. Long, straight swords and lances thrust and stabbed as they cut through the remaining Orcs. The Formorian Horsemen at the front of the attack once again engaged, shooting arrows rapidly from horseback, with deadly accuracy.

With the rush of victory coursing through their bodies, the Elvenii, Dragonborn and Formorian pushed on even harder. The archers picked off individual targets as they presented. The Formorians from the rear picked off those who tried to escape back the way they came. Shamera looked over at Derrell as he brandished Excalibur with expert precision, it cleaved through flesh with devastating efficiency. Shamera watched as Derrell held the sword high, and it glinted in the sun. He brought the sword down on an Orc, Excalibur cleaved through the side of its neck and all the way down to its opposite waist. Derrell thought the sword may have a mind of its own as it parried sword and spear thrusts with ease. He has never wielded such a sword; and to be so light that it did not easily tire him.

It was not long before all the Orcs and Trolls were dead or lay dying. The battle was over, a loud victorious cheer echoed through the canyon.

Four hundred and twenty-six Dragonborn, Formorian, Dwarves and Elvenii lay dead or wounded. The battlefield was now a graveyard. The battle over, the dead lay on the blood-soaked ground. Their souls departed to now walk amongst their ancestors.

Those who could, helped the wounded back to camp. It had been a hard battle against the odds, and the cost of victory was high. Derrell ordered a burial detail for the fallen heroes. Shamera helped the best way he could by using his magic to form a large burial pit. The dead were carefully and reverently placed in the grave along with their weapons. Shamera waved his wand, and covered them the over. Respectfully, some fighters gathered around to pay their respects. Urok stepped forward.

"Brothers, for this is what we are today. As I look around, my heart is heavy and saddened at our losses. Yet, it is happy that we have stood firm and fought side by side and shoulder to shoulder. This day we put away any mistrust we may have had. Today we fought as one. We all have a new Memorial day, and we should remember this day and bury all grievances we once may have had, along with these brave warriors."

Derrell stepped forward and stood next to Urok.

"Those were good words, my friend Urok. A lot of brave men died this day. If I may, The Elvenii have a traditional poem we say when we bury our fallen comrades. We have recited it the same way for hundreds of years. If you will all permit me, I think on this occasion I should amend it slightly so I can recite it for ALL of those who gave their lives this day." Derrell asked politely.

Everyone fell silent. Some nodded their heads slightly in agreement with Derrell's request. He looked around as everyone reverently bowed their heads. Derrell stood erect, clenched his right fist, and placed it over his heart.

We are proud of the way you all stood to fight,
Protecting this land by day and by night,
You band of warriors, who bravely stood fast.
Sleep now in restful peace, with your ancestor's past.
Your bravery and valour, in protecting each other,
Each one a friend, a father, son, or a brother.
Now we now must be away with heavy a heart.
We'll all be remembering you, whilst we are apart.

Derrell hit his fist upon his chest seven times, Artos stood forward.

"I think you have both said everything which needs to be said. However, I will add, we Khul Dwarvian work hard, play hard and drink hard… we've also proved we fight hard too. Tonight, we celebrate their bravery. We should not mourn their death… but celebrate their lives."

It was mid-afternoon, and everyone made their way back to the camp. There was a very sombre atmosphere around the camp. The wounded were being cared for. Urok had sent riders through the canyon to make sure nothing else was coming through to surprise them. He had ordered riders to remain on the far side of the canyon until it was time to leave, it would be their responsibility to prevent, a sneak attack. Urok, Derrell, Shamera and Artos sat around the fire. Artos pulled out his pipe and lit it.

"We will stay camped here tonight and hopefully wait to hear if Merlin and the others have been successful." Derrell said with anticipation.

"I could take a couple of my men and sneak towards the river and observe for a while." said Artos.

"What if you are spotted or even caught? You know they are expecting an attack and will be ready and watching carefully." said Urok.

"We can sneak right under your nose and steal your breath, and you would not know we were there." Artos replied with a sense of pride in his voice.

"Well, you are small enough." laughed Urok. He held both hands palms forward as if to apologise. Artos stared straight at him, his pipe firmly fixed between his lips. He stared at him for a few seconds before he burst out laughing. "Aye, we undoubtedly are."

The three of them sat and laughed.

They turned to Shamera to find he was fast asleep, curled up by the fire.

"Our sleeping hero. Okay, when it becomes dark, take a couple of your men. See what you can find out." Urok said, still smiling.

Later in the night, Artos and two other Dwarvian set out towards Eldermar. The rest of the camp settled down for the night. Guards once again patrolled the perimeter of the camp, and the horsemen were still watching the far side of the canyon. All was quiet under the night sky; it had been about three hours when one guard called out an alarm.

"Who's out there? Show yourself!" Shouted the guard, holding his flaming torch as high as he could, trying to illuminate as much of the darkness as he could. It was Artos who reached the camp first and reported the news.

"Merlin and Elgrin are back with Verazslo. He needs help, quickly now." Artos shouted.

"Where are they?" asked the guard.

"They are a short way behind me." Artos said, pointing back to the way he had come from.

Two Formorian Horseman quickly mounted a couple of saddleless horses and, holding their manes, set off quickly in the direction Artos was pointing. They quickly returned with Verazslo laying across the horse. While Merlin rode behind the other rider. Shamera ran to meet them. He stopped dead in his tracks.

"What's up with him, is he…?" Shamera asked fearfully.

"He's alive, but in need of help. He does not look good." the Horseman replied.

"What happened to him, Merlin?" Derrell asked.

"It looks like she has tortured him, possibly to find out more about Shamera." replied Merlin.

"Where are the Mystics?" Shamera asked.

"They are back there, waiting to mislead anyone following us, in case they spotted us; those Mystics had them running around in circles. I would not have got Verazslo out without their help. I have done everything I can for him. I even gave him some of my elixir. It settled him down, but I fear the worst."

"I will take some of my men and make sure the Mystics are alright and see no one is following behind." Urok said as he whistled for his horse to come to him. He pointed to four of his riders to follow him.

"We need to get him back to Selvenora and to Lord Salogel. He will know what to do." said Derrell with a sense of urgency.

"Which is the quickest route?" Urok asked.

"Overland, we cannot go back to the river. We will all go back to Selvenora together if this sits well with you all? In case we run into any trouble, I would very much like you all fighting by my side."

"Lead the way, friend. You have our battle axes and our hearts." Artos said decisively.

"Thank you, we will set off at first light, we will travel as fast as we can, pray the Gods are still in our favour." Derrell replied.

"How did things go here?" Merlin enquired.

"Not well. Not well at all. We defeated around three thousand Orcs and Trolls, but we lost about forty percent of our combined brave warriors." explained Derrell.

"A heavy loss indeed, but still victorious." Merlin replied.

"Yes, they all fought well. Even Shamera played his part."

"All I did was to fire useless energy balls at them." Shamera said apologetically.

"You helped. Please do not underestimate your effort and value, the granite wall you brought down on the Orcs, gave us a noteworthy advantage."

"You have a natural ability, accept it. You are much better than you give yourself credit for." Merlin added.

"Then why? oh, it doesn't matter." Shamera replied.

"See, you doubt yourself too much, have more faith in yourself, and you will achieve more." Merlin responded, trying to boost Shamera's confidence.

"I was right, just as I suspected. Your Niniane is actually Nimue." Merlin said contemptuously.

"Nimue, wasn't she the one that trapped you in that cave?" Shamera replied looking confused.

"Yes, the very same. We may have won this battle; but, you can bet Nimue's wrath will be great. Her retribution will be swift to follow." Merlin continued.

"Let us not worry about her now, the men are tired and we have Verazslo back with us. Besides if you know who she is, that should be very advantageous. Let's get some rest. We set off for home at first light." Said Derrell.

Chapter 15

Mountains to the east were the backdrop to a very rocky terrain. They had been steadily travelling back to Selvenora for four days. They had decided to take the long way round, fearing going back the way they came would be more dangerous. Verazslo was holding his own, but was still very weak and had slept most of the time. Merlin instructed Shamera with magic lessons, and everyone was on their guard for any reprisal and potential ambushes. It would be dark in a few hours, so they stopped and made camp. Night-time fell; the campfires were lit, which gave a warm, inviting glow to the camp. It was a clear night sky, and the temperature was dropping. Guards patrolled the camp's perimeter. The moon with its stoic grace made its way slowly across the night sky, brining with it a comforting cast of light while everyone slept peacefully below it.

The sun rose above the mountain tops making them look as though they were capped with gold. As the dying embers of the fires faded amongst the ash, a Formorian horseman rode quickly into the camp shouting, "Everybody up, quickly! There are trolls in the gorge."

Shamera and Merlin quickly clambered up the rocky escarpment to a vantage point overlooking a narrow gorge. The gorge was thirty feet wide and somewhere close to eighty feet high.

As Shamera and Merlin stood on the top of the ridge, they could see an army of Nimue's Trolls slowly advancing stealthily through the gorge below. They were around one hundred strong. Their large cumbersome slate grey and warty bodies supported by their hefty, yet short hairy legs and large flat feet were finding it difficult to negotiate the large rocks and boulders of the gorge floor. This was once an old riverbed, strewn with large, jagged boulders which have fallen from the cliff faces.

Shamera looked at Merlin with unease as an icy chill ran down his spine, "There must be at least a hundred Trolls." Shamera exclaimed.

"Luckily for us, they are not the most intelligent of creatures. So… we'll have to even things up, won't we, lad?" Merlin stated as he removed his pointed hat from his head. Before Shamera could ask how, Merlin picked a large purple and red-coloured feather from his hat band, held it in his palm and whispered an incantation whilst slowly passing his wand over it. He took a deep breath and blew the feather into the air. It appeared to hover there for a few seconds, floating on the breeze, before a flash of golden light revealed a large, majestic bird. Its large purple, red, and orange feathers appeared to glow in the sunlight. The birds' wingspan stretched out about six feet wide. It had the powerful and regal head of an eagle and the beautiful body and tail of a pheasant.

"What the…?" Shamera exclaimed as he watched the bird.

"This is the Phoenix, the 'Fire-Bird'. This bird can live for over five hundred years. A rare bird indeed. When it gets old, and it sees its feathers are becoming dull and bedraggled, it constructs a funeral pyre of aromatic twigs it wisely collects. It turns itself towards the rays of the sun, and with a gentle beating of its wings, it deliberately kindles a fire for itself. When it has been fully consumed by the fire and turned into ash, it can once again rise anew from its own ashes. I did not want this one to fall into the hands of Nimue, so I cast a spell to hide and protect it from her evil grasp." Merlin replied.

Shamera watched eagerly as the majestic bird soared high into the sky, twisting and turning, next, in another blinding flash of light the phoenix burst into flames of bright gold. Merlin raised his wand into the air, making circular motions before pointing it down towards the Trolls. The Phoenix let out an almighty ear-piercing squawk as it swooped down towards the Trolls. The Phoenix levelled off its decent and with its wings outstretched it let out another ear-piercing squawk as it flew straight through the line of advancing trolls turning into ashes all it touched. Shamera watched in amazement as the Phoenix again soared high into the sky and made a second run on the advancing Trolls. Again, the majestic flaming bird cut a scorching path through the enemy's ranks. The Trolls were wildly thrashing their clubs around, trying to hit and slay the bird, yet not one club could hit its target. Again, the fiery bird turned all it touched into black ashes, which blew around in the wind and fell to the ground like black snow. The Trolls regrouped and carried on, scrambling over the large rocks and boulders trying to advance and escape the fiery bird.

"It won't be able to keep this up for long as it will need to rest soon, but it will cut their numbers down." Merlin stated.

The Phoenix made two more runs at the advancing trolls. This time it weaved through their ranks, twisting and reeling as it flew amongst them, turning a good half of them to ashes. The Phoenix squawked once again as it soared high into the sky before disappearing into the distance. The remaining Trolls had scattered and hid amongst the rocks, fearing the Phoenix would return and attack again.

"It will find a suitable lair and rest up for a day or so. Transforming like this takes its toll on the bird. Look… it has sent a panic amongst them; look, they are trying to hide amongst the rocks." Merlin said with a look of achievement.

Shamera smiled slightly as he looked towards the high rocky ridge on the far side of the gorge. He gave Merlin a slight sideways glance, smiled slightly as he raised his staff into the air; he whispered an incantation before bringing the staff down hard onto the rocks about his feet. An intense beam of purple light shone out from the staff's gemstone and across the gorge, hitting the large rocky ridge. The ground trembled slightly under their feet. They looked on as the ridge broke loose and fell smartly into the gorge. The Trolls looked up to see the rocks and boulders heading straight down towards them. In sheer panic, they turned around and scrambled as fast as their fat bodies and flat feet could carry them back in the direction they had come from. The falling rocks sounded like a heavy thunderstorm as they piled up and formed a high dam blocking the path across the gorge.

"This should also slow their advance even more." Shamera said proudly.

"Yes, your abilities are getting stronger, along with your confidence, too." Merlin replied with a reassuring smile and a nod of approval.

Urok clambered up the escarpment to take stock of the situation.

"What's the position of the trolls?" he asked.

"Trolls, we have sent them retreating whence they came." Shamera replied.

They watched as the retreating Trolls scrambled hurriedly and clumsily over the rocks, heading back the way they came.

"More will return once they have regrouped. Nimue will not be happy… again." Merlin stated.

"We need to get back to Selvenora quickly. I think we will need Verazslo as well as yourself to defeat this evil." Shamera replied.

"I agree, we need to put some distance between us." said Urok.

Derrell had ridden on ahead to warn Lord Salogel of their arrival and of Verazslo's condition. After five days of uneventful travelling, they finally reached Selvenora. As the Formorian Horsemen approached Selvenora they were amazed at its mountainous beauty, small waterfalls fed into a large crystal-clear stream. The mountain water was so clear, the fish were distinctly visible swimming along in its current. Small birds hovered, drinking nectar from overhanging plants. It differed greatly from the Mirropus plains where they lived. Finally, they reached the iron gated entrance; the gate was already raised for their arrival. Lord Salogel was in the courtyard with Elithrin as the wagon with Verazslo in the back approached.

"I'm glad you are back safe." Elithrin said, smiling at Shamera.

Four guards carefully pulled Verazslo from the wagon.

"Put him in his room straight away, I am glad to see you are unharmed Shamera, I need to see you." Lord Salogel said with urgency.

Shamera and Merlin followed Lord Salogel into the building while four guards stretchered Verazslo to his room. Lord Salogel turned to Shamera and Merlin.

"We need the healing properties of the Anthaepevo, the Snowberry plant. It is a magical plant which solely lives in Avaland and is fairly rare from what Verazslo once told me. Verazslo has found it before. We cannot heal physical wounds brought about by magic, I feel this is our only option." explained Lord Salogel.

"Anthaepevo, Snowberry... I have not come across it before, even reading Mirabilis's books on plants and herbs."

"Mirabilis might have known about it, but unfortunately she's not here and there is no time to get her."

"So, you do not know what it looks like?" asked Shamera

"I would guess by the name it would be a plant with white berries."

"Unfortunately, there are many plants which have white berries." Shamera observed.

"I would think this is one you would have never seen before." Lord Salogel suggested, trying to be positive.

"Avaland, it sounds a lot like Avalon, the magical place they buried my great king." remarked Merlin.

"Avaland is a magical place here, too. Solely those with magic can enter, but with the correct method. Hopefully, you and Shamera can enter Avaland and find the Snowberry plant. All I can remember is it needs to be steeped in the waters from the Cataracta."

"What is a Cataracta?" Shamera asked.

"If it's what I think it is, it's Latin for a waterfall." Merlin replied.

"Latin, what is Latin?" Lord Salogel asked.

"An ancient language spoken by people who invaded Engla land hundreds of years ago. It's strange this language would be spoken here, but they wrote it on the map I took with me to Engla Land." Shamera said proudly. "Where is this Avaland?"

"It's not far, a short ride away, is all."

"Ride... on a horse? I don't ride. Horses dislike me." Shamera replied with a nervous laugh.

Lord Salogel laughed and said, "I'll get one of our riders to take you. I assume you can ride Merlin?"

"Yes, I can ride."

"It is settled. You will leave right away. Verazslo's life hangs in the balance. To enter Avaland you need to ride to the stone arch near to the rings of Tir' Eineth. You will need to use your staff to tap the keystone twice. Next, the stone on its left once, and tap the stone on the right of the keystone twice. Good luck to you both."

Derrell was already sat upon his horse and waiting for Shamera, he was also holding a horse for Merlin. Shamera held on tight as they set off at a gallop for the magical entrance to Avaland. They rode towards the shimmering silver lake and passing it on its right side as they rode on into the woods. They soon came to a clearing. The stone circle which Shamera used to get to Engla land stood before them. Derrell and Merlin slowed their horses to a walk as they passed by. It was again quiet and eerie; the entire sounds were from the horses' hooves and a solitary crow in the distance. The air felt electrified, which made the hairs on the back of Shamera's neck stand on end, and an icy shiver ran down his spine. A short distance past the stone circle, raised on a mound of earth, stood a large grey stone arch. Six thin stone steps led up towards the arch. The aperture was about seven feet high, about four feet wide. Strands of dark green ivy had wrapped itself around the top and sides of the arch, the ivy had also spread down both sides of the stone balustrades either side of the steps. A shaft of light falling through the trees and behind the arch gave it an eerie, ethereal look.

Shamera and Merlin dismounted and approached the stone arch. Shamera walked around the arch inspecting it, he walked through the arch, turned around and walked back through again. Merlin stood watching him, wondering what he was doing.

"Use the staff as Lord Salogel directed. I fear nothing will happen otherwise." instructed Merlin.

"I know. I was curious as it leads nowhere. I think I was expecting it to have a door or something like a door."

Shamera stood in front of the arch, "I think this is the front Merlin, as it has some markings etched upon the stone."

Shamera raised the staff to tap the keystone. As he did, he noticed the stone within the staff glowing. He tapped the keystone twice, the stone to its left once, and the stone on the right of the keystone twice. Both Merlin and Shamera watched as the entrance of the arch shimmered, for a few seconds before showing them a path leading from the arch and through it. They both stood and stared into the arch for a few moments, not even knowing what to expect. It looked very different from their current surroundings. Shamera and Merlin walked through the archway.

A leaf cluttered path led them into the magical grounds of Avaland. As they walked between two grassy slopes Resembling a small valley. They observed ferns with long, dark green, curly tendrils surrounding large moss-covered rocks. In amongst these ferns grew a variety of plants and flowers with an array of shapes and colours. The fragrance from these plants and flowers filled the air with a sweet, heady scent. Taller, tree ferns grew scattered among the plants, their bronzed woody trunks elevated the fronds high above the other plants. Their delicate fronds danced gracefully in the slight breeze.

A variety of colourful winged creatures darted and flew from flower to flower as they drank upon the sweet nectar. Shamera listened to their hypnotic songs as they sweetly sang among the fern trees. *'This is a magical place indeed'*, thought Shamera as they meandered along the path which led them deeper into Avaland.

"Is this like your Avalon?" asked Shamera.

Merlin lifted his nose and sniffed the air before replying, "Not really, but this is undoubtedly a wondrous place. You can feel the magic in here."

"Listen Merlin, can you hear water?" Shamera stopped and cocked his head slightly to the right, trying to determine the direction the sound was coming from. His head turned slightly to the left as he heard the faint sound of falling water. They continued down the path until it came to a fork.

"This way." said Merlin, as he pointed to the right.

The closer they got to the sound of falling water, the louder it became. The slopes of the banks ended, and a rock face lined the edge of the path. Damp, cracked, and broken rocks were home to a thick carpet of multicoloured moss. Green, orange, and red moss thrived as they clung to the rocks and even more ferns grew from the cracks and ledges. They were dripping with water, which seeped through the rock face.

As they walked around a bend, they saw a small wooden, moss-covered bridge arching over a narrow stream. As they crossed the bridge and looked to their right; a wall of stone some eighty feet high arced across the narrow gorge. They followed the path towards the wall of stone. The sound of falling water was getting even louder. The path led them around to the left. There it was. The waterfall. Shamera watched as it cascaded down from the left corner of the rock face; beams of sunlight which pierced the canopy of trees sparkled as it reflected off the fall of water, which crashed loudly upon the rocks at the bottom.

"This is beautiful, but I haven't seen this Snowberry plant yet, or anything resembling it, have you, Merlin?"

"Not yet, but this will undoubtedly be the Cataracta, unless there is a greater one in here."

"Maybe we should split up and search for this mysterious plant."

"I do not know what kind of place this is but, I know it is magical and I know we are being watched."

"Watched by who, or what?"

"Look, those flowers over there."

Shamera looked at the flower bed. "All I can see are flowers."

"Watch."

Merlin rubbed the palms of his hands together; next he cupped them and gently blew into his cupped hands. He opened his hands to reveal four butterflies which fluttered over to the flowers. Several high-pitched squeals emanated from the flower bed and the flowers rose in the air, their skirts bellowing out like jellyfish as they rose even higher.

A high-pitched female voice spoke. "You are not Verazslo, yet you have powerful magic within you."

"This is Shamera. He is Verazslo's apprentice, and I am Merlin. I am a sorcerer from another place, and I am teaching Shamera in Verazslo's absence."

"We are flower fairies, and we live here. It is our job to tend to the other flowers and plants."

"It would appear you are doing a wonderful job. This place is beautiful. We are looking for a rare plant we are told solely grows here. The Snowberry plant, do you know of its whereabouts?" Merlin asked the flower fairy.

"What do you need such a rare and beautiful plant for?" asked one of the other flower fairies.

"To help Verazslo, an evil sorceress kidnapped him and tortured him. Lord Salogel said this plant would help revive him, or we fear he may die." Shamera replied.

"How do we know you speak the truth? I cannot give this to anyone."

"I don't know how we can prove this. Unless you go see for yourselves, we are here with honest intentions." Shamera pleaded.

"Drink this. If you lie, you will die." said a purple flower fairy as she produced a small vial containing a pale-yellow liquid.

"I will gladly drink it." Shamera replied, holding out his right hand.

The fairy handed Shamera the vial.

"You must drink it all, and remember, if you lie, you will die."

Shamera had no hesitation in drinking the contents. He remarked, "It tastes sweet."

The flower fairies flew around Shamera like colourful jellyfish swimming in the air.

"It was merely nectar." laughed one fairy. "If you had refused to drink it, we would have known you were being dishonest."

"Please wait here while we fetch some snowberries." a fairy said as two of them flew off.

They reappeared a few moments later, carrying four white berries. Shamera and Merlin looked on as the waterfall slowed down and appeared to stop. The two fairies flew up to where a beam of light was shining upon the waterfall. As they appeared to take some of the water, there was a bright flash of light. The fairies flew back, and as they did, the waterfall sped up and flowed normally again.

"Here you are. There is enough in here for Verazslo. Our love goes with you. Will you be able to find your own way back?"

"Yes, I think I can remember the way. Oh, how do we close the arch?" Shamera replied.

"Once you both leave, it will close itself."

The fairies flew back to the flower bed and blended in to look like ordinary flowers once more. Without hesitation, both Shamera and Merlin hurried back to the entrance to find their rides still there, waiting for them. As they walked out of the archway, they turned back and watched as it shimmered, and the pathway disappeared.

"What could you see from out here, Derrell?" Shamera enquired.

"Nothing. You walked into the archway and disappeared, what was it like?"

"Magical." Shamera replied.

"Let's get this draft back to Verazslo and get it administered." Merlin said with a sense of urgency as he mounted his horse. Shamera once again held on tightly to Derrell.

As soon as they returned, Shamera gave the draft to Lord Salogel who quickly went to administer it to Verazslo. Shamera and Merlin went to sit in the gardens and wait for any news of Verazslo's recovery. They had been sitting for about thirty minutes when Elithrin appeared.

"My father said he has administered the medicine and now we need to wait. He also asked if he could speak with you, Merlin."

"Of course. Where is your father?"

"He is in the council chamber."

"You look worried Shamera, my father is doing everything he can. And with yours and Merlin's help, he is in the best hands."

"I know. I hardly know him, but it feels like we have a sort of connection." said Shamera mournfully.

"Magic; connected you, therefore, you were chosen."

Elithrin spent the next hour teaching him relaxation techniques and how to control his emotions.

"Remember, you cannot control everything in your life, but you can control the feelings you attach to those events. You are the one who is in charge of your feelings and emotions. Emotions are extremely powerful; therefore, you need to control them. If you let your feelings and emotions control you,

you will lose what you strive to achieve. You cannot concentrate, and your magic will suffer. By controlling them, this will give you better clarity in thinking, and better control of your magic."

Lord Salogel came looking for Shamera.

"Verazslo is still sleeping. We are doing everything we can for him. Merlin would like to have a word with you. He is in the council chambers."

"Do you know what it is about?"

"I will let Merlin explain. All I will say is, it is of the greatest importance."

Shamera went to find Merlin wondering what could be of great importance. He entered the council chamber. Merlin was sitting, waiting for him. He was sitting alone at a long white-marble table in the centre of the room.

Merlin beckoned him over.

"Shamera come in. Come sit, we need to talk."

"Lord Salogel said you wanted to see me, to discuss something of great importance. He wouldn't tell me what. He said you will explain everything to me."

"Yes, well, how can I put it?" Merlin stuttered.

"You look uncomfortable Merlin, is there something wrong?"

"Not wrong, no. I have something to show you. Something which might help us defeat Nimue once and for all."

Merlin reached into his robe and pulled out what looked like a decorative, thin metal strip about two inches wide. It was silver, and about six inches long. It had two intertwined dragons etched upon its surface, along with some other magical looking symbols. Merlin passed him the object.

"What is this?"

"This is what will help us defeat Nimue." replied Merlin with a slight smile.

Shamera gave a little frown as he passed it back to Merlin.

"How will this strip of metal help defeat her?"

Merlin pointed to a large bowl of fresh fruit on the table.

"Use your magic to levitate the bowl of fruit."

Shamera focused on the fruit, and it levitated about two feet above the table. He lowered in back down on to the table.

"Now, give me an arm, it matters not which."

Shamera held out his left arm. Merlin slapped the metal strip against his wrist. The strip quickly wrapped itself around Shamera's wrist. Shamera surprised by this, withdrew his arm swiftly.

"What's this? What have you done?"

"Try to remove it." Merlin said with a smile.

Shamera tried very hard to remove the bracelet, but no matter how hard he tried, he could not remove it. Merlin looked at Shamera and raised his eyebrows and smiled.

"Okay, Shamera, use your magic and raise the fruit bowl up again, even a small amount."

Shamera concentrated, but the fruit bowl remained firmly on the table. Shamera tried even harder, still nothing. Shamera knew he could do this as he practiced levitation and found it easy. Again, he concentrated hard and still the fruit bowl did not move, not an inch. Shamera looked at the bracelet and again attempted to remove it.

"It has something to do with this, hasn't it?"

"Stop, you can never remove it. You cannot even cut it off. The person who placed it there is the only one can remove it. Here, give me your arm."

Shamera held out his left arm. Merlin easily pulled the bracelet apart. As Shamera watched, the bracelet again turned into a solid strip of silver metal. He next turned to the bowl of fruit and with ease levitated it again.

"I have been working on this for a while. The wearer's magic is suppressed all the time they are wearing this bracelet. Now, if we can get it onto the wrist of Nimue, she will be without magic. Without magic, she is powerless. We can imprisoner her, as she once imprisoned me." Merlin said with contempt.

"How are we going to get this on her wrist? She will not let us anywhere near her."

Merlin looked uncomfortable as he stood up and paced around the room. He was pulling his beard through his hands as he tried to think how best to tell Shamera what he was thinking.

"At this moment, I can only think of one way… Merlin paused, well… You will have to be captured by her." continued Merlin awkwardly.

Chapter 16

Shamera looked at Merlin. Had he heard him correctly? His brow furrowed as he tried to process what he had heard.
He cried out. "WHAT! CAPTURED! Why? This is crazy, no. Look what she did to Verazslo, and he was an accomplished sorcerer." Shamera exclaimed loudly. A cold shudder ran through his trembling body. He stiffened and his breathing became shallow and rapid. Panic took hold of him.
"Sit here, calm yourself. Your scared, that's natural, fear is what keeps us alive. Being scared is normal, it's a natural response to anything that threatens us. I'd be more concerned about you if you weren't scared. But you will be alright. She will need to keep you alive. Nimue needs you to give her the staff. She cannot take it from you forcibly, it has to be given freely by you. You will be her bargaining chip. Besides, it will look like you do not yet have any magic she will not perceive you as a threat. Unlike Verazslo, he would have been a great threat to her."
"NO! I'm no one's bargaining chip. What if she tortures me? Sorry Merlin, but I cannot go along with it. I am no match for her. What if she has a device like this and I lose what little magic I have? Which, compared to you and Verazslo, is next to no magic at all. Why can't you be captured?" Shamera replied fearfully.
"Calm your breathing, come on, match it to mine. That's it, nice and steady. I cannot be captured. She knows my magic and she will not let me get anywhere near her. She will know I would be waiting for the opportunity to strike at her. Therefore, it needs to be you. You won't be perceived as a threat to her, and hopefully she will let you get close enough to slap this bracelet on her."
Shamera breathed heavily. He stood up and paced around the room. He felt very warm and was pulling at his clothes and clenching his fists. He stood still for a moment before turning to face Merlin. Shamera's nostrils flared as he bit his bottom lip. His mouth quivered as he raised his shoulders.

"I didn't sign up for this. I wanted to learn magic and hopefully one day I would become a fully-fledged sorcerer. There has to be another way. What makes you think she will let me get close enough? And how do I explain this? Oh, it's simply a bracelet. It doesn't come off, nothing to be concerned about."

Merlin detected the fear and sarcasm in his voice but did not rise to it. He remained calm and replied,

"I don't know if she will let you get close to her, but you pose the least threat. You are simply the apprentice. She will not know of the training you have already undergone, and the bracelet will suppress your magic whilst it is on your wrist. She cannot see the bracelet, nor will she be able to detect your magic. You alone will see it after I enchant it further. Nimue will want to win you over to her side. After all, you are the new keeper of the staff. She needs the staff so she can have greater power. If she gets it, she will become unstoppable. No one can force you to do this Shamera, you need to decide for yourself. But remember, the longer this goes on, the more control of this land she will have. You are our best hope."

Shamera paced around the room again. Intermittently shaking his head, stopping to think, staring at Merlin before resuming to pace around the room again. Shamera had seen battle. He had fought with the Elvenii and the Dwarvian, but this terrified him way beyond what he had already witnessed. deliberately being captured seemed like a crazy suicidal idea.

"I don't know if I can do it Merlin, I'm sorry. I'm not brave, I'm not hero material. I'm just an Ethaenian boy. Before Stefremmus and the Choosing, the most dangerous thing I did was to work in Mirabilis' shop mixing potions. That was hardly a few of months ago. Ever since, my life has been turned upside down. I walked all the way here, ran from dangerous men, drugged, and escaped a crazy man. Travelled through a dangerous forest. Fought a Vark, it's a large vicious killer wild dog, helped slay a dragon. Fought in two battles and now you want me to be captured. What is happening to me? This is now all too much." Shamera's voice quivered as he recalled his escapades.

"You forgot about coming to England to rescue me." Merlin replied, trying to alleviate the situation.

"It's not funny Merlin. I'm scared. I wish I had never been chosen."

"You were chosen because this is your destiny. To appreciate the light and the good times, we must endure the dark and the bad times. Your journey will take you from being someone who is protected, to that of a protector, a sorcerer." Merlin said as reassuringly as he could.

"It's all too much, Merlin. I'm seventeen and I have already used magic to kill. Where's the good in killing?"

"There is never good in having to kill, but in times of war it becomes inevitable people will die. You saved lives during the battle, without your help many could have died. There are things I have done which I wish I never had to do, but they were necessary. You too will experience thing like that, and in time you too will realise that sometimes we all must do things we would rather not. Come, sit." Merlin sat and beckoned Shamera over.

"We will prepare you, and if need be, I will transport myself in and transport you out if the need arises. I will not be far from her lair. But... if you can get close enough to slap this on her wrist, even with your limited powers, you will be stronger than her. No one can force you to do this, but I implore you to think it over. We will prepare you; we will have a contingency plan to rescue you."

"I fear you ask too much of me. How are you going to prepare me? How am I going to get captured and get close enough to her? I'm sorry, but my head... I'm confused. I cannot think straight." Shamera said, fighting back the tears. He had never felt so scared and alone.

"With fear it is necessary that there is balance. Fear must keep you safe and protect you from harm. But you also need to use your fear to take necessary risks. This is something you need to do in life and not just times of war. Trust in yourself and in your abilities, as in these matters, take good advice and guidance from those who care deeply about you. Let's take one thing at a time Shamera, let us first get this settled in your mind.

Elithrin will help you. She's very fond of you, I have seen the way she looks at you." Merlin said with a wink and a grin.

"Stop it." Shamera replied, looking a little embarrassed.

"Oh, I see you are very fond of her, too."

"She's alright." Shamera said shrugging his shoulders but could not prevent a large grin lighting up his face.

"She will help you to stretch out with your mind, to enable you to link with Elithrin's consciousness, even over a long distance. This will enable you to communicate with her and with us."

Shamera looked at Merlin through squinted eyes and a furrowed brow, his lips pressed tightly together. "You have already thought this through, haven't you?"

"Yes Shamera. I will not lie to you. I have already discussed my plan with Elithrin, Salogel and Verazslo." Merlin answered in a soft, apologetic voice.

"So, why was I not involved?"

"Forgive me, that was my idea. I wanted you kept out of it until I had all the details ironed out. I also wanted to be the one to tell you and to give you a choice. Although to be honest, I feel you have little choice, as you are our one chance, our one hope of pulling this off. If I felt you did not have it within you to do it, I would not have brought this suggestion before Salogel."

Shamera said nothing. He stood up, walked over to the window, stared out of it for a short while. Turned, and walked back over to sit back at the table. He placed both elbows on the table and clenched his hands together. He slowly placed his chin on his hands. He sat there deep in thought, not moving, not saying a word. His eyes focused firmly on the fruit bowl, as though looking for inspiration from it. Merlin also said nothing. He left Shamera alone with his thoughts. After what seemed an age, Shamera raised his head, stared at Merlin for a few seconds and leaned back removing his elbows from the table.

"It is a massive thing you are asking of me; I'm not saying I will do it, but... I would like to go through the plan and hear what preparation will be needed."

Merlin looked at him and gave a little smile before gently nodding his head in agreement.

"First, you will need to see Elithrin. She is better placed to inform you what she needs to teach you. Elithrin's teachings will be key to the success of this plan. You will need to block and hide your thoughts from Nimue. She might sense you are doing this. You need to be able to successfully block her probing for the truth. Nimue needs to feel safe around you. This is the easy bit as you will wear this bracelet and she will be able to sense your lack of magic."

"But how do I get it off me and onto her?" Shamera asked, still looking a little anxious.

"The person who puts the bracelet on is the only one who can take it off. You will put it on yourself, here try it." Merlin said as he passed him the bracelet.

"Before putting it on, levitate that fruit bowl."

Shamera successfully levitated it and set it back down again.

"Take hold of the bracelet and slap it against your wrist. It will automatically attach itself." Shamera followed the instructions.

"Now try your magic."

He tried to levitate the fruit bowl once again, but without success. He turned his arm over and found he could effortlessly remove the bracelet.

"It seems to work well." Said Shamera looking a little surprised.

"You need to find Elithrin, she needs to train your mind. You are, without doubt, brave, and noble; you would have been highly regarded and respected in the court of King Arthur. Your heart is as true as any noble knight who served my great king."

"I am no knight, nor a great sorcerer. I don't even know if I am brave or am I just foolish."

Merlin stood up and walked over to Shamera, placed his hand upon his shoulder. "Shamera, you have the true heart of any knight, the makings of a great sorcerer. Believe in yourself and in your abilities. I do not say this lightly. I say this from my heart."

Shamera placed her hand on Merlin's hand and gave it a gentle squeeze.

"You are too kind Merlin, and I thank you for those kind, reassuring words."

Merlin took a deep breath, "Right, lad, find Elithrin. I believe she will be waiting for you in the meditation garden. She has a lot to teach you and you will need to practice."

Shamera stood up. Trying to be brave and not wanting to show Merlin how afraid he was; he sauntered out of the room without speaking. Merlin knew Shamera was afraid, but he also had a belief in his abilities. Shamera must first conquer his fear, this would allow his skills to flourish.

Shamera soon found his way to the meditation garden. Elithrin was sitting at a small table under a willow tree, its long slender tendril like branches arched outwards, stretching downwards towards the ground. Its yellowy green leaves swayed gently in the summer breeze. It looked like a vision of calm amid his head of turbulent thoughts. Elithrin gently beckoned him over and gave him a warm, gentle smile.

"By the look on your face, I can tell Merlin has spoken to you." Elithrin said gently.

Shamera took a deep breath and sat down opposite her.

"Yes... he has told me of his plan. I don't know if I can go along with it. I think he's asking too much of me."

"I know Merlin and Verazslo both believe in your abilities; they have both said they can feel greatness within you. You have come on a long way since the first day you arrived here. You need to believe in yourself more."

"So, what are we going to be doing today? What preparations do I need?"

"We are going to work on your mind, concentration, and emotions. You need to control your emotions; this will increase your ability to concentrate. Also, linking your mind to mine, so we can communicate within our minds. I know it may sound hard, but it truthfully is not."

"Will you be able to read my mind?" he asked curiously.

"No, we can communicate with each other, but we cannot read each other's minds. You will be able to contact me and tell me what is happening to you and reveal her defences. If you are in danger, I will feel it and do what I can to help."

"Danger! Now there's a word that says reassess your choices. Bravery or foolhardy?"

"Bravery and foolhardy go hand in hand. We always need to reassess the situation. Take time to weigh up the danger versus the greater good. This is the brave choice one must make."

Shamera sat and pondered this for a short while, "So, what do I need to do?"

"First, we need to find your happy place, this is a place where you feel safe. A place you can retreat to in your mind whenever you feel threatened or frightened."

"Okay." He said, unconvincingly.

"I want you to close your eyes, listen to my voice, and do exactly as I say without questioning."

"I think I can manage this." He said smiling, then folded his arms.

Elithrin stood behind him and gently placed her hands on the top of his head.

"I want you to close your eyes and think of the place you feel the safest. Relax your mind and breath, deeply and slowly."

He closed his eyes and inhaled deeply. The scent from the nearby plants appeared to intensify. It suddenly transported his thoughts back to Thornbeck Meadow. He imagined himself stood amongst the tall grass and flowers. He could see and smell them as clearly as if he were standing there right now. He inhaled deeply again, and a smile crept across his face. He had not felt this relaxed in a long time. With his eyes closed and imagining he was in the meadow, he turned his head to the right, he was surprised to see Elithrin stood by his side.

"How are you here?" Shamera asked.

"Shhh… concentrate on the vision, be absorbed into it. Make it as real as you can. Listen to my voice and concentrate." She said softly, "Concentrate, smell the flowers and feel the breeze brushing against your face. This is your safe place… your happy place. When you feel this is as real as you can make it, I want you to press your right thumb and forefinger together and press them as hard as you can while still looking around this place. As soon as you are ready, make this place as real as you can, then press hard and hold it for a few seconds." She reiterated in a whisper.

Shamera concentrated hard to make this vision look and feel as real as he could. As he pressed his finger and thumb together,

Elithrin spoke his name loudly in order to break his concentration whilst the imagery was at its strongest, so it was primed for him to return to. Startled, he opened his eyes; he was back sitting under the willow tree.

"Close your eyes again and press your thumb and finger together again and tell me what you are seeing, and how real it seems."

He did as she asked. "I am in the meadow. It's not as vivid as the first time, but…"

"You will need to practise this. You need to practise until you feel you are truly there."

"How long will it take?"

"It all depends on how much you practise and how strongly you want it to happen. The more you practice it the stronger the reality of it will become."

Shamera nodded his head and agreed to practice it regularly.

"Now for the hard bit. Can you remember the first time we dream shared?"

"Ah, that's is what it's called? Yes, I remember. It was very nice." Realising what he had said, he blushed a little and felt uncomfortable, he shuffled in his chair trying to make himself more comfortable. Elithrin smiled at him, which made his face redden even more.

"Before we begin, this will not be easy. This will require a deep connection within your own mind and an internal alignment of your thoughts. Thought transference transcends all physical limitations. It's a sort of merging of our personal energies, this enables us to communicate with each other. We already have mutual empathy; I have felt that. I also feel a strong connection between us. I want you to close your eyes, try to think of nothing, let your mind become blank."

He closed his eyes and tried to think of nothing. He found it harder than he expected.

"First, I want you to think of me, let it induce an emotion and you experience it, let it develop into a strong emotion. When you have done this and you are ready, see your mind connecting with mine. I should be able to feel the connection being made. Don't force it, let it happen naturally. It might take a lot of practice." Elithrin spoke quietly.

Shamera tried to concentrate; but could not make the connection.

"Alright, let me try something else. Shamera, do you like me?"

"Of course, I do."

"I mean, do you have feelings for me?"

Shamera felt uncomfortable and blushed again, "I, erm..."

"I have feelings for you, ever since the first time I saw you. I felt an immediate connection. This is why I gave you my Ordriel." Elithrin said tenderly.

"I have never felt like this about anyone before. I have feelings for you... but..."

"But what?"

"Well, you're the daughter of the Elvenii leader. I am merely an Ethaenian boy."

"No Shamera, you are the next sorcerer, a great sorcerer in the making. I knew how I felt the moment I saw you. I have felt your feelings for me growing stronger. When I gave you my Ordriel for luck, I gave you my heart. This is our way. My father knows I am old enough to decide my own future. My mother was not Elvenii. Sadly, she died when I was very young. My father tells me all about her whenever he can. I still see the sadness in his eyes when he speaks of her. So, for our connection to become even stronger, you must give in to those feelings, if you want to. If not... we must block them out. Or we can never make this connection properly."

"No, I want these feelings. I want to be with you. I wasn't sure what to do, or whether we could be together." He said as he felt a slight sense of relief. He no longer felt as uncomfortable. His feelings were now out in the open. Elithrin stood there and smiled at him.

"We Elvenii are undoubtedly a little more forward regarding our feelings, but, for now I must control them. I am training you for this mission, knowing you are going into a dangerous situation. The mission is one I know you must do; this evil must be driven from our land. And yet, part of me..."

Shamera stood up and slowly approached her. He instinctively placed his hands lightly around her elbows. He slowly drew her towards him and gently kissed her forehead, then her lips.

"Now, I have even more reason to succeed." Shamera stood there looking deep into her eyes, wondering what to do next.

In that moment, the emotion of that kiss evoked a chemistry between them, Shamera's fears subsided, and he once again felt at peace. They stood and embraced each other tightly, neither one wanting to let the moment pass. Eventually Elithrin spoke "part of me never wants you to leave my side...but I know you must go and fight."

She pulled away from Shamera and refocussed "Now we know how we feel for each other, it should make connecting our minds easier. Our emotions will enhance our spiritual feelings. Shall we try again?"

Shamera let go of her hands and sat down. *'Did that just happen?'* he thought to himself. His heart pounded; his stomach felt as though a thousand butterflies had taken off all at the same time. Goose bumps covered his skin. He felt a cold, yet pleasant tingle run down his spine. *'How can I concentrate now?'*

'Okay Elithrin, control your thoughts, take a deep breath. Yes, that did happen.' She thought to herself. She closed her eyes and took a deep, slow breath before sitting beside him.

"I want you to close your eyes. The connection works best when you don't force it. Let it happen naturally. We know it works. We've been there before, remember?"

Shamera thought back to the time he first saw her in his thoughts. A slight smile appeared as the image of her grew stronger.

"Well done, Shamera. I can sense a feint connection." Elithrin closed her eyes and waited for the connection to be strengthened. A few moments passed but made no mental connection.

"Sorry Elithrin, I can't concentrate right now. I've never been involved like this before; my head is all over the place. You seem well versed at controlling your feelings. I don't appear to have the ability."

"Yes, we train our minds from a very early age, meditation, managing emotions. I'm sorry Shamera, sometimes I forget not all people are like us."

"Lately, I wish I could be more like you, some of the experiences I have been through were awful. Emotionally devastating. And now I'm experiencing something entirely different, something fantastic."

"I'm glad you feel the same way for me as I feel for you. But we must put what lays ahead first before our own emotions. We cannot let this get in the way; I wish you didn't have to go but we don't have a choice. Since the day you left for the dragon's heart string, I missed you. Next, you went off to fight with our armies. It worried me greatly and I could stop thinking about you. I had a word with Derrell to make sure he kept you as safe as he could. And I am now to prepare you for the most dangerous part of all. I cannot lie… this…"

"No need to say another word. I think I am scared enough for both of us. I hadn't agreed to do it, but now I know I have to. I must make sure you will be safe, as well as everyone else, including my family. Speaking of which, I've missed them a lot. I'm glad the fighting is nowhere near my region, well, at least not yet." Shamera's heart felt heavy as he thought of his family and his home.

"When you succeed in your mission, we can rebuild and return to normal. You can spend as much time with your family as you want to. You can finish your training and become the greatest sorcerer we have ever had, I will be so proud of you. But we must defeat this evil first. Let's practice a little more and then we can go and have something to eat and relax for a while."

"What do you want me to do?" Shamera said with renewed vigour.

"I want you to think of me. Let it generate an emotion. Once you feel it, I want you to experience this emotion. Let it fill you up. See yourself connecting with me. Don't force it, let it happen. When it does, I will sense it. It might not happen straight away; it will take some practice to achieve the level we need. When we have a good telepathic connection with each other, we will be able to sense each other, and we should be able to communicate easily."

"I'm just afraid that she will read my mind and then she will know what's happening."

"You can put up a telepathic shield by visualising it and willing the person cannot read your mind. Or better still, you can misdirect her by focusing on a misleading thought instead. She will pick up this thought and be entirely fooled. When using a misleading notion, it is important to be careful of your thoughts when we are communicating. You don't want to communicate a falsehood to us. This could jeopardise the entire mission. This is what we will concentrate on later. But, for now, we simply need to practise on making our connection happen."

For a couple of hours, they practiced hard. They managed to make fragile connections before having them break. This happened many times. Shamera tried to control his feelings of failure in not being able to connect with Elithrin.

"Let us stop for a while and have something to eat and drink." Elithrin suggested.

"Good idea. I could do with a break."

"You need to relax more and let it happen. I sensed you were trying to force it too much. We'll try again later. You sit here a while; I will fetch some food."

Shamera stood up, "No, I'll come with you, I'll help."

"You rest here, try a little meditation. It will help focus your thoughts."

Shamera sat back down and watched Elithrin make her way back to the main building. He sat facing the sun; the warmth felt good on his face. He closed his eyes and as his body relaxed, he sank a little into the chair. Slowly breathing in and out, he concentrated on each breath. He felt a sense of calm and inner warmth as he thought of Elithrin and the feelings he had for her. Elithrin's face popped into his head. He thought about how beautiful she looked. Elithrin appeared standing in front of him as she had done the first time. Again, they were in a white room filled with flowing white fabric.

"You've done it." a voice said in his head.

Shamera opened his eyes. He was still sitting in the garden under the willow tree. *'Did what?'* He thought to himself. He looked towards the main building to see Elithrin striding towards him, carrying a tray of food. As she drew closer, he could see she was smiling, "You did it, Shamera." She shouted.

"Did what?" He replied and stood up to greet her.

Elithrin rushed towards him, placed the tray on the table, flung her arms around his neck, and kissed him.

"You did it. You made the connection." She said excitedly leaning on Shamera and hugging him even tighter.

"I did?" He said disbelievingly, holding Elithrin around her waist so he didn't fall, a little lost in her hysteria.

"Yes, you did it. Did you not feel it?"

"I thought I was daydreaming."

"No, you made the connection." Elithrin said elated, then kissed him again.

"But how?"

"You must have relaxed and given in to the emotion, not tried to force it. You did it." said Elithrin jumping up and down.

They both practiced hard over the next three days. Shamera was getting the hang of it and found it was getting a lot easier. He was feeling a lot more relaxed about the mission. Even Merlin noticed the change. Salogel and Merlin stood at the window, watching the two of them walking hand in hand through the gardens, falling deeper in love.

Salogel turned to Merlin. "This is not the time for them to fall for each other. I fear for them both."

"There is nothing either of us can do. Any interference could have a negative effect on his mission." Merlin replied.

"I would never interfere with my daughters' feelings; she knows her own mind. Still, you cannot help but worry about them."

"Adolescent love, yet it might be what Shamera needs, a powerful reason to succeed." Said Merlin with a large grin.

"Love... I see the lad shine brighter these past few days, Elithrin too. I wish it were any other time, they both would be a source of light to shine brightly across our land. I fear the darkness to come if we fail to rid this evil from our land."

It was the fourth day. Shamera had been to see how Verazslo was doing. Merlin was coming out of the room. "He's still sleeping."

"Have the Snowberries not worked?"

"I fear not. He is getting weaker."

"Do we need to get some more? Surely there is something you can do? Is there no magic you can perform?"

"I know of no magic that would help. Perhaps it might be his time, brought on a too soon by Nimue."

"We need to capture her, and bring her here to undo what she has done." Shamera said, his face reddened with anger.

"I'm not sure we could trust her. Nor whether she would help him. But we do need to capture her and bring her to justice."

"I'm ready. When do we go?" His thoughts of Verazslo tinged his tone with anger, possibly even hatred.

"I will see Salogel. His men will have to let slip where you will be so you can be captured. You will leave your wand and staff here for safe keeping. It will also keep you safe. I said it before, I will say it again. You are a brave and noble person, Verazslo was right to place his trust in you."

"I am not a fearless person by nature, quite the opposite. But, I am listening to my instincts and hopefully making the right choices. And of course, there's Elithrin, I now choose to see where future takes me. It is not bravery, but a conscious decision to follow my destiny."

The day had come. Hopefully word of Shamera's trip to Ubatu had reached the ears of Nimue. Shamera went to find Derrell; he had made up his mind to walk into the trap alone.

"I will go alone. I will let no one else die, I cannot let you do this." Shamera said, his voice cracked with fear.

"We have a column of soldiers to protect you on the journey and protect you we will, there is not one of us who would rather stay behind and let you go alone. Besides, we will be arriving one day earlier than we let slip, with less chance of being ambushed, hopefully. And don't forget, I have Excalibur. Also, Elgrin and Krell are coming along just in case we need their skills to confuse the enemy."

Derrell took charge of the one thousand strong column and set off, east, towards Ubatu and the stronghold of Ubatu Robur. After two days of travelling, they finally reached the mouth of the canyon. They cautiously entered, being aware of any ambushes which may lay ahead. As they rounded a bend, Shamera could see the sun glinting off the pure black granite walls of the stronghold. As they got closer, Shamera thought it was indeed an impressive sight.

Ubatu Robur was an old stronghold from the dark-times which was rarely used these days and now merely for training. Eighty feet high and six feet thick, the black granite walls arched across the canyon floor forming the front of the stronghold. Two large wooden gates reinforced with iron were the only way in or out. Two hundred feet high, sheer black granite cliffs formed the rear of the stronghold. Shamera thought they looked very intimidating as they appeared to loom menacingly over the stronghold.

Finally, they had reached the entrance. The doors slowly creaked open. As they entered, in the middle, were four large wooden buildings which would have housed the occupants. Now, they stood derelict. Once everyone was inside, the doors were secured. Derrell gave the order to clean the place up and prepare for the night. Fires were lit, the buildings prepared as best they could for sleeping, and cooking vessels were set up for the evening meal.

Early the next morning, Shamera woke with a start as someone sounded a horn.

'Call to battle!' he heard somebody cry out.

He saw the archers hurrying up to the battlements and the cavalry preparing their horses. Shamera made his way up to the parapet. He looked over the battlements, his body filled with dread. His heart was beating so fast and loud he was sure the enemy could hear it. Derrell shouted out orders for the archers to be ready on the battlements. Shamera could see Derrell's mouth open and close, but in his fearful state, he could not hear any words coming out. He remembered what Derrell and Elithrin had taught him; he took a deep breath and battled to regain control of his emotions.

Three hundred Elvenii bowmen lined themselves up into ranks along the parapet. Their arrows nocked, waiting for the command to fire. Five hundred Dwarvian and Dragonborn positioned themselves behind the bowmen, ready to attack and repel anything coming over the ramparts. Two hundred cavalry waited behind the main gates, ready to ride out and meet the enemy head on.

Facing them were five thousand Orcs and four thousand men in rank and file, forming battle squares outside the range of the Elvenii archers. The enemy outnumbered them ten to one. The enemy had three large trebuchets which were being slowly wheeled into position, edging ever closer to their firing positions. Again, these were placed outside the range of the archers. The Elvenii and the Dwarvian readied themselves for the inevitable battle to begin.

The enemy fired their trebuchets and launched fire balls towards the stronghold. Flaming balls of death flew over the parapets and the heads of the Elvenii and the Dwarvian striking the buildings behind them. Soon the enemy could see large plumes of smoke bellowing from the burning buildings beyond the walls. Both Elgrin and Krell using their gift, made the smoke and flames look worse than they really were in order to deceive the enemy into thinking they had caused more damage than was actually inflicted.

Their strategy worked and the trebuchets were adjusted. This time large rocks and boulders hit the outer walls and battlements. The granite stone of the stronghold walls stood firm and defied the repeated attempts of the weapons which tried their best to breach them. The enemy sent forward their siege towers, each pushed by several Orcs. The towers squeaked and grumbled loudly as they lumbered slowly forward. Enemy archers moved forward and fired towards the battlements.

A large wooden structure was also moving towards the gates. It too creaked and groaned upon its great wooden wheels. Large, wooden shingles overlapped each other and protected the top and sides. This provided excellent protection from the Elvenii archers. Shamera thought it looked like a small wooden house on wheels, it appeared terrifying, nonetheless. The enemy had cut small slits into the front so the occupants could see where they were going. The structure housed an enormous tree trunk tipped with a large iron ball. The battering ram hung from the large iron chains which supported it. The heavy chains would allow the battering ram to swing freely at the gates. The

Elvenii archers returned fire, hundreds of bow strings twanged loudly as they sent arrows flying through the sky, volley, after volley. Hundreds of arrows flew screaming into the sky. The Elvenii arrows looked like a black cloud racing across the sky before raining death upon the enemy. The battering ram now assaulted the gates, weakening them with every strike. The some of the Elvenii bowmen now turned their attention to the battering ram, firing flaming arrows at its wooden housing. The sun was high in the sky as it beat down on the enemy, who were ferociously trying to gain entry to the stronghold.

Shamera peered over the battlements again. The battlefield glistened in the sunlight, the blood of the enemy pooled upon the hard sun-baked ground and shimmered as it reflected the rays of the sun. He looked towards the siege towers being pushed by Orcs and were virtually in position.

The Elvenii archers turned their attention to these and picked off the Orcs and the men standing in the towers, ready to attack as soon as they locked onto the battlements. The Dwarvian had their battle axes ready should anyone breach the defences. The siege towers were now locked into position, and hordes of Orcs and men raced over the battlements. The archers drew their swords and, along with the Dwarvian began hand to hand fighting. The clang of metal against metal rang out and reverberated against the battlements. Swords screeched against armour and guttural screams filled the air as friend and foe fell to ground.

" Their numbers are greater than ours!" yelled one of the archers, his voice barely audible over the din. "We'll be overrun in minutes"

The battle was in full swing when, without warning, the enemy withdrew to a safe distance. A Mage approached the gates under the protection of a white flag.

"What do you want?" shouted Derrell from the battlements.

"All we want is the young sorcerer, Shamera. If he surrenders himself to us, we will let the rest of you live. As you can see, you are vastly outnumbered, and it would simply be a matter of time before we breached this place. There is no need for any further bloodshed. You have my word. Surrender the young sorcerer to us and we will withdraw."

"How can you be certain you outnumber us, you cannot see beyond these walls."

"Our lookouts saw you arrive yesterday. Surrender the young sorcerer and you all live."

"Surrender him to be killed, never!" Derrell shouted back.

"He will not be harmed; I give my word. Nimue wants him alive."

Shamera peered over the battlements and shouted down to the Mage, "How do I know you will keep your word and let these people live?"

"We are not interested in them; we are here for you. As a gesture of good faith, if you give me your word to surrender yourself to me, I will send the Orcs away."

"Alright, I will agree to those terms, but I want to see the Orcs leaving and those machines destroyed before I surrender to you."

The Mage waved his hand above his head and pointed towards the entrance of the canyon; the Orcs retreated.

Shamera watched to make sure the Mage had fully kept his word. He waited until he could no longer see the Orcs.

Shamera kept his word and walked out of the stronghold. The Mage, using elemental magic, destroyed the siege weapons by fire.

"I will spare your people as agreed, as long as you agree to come with no resistance." said the Mage.

"Let them alone, and I will do as you ask."

Chapter 17

Hands bound, Shamera was pushed through the door into a dimly lit room. He was thrown to the cold hard stone floor, he gave a slight whimper as he fell face down. He was then dragged towards Nimue who was already there, waiting for him, "So, this is Shamera. Have you searched him properly?"
"Thoroughly, my lady."
"And?"
"Nothing, he had nothing with him."
"You may leave us." she said, wagging her finger towards the door.

The men nodded, and, as though fearful to turn their backs on her, the two guards walked backwards, keeping their eyes on her whilst feeling for the open door. They quickly left the room, immediately closing the door behind them. Nimue calmly looked down at Shamera who had now got to his knees. Nimue grabbing a handful of his hair, forced his head backwards in order to get a better look at his face. Shamera stared straight back at her. Her long, black, silky dress glinted in the candlelight. A large high rounded black collar framed her pale complexion and her short dark hair.

"And you must be Nimue." He said through gritted teeth.
"Where is my shard?"
"Shard?"
"Don't play games with me, boy. You know exactly to what I am referring." She hissed.
"May I get up and sit in a chair, or do you need me to kneel at your feet?"

She let go of his hair, she then placed both hands either side of his face, cupping his head. She gazed at him for a few seconds and then pointed towards a wooden chair. He gradually rose to his feet and sat down. The room smelled musty and felt cold; it was dimly lit by a few candles scattered around the room. He thought it strange the room had no windows. He felt very uncomfortable; he had never been in a situation like this before. His heart raced whilst it felt like his stomach was doing cartwheels ~~around the room~~. His hands were slightly shaking with his increasing uneasiness. He was in the sorceress' presence, the so called 'Evil one'. Shamera's voice quivered as he spoke. "You won't succeed."

"Do I detect fear in your voice? There is no need to fear me... not yet, anyway. We can still come to an amicable arrangement. Besides, who says I won't or haven't succeeded?" She replied calmly.

He gulped, "I'm not scared."

"Where is my shard?" She said, almost whispering.

"It's not your shard. I do not know where it is. Are you afraid of me? An apprentice. Is this why you need to keep my hands bound?"

Nimue walked over to him. She placed her hand on the front of his head. Pushed his head back slightly and started into his eyes. She stepped back and snapped her fingers. His bindings released. Shamera massaged his wrists. He could see the bracelet on his wrist. He stared at her, hoping for a chance to use it. He knew he would barely get but one chance to do so. He would have to choose his moment carefully.

"You can have powers like mine. I can teach you. I can teach you to become more powerful than you could ever imagine."

"Doesn't it bother you how many innocent lives you are destroying?"

Nimue pretended to think about her answer before replying, "Hmm...no. Rule with me and you can have anything you desire. Are you ready to face your real destiny?"

"Destiny? My real destiny is not ruling with you."

Nimue stared straight into his eyes. "You will reconsider."

"There's just the two of us here. You can tell me, how did you become like this? You can't always have had a blackened heart."

Nimue wondered around the room. Her voice changed to a much softer tone, "The further into this dark world I ventured, the more the light of life became gloomy, gradually getting darker, more distant. I live in my self-created world, a world of blackness, void of colourful light. Somewhere in my past there was a time I lived in a colourful and happy world; of this, I have little recollection. But I remember Sir Pellias, we were in love. We got married. He died... now, I call upon others to follow me into the darkness. I am the potentate of this Hell. I am the one who has the power and control, power to make those who dare oppose me suffer, and the power to crush my enemies underfoot, and then the ability to control what's left."

"Why would people voluntarily follow you into this cruel world of darkness and pain?"

Her voice became more forceful as her pacing increased. She seemed to become agitated.

"For the rewards I can offer, of course. The reward for following me is the love of power and the ability to inflict pain and suffering on those who oppose you. What if I told you there is no right or wrong? Remove your conscience and you become a powerful, unstoppable weapon. This is a cruel world we all inhabit, dog eat dog, a world where essentially only the strongest survive."

"You're wrong. It does not have to be this way. People have been coexisting for a long time. We help each other, not kill each other."

Nimue spun around quickly to face Shamera. "Open your eyes, boy! Look around... If you want something, you just take it."

"No, that's wrong. You must earn it, there is no value in just taking things. That just causes hurt, we learnt from the Dark Times that just taking things leads to unrest. The whole system degrades and leads to anarchy and war." Shamera could see she was becoming increasingly angrier.

"What about your family?" Nimue asked threateningly.

"Leave them out of it. They have nothing to do with any of this."

"They. Have. Everything. To do. With this. And if you do not want to see them harmed, you will do what I say."

Shamera was becoming fearful for his family. His thoughts were becoming more terrifying, and he was losing control of his feelings.

"Why are you doing this?"

"You have something I want. And I shall have it." She shouted.

"Why is it so important you have to threaten and kill people?"

Nimue lifted both hands palm upwards and raised her shoulders. "It's simple… fear and domination. The more people fear you, the more you can dominate."

Shamera rested his arms along the arms of the chair. Nimue looked at him and snapped her fingers. Rope bindings suddenly appeared around his arms and legs, securing him to the chair. Nimue walked over to him menacingly. She placed a hand on his head. The heel of her hand rested on his forehead. He felt her icy cold hand grip his head tightly. She closed her eyes. After a few seconds, she looked at him and said, "Don't go anywhere." And promptly left the room. He struggled with the bindings, but they held fast. He sat and tried to gather his thoughts. He tried to connect with Elithrin but found it more difficult than he imagined. His thoughts kept drifting to his family and wondering what danger he may have put them in.

A voice echoed inside his head. It was calling out to him. *'Shamera, reach out with your thoughts. Call upon Merlin. He will give you the power you need. He can help you. Reach out Shamera, reach out with your thoughts'.* Shamera recognised the voice of Elithrin and tried to connect their minds. He found it very difficult, as he could not relax his mind. He focused his mind solely on Elithrin. He concentrated hard, he managed to control his breathing and relaxed his mind. It was not long before he found they were in the 'White Room', as Shamera called it.

"I was getting worried. How are you?" Asked Elithrin, relieved to be in contact with him.

"Currently, I am tied securely to a chair in a very dingy, smelly room. So far, I am fine, scared, but fine. She has been threatening my family."

"Don't worry about them. They are safe in Selvenora. I promise. You need to connect your mind to Merlin's. Both he and Agnar are waiting close by. They followed you to Melliserin. Relax and remember what I taught you. Reach out to Merlin. You can do it."

Her voice faded. The connection had broken. He found himself back in the dingy room again. He quickly refocused his thoughts again. This time, he focused on Merlin. Again, he concentrated on regulating his breathing and relaxing his mind. He heard Merlin's voice. This time he was not in a *'White Room'* this time Merlin's voice was just in his head.

"How are you holding up, Shamera?"

"*Not well. I'm tied to a chair and can't get close enough to use the bracelet.*"

"*You must gain her trust. Once the bracelet is on her, we can rescue you and take control of Nimue.*"

"*How do I get her to trust me? She suspects everything. If she keeps me tied to this chair, I will have no opportunity to slap the bracelet on her.*"

"*Okay, I have an idea… are you alone in the room?*"

"*Yes.*"

"*Where is Nimue?*"

"*I don't know. She left the room and failed to inform me where she was going.*" he said with a sarcastic tone.

"*Alright, calm down. Slight change of plan.*"

Merlin and Agnar transported into the room.

"Are you mad? If she comes back, she will catch both of you." Said Shamera in a loud whisper.

"Agnar will do his thing when we hear her coming back. Trust us. You need to get her to untie you and be ready at all times. You won't get a second chance." said Merlin.

Merlin and Agnar moved to the back of the room and into an area of deep shadow. There was a sound of footsteps coming closer. Merlin put his finger to his lips. "Shhh."

Shamera watched as Agnar twisted the blue stone on the amulet and watched as they had disappeared into the shadows. Nimue entered the room.

"I have dispatched riders to Helm's Hollow to capture your family and bring them here. Let's see how you feel about watching them being tortured. I told you, I'm done playing with you." she screamed.

"Leave them out of this. It's me you want. You have me. I will do as you ask. Don't hurt my family, please." He begged.

"Where is my shard?"

Shamera had to think fast, he was not expecting to have the threat of his family captured and tortured. Panic had now fogged his mind, he wasn't able to think clearly. He started to tremble, he was cold and scared. This was not going the way he had envisioned it. He looked up at Nimue standing over him, and thinking as best he could said, "I will take you to it. Magic hides it. I am solely the one to retrieve it." His voice was stressed.

"You said you do not possess magic."

"I... I don't. I don't have magical powers... but the Elvenii blessed the place in which they hid it and... and made it so I am the one who can retrieve it."

"And how do I know I can trust you?"

"I don't want my family hurt... please." He pleaded.

"And to think they chose you to be a sorcerer, you will never be a sorcerer. You are too weak." She said insultingly.

"Please, untie me, these bindings are hurting me. Or are you threatened by me? And you call me weak."

"Threatened, by you? Remember, I can kill you as easily as snapping my fingers."

"Killing me would be your biggest mistake. You will never get your hands on the shard of Ellaria. Presently, only I and the Elvenii leader Lord Salogel know its whereabouts, and you can be certain he will never tell you."

Nimue snapped her fingers and released his bindings. Her demeanour changed; she softened her voice as she spoke.

"Look, I don't want to threaten you. I want us to be friends. I'm just used to having to resort to threatening people to get what I want."

Shamera stood up, rubbing his wrists whilst he took a couple of paces forward. As he did, Merlin and Agnar reappeared from the shadows. This startled Nimue. She grabbed Shamera by his throat and placed him between Merlin and herself.

"What kind of treachery is this? Put down your wand or I will rip out his throat." She screamed.

"No, you won't. If you do, the shard of Ellaria will be lost to you forever." Merlin replied.

Without drawing attention to what he was doing, Shamera carefully and slowly removed the bracelet from his wrist. In doing so he almost dropped it, he managed to catch it with his finger tips. He barely had hold of it as he tried to move it through his fingers to attain a better grip. His heart was racing, he would only get one chance to succeed. Once the bracelet was securely back in his grasp, he quickly slapped it against her wrist, Nimue stared at it as it snapped into place.

"What is this?" She screamed, Nimue let go of him to examine what he had placed around her wrist. She clawed at the bracelet, trying to remove it.

As she did, Merlin waved his wand. She fell backwards into the chair. He waved his wand again, and she was bound to it.

"You treacherous little bas…"

Before she could finish the sentence, Merlin again waved his wand a third time and Nimue's lips tightly sealed. The only sound she could make was a faint grunting sound.

"Is my family definitely safe in Selvenora?"

"Yes lad. Elithrin informed me of their arrival there."

"Wield your darkness on your own, you bitch. You dare to threaten my family!" Shamera shrieked menacingly, as he turned to face her.

"Calm yourself lad, what has got into you? We are not out of this yet." said Merlin.

"So, how do we get out of here?" asked Shamera.

"I cannot teleport all of us together. I'll teleport out of here with Nimue. You and Agnar can walk out of here. We can meet up and head back to Selvenora."

"How? How do we walk out of here, Merlin? Have you seen how many of her men are garrisoned here?" Shamera snapped.

"What is the matter with you? You sound as though you are being consumed by hatred. Pull yourself together. This is not like you."

"Don't worry, Shamera. I will make sure they do not see us. As long as you stay very close to me, you will remain invisible to those outside."

Merlin grabbed Nimue by the arm and stood her up, using his cuff they both teleported out of the room. Agnar and Shamera made their way out. As they did, they noticed a lot of commotion. Men running around and shouting the Orcs have vanished.

"Did you see what happened? Those Orcs disappeared, vanished. What do you think happened?" one man said.

"I do not know." came the reply.

As Shamera and Agnar stood back in a recess within the wall, another man came running by, "We cannot find the sorceress. She's disappeared too." the man said.

"I weigh this has something to do with the Orcs disappearing." Another one said.

"I'm leaving, this is our chance, I'm going home." said another, as he finished speaking Shamera stepped forward and suddenly appeared before them.

"Who are you?" said one man, looking very surprised.

"I am Shamera, sorcerer. I, along with Merlin, an even greater sorcerer, have defeated Nimue." he said as Agnar appeared out of nowhere.

The men jumped back in surprise.

"If you truly want to go home back to your families, we will make sure you have safe passage. Or, if you still want to fight…" said Agnar.

"No, please, no more fighting. They forced us into this. Our families threatened. She said the Orcs would destroy them and our villages if we did not fight for her. Please, if you have indeed defeated her, please let us return to our homes and loved ones." Pleaded the man.

"We will have to get word to our armies. It looks like the fighting is over." Agnar said triumphantly.

One man showed them the way out, but as they reached the outside, the men suddenly stopped in their tracks. Merlin stood there before them with Nimue. Merlin had trapped Nimue in what looked like a large ball of blue fire. Shamera walked over to Merlin, "Is everything alright?"

"What is going on here?" asked Merlin.

"They merely want to go home. Nimue has been defeated. She no longer has control over them. They don't want to fight. Apparently, they never did. All the Orcs disappeared. According to one of them, one minute they were there, the next… poof." said Agnar.

"Of course, you have no magic now, do you? When Shamera slapped the bracelet on, it did more than completely stopping your magic abilities. Everything controlled by your magic was also broken." said Merlin, staring straight at her.

Unfortunately, because of the spell placed on her by Merlin, she could not move, nor answer. She stood there making unintelligible noises and shaking her head angrily.

Merlin looked around. He looked at the fear on the faces of the men gathered about.

"You may all leave, but you will have to travel under the banner of peace. Spread the word to your fellow men. We will grant safe passage to those under the protection of the white banner. If any of our armies stop you, show no resistance and tell them Shamera has granted safe passage." he shouted.

Merlin waved his wand and several large white banners appeared, cautiously some men picked them up and marched homeward. Some of them even spat at Nimue, expressing their disgust towards her.

"Come, let us go home." said Agnar, relieved it seemed to be all over.

They began their journey back to Selvenora.

"Merlin, do you not think it was a bit too easy?" asked Shamera

"Easy or not, we have her and she is going nowhere, except with us." he replied. They had travelled for scarcely an hour before being greeted by a patrol of Elvenii and Formorian riders. Shamera recounted their story of what had unfolded and told the rider's men would be marching back home under the protection of the white banners. Some of the Elvenii and Formorian riders set out at pace to inform other patrols the battle was over and to make sure safe passage home was permitted.

Two Elvenii riders rode ahead to inform Lord Salogel of the news, whilst the rest escorted the four of them back to Selvenora.

As expected, the journey back was uneventful. As they approached, the gates of Selvenora opened and they received a hero's welcome, soldiers cheering and waving from the battlements. Elvenii soldiers in full armour lined up with the Dwarves, Dragonborn and Formorian Horsemen to form a welcoming guard of honour. Greeting them at the steps and standing proudly was Lord Salogel, Elithrin and Shamera's family. Shamera felt very honoured as he rode into Selvenora and saw his family standing there. Elithrin ran to meet him. Shamera quickly dismounted and ran towards Elithrin who quickly flung her arms around him and gave him a hero's kiss. She held his hand tightly with both of hers as they walked over to his family.

"Well, what's this?" his mother asked.

"Yes, what is this?" asked Lord Salogel as he looked straight at Shamera.

"Erm, well…" stuttered Shamera as he stood there looking very embarrassed.

"Father, stop it. You're embarrassing him."

Shamera's mother gave him a big, motherly hug. Her eyes welled up as she saw not her child standing before her, but a young man, a hero.

"From what I hear, you have exceeded all expectations son." said his father proudly.

Two guards dragged Nimue before Lord Salogel and asked, "What do you want us to do with her?"

"Lock her up in the guardroom cells for now and double the guard."

Merlin joined Shamera and his family. "Mother, Father, this is Merlin. He is a great sorcerer from another realm. He has been teaching me in the absence of Verazslo, speaking of Verazslo. How is he?" Shamera said as he looked anxiously at Lord Salogel.

"He is still not well, I'm afraid. He is still bed-ridden and weak. You may visit him later for a short while. Please, come and join us in the main hall. We have laid on a grand feast for everyone."

Merlin took off his hat and smiled.

"Hello, Shamera's family. You must be very proud of your son; he is proving to be a skillful young sorcerer. If you will forgive me for a moment, there is something I must attend to."

Shamera turned to Lord Salogel. "We need to talk about Nimue. I have an idea which will get rid of her forever."

Elithrin led the way to the main hall, followed by Shamera and his family.

"You have become quite the young man in these past few months, and the adventurer too from what I hear." said his mother.

Shamera smiled, "Where's Gwen?"

"She's somewhere playing with Elvenii children." Said his mother.

"She's in the gardens. They are taking it in turns riding a small pony." Elithrin said.

"Can we go there first? There is something I need to do." asked Shamera.

"Of course." replied Elithrin.

As they walked out into the gardens, Gwen spotted her big brother, jumped off the pony and ran over to him. She jumped up at him and gave him a big hug.

Shamera kneeled so she could give him a better hug. As she hugged his neck tightly, Shamera sneaked his wand out of his back pocket and waved it towards the pony.

"I've missed you. Are you a sorcerer now?"

"No, not yet. I still have a lot to learn, so what are you up to?"

"We are playing with this pony. He is lovely."

"What pony?"

"This…" As Gwen turned to point at the pony, she saw a small white unicorn standing in its place. Her face lit up with the biggest of smiles, her eyes widened as her jaw dropped.

"Did… you do this?" She squealed in surprise.

"Of course, you asked me for one, remember? The magic will last about an hour. Have fun, little sister."

Gwen ran back over to the other children whilst Shamera accompanied the others and went into the Great Hall. A great feast indeed, long tables festooned with meats, fruits, large jugs of mead and ale. Shamera looked over at Artos and six Dwarves who were drinking heartily and singing Dwarvian songs, often with their mouths still full of food. Urok was sitting with some of his men, and the Dragonborn enjoying the feast and drinking copious amounts of mead. The Ethaenians and the Mystics were sitting, enjoying themselves, too. They spotted Shamera and his family and beckoned them over. They sat down with the rest of them to eat.

Urok stood up on his table and banged a metal serving spoon against a large serving tray, "Can... can I have everyone's attention, before we've all got too drunk..."

"Too late for you pal." shouted one dwarf whilst laughing loudly.

"Before we all get too drunk, we should pay our respects to two sorcerers who saved us all from the clutches of the evil one. *'Burp'*. Oops, sorry. So, raise your tankards to Shamera and Merlin."

Everyone stood up and shouted, "Shamera and Merlin!"

Shamera stood up embarrassed and gave a slight wave to everyone and quickly sat down. As he sat down, Lord Salogel approached.

"Sorry to interrupt. Could I see you please, Shamera?"

Shamera gave his apologies and followed Lord Salogel out of the hall and into a small anti-chamber close by. Merlin was already there. Shamera could see by the pained look on Merlin's face something was wrong.

"What's the matter? She has not escaped, has she?"

"Please, come sit."

Shamera sat next to Merlin and Lord Salogel sat next to Shamera. Lord Salogel slowly handed Shamera a piece of folded paper. He slowly unfolded the paper and he read.

Shamera, I'm afraid the debt of life must now be paid. Forgive me, for I am the one to pay it. My life is coming to its end. In comparison, yours is at its bright beginning and you are destined for great endeavours. I want you to live your life by the code and beliefs Mirabilis, Merlin, and the Elvenii have and will teach you. I truly believe you will become the greatest sorcerer this world has ever seen, of that I have no doubt. To have watched you grow up, albeit for a brief time, can honestly be described as a privilege. You should not mourn my death. You will carry on my work and my magic will live on within you, alongside your own. I leave you my magic ring. This is the greatest gift I can bestow upon you, my young apprentice. Goodbye Shamera, my friend, and take good care of yourself and of this land. Make everyone proud, I know you will. And signed, Verazslo, Sorcerer.

"I need to see him, please. Where is he?"

"I'm sorry Shamera but he has passed over. He died quietly in his sleep a few moments ago. We found this letter and ring next to his bed addressed to you."

As Shamera looked at the letter, his eyes welled up and tears rolled down his face. He felt numb. A shivery feeling spread across his body and made him shudder.

"He's dead because of me. I didn't truly know him. The last time I saw him was at the Choosing. It was a beautiful day, and I was so excited when I was chosen. Now, I don't want it. I've killed, seen death, felt so frightened I could barely breath."

"You cannot blame yourself Shamera, all this would have happened even if they chose someone else in your stead." said Lord Salogel.

Merlin looked at Shamera, took a deep breath and said, "There are times in life which will challenge our very being. They shape and transform us. They even force us to question our own existence. This is what makes you that person. You can skulk away and hide from it, or you can rise above it, accept the grief, and become the person you know you are. It will take great strength and courage, and we are all here to help you through it. I have nowhere to go. These great people have said I can stay here with them. I can become your teacher if you so wish. Here, place the ring upon your finger and honour his memory by becoming the person he believed you would become."

Shamera sat there staring at the ring, tears still running down his cheeks, his blue eyes reddened with sorrow.

"I want to kill her!" He said, as he stood up, his face and voice full of rage.

"Wait, please sit back down." Beckoned Merlin.

"None of this would have happened had it not been for her!"

"Revenge like this is not right. You are not a killer. You are angry right now, a great king once told me. Never make a decision whilst you are angry. Your mind is clouded, and you will never make the right decision." Said Merlin, hoping Shamera would see reason through his anger.

"She cannot get away with this. She has to be severely punished."

"Both myself and Merlin have discussed your idea of putting her in Merlin's cave and trapping her there as she did to him. He has agreed this is a great idea. This might ease your sadness, knowing we will trap her in there for eternity." Lord Salogel replied.

"Remember where you found me? In the cave. She will have a taste of her own medicine and a millennium and more to think about her crimes. Killing her would be the easy way out for her. Trust me, I know; this would be the ultimate punishment."

"When do we go?"

"We can leave tomorrow night. Do what we need to do and come straight back."

"I did not know Verazslo particularly well. Why do I feel like this?" asked Shamera.

"Grief is the price we all pay for love, for caring, for being of good heart." Lord Salogel replied softly. Shamera looked at Verazslo's ring, a gold ring with a red gemstone set in the centre of the band. Shamera placed it on the first finger of his right hand. As he did, he felt a slight tingle flow through his body, as an icy shiver ran down his spine.

"This ring has magical properties; I can sense it." Merlin said, observing the ring.

"I know you are upset, but I think it best you go and re-join the feast, I'm sure your family and Elithrin are missing you." Said Salogel softly.

Shamera reluctantly re-joined his family and Elithrin. Saddened by the loss of Verazslo he managed to put on a brave face. Elithrin stood up and walked over to greet him. She sensed something was wrong, "What is the matter?" She whispered.

"It's alright, I'll tell you later. I don't want to spoil my enjoyment. We haven't seen each other in ages and this is the first time I have ever been away from them for this length of time. Let us just enjoy the rest of this feast."

They sat and drank mead and enjoyed the feast. Shamera watched as everyone laughed heartily with each other. All nations for the time being were enjoying each other's company, and celebrating victory. His mum kept asking how his training was coming along. His father would change the subject when questions of battles or fighting were asked. And as for Gwen, all she wanted was to eat cake and ask when Shamera would conjure up another unicorn. Merlin joined the party and called Shamera over to see how he was doing.

"I'm okay, this festivity has been an emotional uplift that I think we all needed to share. Sitting here I could see that it has raised everyone up to a higher plane of acceptance of each other. All petty differences have been put aside, as everyone has come together for a common cause. All I want to do now is to take that evil thing, out of the Second Realm once and for all. For everything to get back to normal and to continue my training the way it should have been from the start."

"You have become the kind of young man others will want follow, you are a natural leader, and that will go a long way in making you a great sorcerer that everyone will be proud of, especially Verazslo. Speaking of which, Salogel wants us to lead the funeral procession to Avangard where he will be laid to rest."

Shamera said nothing but with his eyes welling up, nodded in acceptance. Elithrin felt Shamera's pain and came over to join him, "We need to say goodnight to your family, I will arrange for them to be taken care of."

Tomorrow came and it was time for the funeral procession to take Verazslo to his resting place. The procession was led by Lord Salogel, Shamera and Merlin. They were followed by representative of the Elvenii, Dwarves, Dragonborn, Horsemen of Mirropus, and the Mystics. The ornate golden hearse was drawn by two white stallions, the wrapped body of Verazslo laid upon a bed of flowers. They slowly made their way to the archway which led to Avaland, the only noise was from the slight creaking of the hearses' wheels. Even the birds were silent, it was as though even they were paying their respects. They finally reached the arch, and Shamera stepped forward. He raised his staff and tapped the arch stones in the correct sequence. The archway shimmered and a host of flower fairies flew out to greet them.

"We will take him from here." said a blue fairy, softly.

A small choir of Elvenii started to sing in Elvish, thier farewell song echoed hauntingly through the woods. The fairies hovered over Verazslo's body, and slowly it rose into the air. Then, it gently floated forward towards the arch. A yellow fairy spoke in a high pitched, yet soft voice.

"Please do not mourn Verazslo, but go forth and celebrate his life. Proclaim his accomplishments and the good he did across all our lands. And you Shamera, continue in his light, become the sorcerer he once was and make the Second Realm proud."

Verazslo's body glided effortlessly through the arch surrounded by the flower fairies. The archway closed once more, and the procession made its way back home. Shamera bowed his head in reverence to the grief he was feeling.

"At times like this, we must accept the dark so we can appreciate the light. Let this time of mourning envelop you, think of Verazslo and let it start the healing process." Merlin said offering some words of comfort, but Shamera was too hurt to hear them. Tears of pain and of anger ran down Shamera's cheeks, for the first time in his life he was experiencing hate.

Elithrin was waiting for Shamera's return, "Come, let us walk in the garden."

"I am sorry Elithrin, but I do not feel like it." He replied, his voice filled with hate.

"I am sorry Shamera, but you need to walk with me. We need to transform this hatred I am sensing into a positive emotional feeling. If not, it will poison you. Do you want to become like Nimue? To hate is to fail in seeing that there are alternatives."

"What alternatives?" Interrupted Shamera.

"If it wasn't for her, we may never have met and fallen in love. I can see things from your perspective, I feel it too. Let me help you, please do not let hatred poison your heart."

Shamera wiped away his tears and accompanied Elithrin through the gardens.

"Let's sit here a while, and talk." Suggested Elithrin.

Shamera sat and Elithrin stood behind him. Placing her hands on his shoulders she spoke softly, "Close your eyes, and feel my energy. Kardia is the affective centre of our being, our heart is where love resides. If hatred is allowed to reside there too, it will in time take over and blacken your heart. There will be no room for love, compassion and forgiveness. You must make a conscious effort to remove this hatred and replace it with forgiveness. You must choose to forgive, it has to be absolute. Purge your heart of all ill-feelings, feel your heart lift with love. It is not easy, but it is not impossible." Elithrin continued to pass positive energy through his body. Almost one hour had passed.

"You're right, I can pass through this grief within my heart, and keep my love intact. You are my salvation."

"Now imagine you are holding a balloon, tie that hatred to the string and let it go. Watch it fly away, feel it leave your body." she said again softly.

He smiled, and as he imagined letting go of the balloon, he felt his heart lift.

"The paths we take should all be forward, never going back. Only when we practice true forgiveness, can we fully heal ourselves. Inner healing will bring with it inner peace. It's time to release the anger, the forgiveness will come in time. Now, shall we go and find your family? I think they will want to see you before they leave to go home."

Shamera smiled as he reached out for Elithrin's hand. Together they walked back to the main building. Shamera's family were almost finished packing.

"I understand you will be remaining here to finish your training. We are so proud of you, you turned out to be quite the young man and hero. We are glad this Nimue business is over, we can all settle down and get back to normality." Said his mother, then she gave him a big hug. He smiled as he felt the love from the hug only a mother could generate.

"I will come and visit you soon, I promise."

"And bring Elithrin too, you have picked a good one there." She teased.

"Mother!" he replied, feeling very embarrassed.

"Leave the lad be mother." said his father seeing Shamera's face redden.

"Lord Salogel has organised an escort for us, we told him it wasn't necessary, but he insisted. So we will be travelling back home in style." Beamed his mother.

Shamera stayed with them until it was time for them to leave. His mother gave him another rib crushing hug and kissed his cheek. Gwen also gave him a hug; on the condition he brought her a unicorn she could keep. His father also gave him a hug and made his promise once more to come home and visit soon.

"May the ways be good, and your journey home be a safe one. I will visit soon." said Shamera forcing a smile. He would like to have gone with them, but he one last thing to attend to.

For Shamera, the evening came all too slow. The pale-yellow crescent moon shone like a giant dragon's claw amongst a myriad of diamonds in the night sky. Derrell, Vesryn, Hethoral and Theronas accompanied Merlin, Shamera and Nimue to the stone rings.

"Where are you taking me?" Demanded Nimue.

"Do unto others as they do unto you." Merlin replied.

"You have not quoted the golden rule correctly Merlin, have you forgot your scriptures already?"

"No, merely giving you a clue." Merlin replied smugly.

Nimue appeared to give his quote a little thought, then replied, "You cannot imprison me, I am way too powerful to allow that."

"Whilst you wear that bracelet, you have no power."

"Are you sure about that?" She replied, there was a confidence to her tone.

"If you had any powers you would have used them to escape and been long gone. Now, be silent or I will seal your mouth again." Shamera interjected.

Nimue gave Shamera a sideways glance, smiled then made a slight 'Huh' sound.

She remained silent the rest of the way. Her brow creased and a tense scowl showed her displeasure. As they approached the stone rings they appeared to have a slight incandescent glow in the pale moonlight. Everyone dismounted. Derrell and the others watched as they entered the ring and shouted, "We look forward to seeing you both back here soon!"

"Once we have taken care of her, we will be straight back." Shamera replied.

He raised his wand, held his staff in front of him and recited the incantation, but nothing happened. He looked at Merlin and shrugged his shoulders.

"Did you recite it correctly?" Merlin asked.

"I think so. I will try it again."

Once more, Shamera held his wand high and again recited the incantation. Again, it did not work.

"Take your time and try again. Concentrate, don't be distracted by her." said Merlin, looking straight at Nimue with mistrust.

Shamera slowly raised his wand and recited the incantation once more. This time, it appeared to work. After a few seconds, once again, in a bright flash of light, they were thrown forward onto their knees.

Shamera was the first to stand up. He shook his head and rubbed his eyes, then looked around.

"Merlin! where is Nimue? and why is it daylight?"

Merlin rose to his feet and said, "I stood her next to you." Merlin continued to look around, but she was nowhere to be seen.

"Remy!" called out Shamera, but there was no answer.

Shamera bent down to pick up his staff. It had disappeared. Only the shard of Ellaria lay on the grass. He picked it up and, with a slight look of confusion; he placed it in his pocket.

"This is most strange." said Merlin, still feeling a little unsteady on his feet.

"Merlin, look, there are some people walking this way."

"They look like… They can't be." exclaimed Merlin.

"Can't be who Merlin?"

"Druids."

"Good evening, friends." Called out the lead man, dressed in white robes. He used a long staff to aid with his walking.

"Tell me, where exactly are we?" asked Merlin.

The Druid looked at him slightly confused.

"Albion, of course. Are you strangers to these parts?"

"What's going on Merlin, where is Nimue?"

"Nimue! you dare to speak her name out loud!" shouted the man as he raised his staff towards Shamera.

Shamera took a step back and raised his wand. The man stopped in his tracks; he lowered his staff, and he took a step backwards.

"You're a sorcerer." the man said.

"And who are you?" Shamera asked.

"I am Galiuss, a Druid healer. We were on our way to Avebury. And thereafter, we head back towards Camelot. Arthur is not himself anymore. Nimue and Morgana have bewitched him with the use of dark magic."

"Arthur Pendragon lives?" asked Merlin, as he stumbled around, mystified. He looked at Galiuss and asked, "What year is this?"

"This is the year of our lord, five hundred and two."

Merlin looked straight at Shamera; his skin tingled as a cold sensation ran through his body. His heart felt like it was missing every other beat. His eyes widened as his knees buckled slightly.

"It has somehow transported us back in time, back to the reign of King Arthur. I'm going to get to see my King again!" Merlin said excitedly.

Dear Reader,

Thank you for embarking on this journey with me. I hope you enjoyed reading this book as much as I enjoyed writing it. Your thoughts and feedback are incredibly valuable to me and can make a significant difference.

If you enjoyed this book, please consider leaving a review on Amazon. It's quick, easy, and absolutely free. Your review not only helps other readers discover my work but also fuels my passion for creating more stories for you.

Visit my website at **www.tsjames.uk** to stay updated on my latest books, exclusive content, and more. Join our community of Beta-Readers and be the first to read our new releases.

Thank you for your support, and happy reading!

Warm regards,
T S James